# WOMEN ON
# THE BRINK
## STORIES

G. ELIZABETH KRETCHMER

Cover Design by Maria Aiello
Edited by Erin Curlett
Cover Art by Lindsey Surin

The following stories have previously appeared, in slightly different versions, in other publications as follows:
Skydancer, *High Desert Journal* Issue 9, Spring 2009
Liar's Game, *The Chaffey Review* Volume 8, September 2012
Bridge Out, *SLAB* Issue 10, Spring 2015

*This is a work of fiction. Names, characters, places, brands, media, and incidents are either the product of the author's imagination or are used fictitiously. Any resemblance to similarly named places or to persons living or deceased is unintentional.*

PRINT ISBN 978-0-99610-383-1
EPUB ISBN 978-0-99610-385-5

Library of Congress Control Number: 2015915778

# Table of Contents

*For anyone who ever dreamed of running away*

*"May your trails be crooked, winding, lonesome, dangerous, leading to the most amazing view."*

—EDWARD ABBEY

# AUTUMN

# SKYDANCER

# Inventing Wings

—RYAN BRADLEY

There's a reason we wouldn't stop
until we figured out a way
for us to lift our feet from the ground,
to soar like birds and have the best
of both worlds.

There's a reason we are always asking
for something more, something new,
a reason we hope and believe,
why "faith" is even a word at all.

There's a reason we ready
new generations, why we love,
why we gravitate to one another
for companionship and more.

There's a reason we tell ourselves
we aren't ready. It's the only way
we know to keep us searching.

**AUNTIE HAD A WAY** of looking through Marisa's skin and deeper, maybe into her soul. There was something about those black eyes, not blinking, not glancing away like most people would. But not staring either, rather inspecting Marisa in a way that made her feel like her skin didn't fit right—an itchy, too-tight sweater—a way that made her examine herself: first her appearance—her wavy hair, her skin much paler than the women in the clan—and then her thoughts, her opinions, her ambitions, how she spent her days in the sky, escaping from the cars and espressos and souvenir shops, navigating through dense fog, between granite cliffs, and above ribbons of Alaskan ice and rock—and finally into a personal void, where there should have been more friends and lovers—and love—but where instead there were fears, selfishness, and terrifying shame.

It was crowded in Marisa's shabby, three-room cabin. Auntie sat in the rocker, wrapped in a crocheted blanket with her long braid dangling across her right shoulder, her knitting needles already clacking so early in the morning and her foot swinging to a beat that traveled from a pink iPod through earbuds into giant, wrinkled ears. Twenty-year-old Marisa paced back and forth in front of the fireplace, arms crossed tightly around her stomach, refusing to turn around. And the baby squawked.

Marisa had awakened earlier, when the room was still dark, after what seemed like only a few minutes of rest. Embers popped in the fireplace and wind rustled the leaves of the aspens outside. She was sweaty where the baby lay resting against her. She listened to the baby's breath, steady as a first snow. But then she wondered for a fleeting instant, just the time it takes for a bird to flap its wings, about the freedom she might have had if it were different, if she had awakened to find no breath.

"Good morning, Sunshine." Auntie had startled Marisa out of the fantasy. The old woman had been watching. And when she'd spoken, the baby began to cry, and the cycle began again. First the cry for milk, then the refusal of Marisa's breast. Cry, refuse. Scream, refuse. It was the same routine each time, the same battle. The thought of forcing her nipple into the baby's mouth didn't feel right to Marisa, a former tomboy who had preferred tree forts and snowball fights over knitting and babysitting when she was a girl. Now, breastfeeding was simply not in her makeup: the burning and stinging, the tenderness and bleeding, the cracked nipples, the sucking that made her flinch. And the relentless colicky wailing afterward.

It was not second nature to Marisa to be a mother, despite Auntie's predictions.

Now Marisa continued to pace and the baby continued to cry.

After a few minutes, Auntie pulled one of her earbuds out and spoke. "Don't worry, you'll get the hang of it. It always hurts the first week or so. Have I told you the story of Otter? Don't worry," she said again. "You and the baby will adjust to each other and your inner Otter will emerge." Auntie still clung to her ancestor's beliefs, and it was rare for a conversation to flow from beginning to end without some bit of tribal wisdom. She hesitated, then put the earbud back in.

"You don't know what you're talking about," Marisa said. "This has nothing to do with some stupid inner otter. I'm in pain, okay? I haven't slept one bit." It might have been an exaggeration, but that was how she felt. Meanwhile, the baby's face was growing red as Indian paintbrush. "She's been at it every night, crying and screeching." Not like Auntie would have noticed, the way she snored all night long in the back bedroom.

"I never should have kept her."

Auntie's knitting needles stopped, strands of pink yarn dangling mid-air. From behind her oversized tortoiseshell glasses, the same ones from a decade ago, her black eyes once again pierced right into Marisa, the way her knife had dug into the raw fish the night before. Now Marisa felt a little like that fish must have: alone, gutted, and empty.

These selfish feelings were wrong; this much Marisa knew. She should be cooing over her infant, holding her into the early morning hours, refusing the temptation to set her down and let her howl. She should soothe her with a tender voice, rock her, walk her through their little world of knotty pine walls and dirty windows, soft fur blankets, September breezes, and sunshine that threatened to disappear below the horizon earlier and earlier each day. Instead of covering her ears from the racket, she should be inviting friends and all her cousins to the house, all those loving arms and sweet voices and gifts of clothing and toys and fabric books, the sounds of laughter and tinkling rattles.

She should, by now, have come up with a name for the child.

"Aashka," Auntie said, as if she had been reading Marisa's mind. Auntie had once said that name meant *blessing*, but right now the baby felt more like a curse to Marisa. Auntie stood and set her iPod into its speaker dock, and the hip-hop music blared.

*Let me feel ya, baby, all over my body*
*Let me feel ya, sugar, till I scream out loud.*

The baby's cry grew more frantic, and Marisa—her skin crawling from these lyrics—lunged to turn down the volume. She pulled her t-shirt with its dried milk stains up and over her head and tossed it into a heap of clothes in the corner. Her breasts hung heavy in the nursing bra, and with the lip of her sweatpants digging into her stomach, her skin flapped over the waistband. She took the last clean t-shirt out of the laundry basket, an extra-large brown one with a rip in the back, and slipped it over her head, then sat down on the floor to put her hiking boots on.

"Where do you think you're going?" Auntie asked.

"To the store. To buy some bottles and formula. I can't do this breastfeeding crap."

The chair squeaked as Auntie lifted herself out of it for the second time and picked up the baby.

"There, there. It's okay. Auntie's here. Mama loves you, too. Poor thing. But don't you worry, now. Everything will be all right, little Aashka."

"Stop calling her Aashka. It's a stupid name."

There was a knocking sound, and Marisa cocked her head. Norman and Lucy, her two best—but not necessarily close— friends, had said they'd stop by to see the baby, but so far they hadn't come. Marisa looked out the window. No one was there except for a woodpecker on a nearby spruce tree. Meanwhile, Auntie hummed, her voice now low and velvety. It was the same voice that had coached Marisa through the contractions and the pain and the delivery.

"I know, little butterfly, you're hungry. I know," Auntie said. The baby's screech subsided into wet sobs and gasps. Marisa felt something tugging at her, and she stiffened. Auntie went on. "Mama's right here, baby. See? Right here by the window." Auntie's warmth and the baby's powdery smell closed in on Marisa, but still she would not turn around.

"Mama's almost ready for you," Auntie said, and the crying stopped, except for the long, intermittent sniffles.

It wasn't that Marisa didn't have a heart. As a child, she had been the one to bring home the owlet with the broken wing and the ptarmigan with the broken leg. The cat with a maimed ear. Once, she'd even found an abandoned wolf pup. Auntie encouraged Marisa to care for the pup and later remarked how Marisa would someday make a fine mother. But that was long ago, and it was different now. An animal didn't require the commitment of a lifetime.

A lifetime.

Auntie switched songs on her iPod. Now it was Tchaikovsky, with the sad, steady beginning of bass and cello, soon followed by woodwinds and trumpets—the increasing volume and the quickening pace—and then came the soothing buzz of violins. These were the sounds, unlike Auntie's hip-hop, that hinted at what life was like before the baby was born. It was Uncle who suggested, when he'd first taken Marisa up in his ancient De Havilland Beaver years earlier, that he thought of himself as an orchestra conductor. She had been strapped beside him, shaking, and he'd told her to listen to the propeller as it began to spin, slowly at first and then accelerating to a dizzying speed, and to imagine string instruments in harmony. He'd said to think of the loud vibration of taxiing and the higher pitch at take off, when your heart quickens and the plane angles up into the sky, as the violins and flutes and oboes. Her heart had been pounding that day, as the plane bounced through air pockets and then headed for the sharp edges of the mountains, but Uncle kept telling her to listen to the music as he named each peak, explained the controls, and even pointed down at a miniscule herd of caribou far below. Eventually, she'd relaxed when his plane leveled out high above the interwoven riverbeds and the parallel ridges, when he'd offered her the cookie tin and a sip of his milky coffee. And then, when it came time to land, she'd begged Uncle for more time in the sky, just the two of them, away from Auntie and all the cousins and her mother's empty room.

Now, as the music played, Marisa wished she were back in the plane, but this time flying solo toward those snow-capped peaks, a bush pilot extraordinaire carting bananas and propane gas and computers to those who lived in isolation, or searching for missing hikers lost somewhere in the infinite tundra, or delivering climbers—some tense, some arrogant—to Denali's base camp and coaxing them out of the plane as Auntie had coaxed the baby from Marisa's own body, just a few days ago. She opened the door, and the wind came inside, and the baby began to cry again.

"Marisa, she's starving," Auntie said. "You have to feed her. Now."

"Maybe she's pooped in her diaper." Auntie stepped behind Marisa.

The baby blanket rubbed against Marisa's elbow, and in her peripheral vision she saw the baby's mouth open and fists clench shut.

"You have a lot to learn about being a mother," Auntie said. "This isn't the cry of a dirty diaper. This is her cry for food. Come on, Marisa. Let me help you."

They'd been through that before. Auntie was reaching one hand out, toward her, and Marisa's breasts still hurt from the last time "Don't," she said. "I don't want you to touch me again. I don't like to be touched."

Auntie laughed. "Well, now's a fine time to figure that out. Seems to me that's how you got yourself in this predicament in the first place."

Marisa wasn't just figuring this out. Even when she and Brad had made love—if it could be called that, on a snowy night when he was stranded in her little town—the lights were out and the covers were pulled up and over their bodies, up to their shoulders, and even then she had kept her t-shirt and socks on. If she could have, she would have worn all her clothes throughout the ordeal. She'd been seduced more by his predicament and his travel stories than by his hands, and she'd lain there trying to think unsuccessfully about something other than what he was doing to her. She'd known him a while by then—but only as his pilot, bringing him out to base camp and back—and that night she imagined climbing mountains, or trekking through jungles, or flying off to sunny beaches with him. She'd turned her head and looked out at the sideways snow and listened to the moaning wind, and she'd wondered why she wasn't enjoying his touch, his sex. She'd been anxious for it to end, so that, after he left her bed, she would have her body to herself again, to hibernate for the rest of the year inside her soft, warm clothes—the same way she did, fifteen years earlier, when her mother breezed out the door that last time.

Marisa had been only four then, too young to name the expression on her mother's face, and too young to recognize that the excuses made for her mother's retirement from parenthood were nothing more than frozen lies that would eventually melt. Marisa had missed her mother, then hated her. Only now was she beginning to understand her.

Auntie ignored Marisa's request to leave her alone and reached out, first, to the base of Marisa's neck, lightly squeezing where all the worries were trapped. Marisa cringed at her touch, though. Auntie was just another in the long parade of hands, ever since that night with Brad, ever since Marisa's body no longer belonged to her. After Brad came the doctors, and then the women in the grocery store who had to touch her belly, and finally the baby forcing her way out. Marisa had learned, while growing up without her mother, how to live without touch, and she liked it that way.

"I guess privacy, once you have a baby, is impossible," Marisa said. "I wish I'd understood that sooner. Really understood it."

"What good would that have done?" Auntie asked as she closed the door and herded Marisa back into the room.

"Things would have been different."

The baby quieted as if hearing Marisa's thoughts.

Marisa switched off the music, plopped down in the rocker, and lifted her t-shirt as one last draft chased into the room after her. Auntie placed the child in Marisa's arms.

"Good girl," Auntie said. She settled a pillow behind Marisa's back and another under the arm cradling the child. "Now turn her toward you, her whole body." Auntie nudged the baby in to face Marisa. "And put your hand here." She adjusted Marisa's position, and reminded her to stroke the baby's lower lip.

Marisa blushed. She wondered if her mother had trouble with this. She tried to remember her mother's face, her skin. She could only come up with a faint vision of her neckline, above a white terry cloth robe.

"Okay, now wait a minute. Just wait," Auntie said. "She'll know when." Her voice sounded like springtime, cheerful and out of place.

The child's warm breath tickled like fizz from a glass of 7-Up. She started to suck, and after the initial pain subsided, Marisa relaxed and watched as the baby's long lashes fluttered and her eyes closed.

"This is different, isn't it?" Auntie said after a while. "Tough old Marisa, flying those airplanes in her big important job. Carrying a .44 and a knife in her survival kit. Scrabbling in the forest in nasty weather. This is different, isn't it? Not like hanging out at the Elkhorn Tavern with Uncle and those old farts."

Marisa rocked for a few minutes, then glanced up at the microwave clock in the kitchen. "How long do we do this for?"

"Till she acts a little drunk," Auntie said. "She'll know when to stop. Your job is to just sit and give."

Auntie began a story about Otter. Marisa had heard all those stories about the bear and the raven and the coyote, passed around the clan for generations like pipes. When she was young and had first come to live with Auntie, the stories were exciting and mesmerizing. They had lulled her into a sense of comfort and belonging. But now that she'd grown up, they were plain irritating. Uncle was her mother's relation, not Auntie, and Marisa would rather hear his flying stories, the adventures and near misses—like the time he couldn't land on the frozen lake and smashed into an enormous snowdrift, the plane scattering in all directions. How he hiked out on foot, dragging the remnants of his gear on a sled that scraped behind him for miles through whiteout conditions. How he defied all odds.

"Otter gives us energy and joy," Auntie said. "She plays around, has fun with her young." She peered over her glasses. "She creates space in her life for others to enter."

As Auntie went on, Marisa leaned her head back on the rocker, wondering again what had happened to Norman and Lucy, why they hadn't come to visit. She wished she were at the bar with them, and with Uncle, too. Or, better yet, out at Uncle's hangar, tinkering with the parts and debating weather patterns. She could be with him now, fingering the maps spread across the big wooden table or replenishing the metal survival box with flares and water and matches, or crouching under the plane, inspecting the gear legs and bolts. Sniffing the air with Uncle, as the wind brushed past. Climbing into the plane. Waiting for his thumbs up. She could be cruising down the runway faster, then faster, and sailing upward toward the afternoon sun shining like a star through the treetops. She could be flying toward the ridges of mountains layered in shades of gray. That was all she really ever wanted to do, the only place she ever wanted to be. The only place where she could forget about her past.

Marisa shifted in the rocker. Her right arm, the one holding the baby, was getting numb, and her back had stiffened. The baby's eyes were closed, but she was still sucking. Auntie sat across the room at the table sipping a cup of tea. Watching.

"Most women have Otter in their blood," Auntie said. Marisa rocked back and forth. "It's what makes the sisterhood strong. Otter makes you playful and helps you let your new life unfold, helps you move into the river of life so the current can take you to new places."

Marisa yawned.

"But I suppose," Auntie went on, "that Otter doesn't whisper these words to you yet, does she?" Her eyes locked onto Marisa's, and then she laughed. "It could be that you need a man. A man who sticks around."

Marisa stood, cringed with the aches in her back and the stinging in her breasts, and handed the baby to Auntie. Then she reached for her Seattle Mariners sweatshirt and her backpack.

"Don't be too long," Auntie said.

Marisa stepped out to the cabin's front porch and breathed in the fresh scent of spruce. She took another breath, letting the air tingle in her nostrils and down her windpipe. She took another, and then another, and headed off for town.

She walked past the West Rib and some closed gift shops and the ice cream shop, where a little girl stood outside with chocolate smeared across her face, and she brisked past a vacant storefront until finally arriving at the Elkhorn.

It took a minute for her eyes to adjust to the dark, wood-paneled interior. The baseball playoffs were on the television, and George and Howard—Uncle's retired pilot friends— were back in the corner playing darts, as usual. But where was Uncle? She needed to see him. He was the only one who understood what it meant to fly. The addiction to flying. And the withdrawals when you stop. Marty, the bartender, came out of the men's room and smiled when he saw Marisa. He adjusted the Cubs hat on his bald head, cinched up the waistline of his baggy jeans, and wrapped his scraggly arms around her.

"Welcome back, Little Pilot," he said. "Or should I now call you Little Mama?"

"Where's Uncle?" she asked.

Marty shrugged. "Not here."

She sat down on a barstool anyway and pulled her laptop from her backpack. She didn't particularly like being in bars, but at least Marty had free Wi-Fi. She powered on her computer.

Most of her e-mail was junk, except for one message from a client who needed a pilot next month. She wanted to reply that yes, she'd take the job. But it had already been decided for her. Uncle would handle all the flights for the first six months. "And then we'll see," Auntie had said.

Marisa deleted the rest of the junk and those annoying jokes that her cousins were now always sending her about parenthood. It didn't surprise her there was nothing from Brad, but it was a disappointment. By now she would have expected something from him about the baby. He'd known perfectly well when the due date was. And she'd already sent him one e-mail since the baby was born. What the hell, she thought. She drafted another note.

> From: Marisa
> Subject: Checking In
> Date: September 28 11:36:12 AM AKDT
> To: Brad
>
> Hey Brad,
> Just thought I'd check in. Aashka and I are doing well.

She stared at the screen and wondered what he thought about the name. She wanted to tell him to get the hell up here, not for her sake but for the baby. Wanted to say this was damn hard and he should be here helping. It was his responsibility, after all. And maybe—though she'd never admit it to him or anyone else—maybe there was a part of her that wished he were there for her, too. Sure, Marisa could do it on her own. Her mother didn't have a man around to help her, either.

Then again, look what happened there.

> Your baby's beautiful.

Marisa thought she might even be able to get used to being touched by him again. Better than Auntie's hands all over her breasts.

> Let me know how you are.
>
> Love,
> Marisa

She pressed SEND quickly, before she changed her mind. But the message bounced back. It was undeliverable.

"Shit," she said aloud.

Marisa scrolled the phone book on her cell phone for Brad's number. She hadn't spoken to him for months, so at this point she had nothing to lose. His phone rang four times, and then an automated voice told her the number was no longer in service. She slammed her hand down on the bar, then packed up her stuff and raced out the door.

Taking the front steps to her little cabin two by two, Marisa was anxious to just throw herself down on her bed and check out for good. But when she opened the front door, she froze. Auntie was sitting in the rocker, with the baby swaddled in her pink blanket and crying again. Three of Marisa's cousins had come to visit with their fidgety babies and toddlers.

"There you are!" Auntie said as Marisa tried to catch her breath.

She set her backpack down and took the baby from Auntie without a word. She walked back to the bedroom. She lifted her t-shirt and adjusted her position as Auntie had taught her, and the baby began to nurse. But it still hurt. It hurt like hell.

Auntie clanged around in the kitchen, and the cousins chirped and chatted in the front room, while Marisa waited impatiently for the child to finish. Finally, both breasts were drained and the baby fell asleep on her back. Marisa lay down and listened to the steady breath.

After a few minutes she shifted away, trying not to wake the baby. She stood and studied the spiky black hair, the long lashes, the round little nose, and the heart-shaped lips. Aashka, curled up like that, was no bigger than a loaf of bread, so small she could fit inside a backpack. Marisa watched the rise and fall of the baby's chest, the way her fingers squeezed and released those tiny fists. She rested her hand over the baby's heart and felt it pumping, a rapid little beat that mirrored the pounding in her own chest. She pulled the pink blanket up to the baby's chin, then hesitated and glanced at the doorway, where she expected to see Auntie watching.

But Auntie wasn't there. Marisa and Aashka were alone in the bedroom. She pulled the blanket higher, up and over the baby's face, and let it drop. The baby continued to breathe, and a miniature crater in the blanket formed above the baby's mouth, deepening with each inhale and then relaxing with the exhale.

Marisa wondered how long the baby could breathe under the blanket. She looked toward the doorway again. She realized she was holding her own breath. She returned her gaze to the blanket rising and falling, then reached for the baby, slid the blanket down from the baby's face, and tucked it tight around her neck. She then kissed Aashka's cheek.

Once again, Marisa breezed through the front room of the cabin and out the door, not bothering to explain her departure. When she got to the hangar, Uncle was tinkering with the plane, wearing his old plaid jacket and baseball cap. He smiled when he saw her.

"What took you so long?" he asked.

He picked up his old saddlebag and pulled out a thermos of coffee and the old cookie tin that he'd brought to work every day for as long as Marisa could remember. On its lid was a painted scene of an airplane much like Uncle's Beaver, set against a cloudless sky, with trees edging along the bottom. The plane trailed a banner that read SKYDANCER.

"Here, you'll need these," Uncle said. "Got a fresh batch of sugar cookies in here." She took the thermos. But she waved the cookie tin away. It reminded her too much of her childhood, her past. Her mother.

A cold drizzle began to fall, and the sky had become a flat, brownish gray that cast a sepia hue over the landscape. It was no longer like the picturesque sky on the cookie tin. But Marisa didn't care. She climbed in and started the plane. She checked the instrument panel, fastened her seat belt, and waited for Uncle's thumbs up. As she taxied, Marisa took a deep breath and sank back into the vibration of the seat. She heard the orchestra warming up, first with the low bass notes and gradually ascending to higher pitches, and then at take off the violins and woodwinds. She felt lighter herself as the plane rose into the sky. The town grew smaller and smaller in the distance now, and the wipers slapped at the rain as she blinked back tears.

What had happened in the cabin? Sweating, Marisa pushed in the throttle and glanced at the instruments, but what she saw was a pink blanket pulled over Aashka's face. She saw herself standing, immobile, waiting for Auntie to step in, to stop her. She thought of her mother again, wrapped in her robe—a cool woman who didn't demonstrate much love and who eventually abandoned her only child—and she wondered how long her mother had wanted to leave, how long it had taken her to muster the courage to run away—or if it was courage at all—and whether she had also once imagined pulling a pink baby blanket too high. The horror of it all made Marisa woozy. She felt her milk let down again, already, and she pulled back on the yoke. The plane rose higher still, and Marisa wondered whether abandonment, like black eyes, was hereditary.

She took a deep, long breath and leveled out the plane. It had taken longer than usual to rise above the thin layer of clouds and memory, to leave behind the stories about Otter making space for others. But finally, it seemed she had, and meanwhile the sky had become tinged with evening pink. Marisa checked her fuel, and her heart thumped like a happy dog's tail. She could bank to the northeast and make it to Fairbanks. She could turn south toward Anchorage and run away to the mainland. She could head out to base camp where surely something was happening.

Unbuckling her seat belt, she reached down for Uncle's thermos and poured coffee into the blue plastic cup. She guzzled it and poured another cup and drank that one, too. Then she screwed the cup back onto the thermos and set it back into Uncle's organized bin of tools and trinkets. There, she found the old faded picture of Auntie and their seven happy children, arms wrapped around one another's shoulders and waists, with five-year-old Marisa sitting cross-legged in front of the group, tight-lipped and separate and alone. She had always hated that photograph. And now she hated it even more because it brought everything back yet again.

Had it not been for Aashka, this plane would have been hers by now, and the picture would have been gone.

She stared at it once more, then shoved it back where she'd found it and looked out the window at the cold and darkening sky. She was too high to see the caribou down below or even the golden eagles perched on a ledge somewhere. She was too upset to think, right now, about where the abandonments of her past and the responsibilities of her future might lead. Tonight, she could only do what came naturally to her, so she pulled back on the yoke once more, guiding the plane higher and aiming away from town toward the desolate mountains she called home.

# LIAR'S GAME

# At the Church of St. Absolut

—LEA GALANTER

A lie is merely a truth misunderstood
a confession made to anyone who will listen
purged with prayer in some wayside church
and absolved of sin by the holy man of spirits

Confession is good for the souls of those who wander
finding sanctuary in a mirrored shrine
and an altar for hair-shirt stories woven of myth and mire

Bring your silences and your songbird secrets
sing out the sorrows of your divine contrition
penance is more than sacks and cigarette ashes
healing more than holy water and three hail bloody Marys
served by a steward who makes sacraments of our
        offenses

Do not suffer the wretched commandments of your
        conscience
but dive freely into the font of avowed revelations

**ON WEDNESDAYS,** Ron Major would shut down the lumberyard early and lead us over to C.J.'s, down the street from the train station, for a bottle of Wild Turkey and an afternoon of liar's poker. We all went. I had to; it was part of the job. We'd file into the dim bar, paneled in the same dark walnut that decorated my husband's sanctuary at the church, and we'd take our positions at the old, round table in the middle of the room, waiting to get started like communicants at the altar. Walt, a freckle-faced guy with biceps bigger than my thighs, always sat to my left, and next around the table came Bill Spitt and Bill Chew, both of them with pregnant wives and lawns to mow and bills to pay back home. (Spitt and Chew, by the way, were their honest-to-God names; I know because I did the payroll.) Then came Ron, seated on my right, wearing his usual short-sleeved white shirt and clip-on tie, with a cigar in his pocket protector next to the blue ballpoint pens. And of course, me, with my back to the door, my silk scarf shoved deep in my pocket, and my top two blouse buttons finally open so I could really breathe.

We were the only customers in the tavern at that time of day (that time when you notice how badly it reeks of stale smoke from years ago, or from last Wednesday when Clarence the bartender broke the rules and let us light up, like he did every week). He'd already have the bottle set in the middle of the table and the pretzel bowl filled before we even arrived, and once we were seated the guys would take their first round of shots and light up whatever it was they were smoking, and then we'd get to playing.

We each brought our own stash of single dollar bills for liar's poker. We'd laugh and bluff, smirk and swear, and gladly take each other's hard-earned pay. And we'd listen to Ron's stories all afternoon, till 5:00 sharp—when the train would blast its whistle and rumble into the station, and the phone behind the bar would ring. I'd always jump at the sound, surprised at how quickly the time had passed and scared that this might be the time I'd be found out. But it was always Ron's wife, a Scandinavian woman named Ursa, calling to ask Clarence to send Ron directly home.

There's something about poker that brings out the stories—stories that people want to tell and that others want to hear. Stories, too, that make you wonder. Back in my former life, when I wore my hair spiked and dyed magenta, and when I smoked Virginia Slims, and when I insisted I *was too* a virgin, I was a sponge for any good tale. One time, when I'd headed out to Vegas with my roommate to escape those suffocating classrooms and midterm exams, I met a guy in aviator glasses whose name was McFinn. Sure, he was cute: blonde hair, broad shoulders, and a smile straight out of a toothpaste commercial. But what impressed me most (besides all those chips stacked in front of him) were the stories he told, like how he earned the tooth on his gold chain by wrestling a man-eating shark, and how he'd made a half-million bucks playing church bingo, only to donate it all to an Appalachian orphanage, and how he then became a swimsuit sales rep because he wanted to help women with their self-esteem. I thought I could play Five-card Stud and Texas Hold 'Em forever, drinking whiskey even cheaper than Wild Turkey and listening to him spin those yarns.

Ron's stories weren't so glamorous but they still were plenty interesting. His were always set in the great outdoors, like the one about the moose charging him in his Old Town canoe on the Allagash River up in Maine. Or the time he got trapped—and almost drowned—under the same canoe just below Little Wildcat Falls. Or the time he chased a wolf away from his cabin in the Upper Peninsula, when lo and behold the wolf stopped, turned around, and chased him right back through the cabin's screen door.

I guess I'd been a sort of a wolf myself, chasing after McFinn. One night I chased him right up to his penthouse suite. He asked me to model a size four red-and-black bikini, and when I came out of the bathroom, the lights were turned low and the Brut was poured. He checked the fit and told a few more stories and, well you can pretty much figure out what happened then. I didn't hear from him until a couple of months later, till after I'd started dating Ian—the new pastor fresh out of seminary at my parent's church. A package came in the mail one day while Ian was visiting. I opened it at the kitchen table, careful not to knock over our glasses of raspberry lemonade, and pulled out that size four swimsuit, along with a deck of cards, a set of poker chips, and a photo of McFinn modeling a pretty tight Speedo. I started to explain, but Ian held his index finger to my lips and shook his head. "Don't want to hear about that, not now, not ever." That pretty much became his mantra during our entire courtship, and then our marriage. He was happy with who I had become and didn't need to know anything else. His acceptance of me had been adorably fresh, at the time, and I didn't mind his reluctance to hear about my past.

And now, even though Ian still didn't want to hear my stories, I think he would have enjoyed Ron's, if the situation had been different, if I could have brought him into the bar and introduced him to the guys. Except, of course, for the way everyone reacted to the one Ron told that hot September afternoon.

The guys had already gone through most of a bottle, the afternoon sun was blasting through the window down onto our table, and time was running thin. Walt had been the big winner that day, having cheated each of us out of at least six or seven dollars, and I was (as usual) hoping Ian wouldn't notice that I'd run short of cash or figure out why we always had tuna-noodle casserole on Wednesdays. We each dug out one last dollar bill, folded it in half lengthwise and then in half again, and tucked it neatly inside the palms of our hands so that we couldn't see each other's serial number. It was my turn to bet first.

"Five twos," I said, pretty sure that—among the five of us—at least five twos could be found in the collection of serial numbers on the bills we held.

Walt scoffed, but then he only raised me a little (five fives), and I was tempted to scoff right back but I didn't—maybe because it just wouldn't have been right, or maybe because I was just too tired. So off we went with another round of gambling. By the time it got around to Ron's turn, we were well past the bets of five-of-anything.

"Ten aces," he said, and while it was certainly possible there were ten ones among the five of us, I knew he was stretching his luck by the way he held up his unlit cigar and started a story. Chances were good he didn't have a single ace, which meant it was up to the four of us to produce ten of them in order for Ron to win this round.

"So I was camping in New Mexico a few years back," he said, "up above Taos, with a bunch of Cub Scouts. I was practically dead after a long day of caving, campfires, and sticky marshmallows, and I had to share my tent with four of the kids. But it was a clear summer night, no mosquitoes for miles, so I slept half-in, half-out of the tent." He gestured toward his crotch when he said this.

Walt asked what he meant, and Ron rolled his eyes and shook his head and explained that it was his bottom half, *everything below the belt*, that protruded out through the tent door, and I wondered if everyone else was wondering what I was—whether or not Ron was clothed. Once, in a prior story, he'd revealed his tendency to sleep in the nude.

It was my turn to bet, and even though I was pretty sure he didn't have any aces, I couldn't call Ron just yet. But in liar's poker you either have to call or raise. "Ten sixes," I said, although I didn't have a single six. Now it was Walt's turn.

"So anyway," Ron glanced at me and then went on. "I wake up in the middle of the night and hear this heavy breathing."

I can't help it, but when I'm at the yard or the bar with these guys, I kind of regress to my wilder self, like a trapped feral animal that has escaped from its cage for a while, adrenaline surging. When Ron mentioned *heavy breathing*, and raised his eyebrows the way he did, my imagination started to heat up, and apparently so did everyone else's. Ian would say I shouldn't even be listening to this story, with the looks on the guys' faces—smirks of anticipation—and the lusty grunts they were making for sound effects as they waited to hear what the heavy breathing was all about.

"There's all this noise and twigs snapping and so on," Ron said. He was actually breaking a little beaded sweat along his hairline, and trying to stifle a smile.

So was Walt, who reminded me of a dog waiting for its food, practically salivating at just a hint of something decadent. The Bills looked at each other, grinned, nodded. I folded my hands on top of my dollar bill and stiffened. It was the way Ron was telling the story, not just his insinuation of what might have been happening out there in those woods, but also his gestures, his theatrical expressions, and the twinkle in his eyes, which made the whole thing so sensual, so arousing.

"But remember I'm half in, half out of the tent. No way I can move," Ron said. "I've got no choice but to lie there and listen, hoping the kids don't wake up and figure out what's going on. I'm thinking if I move even one muscle, I'll wake them, and that sure as hell..." He nodded at me, and winked. "Sorry, Brinn. Poor choice of words." Even in the bar, they were always respectful of my situation as a pastor's wife. "So instead I just lie there holding my breath and waiting it out."

By this point, I couldn't even look up at Ron. My cheeks were hot and I knew my neck was flushing.

One of Ian's recent sermons came to mind; he always had me read his messages before he delivered them to the congregation. And this one, like so many of them, involved truth and lies—Ian's biggest hot buttons.

*Satan tells us lies every day,* Ian had written, *about what we need to be happy.* Sex. Alcohol. Money. In so doing, Ian said, Satan convinces us to do whatever we need to do in order to get whatever we want, which often means lying to our loved ones, and to ourselves, and to God. *Remember, lies aren't just about telling an untruth. Lies are also omissions of truth.* And every time we fail to talk to God, and when we fail to confess our sins, Ian said, Satan is turning us away from our Lord and Savior. *Satan is the father of all lies, and he's the one we should turn away from.*

I had shivered that Sunday morning when I read Ian's words, thinking about all the omissions of my past that Ian had never wanted to hear about. And my omissions of the present, like the Wednesday afternoons I spent drinking and gambling with the guys from work. I knew it was wrong for me to keep this secret from my own husband. And yet I returned to the bar every week, and when I did, it almost felt like I was returning to myself.

Ron took a break from his story to watch a grand slam on the TV above the bar.

Walt pushed back from the table. "Nature's calling," he said.

Just as Ron always began telling stories whenever he made a wild bet, Walt had a tendency to leave the table whenever he thought he was about to lose. He slipped his folded dollar bill into a napkin, set his empty shot glass on top, and studied what he'd done. "Oh, twelve sixes," he said, and then he hurried off to the restroom. Bill Spitt and Bill Chew watched him go and then examined their own bills.

A bet of twelve sixes was pretty gutsy, and while it's not technically *lying* if you make an unlikely bet when you don't have many sixes—or whatever—in your own hand, it *feels* like a lie. And when everyone shows their bills at the end of the round, and they see that you never had any sixes at all, you feel like you've been caught in one. I guess that's why they call it liar's poker.

"Sure enough," Ron said, continuing with his story in Walt's absence, his eyes sparkling the way they always did when he really got going. And when he'd had a lot to drink. He paused just long enough to pour everyone another shot.

"The next thing I know," Ron said, "there's this heavy weight on my left shin, for just a moment. And then comes this piercing pain. That's when I scream bloody murder."

Until now I'd been imagining some sort of tryst in the woods, but now I wasn't so sure what the story was about. Bill Chew interrupted my thoughts.

"I fold," he said.

"You can't fold in liar's poker," the other Bill said.

"Well I do," Bill Chew said. "It's the last round anyway. So who cares?"

"Good point," Bill Spitt said. "Then I fold, too."

Ron shot a look of distaste at both of them, then downed his shot of whiskey. He flattened his hands on the table and leaned in toward me. "I'm writhing in pain," he said, his face growing red. We were back in his story again. "I'm moaning and crying Jesus this and Jesus that—sorry, Brinn—and the kids all wake up. Flashlights switch on..." His gaze drifted to a distant place, and he paused, and we waited, and then he came back to us, head ducked low and eyebrows knitted together. He lowered his voice to a near whisper. "And there's *blood* everywhere."

"Blood?"

"Blood! All over my leg, all over the tent. The kids are going berserk." He looked around at each of us. He was reliving the experience, his face crumpled with pain, his eyes narrowed. Or he was doing a great job acting.

We waited for enlightenment. It's pretty hard to admit to your boss that you have no idea what he's talking about, or that you think he's lying. And I know the Bills felt the same way. I could tell by how they scratched their heads and picked at their fingernails that even they had grown uncomfortable, and maybe a bit bored.

And then Ron started to laugh, his shoulders jerking as small grunts burst out from somewhere in his gut. "Don't you get it? Don't you see?" He was laughing even harder now, all by himself, and the three of us shook our heads.

"You don't? It was a damn bear! A bear that tripped right over my leg and then turned around and bit me, sure as you might kick a table you bump into in the middle of the night! Get it?" He slapped the table a couple of times and laughed even harder until the sweat streamed down his forehead and his eyes began to fill with tears. The shot glasses jiggled with his slap like they were laughing along with him, and I forced a couple of chuckles, too. But it's hard to laugh at a big fat lie; there was no way a bear would trip over him, then turn back around to bite. But what made it even harder for me to laugh was the admission to myself that I'd actually thought something indecent had been going on in the woods—an orgy perhaps—before the alleged bear dropped by. My mind had unnecessarily been in the gutter.

The building shook, and the 5:00 train screeched into the station, and Ron stopped laughing. He turned toward the window, where I figure he probably saw the imaginary bear instead of the train, and I closed my eyes to try to finally see the whole scene as it was meant to be seen. I still couldn't.

Walt came back then, swung his chair around backward, and straddled it like a cowboy. "What'd I miss?" He'd undone a couple of buttons on his shirt and now wiped his hand over his face, and I couldn't help but wonder if he'd used soap in the bathroom. He studied his napkin again and then carefully moved the full shot glass and slid his dollar bill out and inspected that, too, until he finally seemed satisfied that all was as he'd left it, and I noticed for the first time in all these years that he wore a gold chain a lot like McFinn's, except that Walt's chain had a cross dangling into the hairy shadows beneath his shirt.

"What'd you miss? A bear tripped over Ron," I said, "and then turned around and bit him. And the Bills folded."

"No shit," Walt said. He shot the same disgusted look toward the Bills that Ron had, then turned his attention to Ron. "Liar."

I admit it, I had to wonder, too, and I wished I could've gone home to share the bear story with Ian to see what he thought about it. But then I'd have had to tell him about the bar and the poker and everything else, of which he wouldn't approve, and probably what I'd actually thought had been going on in the woods, at which he'd be appalled. So this story would be buried in my silent memory along with so many of my other stories. Right alongside McFinn.

Most of the time these guys were respectful of my position as a pastor's wife, but occasionally they ribbed me about it and asked how I

wound up with such a straight and narrow kind of guy. I made up some
sort of explanation, but the truth was that I couldn't explain why I fell in
love with Ian all those years ago. Love just doesn't always make sense.
He was handsome and kind; he treated me right. I knew you have to
make compromises to make a marriage work. But I also knew I'd always
be able to trust Ian, which you can't say about a lot of people you meet.

Ron looked back down at his own dollar bill. It was his turn. It's hard
to beat twelve sixes. It was past 5:00 now, and the phone hadn't rung yet.
We'd never actually met Ron's wife, and he didn't wear a wedding ring,
so I had to wonder about that, too, whether Ursa even existed, and also
whether that was even her real name. After all, who in her right mind
would take on his last name—Major—if her first name really was Ursa?

Ron looked back at Walt and they stared at each other head-on. The
Bills had crossed their arms and leaned back from the table, balancing on
the back legs of their chairs. Ron emptied the bottle into his shot glass
and gulped it down as he glanced up at the television. The Cubs were
down by four in the eighth inning of their last game of the season. He
checked his watch. "Twelve nines."

Walt didn't react, as if he hadn't heard what Ron had said. But I was
thinking *twelve nines*? What was the likelihood we'd come up with twelve
nines among the five of us—or among the three of us now that the Bills
were out?

"Twelve nines, I said," Ron repeated.

I could have gone the honest—and possibly smart—route and called
Ron. Or I could have lied again, too. The odds were stacked against me,
and no matter what I did, and no matter what happened, I'd never be
able to tell this story except during silent confession in the front pew on
Sunday morning, when I'd be praying to God to please keep holding on
to my little secret about being a lying, cheating, gambling pastor's wife.

I was about to bluff when Ron turned his chair out from the table,
scooted toward me a little, crossed his legs, and winked. I glanced down,
and he pulled up the hem of his left pant leg, high enough for me to see a
nasty scar on each side of his naked shin, a scar that sure enough
could've been made by a bear's sharp bite. Then he pulled out his wallet
to pay the bar bill, and he angled it toward me so I could see a photo of
him with a blond woman with big blue eyes wearing nothing but a
Sports Illustrated-style bikini (not unlike the one McFinn had sent me)
inside the plastic photo holder.

"That's Ursa," Ron said.

I had no choice. No matter what scars and secrets might be hidden behind aviator glasses and polyester pants, you can't deny what you actually see any more than you can believe what you can't. It makes you wonder if you ever really know what's true and what isn't.

It was now 5:09, and the phone behind the bar finally rang. Walt lit up another Camel, stuck it between his lips, and tossed his dollar bill into the pot. I threw mine in, too. Bill Spitt and Bill Chew drained the last drops of Wild Turkey from their shot glasses. Ron lit up his cigar—even though I wished he'd wait till he was outside—and gathered the pile of cash from the middle of the table. I buttoned up my blouse and tied my scarf into a neat little bow.

Clarence picked up the phone, and the five of us watched him, waiting to hear what Ursa had to say, as we sat at our table—one woman of faith and four drunken men, gathered together in a precious circle of fellowship, sharing a secret communion of sorts beneath a dissipating halo of smoke and lies.

# FLOAT AWAY

# In Algiers the Wind Howls

—ELAINE NUSSBAUM

The Mississippi runs deep and wide
He played a sad song—Miles Davis.
Lyrics about a woman on a long white table
You can't be sort of dead.

He played a sad song—Miles Davis.
Anna Karenina. The Awakening. They don't end well.
You can't be sort of dead.
The Adventures of Huck Finn or Peter Pan.

Anna Karenina. The Awakening. They don't end well.
That's where it's at for cats like me.
The Adventures of Huck Finn or Peter Pan
Dixie Land, New Orleans.

That's where it's at for cats like me.
Others twisted, turned, some broke free.
Dixie Land, New Orleans.
You've got to take what comes to you.

Others twisted, turned, some broke free.
She ran to the mighty Mississippi.
You've got to take what comes to you.
Time seemed to stop, the river flowed.

She ran to the mighty Mississippi.
Water slurps, hungry for us too.
Time seemed to stop, the river flowed
The river our ticket to the entire world.

Water slurps, hungry for us too.
Maybe we'll go all the way to New Orleans.
The river our ticket to the entire world.
He looked out towards the Mississippi.

Maybe we'll go all the way to New Orleans.
An old weathered boat floated by.
He looked out towards the Mississippi.
The boat looked frail, I can't swim.

An old weathered boat floated by.
We'll get further than we are now.
The boat looked frail, I can't swim.
That's all we can hope for.

We'll get further than we are now.
The boat rocked and creaked.
That's all we can hope for.
Water thick like rowing through a swamp.

The boat rocked and creaked.
The water slurped and gurgled.
Water thick like rowing through a swamp.
Bald eagles, crows, black wings.

The Mississippi runs deep and wide
Lyrics about a woman on a long white table.

**WHEN TORO,** our neighbor's black pit bull, growled at me from behind his owner's screen door, I picked up a smashed beer can and hurled it at him. He snapped his sharp little teeth. Poor guy. So stupid he couldn't even realize when something big stood in his way.

I sure was gonna miss him.

Raina, who technically was my mother, staggered into my room last night, her breath reeking of stale smoke and nasty old beer, and she woke me up to say we were gonna be moving across the river to Davenport, Iowa. Tonight.

*It's all for the best, Frankie. I promise.*

Yeah, right. That was her standard mantra, and I pretty much knew not to believe it. I also knew not to ask any questions about the man's voice I heard out in the hallway. Instead, I pulled up my covers and grabbed Boo, my stuffed teddy bear with the missing eye that I'd had since I was a little bitty baby, and I turned toward the wall until she left. I knew a middle-school girl shouldn't be hugging teddy bears anymore, but it felt good.

But Boo couldn't fix things, and when I woke up this morning and stepped outside to check the weather—it was cold, and the air tickled the inside of my nose and there was gauzy dew everywhere and dust floating around in the hazy sunlight—I discovered a pile of flattened cardboard boxes in the dirt, along with a roll of packing tape, a permanent marker, a box cutter, and an empty bottle of Beefeaters.

It hadn't been a bad dream. We were in for another move.

I knew not to expect any more from this one than any of the others. It wasn't like we were running off to someplace lovely like Oregon or

Alaska, which my friends Beth and Ryan had told me all about, or even to a big city like Chicago where my grandpa lived in that fancy high rise overlooking Lake Michigan. No. This move was just another lame attempt by my mother to find some sort of new way to make it.

At least we'd get out of this trailer dump, though. And I could always hope for something better, couldn't I? By moving to a new school I might finally escape from that god-awful nickname assigned to me back in fourth grade, a nickname that has stuck to me like roaches to the floor of a roach motel.

Swamp Girl.

I remember exactly when that name came up, thanks to that big-ass boy with the gold, wire-rimmed glasses, khaki pants and an Izod polo shirt who was now always in the local news as the star junior varsity quarterback at the high school. Eric something-or-other. I'd been lined up with my classmates at the elementary school, waiting to go back inside after recess, when a bunch of white kids from the middle school on the rich side of town came over. I never did find out what they were doing there, but that wasn't what mattered.

"Hey, Swamp Girl," the wire-rimmed boy called out, loud enough for the whole world, or maybe the whole universe, to hear. His bully friends laughed their butts off and so did all the kids in my own class. I didn't know if they were making fun of the color of my skin or the fact that I lived in a trashy trailer park; either way there weren't any swamps around here so it was a stupid name, and I decided it was best to pretend I didn't hear them. I bent down to retie my shoelaces. But the damage was done. For the rest of the day, and pretty much the rest of my life, I was known at school by that name, which meant the end of any chance of new friends.

And that wasn't the only thing bad that happened that rotten day. Back then, Raina was still sober in the afternoons, and when I went home to tell her what had happened at school, and when she wrapped her long, slender arms around me and kissed the top of my head, I noticed a ring of bruises around her wrists and in the creases of her elbows. I ran my fingers across those marks and wanted to ask about them, but something inside told me not to, the same way I knew not to ask about some of the strange things I'd found in her room, including the bloody underwear. Raina had been going out at night with a lot of different men, and I knew those bruises and scars and bloodstains had something to do with them. When Raina told me that day not to let those boys at school hurt me by calling me names, I wondered how she could possibly mean it when it was obvious that grown-up men were hurting her.

"Aw, Sugar," she said to me. "You gotta learn to let those kinds of things roll off your shoulders. You gotta let everyone know who's in charge."

I pretty much didn't trust whatever she said after that.

Now, thinking about our upcoming move and the possibility of shedding that nickname, the irony of her words finally struck me. I had just learned about irony in language arts last week, and I hadn't quite grasped the concept. But as Toro yapped at me from next door and a strand of ants circled the gin bottle in the dirt, I realized this was a perfect example of that term. My mother, the hooker/alcoholic/drug addict, who let men dope her up and beat her up, had told me that you've got to let others know who's in charge when in fact she hadn't been able to do just that. I probably could've earned some extra credit if I shared all that with my teacher. Except I wouldn't have the chance to do that if we were really moving away later that day. Besides, I couldn't tell my teacher the truth about my mom.

I picked up the packing supplies and headed for my room, and then an image of Libby flashed before my eyes. A rock the size of a football swelled up in my gut.

Tyler Libertone. My one and only friend these days. A boy who, even when he was completely grown up, would never hurt me the way so many men had hurt Raina. I knew that about him. And now I was going to have to leave him behind.

I stuffed the marker and box cutter into the back pocket of my jeans, then sprinted right out through the door and straight out of the trailer park, my heart racing as fast as my legs. I had to see him one last time.

It was nearly three miles, past the corn maze that would be opening in just a couple more weeks, and past the field where I'd stolen a pumpkin last year, where once again a fresh batch of them was scattered about. They reminded me of fat orange cats lazing in the sun. Finally I came to the intersection with the old Shell station, Wilson's Feed Store, Lonnie's Diner, and the library, which gave me an idea.

I started up the library's crooked stone steps, and there was that man I'd seen around town lately. The one with a patch over one eye, which reminded me of Boo. He had smooth, dark skin—like chocolate fudge, my favorite flavor—with one vanilla-white spot on his left cheekbone. I envied his skin color; whether you called him black or African American or one of the naughty names, at least it was clear which group of people he belonged to.

Unlike me. Raina had been adopted when she was a baby, and all I knew was that her mother was white and her father was from a foreign country, somewhere in the Middle East. As for my own father, I'd been told he might have been Italian but nobody, including my own mother, knew for sure. In other words, I was a mutt without a history.

I sat down on the top stone step, a safe distance from the eyepatch man. He smiled and nodded at me, then did exactly what I'd hoped he'd do. He pulled his shiny brass trumpet out of a velvet-lined case. After slipping a mouthpiece into one end and fitting a silver cone into the other, he blew through the horn. It reminded me of a sleepy police siren. Then he played a sad song, and when he was finished, he looked over at me again.

"Miles Davis," he said. It was the first time he'd ever said anything directly to me.

"Nice to meet you, Miles." I measured the distance between us.

He laughed. "No, not me. Haven't you ever heard of the great Miles Davis? That was one of his tunes."

"Oh." I had heard of Miles Davis; Raina sometimes played his music. I just wasn't thinking about him now, with so much else on my mind. I watched the musician's fingers dance on the three little trumpet pads, as though they were itching to keep on playing. But the man looked like he was waiting for something. Soon enough a young couple walked out of Lonnie's hand in hand, and the woman dropped a five-dollar bill into the open instrument case. The trumpet player thanked her, then played another song. He was like a wind-up doll.

"Was that Miles too?" I asked when he'd finished.

"No, that was Bix Beiderbecke. Another of the jazz greats. He lived right over there." He pointed west. "Right across the river, in Davenport."

I had lived near the Mississippi all my life but had never been over the bridge. I wondered if I'd run into Bix over there after we moved.

An old woman hobbled over and dropped a couple of dollar bills into the trumpet case, and as the musician lifted his trumpet to his lips again, my stomach began to growl. My fingers wanted that money as badly as his fingers wanted to play.

"Hungry?" the trumpeter said when his next song was done.

I didn't know my stomach could be that loud.

"I'll tell you what," he said. "I've got enough here for you to go into the diner and buy us a big plate of biscuits and gravy. We can share it. All you have to do is name this next artist."

*Never take nothing from a man you don't know, unless you're truly desperate. We ain't beggars.* Raina's words echoed inside my head. But my churning stomach had other ideas. The trumpet player was blowing into his horn again, this song even sadder than the first one, and then he put the trumpet down and sang some lyrics about a woman lying on a long, white table and about having to let her go.

"She died?" I asked when he was done. "Is she dead?"

He looked at me, puzzled. "You mean in the song? Is the woman in the song dead?" He scratched his head. "Well, yeah, I guess she sort of is."

"You can't be sort of dead." When my grandmother died from cancer, she was definitely 100 percent dead. Which meant my life was 100 percent screwed from that point on. And I couldn't name the artist any more than I could name the man. I told the trumpet player I'd better get going.

"You play real good," I said. With that, I stood up and darted through the library's wide double doors, anxious to see the library lady. She was always nice to me.

But she wasn't there. Instead, a man standing behind the desk peered at me over his glasses.

"Where's Mrs. Whitcomb?" I asked.

"She has today off. Can I help you?"

I looked around. Mrs. Whitcomb would have willingly helped me find what I was looking for. But I didn't know if I could trust this guy. I guess that's one thing Raina taught me: being careful about trust.

"Looking for books about running away. I mean, about runaways." I forced my chin up and my shoulders back as he gave me a quick once-over.

"Runaways?" he repeated.

I nodded.

"How old are you?"

"Why?" It wasn't like I was trying to buy liquor.

"I'm wondering whether to steer you toward adult fiction or children's literature."

Children's stories? Was he kidding?

"I'm sixteen."

Which of course wasn't true, and usually I wouldn't lie. But I kind of wondered if librarians had those secret buttons, like bank tellers did, to contact the police. Did he think I was going to run away? And if he did think this, would he report me?

"How about *The Adventures of Huckleberry Finn*?" He asked. "Or *Peter Pan*?"

"Don't want any books about dumb boys," I told him. Which reminded me I needed to get a move on here. I still needed to get to Libby.

"Well, there are also some very classic stories about grown women who run away from their lives. *Anna Karenina. The Awakening.* But they don't often end well."

"Any about teenage girls? With happy endings?"

The man sighed at me.

"What? No such thing as a happy ending for a girl?"

"I'm sure there are. But not here in this library. Our selection is limited. I can order something for you, though, from the city."

I reached into the back pocket of my jeans, where I always kept a tube of cherry-flavored ChapStick and my library card. I slapped the card down on the librarian's desk. "Never mind. I won't be needing this anymore."

Something about turning in that card made my eyes fill up. Or maybe it was that suggestion about there being no happy endings for girls. Whatever, I'd felt both anxious and numb at the same time, which had been happening a lot to me lately. There was only one way I knew how to fix that.

I ran to the bathroom and into a stall. I unzipped my jeans and pulled them down, and then, with the box cutter from Raina, I drew a thin red line just below my right hip bone. At first the line wouldn't bleed, but I knew I had to be patient, and sure enough eventually the blood started to flow. Proof that I could still feel pain. It sounds really weird, but cutting made me feel better. More human. Alive. Maybe even stronger.

"Change your mind about breakfast?" the trumpet player asked as I came down the steps, after I'd blotted the blood with toilet paper.

"No. But I do have a question for you," I said.

"Go ahead. Shoot."

I asked him if he made all his money just sitting there a couple of hours a day playing his horn.

"Why do you ask?"

"Don't know. Thinking about finding a way to make money. An honest way." I would never resort to Raina's way of making money. Ever. I'd die before I did that.

"Good luck with that," he said to me. "Especially around here. You'd better get to a bigger city if you want to find something to do. Unless you have a real special skill."

Same thing the librarian said. I needed to get to a big city for the right books.

"Then what are *you* doing here?" I said. "Not that you don't have a real special skill."

"Me? I'm just passing through. I've got some family here."

"Where are you going, after this?"

"Dixieland. New Orleans. Now there's a real city. That's where it's at for cats like me. "

He looked west again, toward the river, and I followed his gaze, focusing not so much on what he might be looking at but on all the thoughts whirling around in my head and trying to come together into a single mass, like a bunch of stupid gnats drawn to a bug zapper.

Accepting a ride from a stranger would not normally have been a good idea, but I'd struck out in the library and time was slipping away. Also, as Raina sometimes said, *you've got to be willing to take a few risks if you're going to take charge of your sorry life.* And my shoes, at least a size too small, were hurting my feet after all that running to get to town. So when the musician offered me a ride across town to Libby's neighborhood, I took it.

Libby lived in the rich area, probably close to wire-rimmed Eric. I couldn't exactly just saunter up to the door and ring the bell, especially with a blood stain on my jeans from earlier. His parents wouldn't want someone like me loitering around, I was pretty sure, and I didn't want the neighbors to call the cops because some stranger girl was lurking around. I waited for the jazz player to drive his old beater away, then circled around to the back of Libby's house. I located what I thought might be his bedroom window, the one with the shades drawn shut. He liked his room dark and quiet, he'd told me. He was a loner, I had learned, like me; the only person who understood how you sometimes have to hide away in a bathroom stall during lunch to avoid having to sit by yourself in the lunchroom, or how you bury your chin to your chest in the hallway, trying to make yourself invisible—and deaf—to the taunts of the other kids. Anyway, I picked up a few pebbles from the garden, and I tossed one up at the window. Nothing. Another pebble. Nothing.

*You gotta let them know who's in charge.*

I smoothed my thick hair as best I could while I worked up the courage to go around front and ring the doorbell. When I did, a gorgeous woman with blonde hair and a few freckles sprinkled across her nose answered the door. Her smile made me nervous.

"Is Libby here?" I asked.

The woman shook her head. "He's at a Homecoming planning meeting. Can I help you?"

Shit. Homecoming. Somehow I always forgot that Libby was in high school and so much older than me.

"When will he be home?"

"Soon, actually. He has homework to do this afternoon. Would you like to come in and wait?"

As much as I would have loved to step inside, feel that cold marble floor beneath my feet, and inhale whatever that delicious aroma was, and even though the woman seemed kind enough, I didn't have the nerve.

"No, thank you. Could you just tell him Frankie was here? And to meet me at the normal spot as soon as he can?"

"The normal spot?"

"Yes," I said. "He'll know. Thank you."

I felt heat rushing to my face as she looked at me. I turned and ran down the front steps before she could ask me anything else. This taking charge business can be hard. Which was probably why Raina was so lousy at it, too.

I ran and ran in my toe-pinching shoes all the way to my little river. It was nothing like the great Mississippi, but that's why I loved it so much. There was a secluded little path I'd found, hidden behind a broken chain-link fence. It zigzagged among scraggly brush and willow trees whose branches swept the ground. I went there almost every day to hear my thoughts and feel the fresh breeze sweep along my bare skin; it was where I went to feel safe. The squirrels sassed at me from the branches overhead, and a bald eagle showed up every now and then, which used to creep me out, the way it would fly around and stare at me, like maybe I'd taste pretty good. I used to wish I could shoot it right out of the sky.

But over time, I got used to that bird and was pretty sure it got used to me, too, and I almost thought of it as my pet. Now it swooped down close to say hello again. Or to say goodbye. And then it flapped away.

I killed time as I waited for Libby by breaking cottonwood twigs into little pieces and floating them like boats downstream. I put each one into the river at the exact same spot, but they all chose a different path through the pile of rocks clustered together like a barricade. Some of the twigs got caught up, stuck, pressed in place and held there. Others twisted and turned and somehow broke free, moving on. Like people. Raina was one of those people that got caught up. I wanted to be one to break free.

One of the twigs had a little offshoot branch with a leaf waving on top like a flag. I watched it float a ways and then capsize under a splash of frothy water. Then I picked up another twig, and there was a little brown ant crawling on it. I could have shaken it off, and probably should have, but I wanted to see what it would do.

"You've got to take what comes to you," I whispered, kneeling down and setting the twig into the flow. "Let's see what you're gonna do, little ant. Let's see who's in charge." It danced back and forth, frantic, as the twig got jostled around and then, in the glare on the water, I lost sight of the little guy. I didn't know for sure where he went, but I had a pretty good idea.

Then, a late afternoon shadow came up from behind and swallowed me.

"Hey," Libby said, his voice deep and soft as fur, his hands resting gently on my shoulders.

"Hey," I said as I turned around.

I tried not to melt like bacon fat in his presence. With his blonde hair and green eyes, narrow nose, and perfect lips, I'd always thought Libby looked like a god.

"Got your message," he said. "What's up?"

The fact that he was actually there suddenly caught me off guard. Even though I had gone over this conversation a million times that day, I felt tears coming on. I bit my lip hard, and I clenched my fists so tight that my nails dug into my palms. Then I took a deep breath.

"I'm moving. To Davenport. That's what's up."

He was still smiling, like he didn't hear me right. "You're what?"

Time seemed to stop, even though the river kept flowing.

"I'm moving to Iowa. Tonight."

Now his smile twitched.

He was so handsome. A real man, Raina would have said. I looked down and saw that his fists were matching mine.

"You're moving tonight? Just like that?"

"Come on, walk up the river with me a ways," I said. We walked upstream, farther away from the real world.

Tall grasses swayed along the bank, and something skittered beneath a fallen branch. The waning sunlight reflected off the ripples in the water. I tugged down my sleeves, a matter of habit to cover up the scars on my wrists. Not that it mattered. Libby knew I was a cutter. In fact that was how we met.

It wasn't even two months ago when Libby's high school freshman football team was about to practice one morning on the middle school field, and there they all stood waiting in their green and silver practice uniforms, looking so fresh and mature and handsome. It was orientation day for our middle school, and an annoying cluster of middle school girls surrounded the boys like homeless cats waiting for handouts. Swamp Girl here had just started cutting, and I was afraid to let anyone see me for fear of what they'd call me next, so I was dawdling in the shadow of a maple tree until it was time to go into the school. And then I heard someone call out.

"Ew! Look! There's that weird Swamp Girl!"

The gaggle of girls all looked in my direction, holding up their fancy cell phones and taking pictures of me like I was some sort of zoo animal, and then along came one of the football players. I hadn't noticed him until just then; he wasn't coming from the crowd of players and their groupies but from another direction. I'm normally not the type to be afraid, but he had broad shoulders and was making a beeline right for me, and when he got to within spittin' distance I realized he stood at least a head taller than me. As I noticed an angry scratch down his jawline, I also saw that he was holding out a hand.

"Hey," he said. "Come with me."

I still didn't know if I could trust him, but like I said, he had a soft voice. And I figured at least he'd take me away from the staring students. We crossed the parking lot and went around a tall hedge.

"I'm sorry for what they said. They're just a bunch of jerks," he said to me.

"But they're right. I am weird. See?" It was stupid of me to do it, but I don't always make the best decisions. I showed him my wrist with the fresh scars.

He looked down at the red line like he was looking down at a broken bird. Then he pointed at his ear and his jaw.

"And I scratch when I'm nervous. See? I guess I'm weird, too."

I looked at him closer. The scratches extended from the whorls on his ear all the way down his jaw to his neck. They looked painful and raw. Like my arms.

"I don't think you're weird," I told him. I wanted to add that I thought he was beautiful, not only in appearance but in his heart. If scratching was a sign of nervousness, then that showed he must be sensitive and true. But of course I couldn't say all that to him. I would've scared him off.

Now here we were at the river, on moving day, the cutter and the scratcher. I wanted so badly to finally tell him how I felt about him. How I loved him.

We walked, single file along a narrow stretch of trail, the silence jabbing at me sharply.

"I know this might not be a big deal to you," I said, even though I suspected maybe it was. "Because you live in one of those fancy houses in the middle of town. But this might be the first time I'll ever get to live in a real house. My own bedroom. A kitchen with a dishwasher. Cable TV, a front lawn. I can see it now. Look."

I stopped walking, and Libby stopped behind me, and I held up my two hands to form a window for us to look through, to help us both envision this dream house a little more clearly. I guess I hoped that by showing it to him this way I could convince myself—and Libby—that it was true, that things were going to be all right, even if I knew it to be a lie.

"Look. There's a white car in the driveway and an electric lawn mower in the yard and tulips and daffodils, and nice next-door neighbors with a dog and kids to hang out with, and—"

Libby leaned down and looked through my imaginary window, but then he turned and kissed me right then, right in the middle of my sentence, for the first time ever. Right on my mouth. Gentle, his lips soft as marshmallows. His eyes closed, his blonde lashes resting against that pure white skin. He pulled back, smiled, and came back in for another kiss the way that eagle sometimes swooped down around me for a second look. He placed his hands on my shoulders and then slid them down my arms to hold my hands, and that swish along my skin gave me the biggest goose bumps. This time, I closed my eyes too. It was the first time anyone ever kissed me nice like that. Not hard and messy. No tongue. Not at all like the johns and pimps and dealers that tried to come after me when they were done with Raina. I wanted this kiss to last forever.

But then Libby pulled back again, and I noticed how clear his skin was that day. No scratches. It had been clearing up so nicely ever since we became friends, and in my own way, I took credit for that.

"Frankie," Libby said. "What about us?"

And then, sure enough, he did it. He scratched his ear, and his jaw. Hard.

He scratched again. And again, until blood started to pool at the surface of his skin. His nervous tic was back, and it was all my fault. I wanted to shout at him, tell him to stop.

"Libby," I said, and then I wasn't sure what else to say. "Libby, you'll be fine without me. You've got your football games, your Homecoming dance, your driver's license. You'll probably forget all about me in no time."

I felt like a traitor to myself for saying that, and to him, too. He climbed up on a nearby boulder and I climbed up beside him, wrapping my arms around my knees. And then, because my thoughts were tangled in my brain like the string and tape and bottle caps in Raina's kitchen junk drawer, I blurted out the stupidest thing ever.

"I love you, Libby, and I wish I could put a spell on you so that you'll always remember me." I wiggled my fingers at him to cast the imaginary spell.

He laughed, then slid down off the boulder and reached up for me. "Come on."

He ran along the trail, and I followed him, toward the strip of flattened rock that jutted out above the rapids, where the river tightened and cut deep into the earth, a place that I'd always thought would be a good place to end it all. Jumbled rocks waited for us down below, and the water splashed and slurped as though it were hungry for us, too.

Libby reached out, folded up the cuffs of my sleeves, and lightly touched his lips to each of the pink scars on the inside of my forearms. Then he turned me around to face the river and he stood behind me and wrapped his arms around me tight. This was it, I thought. He was about to cast us off the ledge together, down onto the jagged rocks, into the frenzied water, which roared like a thousand voices below. He smelled like Dial soap and earthy cattails, and for one crazy second I was fine with the idea of a lover's leap. It was I who had become caught in his spell, rather than the other way around.

But of course he didn't push us off the rock. And when I started to shiver from the cold water spraying up at us, he said we'd better go back.

"But before we say goodbye, there's something I need you to do for me," I said.

I told him where to drive, along the highway heading west, toward the Mississippi. I said to turn off onto a frontage road when we got to the river.

"Where are we going?" he asked. "I need to get home. My mom's probably worried about me. I've missed dinner. And I'm supposed to be doing my homework."

Screw your homework, I wanted to say. "Don't worry. I know what I'm doing." I really didn't know anything for sure. Finally we came to the empty gravel parking lot I'd been looking for. "Here we are. Pull in."

I opened his glove box and rummaged around inside it, looking for a flashlight. There was a small packet of Kleenex, a couple of city maps, a tire gauge, and, hooray, a flashlight. I left the tire gauge but took everything else and got out of the car, directing Libby to follow me, and I led him down an overgrown path to a rickety old dock. An old weathered boat was tied to it.

"Frankie, what are we doing?"

Libby had stopped before reaching the dock and now stood above me on the path, his windbreaker scrunched in one of his hands.

"Come on!" I called to him. The sun had by now set below the western bank of the river. The sky was purple, like a bruise, but Libby's face was in shadow. I shone the flashlight at him. "We're running away."

"What?"

"You heard me. We're hitting the road. Well, actually the river."

He fumbled for words. "How...how did you even know this place was here?"

"Raina brought me here a couple of weeks ago. For some sort of drug deal."

"You've been planning this for a couple of weeks?"

No, I hadn't. The idea had actually just started to form, in a hazy sort of way, when he asked what we were going to do about us. And then it became more solid, like Jell-O, after it's sat awhile. I knew this was the only way Libby and I could be together.

I shone the light up at him again and caught him scratching.

"You and me, a couple of misfits stuck in the wrong time and wrong place. Now's our chance, don't you see? We'll just take this little old rowboat here and float downstream till we get somewhere good. Like Huckleberry Finn and Injun Joe. Isn't that who Huck ran away with? Or was it Tom Sawyer?" I should have checked that library book out after all. It would have been nice to have something to read on the boat. "Anyway, we'll make a new life and start over. Just you and me. Maybe we'll go all the way to New Orleans. I hear that's where it's at."

"Frankie."

"It'll be better," I said, trying to convince both of us, recalling Raina's words from the previous night. *It's all for the best.*

"Frankie." He walked toward the boat but still stood a few feet away, as though afraid I'd snatch him, like he was a housefly falling prey to a black widow spider. Or maybe he was afraid he'd really get into the boat with me and take up the oars and begin to paddle. Maybe he was as afraid of his own dreams as I was of mine.

"Frankie, I can't run away."

"Why not?"

"Why not? Why *not*? Well, let's see. For one thing, I'm supposed to be at school tomorrow. And like I said, my mom's probably already worried about me right now."

Lucky for him. At least he had a mother who worried.

"Forget about school. You don't need that, Libby. You've learned everything you need to learn in school. Sometimes you have to just take a chance in life and figure the rest out on your own. Stick with me, I'll show you what you need to learn. Just you and me on this little rowboat. Our own little home."

"A stolen rowboat."

"It's just an old boat. It's not like we're stealing a car or something." The boat was so frail that I did actually wonder if it was even seaworthy. *Seaworthy.* I liked that word.

He shook his head. "You're crazy."

"No, I'm not. And besides, I don't have a choice. I have to go."

"No you don't."

I thought about that for about a half a second. "Okay then." I crossed my arms like Raina did whenever she was trying to sound smart or important. "Okay then, we won't steal a car or a boat or run away. I'll come live with you."

He shifted his stance. "Um. I don't think that'll work either."

I asked why not.

"It wouldn't be cool, Frankie. That's why. Especially not with my mom. You're just a middle school girl."

That was the first time Libby had said anything so dumb, and so grown-up sounding, and it stung worse than any insect bite I could imagine. No one understood that I wasn't just a normal thirteen-year-old girl, not even Libby. I'd seen more than a lot of people did in their entire lifetimes, I was pretty sure. And the thing was, I wished I could be just normal.

"I'm a lot more mature than those girls in your stupid school."

"I'm not saying you're not mature," he said. "But you can't just move in with my family. You have to live with yours."

"I don't have a family. And besides, I thought you loved me."

I blinded him this time with the flashlight. He squinted and held his hand above his eyes.

"I know you never exactly told me you love me," I said. "But I can tell you do. The way you kissed me."

"I'm a teenage boy, what did you expect? You know, hormones?"

"Nope." Uh-uh. I wasn't going to let him get away with that excuse. "Nope. You're not getting off that easy. I know about men. Trust me. This was different. *You* were different. You kissed my wrists." I turned off the flashlight. "Say it. Say you love me."

In the dim twilight, I saw him scratching his neck, pulling his collar up, then scratching again. Without me, he'd scratch himself down to the bone.

"Say it."

He looked out toward the Mississippi, toward Iowa, toward the west and Oregon where someday I wanted to go. But he did not look at me.

"No. No, I'm not going to say it. But it's not because I don't. I'm just not going to say it, Frankie."

I couldn't believe what I was hearing, or rather not hearing. "I thought you were my friend. I thought I could count on you. But as it turns out, you're no better than the rest." *All men are alike*, Raina would say. *They're all dicks*. Maybe Raina was right after all.

"Fine. I'll go by myself."

"What?"

"I'm running away. Without you."

"Frankie."

But he didn't say anything else. After a long minute, he reached into his pocket, pulled out his wallet, and retrieved his driver's license. Then he came a few steps closer and handed me the wallet and his windbreaker.

"Here, take these. You'll need the money. And you're already cold." Then, he backed away.

Which meant he was really going to let me go, which meant now I couldn't turn back. My eyes started to sting from the cold wind or something.

"Do me one favor," I said as I pulled the jacket on. It smelled like Libby, and I struggled through a storm of tears to get the zipper to work. "Well, two favors, actually. First, find a way to get a hold of Raina and tell her I'm gone. But that I'm okay. And second, watch out for me until I get going onto the river, will you? I can't swim."

He started to scratch, then stopped. He looked down at me in the boat, finally, and I waited for an entire lifetime for him to come toward me one more time and bend down and give me a last kiss. At least I deserved that, didn't I?

It was only now, in this unreal silence, that I noticed the boat reeked of fish. Probably some old guy used it now and then to catch his catfish dinner. He'd go hungry now. Or have to buy his fish at the store. I didn't much care about him though. I had more worries than some old fisherman, including the fact that I hadn't eaten all day and sure as shit didn't know how to catch a fish. This whole idea of running away on a boat was beginning to sound crazy even to me, but I had no better answers to offer myself.

"You won't get far," he said. "Not with all the locks and dams."

"I'll get farther than I am right now," I said. "That's all I can hope for."

I unhooked the rope that tied the boat to the edge of the rotting dock and pushed off with an oar. The boat rocked and creaked. I stretched to place a hand on each side of the boat to steady myself, listening to the water's gurgles and inspecting the floor for any leaks, while trying not to think about what I'd do if the boat started to sink. And also trying not to think about that last kiss that Libby never gave me.

He walked backwards up the path, away from me, and stood there in the night's shadows watching me. I thought I saw him lift his arm to wave, although it could have just been my imagination.

I slipped the oars into the water then and aimed the boat downstream. The oars were heavier than I thought they'd be, and the water felt thick, like I was rowing through a swamp. The boat tacked back and forth the way

Raina walked when she was drunk, but eventually I got into a rhythm. I looked back toward Libby one more time. He was much smaller now.

And then I drifted.

At first, I listened to the water lapping against the side of the boat, and then I heard the motor of a car on the frontage road that ran alongside the river, and sirens in the distance, reminding me of Raina and that ratty tin can trailer. I figured Raina would still move, even without me. Then I thought of poor little Toro, and my stuffed Boo, left behind.

When the boat caught into the river's stronger current, I leaned back against the bow, resting a dilapidated old seat cushion behind my head, and I let my mind wander back to my little river. Its rush of water like thunder, its roily rapids beneath the ledge, those annoying squirrels. I saw my bald eagle, black wings spread wide as it watched over me, and all those cottonwood trees and their fallen branches. I saw the twigs floating downstream through the jumbled rocks, and then the ant on one little twig, all alone, dancing as it was jostled in the water, dancing to the music of the river. And then I became the ant on the little river, and I floated away.

# ALLIGATOR
# POETRY

# Sensing Miracles

—MARY SALISBURY

There are borders between us.
All of us crossing through desert
and snow, carrying peaches.
Longing for our own torch of peace
to light the way to shore.

**I LAY SPRAWLED** across my new king-sized Ralph Lauren duvet—another gift from Hugh—trying to figure out why Sylvia Plath chose the oven and Virginia Woolf decided to drown, and also where on earth Charlotte Perkins Gilman even found chloroform. Meanwhile, the phone rang: more pleas for money.

I liked giving my husband's money away. I also enjoyed talking to the telephone solicitors, most of the time. But not today. Today I felt like that woman in Ezra Pound's poem who was *dying piecemeal of a sort of emotional anemia*. What if *I* committed suicide? What if I, like Virginia Woolf, just disappeared one day? Would anyone even care? Sometimes I wondered if I was going mad when these thoughts, and the darker ones beneath them, ambushed me. They were mean little SOBs, these thoughts. Opportunistic predators.

It was that nasty e-mail from my younger sister Veronica that got me riled up this time, a venomous missive that pinched nearly as badly as those real pinches from forever ago when we shared a small bedroom, adorned with frilly lavender bedspreads and curtains. Every night after the lights were turned out, Veronica would reach across from her twin bed to mine and pinch the skin of my forearm so hard it would make me cry. Mother always said Ronnie was jealous of me, but I never understood why.

And now, four decades later, the jealousy—and the pinch—hurt as badly as ever, but Mother was no longer around for comfort, so on days like this I turned to the likes of Woolf and Plath for whatever pitiful solace they had to offer. Which wasn't much. I rolled over and woke up my laptop to reread the e-mail thread. First, the one I'd sent to Veronica.

From: Gillian Blake-Moore
Subject: We're Disappearing
Date: September 18  2:27:13 PM PDT
To: Veronica Berg

Ronnie,

I just read another article about the disappearing middle class, and I'm so sick of all this. It sounds like we're just going to be Photoshopped out of life. Deleted. Poof! One day we're here, the next day we're gone.

Here's a link for you if you feel like getting depressed. www.broadviewreporter.com/tag/disappearing-middle-class.hi52587.htm

Speaking of depression, I've been thinking about you all day and figure you must be beyond your wits. Was Sissy really suspended? Well tell her Aunt Gillian says she'd better snap herself into shape. Or else.

I'm reminded of a Kenneth Koch poem, *One Train May Hide Another*. Here's a line for you to think about while you're dealing with life's woes:

"When you come to something, stop to let it pass
So you can see what else is there."

Hugs,
Gillian

What was wrong with that?  But here's what my beloved sister wrote in reply.

From: Veronica Berg
Subject: We're Disappearing BUT YOU'RE NOT
Date: September 18  2:41:10 PM PDT
To: Gillian Blake-Moore

Gillian, obviously you won't be poofed out of anywhere! I immediately read that article you sent (although I have far more pressing concerns) and the writer made it perfectly clear that anyone earning more than $250,000 will be just fine through all this financial mumbo jumbo! Which, of course, means you. (Don't try to tell me Hugh doesn't make that much; I know for a fact he rakes in a lot more than that.) So please at least call a spade a spade. You're not middle class!

If you're worried about me, say so, and I'll tell you thanks but no thanks. Please just don't try to pretend you're still one of us. When was the last time you made chicken soup from a carcass to stretch through the week?

Veronica was so tense these days! I was just trying to help, to let her know I'm here for her, to listen or maybe even offer financial advice. And while my husband did indeed earn an embarrassingly large salary, I certainly didn't think of our family as *rich*. Upper middle class at best. More importantly, I thought of myself as the same person I was way back when, just a simple middle class gal from the Hoosier state, and I didn't see why Veronica couldn't think of me that way, too.

On a more important matter (from my perspective, at least), you haven't heard the half of our problems! While I was out on the back porch talking to Legal Aid about Sissy getting caught with pot, that damn daughter of mine vanished. Ran off with her backpack, that anthology of poems you sent her last year, and those awful big black boots she wears everywhere. All gone. Just like that. Lingerie: gone. Socks: gone. Of course she left her school books strewn across her desk. And she didn't even leave a note. So I'm sorry to report that I won't be able to share your "concern" (or was it a threat?) with her.

Sorry to sound so harsh. I'm just so stressed. This is the sort of crap those of us who live in the real world have to deal with. We don't have time to get depressed.

By the way, stop sending us poetry.
V.

Well, well. Of course Veronica's life was challenging. But did I really deserve to be dumped upon like this? And what was that comment about not sending poetry anymore? Was Veronica the only one who had the right to read or share or discuss poetry, just because she was an English teacher? Or was she somehow blaming me for Sissy running away, since she took the book I had sent her? Here we were, two sisters living thousands of miles apart, each one still derailing the other, whether intentionally or not. It felt like our relationship was becoming more and more diluted, like a cube of bouillon dissipating in a pot of boiling water.

I heard something, and when I sat up and looked out the picture window, I discovered what it was. Seattle raindrops were plinking off the surface of our swimming pool down below. I hoped Rosa would remember to shut all the windows before leaving. I lay back down and tried to recall the words from that Rachel Wetzsteon poem. The only line I for sure remembered was about petals scattering in the wind, "like versions of myself I was on the verge of becoming." What was it that I had been on the verge of becoming before marriage and children and wealth? I couldn't remember any more.

Jackson. That's what I could do. Write to my brother. Maybe he would explain what was going on with Veronica.

> From: Gillian Blake-Moore
> Subject: Veronica
> Date: September 18  2:50:53 PM PDT
> To: Jackson Blake
>
> Hey bro,
> How are you? I'm sorry I haven't been in touch lately! We have just been so busy, what with Henry's college apps and Sarah's application to the National Youth Orchestra and little Mulu Ken's soccer games every weekend. Hugh's been traveling a ton, too, mostly back and forth to South America. Oh, how I wish I could go with him, but there's just so much to do.
>
> That last line was a lie; I had no desire to travel or do much of anything these days. And I really wasn't all that busy, either; Henry and Sarah had reached that age where they didn't seem to need a mother anymore. But Jackson didn't need to know these truths.
>
> I'm worried about Veronica and thought you might know what's going on. Obviously Sissy's a big part of the

problem; did you know she's run away? I feel like picking up the phone and calling our sister, but no matter what I say or do I always seem to upset her. Have you noticed the same?

I've been thinking about you and Wanda a lot lately, too, and wish I lived closer so I could help out. How are Wanda's treatments going? Please give her my love and tell her I suggest she read Joan Halperin's poem, *Diagnosis*. She might find it comforting to know she's not alone.

Also, I'm wondering if you'd like me to send you a link to an article about the disappearing middle class. I already sent it to Veronica.

Hugs from your big sis,
Gillian

I decided to haul myself off the bed and face the day before the kids got home from school. Making my way down the curved stairway step by step, I absentmindedly trailed my fingers along the cherry balustrade and instinctively checked for dust. I think I was subconsciously hoping that, for just this once, there'd be something wrong or dirty or out of place around here. But of course there wasn't, and for a fleeting second I looked around to see what I might do to upset this little world of perfection. I stopped momentarily, on the fourth step down, and gazed out through the foyer's arch-shaped window, through the gray drizzle and over the rooftops of the lower elevation, smaller houses to the crowded highways and the lines of school buses. My children would not be on those buses.

Why? Because they had always *refused* to ride them. I didn't understand why; they were perfectly adequate methods of transportation when I was a school girl. But my children wanted me to drive them to and from school, and while I didn't like their propensity toward snobbishness, I did, for the most part, delight in the role of mother-chauffeur-slave. It meant I got to spend more time with them. Until Henry turned sixteen.

Hugh had insisted on getting our son a BMW, overruling my desire to have our children live like normal kids. Then Henry—a child who always had craved responsibility—insisted on driving himself and the other kids to and from school ever since. So I got fired from that job.

In fact, Henry and Sarah were doing so much for themselves these days that I sometimes felt like I was slacking off. It was as though my little family's universe had shifted but still remained in holistic balance. And while some parents can't wait until their kids aren't as needy as they once were, I was having the opposite problem. I was bored. I had become a human vacuum, wandering through this hazy thing called life.

I started to recall Charlotte Perkins Gilman's words, right before she'd killed herself. *When all usefulness is over*—until I was interrupted.

"Good-bye, Miss Gillian!"

Rosa's call, echoing from somewhere else in our sparkling, cavernous house, brought me back to my right mind, thankfully before I missed a step and tumbled to the marble foyer floor and—what? Before I tumbled to the marble foyer floor and killed myself? Maybe it would have been a blessing.

"See you tomorrow!" Rosa called again.

"Wait!" I called, and I hurried down the rest of the steps, but by the time I made it all the way down the hall to the mud room, which never had a trace of mud in it either, Rosa was already out the door.

That's the trouble with such a big house: You can't even say a proper goodbye.

It wasn't that I was ungrateful; sometimes I just longed for that little two-bedroom house where I grew up in the Midwest, even if it did have Formica countertops instead of slab granite, and linoleum floors instead of hardwood and marble. Even if I did have to share a bedroom with Veronica. At least we could find one another.

I stood at the window and watched Rosa backing her rusty little Ford Focus out of the driveway, and my heart felt as though it were weighted down with a thousand of our cold marble tiles. Rosa had been with our family since before Sarah was born, since before we'd adopted Mulu Ken, since before my mother died. Rosa had been like the big sister I never had, there to celebrate good news or offer comfort in times of sorrow.

"There, there, Miss Gillian," Rosa would say whenever I got upset, and she'd set down her dust cloth or her mop and sit down to listen to all my *rich life woes*, as Veronica would call them. Or sometimes Rosa would read a poem I'd just penned. She never asked what the poem meant or suggested any changes, as Veronica would. She also never charged for the extra time. She was far more than a maid, which was what Veronica had called Rosa last month when she left that spiteful message on voicemail.

I hadn't picked up when the phone rang that day either. Like today, I'd been in bed with a bad case of what I called the alligators, those dark thoughts that swarmed about, closing in, snapping their big sharp teeth at me, much like they had been today. I had never told anyone about these feelings, or the way I thought of them metaphorically as primordial reptiles. They'd think I really was loony. But I knew I wasn't. Just as Sylvia Plath described her own depression as an owl's talon clenching her heart, my dark thoughts reminded me of alligators.

And on that particular day when Veronica had left that scornful message, the alligators had been circling my bed and I'd let the phone ring because I knew I couldn't talk to my sister and act like everything was all right. But listening to her voicemail wasn't exactly chicken soup for my despairing soul, either.

"Are you trying to tell me you're *too busy* to pick up my call?" That was the first thing Veronica had said, and normally, when she made comments like this, I could let it slide. But then she said something about how I obviously wasn't busy cleaning the house, because I had *Rosie the Maid* for that. It was only then that she revealed the real reason for her call. Dad was in the hospital. *Maybe you'd like to come visit if you can tear yourself away from your poems.*

Okay, so maybe I wasn't Maya Angelou. Maybe I hadn't even published anything yet. But I still had a right to write, didn't I? And was it my fault that Hugh and I were financially comfortable? Did I really deserve it whenever my sister unfurled her scorn at me?

I sat down that very afternoon and wrote an old-fashioned snail mail letter to my sister, and I was so upset I kept a copy of it, which I've reread so many times that I now knew it by heart.

> Dear Ronnie,
>
> I'm sorry you are so jealous of me. You seem to forget that we were both born and raised in the same middle class home where we did our chores and said our prayers and practiced the golden rule. Just because we each grew up and took a separate path, and mine led me to a man with a lucrative law practice, doesn't mean I'm a different person than I once was. I am still your sister, and I wish our differing financial situations didn't have to drive such a wedge between us.

And just because I have a housekeeper instead of a job doesn't mean I am some sort of spoiled rich bitch. It's not as though I just sit around take, take, taking from the world and not giving back. Obviously I could have been doing my own dusting and sweeping and dishes and vacuuming and mopping all these years. I could have been doing all that quite well, thank you very much. Or I could have been working in an office somewhere. Did you forget I have a business admin degree? But instead I chose to spend my time, and my resources, doing other things.

Like adopting Mulu Ken, who you may recall was once a starving orphan in Ethiopia. And employing a needy Hispanic woman who is far more than a housecleaner, by the way. She's a lovely woman. And don't forget that Hugh and I have donated quite a bit of money to higher education and other charities.

As I wrote the letter, I actually thought about letting Rosa go just to prove a point to my sister that I *could* do my own housework. But I loved Rosa too much to do that. And Rosa did need the money; she'd been trying for so long to hoist herself over the ledge of poverty and I was happy I could help her. Another option, of course, would have been to convince Hugh to downsize. But that would be crazy to do something like that just to please my sister. Besides, he'd never go for that. He needed to uphold an image for professional purposes, he often said.

I am so tired of being resented. If only people understood what it's like to be me. If only at least my own sister understood.

I never heard back from Veronica in response to that letter. Now, as I watched Rosa's little car disappear down the hill, I longed for her to come back. I wanted to tell her about today's e-mail from my sister. Or maybe what I really wanted was to forget about Veronica and listen to one of Rosa's stories, about her family back home, about the border crossing, about the struggles she'd faced ever since coming to America. To listen to Rosa, a woman of meager means, tell her stories with such love and gratitude and hope in her eyes.

But she was gone, and the putt-putt sound of her dying car was soon replaced by the booming bass sounds from Henry's Beamer. The floor vibrated beneath my bare feet, and my heart felt like it was vibrating too. Now that I'm not driving them to and from school anymore, the highlight of my day is when they come home. I hurried into the kitchen, hoping it would look like I'd been busy doing something productive today, and began to set a platter of food out for the kids: Beecher's Blank Slate Honey cheese, local Honeycrisp apples, gluten-free rice crackers, and organic chocolate almond milk, of course, to drink.

Sarah sashayed into the house first. She had a dreamy look in her eyes.

"Guess which 9th grader just got invited to Homecoming?" She twirled in a circle, the sides of her lacy cardigan fluttering around her like angel wings. "By the captain of the football team!"

Before I had a chance to race through the list of how a mother is supposed to feel when her only daughter gets invited to her first dance—by an upperclassman—Henry sauntered in and tossed his backpack on the table.

"Hello, Mum," he said. He'd been perfecting his British accent ever since he visited Oxford last spring break. He gave me a kiss on my cheek.

The thing is: every afternoon was like this, a present day version of Ozzie and Harriet—which I only knew from reruns, given that I wasn't old enough to have watched it the first time around. Three perfect kids who greeted me warmly, washed their hands before sitting down at the table, and were willing to spend a few minutes with me to tell me about their day. I knew I didn't deserve this, and I knew I should be grateful that this is what I had. There was no excuse for my alligators.

"Wait, where's Mulu Ken?"

"Oh, sorry Mum," Henry said. "Forgot to mention that MK's gone home with his pal Alex." I watched his Adam's apple bob as he swallowed his apple slices. "I cleared it with Alex's mum. No worries. She said she'll have him home right after dinner."

Utterly perfect kids. If Virginia and Sylvia had been in my shoes, might they have lived longer, happier lives?

The phone rang then, for the umpteenth time that day. I ignored it. I didn't want to interrupt this precious time.

"Aren't you going to answer that?" Sarah asked. When I shook my head, she lunged for the phone and hit the speaker button.

"Hello, this is Children With Hair Loss calling to—"

Sarah hung up.

"Why did you do that?" I asked. Sarah and Henry looked at one another, then both rolled their eyes.

"Are you kidding?" Sarah said.

Henry walked to the desk at the edge of the kitchen and picked up my mom's old Longaberger basket. "She hung up because of this, Mum." The basket was overflowing with mail, including free return address labels, American flag pins, and even coins—with requests for money from all sorts of organizations.

"What about it?" I asked.

"Mom," Sarah said. "You're becoming obsessed with giving away money. It's not that it's bad to give to charities. But some of these people are just scam artists." She tightly wrapped the remaining cheese in Saran Wrap and set it in the fridge. "Besides, you've got to find something else to do with your life besides answering junk mail. Go out and get a job or something. Find your passion."

She stood across from me, exactly my height, and met my eyes with hers. Her expression was not cruel, but those last three words were as sharp and serrated as the knife that remained on the cheese cutting board. Didn't she understand that she, and her brothers, and her father, had been my passion? Didn't she give any credit to my previous, albeit short, life as a bookkeeper, or to my desire to write my own poetry? Maybe I wasn't that good yet. Maybe I wasn't winning awards with my words the way she was with her music. But still. I was flabbergasted, and at a loss for words, too.

She turned to wash the cutting board and knife at the sink, and Henry cleared the rest of the snacks from the table. I simply stood there and watched them as though I was a mere audience member and they were the important actors on the stage. When they completed their tasks, Henry said they were heading upstairs to do their homework.

Why? I wondered. Why did they have to be so goddamn perfect? Why did they have to clean up every crumb in the kitchen? Why did they have to study so hard and get straight A's? I watched them go and found myself resenting my own children. Being around them had made me feel unnecessary, inferior, and lonelier than I had before they'd come home. How sad was that?

Just as Veronica was jealous of me—her own sister, I had become envious of my own children. And maybe I was also a bit jealous of Veronica, too. At least Veronica's life was normal.

"Dinner at 6:30?" I called after the kids. "Spicy jambalaya? With Rosa's jalapeno cornbread recipe, and homemade peach cobbler for dessert?" At least I could still cook.

"Sorry, Mum. We've got to head back to school at 6:00 for a Homecoming meeting," Henry called back. "Mandatory."

A mandatory meeting at dinnertime? I watched him take the stairs up two at a time. Damn it! I had been looking forward to dinnertime; it had always been the highlight of my day, when I could produce a fabulous meal for my family and feel like I'd accomplished something. But not so much anymore. My perfect children were too perfectly involved in school and in their own lives.

Well at least Hugh would come home to appreciate my efforts.

I began to busy myself in our bright and airy Tuscan-style kitchen. The rain had stopped and a ray of light filtered in over the sink. I set the butter, sugar, eggs, and cornmeal out on the island, and chopped peppers on the end-grain cutting board, and then decided I'd text Hugh to confirm he'd be home by 7:00 p.m.

As I waited for his reply, flipping through the mail Rosa had left on the counter, a new e-mail came in on my phone.

> From: Jackson Blake
> Subject: Veronica
> Date: September 18  3:22:08 PM PDT
> To: Gillian Blake-Moore
>
> Hey Sis,
> Sarah's joining the National Youth Orchestra? Don't know what that is, but it sounds impressive, and way out of my league. But then I wouldn't expect anything less from your kids.
> Regarding Ronnie: I don't know what your problem is with her. She acts fine to me. Obviously it's upsetting when your child gets caught smoking weed in the school parking lot and then runs away. On top of Walt losing his job. I think it's just that she has so many problems to deal with, something she figures you'll never understand.

Wanda says hello and will call you sometime when she's feeling better. This chemo's taking a harder toll on her than the last one, but some say that's a sign it's working.

Jackson

The house phone rang then. My mother used to say dinnertime was the busiest time of day for interruptions. I answered it quickly, thinking it would be Hugh calling instead of texting, saying he wanted to hear my voice. But it wasn't him.

"Hello, this is the Society for Diversity in Landscaping calling."

The Society for what? Although I was indeed curious, Sarah's words were still echoing in my mind, so I hung up, and then immediately wished I hadn't. What she didn't understand was that it's lonely, living way up here on the hill in our huge house with my housecleaner and my perfect little world. It's lonely being in the top 1 percent. At least all these solicitors give me an opportunity to have an uplifting, even hopeful conversation with someone.

I looked back at Jackson's e-mail. What exactly did he mean when he referred to *my* problem with Veronica?

I tried to ignore Sarah's words. I tried to ignore Jackson's. But they were like Tolstoy's proverbial white bear in the forest. The more you try not to think of it, the more you do. Anger began to bubble up inside me, and I began to take it out on the cornbread batter, beating it harder than I know I should have. I whipped and whipped until my forearm cramped.

Damn it, Jackson! You're the one who has it *all* wrong. *I'm* not the one with the problem.

I shoved the cornbread into the oven. Next, I started slicing peaches with a vengeance. It's a wonder I didn't slice off a fingertip. Thankfully, I put down the knife when a text came in.

Hugh: *Bad news. Must work late. Don't wait for dinner. Love.*

Really? This could not be happening. I wiped my hands on a towel.

Me: *Hugh! I asked you this morning about these dinner plans. Can't you just go to work early tomorrow? I can hold off till 8 for dinner.*

Hugh: *No can do. Sorry, sweet pea. Love.*

This was not good. I did not want to be alone tonight. My anger was quickly replaced with a heaviness, the debilitating weight of marble again. The alligators were congregating and threatening to move in, perhaps closer than they had ever before.

I'd been trying to hold them at bay all day by visiting my favorite bookstore in the morning, taking a bubble bath at noon, indulging in a glass (or was it two?) of pear cider—which I rationalized was fine since it had less alcohol content than wine—and I'd lain down with Sylvia Plath. But it had all been for naught. Rosa went home. The kids were busy. Hugh had important things to do. Only the alligators were here for me.

And now they were rumbling. Bellowing. Growling. They sounded ravenous. I wondered if maybe I did need to get some professional help.

I looked into the oven at the cornbread, then imagined what position Sylvia had sat in. I turned the oven off, leaving the half-baked cornbread inside. I threw the peach slices and pits into the compost bin under the sink, ran upstairs, and dove under the covers. I prayed for sleep to come, but it didn't, because sleep never comes when you really need it.

I waited for Mulu Ken.

Finally, I heard him come in through the front door. It was dark inside and out by then. He was much later than I'd expected. But I couldn't be angry with him as I listened to him whistling his way through the kitchen. MK somehow always gave me a jolt of energy and hope, this time just enough to haul myself out of bed. I put on my happy Mommy face and went downstairs.

"How was your day, MK?"

I kissed him on the forehead, and he retrieved the imaginary kiss in his fingertips and placed it in the front pocket of his jeans.

"It was good, Mama Gill."

It had been seven years since we'd adopted him, but he still insisted on calling me that. I understood why; his African birthmother, now deceased, would always be his true mother. But just once I wished he'd use the word *mom* for me.

"Did you get enough to eat at your friend's house?" I asked.

"Mm-hmm. And I finished my homework while I was there, too."

"Then let's go up," I said, and I shepherded him up the stairs. I lay on his bed, waiting as he took his evening shower and brushed his teeth, studying the posters of Africa he'd hung on his wall and wondering what his life would have been like if his mother had lived. If he would have been happier there, with her, than here with me.

After he was tucked into bed, I sat by his side and listened to him recount more about his day, his black arms skinny as licorice crooked behind his head, his smile stretching his cheeks wide.

"I got a B+ on my marine wildlife report," he told me. "Mrs. Taylor says my writing's getting better."

I smoothed his hair back from his forehead.

"And a girl in my class said she thinks I'm cute."

I felt the same pang I'd felt earlier when Sarah told me she had been asked to the dance. Was I already losing MK to girls and the rest of the world? "What did you say to her?"

"I thanked her," he said.

I laughed. "Well, she's right. You are cute. Very cute." I gently wiggled the lobes of his ears, a secret gesture of love we shared with one another.

"Now tell me about your day."

I was caught off guard by his request. I could not tell him that I'd lain around all day being depressed. Or that my sister and I were having a spat about trivial matters. I couldn't tell him the alligators had been to visit. Before I had a chance to figure out what to say, he had something else to say to me.

"Oh, Mama Gill, I forgot to tell you about the dinner Alex's mother prepared for his family. It was fantastic. We should have it sometime."

I thought about the cornbread, now cold and abandoned in the oven, and the peaches in the trash. I recalled Hugh's text and Henry and Sarah's oh-so-important obligations. I did not really want to hear about somebody else's family dinner, but I didn't know how to stop him from going on.

"It was fried chicken from a place called KFC," MK said. "Finger-licking good, they say. And it was." To prove his point, he licked his fingers even though any remnant of batter, meat, or grease would have been washed down the shower drain. "Could we have that for dinner sometime, Mama Gill?"

KFC?

I laughed. Every day I lovingly labored over sometimes-complicated, always-savory and healthy recipes for the family, never once having thought about serving fast food to them. I hadn't had KFC since I was a young girl, but now that I thought of it, I remembered how exciting it had been whenever Dad would come home from work with that big red and white bucket, along with sides of coleslaw and sweet buns. Ronnie and Jackson and I would practically trip over one another on our way to the kitchen, and we always fought over who got the last drumstick. The family sat around the table laughing and talking and doing what families are supposed to do at dinnertime: connecting over a meal.

I kissed Mulu Ken good night on the forehead, watched him stuff the invisible kiss under his pillow, and retreated to my own room once again. I sat down at my vanity with the gilded mirror and began to brush my hair, 100 strokes before bedtime, as I'd done ever since I'd been a child. Maybe, I thought, happiness is inversely related to money, and that was really my whole problem. The families I'd known with money tended to get divorced or fight over estates or otherwise lose touch with each other. Maybe the ones without much money—the ones who ate KFC for dinner—were a whole lot better at staying put, dealing with whatever life throws at them, and appreciating simple things. Like buckets of crispy chicken legs.

I then began to remove my makeup with Noxzema, like Sylvia Plath had religiously done every night, and just when the cream was slathered over my eyelids, I heard Hugh's voice.

"Sorry, love."

I kept my eyes closed as he took the cleaning pads from my hands and gently wiped my eyelids for me.

"Keep your eyes closed for one more minute," he said. "I brought something home for you."

I couldn't imagine what it might be. Another diamond necklace? A new tennis bracelet? I didn't want another bauble as an apology for a missed dinner. I heard a whimper then, and he released his hands from my eyes.

A black Labrador retriever puppy was sitting on the floor next to him, a blue leash held down by one of Hugh's feet.

"My admin's dogs had pups," he said. "They're from a perfect lineage. Show dogs. I told her I wanted the best one for you. That's why I was late."

I was not simply speechless; I was thoughtless, too. Completely blank, as though I had not only wiped away the makeup from my skin but also the thoughts beneath it. Yes, the puppy was adorable, and yes, Hugh was a dear for thinking of me and for surprising me. But I didn't want a dog from a perfect lineage. I didn't want any more perfection, period. If I'd wanted any dog, it would have been the sickly runt of the litter. But I didn't even want that. As I tried to figure out what to say, I heard an alligator rustling.

"I'm tired, Hugh. Let's talk about this in the morning."

He hesitated. No doubt he was startled that I hadn't oohed and aahed over the puppy. He leaned over and kissed me on the forehead, then led the poor thing out of the bedroom.

The next morning, I got up to make blueberry pancakes for everyone. I cleaned up the dog pee and poop that landed just beyond the newspaper I'd set out for the puppy. I listened to Hugh regale me with his upcoming calendar commitments.

And I read the astonishing e-mails that came in from my beloved relatives.

> From: Sissy Berg
> Subject: (no subject)
> Date: September 19  8:34:17 AM PDT
> To: Gillian Blakemore
>
> Dear Aunt Gillian,
> You may have heard about some trouble I got in. It was really stupid what I did and I'm sorry for all the trouble I've caused. Anyway, Mom talked to a lawyer last night who thinks she can get me off the possession charge but we can't afford her. Mom said forget it but I wondered if maybe you'd be willing to help? She (I mean the lawyer) wants a $4,000 retainer and I promise someday I'll pay you back if you decide to help. If you could just send me some money through PayPal, I'd really appreciate it.
>
> Love from your niece,
> Sissy
>
> PS Please say hi to H, S, and MK for me.

So. Sissy had returned home, and Veronica wanted money from her rich sister for legal fees, but was too cowardly to ask for it herself so she put her daughter up to the stunt. Was that all I was good for these days? Charity?

> From: Jackson Blake
> Subject: Middle Class
> Date: September 18  8:52:20 AM PDT
> To: Gillian Blake-Moore

Hey Sis,

I finally checked out that link you sent Ronnie. You're right, things are getting worse. What I'm most worried about is that my employer is talking about more radical changes to our healthcare coverage. It all started with Obamacare and it's gotten worse ever since. Wanda and I are nearly as worried about finances as her cancer. You have no idea.

Yeah, I think the middle class will disappear in our lifetime. What I'm not sure about is whether it's better to be one of the peasants or the aristocrats. Good luck to you and your kids! LOL.

Jackson

And what, exactly, was that supposed to mean?

The puppy whined, which was what I felt like doing, too. Hugh had sequestered it inside a dog crate, and clearly it wanted to be out and about. I let it out. It sniffed around the kitchen, then lifted its tiny hind leg and peed on the corner of the island.

Go ahead and pee, dog. LOL.

Hugh, who had gone upstairs to shower and get dressed, came back down.

Somebody said, "I don't want the dog."

It was my own voice that had spoken the words, although I didn't even know the thought had been forming in my head.

Hugh looked at me as though I'd said I didn't want him. "You don't?"

"No."

Something hung in the air between the two of us. It felt a little like guilt, but not exactly. It might have been freedom. I wasn't sure. He poured himself a cappuccino. I watched him do it.

"So, love, what *do* you want?" he asked me.

"I don't know, but not a puppy."

"You seem unhappy." He was still handsome after all these years: his shoulders broad, his abs strong, his butt firm in those designer slacks. He still had a full head of thick hair, and his face was tanned and unblemished. I hated him for all that. Whenever I looked in the mirror, I saw old, fat, grumpy—even if I've just had my brows waxed and my nails done. He, on the other hand, was more dashing than ever.

He was right: I was unhappy. But to admit that was to admit weakness. You don't just walk around telling people you're unhappy when you aren't even sure why you are. Especially when you have a virile, successful husband who would give you whatever you want, and three fantastic kids, and a beautiful home, a housecleaner you adore, and abundant financial resources. When you and your family are perfectly healthy. You don't go telling people about alligators.

But as it turned out, I inadvertently had.

"What does this mean?" Hugh asked. He pulled something out from the back pocket of his slacks. It was an envelope, one with a clear window on the front, the kind bills come in. His brows were furrowed.

"How should I know?"

Then he flipped it over, and I saw what it was. Yesterday, I'd jotted down some thoughts. A poem. About alligators. Those words hadn't been meant for public consumption, not even for his eyes. Especially not for his eyes; he wouldn't understand. I must have left it on the nightstand, along with some poetry collections, by accident.

He handed it to me, and I reread what I'd written.

ALLIGATORS

They come every so often,
Catching me by surprise.
Slowly, stealthily,
As though they smell my blood.
They feed on my raw
Desire to love
Or be loved,
To give
Or be given to.
To live.
They surround me.
They drown me.
One day
They will
Devour me.

Not exactly Plath, perhaps.

"I'm worried about you," he said.

"Me, too."

"I want you to see a therapist," he said.

"I'll think about it." But I knew I probably wouldn't, because as long as I lived in my perfect house with my perfect family, there would be nothing the therapist could do or say that would change anything. You can't fix perfection.

After Hugh left for work with the puppy, and the kids left for school, I wandered back upstairs, each footstep feeling as though someone had strapped twenty-pound weights to my feet. I didn't even know why I was going upstairs, or what I would do when I got there.

Our house was deathly quiet.

Maybe I should just do it, I thought. If there is no purpose in life, why live it? The truth was that Hugh and Henry and Sarah no longer needed me; they didn't even seem to care if I was around. Mulu Ken did, but he didn't think of me as his real mother, and with the way his brother and sister doted on him, I knew he'd survive. As for Rosa? Yes, she would miss me, but she'd light a few candles at her church and say a few prayers and then she'd be all right.

Veronica and Jackson? Fuck them. I had been starting to wonder lately if I'd ever had a good relationship with them. Maybe I'd been deluding myself all these years.

I went into the bathroom and stripped off my clothes. I took a long, steamy shower, morbidly musing that at least they wouldn't have to wash down my body upon my death. I slipped a comfortable flannel shirt and leggings on, skipping the bra. Who needs a bra when you're about to die? Did Virginia Woolf wear one when she wrote she was "doing what seems the best thing to do?"

I opened the medicine cabinet and began to pull various bottles down from the crowded shelves—vitamins, Tylenol, expired antibiotics, Hugh's over-the-counter sleep aid. The phone rang.

Let it ring, I decided. Let it ring.

But the damned answering machine didn't kick in, and eventually it felt like the phone was taunting me, keeping me from figuring out my recipe for death.

"Hello?" My mouth was dry, my voice hoarse.

"Good afternoon. This is Pacific Northwest Wildfire and Disaster Support—"

I was about to press END, but something stopped me. Maybe it was the name of the organization, someone who'd never called me before. Or the smooth, friendly, almost timid voice of the woman on the other end of the line. She was not a professional solicitor.

"I'm sorry to bother you. I'm sure you're busy."

Yes, I thought. I'm so, so terribly busy.

"This calling program is highly unusual for us, but in light of the disaster we're facing, we're reaching out to residents of select zip codes in the Pacific Northwest with the hope they'll be able to help us."

Select zip codes, right. I knew exactly what that meant. They were reaching out to those with affluence. Veronica wouldn't get this phone call if she lived around here. Or Jackson. All this woman needed from me, all anyone needed from me, was money. And it wasn't even money I'd earned. It was Hugh's money. I was just the clearinghouse.

"Disaster?" I asked.

"Yes, the massive wildfires raging throughout Central and Eastern Washington and Oregon. They're unprecedented in size, and we're only ten percent contained. Communities have been ravaged, and we're looking for folks who can help in any way possible. Donations, of course, are always helpful."

Of course.

"But even more than that—," she said, before I had the chance to hang up or offer a pledge"—we're looking for manpower. Or womanpower, I should say." There was a hint of humor in her voice. A tasteful, subtle hint. "We're actually looking more for time and talent than money."

What an odd thing for a telephone solicitor to ask for. What was the catch? I hesitated, thinking that I certainly had time. All the time in this big old lonely world. But talent? I shook my head as though she could see me. Sorry, I had no talent that anyone valued. Not anymore; it had been nearly two decades since I'd held any sort of job, such as it was—bookkeeping for a local restaurant chain. And it was clear that my lame attempts at writing poetry didn't demonstrate any talent, although even it they had, I wasn't sure how poetry could help put out the fire. But there was one thing I could do, for whatever that was worth.

"I can cook."

The woman paused, and I realized then how foolish I had sounded. I was about to tell her I'd been joking.

"Really?" The tone of her voice had perked up. Then she let a small laugh of what sounded like relief. "You're the first person who's offered any sort of talent since I started making these calls. Everyone else just wants to donate money and get off the phone."

I looked out the window. Another gray day in Seattle, where wildfires were merely an abstract idea. A pair of mallards flew into the yard and landed in the pool. A happy couple.

Everyone else wants to get off the phone because they have things to do. They have more purpose in their lives. Or, more accurately, they have a sense of self. That's why they don't want to listen to this woman talk about out-of-control wildfires. But because I was feeling more and more like a blank sheet of paper in a half-used spiral notebook—a notebook from which all the used pages had been ripped out, but which still contained a healthy number of pages waiting to be filled—I had the time and the interest, or perhaps the bona fide need, to listen to what she had to say.

"So what exactly would you want me to do?"

I listened closely to the woman's voice on the other end of the phone, telling me about the firefighters who had come from all over the country to fight the blazes. This organization was looking for volunteers to tend to the firefighters' needs: lodging, laundry, medical.

"And food." My heart started beating wildly, the way Mulu Ken had flailed the first time he'd jumped into our pool. Yes, I could cook. I could do food. I could tend to the tired and hungry stomachs each morning and each evening, filling them up with delicious nourishment while they, unknowingly, filled me up with purpose.

I could do this. It would just be for a while, just for as long as the fire lasted. Those medicine bottles would wait for me.

"It's hard to say how long you'd need to be here," she said after I'd asked. "We'll take however much time you can give us."

It was a mutual feeling. I'd take however much time they could give me.

After hanging up with her, I began to pack my casual clothes, first filling one suitcase and then another, all the while trying to figure out how I'd tell the family what I'd decided to do. I imagined MK's bright smile as he remembered the volunteer organizations that had come to help his fellow villagers. I envisioned Henry and Sarah looking at me with pride for coming up with a passion and something to do. I anticipated Veronica's hesitation on the phone when I called to tell her and her inevitable question of why in the world I'd go off and do that sort of thing. And then I saw Hugh's look, first of confusion, and then a bit of a pout that I'd be leaving him for a while, and then his concern about whether there would be a suitable place for me to stay way out there in the middle of nowhere.

This was when I knew, for sure, this was what I had to do. My decision to leave wasn't just to help remedy disaster for a community ravaged by wildfire. It was to address the disaster that had become my life.

I dragged the suitcases out of the closet and into the bedroom, and I felt something behind me. I turned; there was nothing there. But I knew what I'd felt. The alligators. They were lurking there, somewhere, and I realized I wouldn't, and couldn't, wait for the family to come home to tell them about my plans. I had to go now.

I sat down and wrote them a letter.

> Dear Hugh, Henry, Sarah, and MK,
> I know this may come as a surprise to all of you, but I have made a decision to go away for a while. You may have suspected I've been unhappy lately. In truth, I have felt as though I'm on the brink of something—something that I can't quite name. All I know is that I need a change, and right now I'm heading to eastern Oregon to volunteer in support of the firefighting efforts there. It's urgent, which is why I've decided to leave right away.
> Don't worry about me; I will call you when I get there. I know you'll all be fine here. I love you and I will miss you all.
>
> Love you,
> Mom
>
> PS Hugh, please don't send me any money.

I took off my diamond ring and earrings and locked them inside the safe in our closet. I placed the letter on Hugh's dresser, next to a wooden bowl filled with his cuff links. And I only glanced at all those dead poets stacked on my nightstand.

By nine o'clock that night, I had traded in my Jaguar XKR for a Ford Explorer with nearly 100,000 miles and gotten cash back. I had stopped in Walla Walla for dinner at a KFC. And I had found my way to eastern Oregon. I was still twenty miles out from my final destination, and probably forty or fifty miles from any fires, when I pulled the car over onto the highway's shoulder to stretch my legs.

There had been an early snow, and the ground was completely white. I got out of the car and, although the air was vaguely smoky even at this distance, I felt more clear-headed and alive than I had for so very long. I trudged through the snow into the woods, blazing a path among the trees where no one had yet walked. It was remarkably peaceful there, and far less lonely than back in the city where I'd lived for most of my adult life. I listened. A bird—perhaps an owl—flapped enormous wings. A clump of snow dropped from a branch and softly plopped onto the ground beside me. But there were no other sounds, no other movement, and as far as I could tell, there were no alligators for miles around.

# WINTER

# ACCELERANT

# Fond Litter

—PATRICIA REYNOLDS SØRBYE

She wants to speak so many words at once
That they all rush out and get stuck sideways
Straining against the opening in her spirit
She is worn and hopeful and sad and hungry
The arms wrap around and press us together
It's all right, I understand
The pressure increases suddenly
I am sorry, I love you
Release.

And the log jam breaks
And all of the colorful, frolicking adventures tumble
      forth
In terror and joy
The scenes cast by madmen
Costuming mismatched, festive and hilarious
      As an Apache raid
And the food comes, and is wolfed down
Between sips of me and declarations of love and
      wonder
Mouthfuls of coleslaw and apology

And all through, a running narrative
On the method of private, multi-level communication
At opposing axes
In one spate of dialogue
As the tea and the bacon disappears
And the weary, tattooed waitress smiles

Provides her level of comfort
And I am glazed and unbalanced
By the din – emotional, decibel, cultural

And then laying down the paper & metal to pay
Remember the scarf and a tip
Step out into the swirling world
Where she will be dragged away
Through the layers of cigarette smoke
On down the current
A pale face bobbing once above a wave
Then a small, gunmetal splash
And she's gone...   *and she loves me.*

And even now
My tissues continue to quiver
With the low harmonics of her presence
Though she has sunk below the surface
        Of a dark, windy lake
And is gone.

**JUSTINE LEANED** against the railing and flicked lit matches into the hotel lobby's koi pond, watching the fish dart anxiously every time a flame sizzled on the water's surface. She was exhausted. First there was the pre-dawn inventory, then the multiple missed calls from her grandmother, and now the drunken accusation by Robb "BB" Jones, the senior partner of the accounting firm where she worked. She wondered why the fish didn't just swim away to serenity in a dark, calm corner in the pool, why instead they were so drawn to the fire.

Her phone chirped: an incoming text.

> Charla: *I wouldn't do that if I were you. You're scaring the fish.*

Charla may have just been teasing, but Justine was in no mood to even offhandedly worry about some stupid fish in a grand hotel lobby. Maybe she was doing them a favor, giving them some excitement, so they wouldn't die of boredom like Grandma Miriam apparently thought she, Justine, would soon do unless she found a nice young man and settled down.

Ignoring the text for the moment, Justine lit the final match in the book and blew at it gently. The flame leaned away from her as the koi circled beneath her, like hungry worries desperate for resolution. When the match burned halfway down, she flung it into the water. A wisp of smoke rose from the ripple she'd created.

Now she texted back to her friend.

> Justine: *Stop watching me.*
> Charla: *I'm not watching you.*

Justine: *Yes you are. I can feel it. It's kinda creepy.*
Charla: *Well I'm just worried, that's all. And I'm not the creep. I saw the way BB had you pinned against the far wall of the banquet room. Why do you let him do that to you? It's such BS. You need to toughen up, my friend.*

How do you respond to a text like that? How do you know why you do the things you do? Or why you let others do things to you, for that matter? BB was notorious for getting drunk and holding new female staff accountants hostage at the annual Christmas gala, and this year apparently Justine was his target. She closed her eyes and tried to forget the reek of his breath—some beastly blend of whiskey, stale coffee, and cheap cigars. She had endured it as long as she could because, despite all the laws about sexual harassment, she knew that sometimes you have to suck up and do whatever it takes, within reason—however reason might be defined. Or maybe Charla was right; maybe Justine had endured his lecherous behavior because she was too cowardly, or even too lazy, to push him away.

Which is practically what she had to do after his last comment.

*They're saying you're the one who started it.*

He'd grinned when he said it, leering and smug, and she'd put up her hands as though preparing to push him back, if necessary. When she excused herself to the restroom, he barely stepped back enough for her to escape.

"It was your dress, you know. That's why he picked you."

Justine startled at the sound of Charla's voice behind her. She adjusted the slinky silver knit around her hips as she turned around.

"Don't sneak up on me like that! Besides, you're the one who told me to dress up, Charla. I thought this dress might accrue some holiday goodwill."

"I told you to dress up *conservatively*. What that dress has accrued is some material interest."

Justine half-laughed. Her friend meant no harm, certainly, but Justine didn't like the accusatory tone. For the second time in one evening she was being blamed for something she hadn't done, or at least hadn't meant to do. And the funny thing was she was starting to feel like she *had* done something wrong, the way you feel when a police car is following you even when you know you've been doing everything right.

"Well I don't think it was the dress that sparked his attention," Justine said.

Charla threw a quizzical look at her.

"I was at the Lichtenstein Chocolate Company this morning."

"You were assigned to that inventory? You lucky bitch! I would've died and gone to heaven to be put on that account. So prestigious. And all that candy."

"Yep. Counted thousands of chocolate Easter bunnies in the warehouse, and it's not even Christmas yet," Justine said.

"God. I heard you get as many free chocolate samples as you want when you do that inventory." If that was all Charla had heard, then that was a good sign. Word hadn't gotten out about the fire yet. "I suppose you refrained from eating anything, knowing *your* will power."

Justine couldn't help but scan down her friend's chunky figure. "No, I ate a few little bunnies, mostly as a pick me up. The inventory started before dawn, and I worked until at least two in the afternoon."

"So that's why you didn't call me. I thought we were going to have lunch together."

Charla sounded like Justine's grandmother just then. Which reminded Justine that she hadn't called Miriam today as she'd promised she would, and she hadn't listened to the multiple voicemails from her grandmother either. She didn't have to listen to the messages to know what they'd say. *Where are you?* Or *are you still coming tomorrow in time for lunch?* Or *can you remind me how to work the remote? By the way, when is my next doctor's appointment?* Or, even more likely, her grandmother would have left the standard lecture about how Justine was far too busy for her own good and *why didn't she ever answer her phone?*

"Sorry." Justine yawned. "The inventory went longer than I thought it would, and then I had to stop by Nordstrom's to pick up a couple of Christmas gifts that I'd ordered, and I barely got to the gym in time for my cardio pump class. And I'm supposed to head downstate in the morning to take my grandmother Christmas shopping." She yawned again. "Sorry, but I'm exhausted. I think I'll go home soon."

"Good idea. I'll go, too." Charla drained the last drop from her wine glass, and the two women turned to leave, when BB came into sight. He was flanked by two men in suits, and all three were heading directly toward Justine.

"Who are those men with BB?" Charla asked. "They look serious."

"No idea."

"We need to ask you some questions," one of the men said in a delectable British accent after BB introduced them to Justine as insurance adjusters.

"Um, I think I'll get another glass of wine," Charla said. She hobbled away on her ridiculous six-inch heels.

The British adjuster, a tall and handsome man who introduced himself solely as Barnes, extended an open arm, gesturing for Justine to sit in a nearby gold velour chair. She adjusted the neckline of her dress as she sat, hoping he and his colleague didn't see the soggy matchsticks in the water. Or the heat rising beneath her skin.

"As you've probably heard, Miss Davis," Barnes said, "the old Lichtenstein warehouse was consumed by a significant fire at approximately three o'clock this afternoon." He glanced at his watch. "Less than six hours ago. We, as representatives for the insurer, were contacted at about four-thirty. We won't have access to the scene to conduct our onsite investigation until the fire department leaves, but we are conducting preliminary interviews with key witnesses while everything is still piping hot in their memories. So to speak. And your name was given to us as one of those key witnesses."

Justine had only partially listened to the adjuster's words; she had been caught up by the sound of his voice instead. And his good looks. Maybe her grandmother was right. Maybe she did need to find a man.

But did he say *witness*? Although she liked the way Barnes said the word, his white teeth lingering with the double *s*, Justine wasn't a witness. She hadn't seen the fire. She'd merely been the lowly staff accountant helping with the audit of the year-end inventory.

"Okay," she said. God, she was such a dweeb. More heat rushed to her cheeks. But what else was she supposed to say?

"Here, take a look at these." Barnes showed her some photos on his cell phone, and at first all she could see was his strong hand, his long fingers, his masculine knuckles. When he leaned a bit closer to her, she forced herself to focus on the images. She could tell that he'd taken the pictures of the warehouse from across the street. Dark smoke billowed above the old brick building, and flames shot out from upper-level windows. In the foreground were hundreds of foil clumps piled up alongside the curb.

Her phone chirped.

Charla: *What's going on over there? Don't look now, but I'm watching you from the bar.*

Justine ignored the text. "What are those foil clumps?" she asked Barnes, pointing at his phone.

"Melted chocolates, I gather. They apparently were flushed out of the building and into the gutter by the fire department's powerful hoses."

Chocolate bunnies! Hundreds, or thousands, of them, which she'd just counted earlier that day.

"So, am I in some sort of trouble?"

Her phone chirped again. She and Barnes both looked at it.

"Do you need to get that?" he asked.

"No. It's just an annoying friend."

Barnes smiled. "Back to your question, no, you're not in trouble. Not at all. In fact, all fires are considered accidental unless, and until, they can be ruled intentional. It's far too early to know anything; we have a lot of work ahead of us. But of course when a sizeable asset like this is destroyed—and at a landmark facility operated by a multinational corporation, with millions of dollars on the line—we need to be very careful. You'd be surprised how many people think about cashing in on their insurance proceeds by burning down their properties, even properties with sentimental or historical value. Especially when they're family assets, if there are no heirs to assume the reins of the operations. And it's not only just for the money. It's an unfortunate way some people create space for change in their lives. So we need to look at all the possibilities."

Justine, like everyone else in the city of Chicago, knew about Lichtenstein chocolates, and not just because of the inventory or, now, the fire. The company, which had been around for more than a century, was a privately held family business, and the names of the individual shareholders—along with the candy recipes—had always been kept secret. But what everyone did know was that the chocolates were sinfully delicious, having been endorsed by nearly every major political, entertainment, and sports icon in the Windy City—including Al Capone, Barack Obama, and Oprah. Justine couldn't imagine how anyone would ever consider destroying such a legacy, even for all the money in the world.

"Tonight," Barnes continued, "our questions are only preliminary. We may very well follow up with you down the road. And I'm sure the fire department investigators and CPD will also want to speak with you after they've been able to get into the remains of the building and begin their site analysis."

"CPD? You mean the police?"

"I would expect some sort of police involvement, yes."

BB's earlier accusations echoed inside her head, and suddenly she thought she might faint. She should have had something to eat along with those two—or was it three?—mojitos.

"I wouldn't worry," he said, his face softening and his smile reappearing. "All I'd like to ask of you now is that you be as candid and forthright with us as possible."

This time when her phone chirped, she turned it off and put it in her purse. Now was not the time for girlfriend gossip, although she wasn't sure if there ever was a good time for it. She wasn't the type to gossip. She also wasn't the type to get in trouble.

There was no reason to be worried, of course. She had not done anything wrong, unless of course she should have detected a risk of fire somehow. But that wouldn't make sense. Still, something about this whole thing gave her reason to feel guilty, as though she had some sort of shadow self who'd gone off and started a fire when she wasn't paying attention.

BB, who had been remarkably quiet until now, cleared his throat and loosened his tie. He pulled a handkerchief from his pocket and dabbed at his forehead and his leaky eyes. Funny, she thought. Neither she nor her boss, both auditors for a living, liked being audited themselves.

Barnes and his assistant began their inquiry of Justine. What, specifically, had she done in the warehouse? Who had been with her? What parts of the building had she accessed? Could she describe the general condition of the property? Did everything seem well organized, or was it cluttered? Did she observe any open doors or windows, or anything that might have struck her as suspicious or dangerous?

Justine felt stupid saying *I don't know* to most of their questions, thinking it reflected poorly on her professional competence and maybe on her overall intelligence as a human being. Or that it made her appear culpable. But it was the truth. She didn't know much at all. She'd been focused on counting chocolates, as she'd been instructed.

"She's just a staff accountant, and a brand new one at that," BB finally interjected, his voice heavy with ennui as he studied the pool of water behind Justine. His tone implied that being a new accountant was no more important than being a koi in a pond. "She's not even a CPA yet, and she's certainly not an expert in matters of risk and safety."

"Thank you, Mr. Jones, for that clarification," Barnes said. "In fact, thank you for your time. But you don't need to stick around any longer."

"Like hell I don't," BB said.

The two men exchanged adversarial glares, and Justine found herself siding with Barnes. She didn't know him one bit, but she had a better feeling about him than BB. It wasn't just that he was so good-looking. He was also polite and treated her with far more respect than BB had a short while ago.

"You're doing great," Barnes said to her, ignoring her boss. "Just give us your straight answers as best as you can. Once again, did you notice anything suspicious?" His eyes were lagoon blue, and she found herself thinking that, if she were a fish, she'd swim right into them. Yep. Too much alcohol. And too much time spent without male company. She definitely needed to work less and get out more. But right now she needed to concentrate.

"It's hard...to remember. But nothing comes to mind as unusual. Then again this was my first inventory assignment ever. I've never even stepped foot in a warehouse until today. Not counting Costco."

Barnes made a note. "Okay, that's fine. Now I have one more question for you. Why were you, and not a more senior member of your team or, better yet, a representative of the Lichtenstein Company, the last person to leave the building?"

"I don't know." This was also true, and she hadn't given it a moment's notice until now. "We were all walking out together: there was BB, and the president of the company, and my supervisor, and then the warehouse manager. We were all going to go have a late lunch together, but then I went to check the time on my cell phone to be sure I had time to join them, because I had so much to do before tonight's party, and I couldn't find it. My phone, that is. Which was weird, because I always keep it in my purse. But it wasn't there. So, just before the door slammed shut, I ran back in to the conference room and everyone else waited outside."

"The conference room?"

"Yes, it's where we'd set down all our stuff before the inventory. I assumed my phone was there."

"I presume you found it?" Barnes said, pointing to her purse. "Your phone?"

"At first I didn't, and then I saw it, or at least what I thought was my phone, sitting in the fake soil of an artificial potted tree in the conference room. I remember thinking how weird that was, and wondering how my phone landed there. I picked it up, and I thought it smelled funny." What an odd thing to say, she knew. "Anyway, I picked up the phone and brushed it off, and then I realized it wasn't mine. I wasn't sure what to do with it." She knew this next part was going to sound really stupid. "So I tossed it back in the plant."

They looked at her quizzically. "I know, I know. Lame, huh? Don't ask me why I did that, because I really don't know. Anyway, I retraced my steps, trying to figure out where I might have left my phone, and I went into the ladies room." This was even more embarrassing. She decided she'd better avoid too many specifics. "I'd gone in there right before we left the building. I did find my phone there, and I headed for the exit once again, and this time, I remember thinking the warehouse seemed really dark and creepy, with all the lights off except for the little Exit sign lights. It gave me the heebie-jeebies being there all alone. I hurried back outside, and that was that. Oh, except I told the group that I wouldn't have time to go have lunch with them after all. I had some errands to do and I wanted to get a workout in."

She could have sworn Barnes glanced at her dress just then.

"So I got in my car and left."

Barnes was typing quickly into his iPad.

"Did I say something important?" she asked.

The other adjuster said, "Probably not. Unless—"

Barnes, BB, and Justine waited.

"Unless there was something in the soil. That part of your story is strange."

Barnes nodded. "Right. The way that phone smelled, too. Can you describe it more specifically? I'm thinking the soil might have contained an accelerant, and whoever started the fire might have placed the phone there on purpose."

"Accelerant?" Justine asked.

"Yes. An accelerant is anything that makes a fire burn hotter, faster. If someone had placed a cell phone there, Miss Davis, the battery could trigger an explosion once the fire started. We'll know more after they bring the K-9s in." Again he asked her if she could describe the smell.

She was not exactly an olfactory expert. "I don't know. Like chemicals I guess. I can't explain it. It just didn't smell like an ordinary phone. Is it bad that I touched it?" She looked at the palms of her hands. "I mean I took a shower after the inventory."

Another embarrassing thing to say. She hoped none of them, and especially BB, was now envisioning her in the shower with water streaming down her naked body.

"I'm sure you'll be fine," Barnes said. "Anything else?"

She shook her head. "No. Except...except as I was pulling out of the parking lot, I thought it was weird how everyone was just milling about in my rear view mirror, watching me drive away. They had seemed so anxious to go get lunch, but then they were just standing around."

Both adjusters made some notes in their twin electronic tablets. Barnes fished a business card out from his jacket pocket and handed it to Justine.

"Well done, Miss Davis. Call me." He flashed his smile one more time. "I mean, if you think of anything else you want to say."

As Justine turned onto her grandmother's long, icy driveway the next morning, she noticed how the gate had finally fallen off its hinges, and how the fence paint seemed to be even more chipped and peeled than when she had last visited a few weeks earlier. The next thing she noticed was that the house was dark except for the array of Christmas lights around the doors and windows, which were illuminated even at this hour of the day, although only half of the bulbs seemed to be working. She looked up at the gutters, clogged with dry leaves and twigs, and then up toward the chimney, caked in creosote. The whole place—what was once a gorgeous Victorian spread just two hours south of Chicago—was an absolute wreck. It looked almost abandoned.

Miriam stood inside the frosty storm door with her walker, hugging herself in a thin cardigan sweater, waiting.

"Hi Grandma!" Justine lugged two shopping bags full of groceries into the house, set them down in the foyer, and delivered a kiss to her grandmother's cheek.

"Where have you been?" Miriam asked. "I've been worried sick about you in this ice storm."

It wasn't an ice storm, just a cold spell that had frozen the previous layer of snow. The roads were fine.

"Sorry, Grandma," Justine said as she looked around. The drapes were drawn shut, but other than that Miriam's house looked the same as ever with stacks of New Yorker, National Geographic, and Smithsonian magazines lining the walls. Miriam had saved the magazines over the years just in case Justine ever needed them for a school project, and she still hung onto them even though Justine was now out of college and out in the working world.

"Why are all your drapes drawn and your lights off, Grandma? And why is it so cold in here?" She rubbed her hands over her arms.

"I'm keeping my costs down. Saving money."

"Aw Grandma, you shouldn't sit in the dark, freezing. I'm going to turn up your heat."

"No, don't touch that thermostat. Please. We'll be leaving soon for lunch and shopping. I just want to finish my tea. Meanwhile, if you're cold you can put on one of my sweaters. I don't know why you young people insist on running around without proper clothing these days."

An assortment of raggedy cardigans, in varying shades of beige, hung on a row of hooks near the back door. Justine picked the one that smelled the least like Grandma's foundation makeup. As she put it on, she surveyed the living room and noticed the fireplace was stuffed with old documents, yellowed photographs and negatives, and a reel of film.

"What's all this?" Justine called over her shoulder. She was tempted to reach in and look more closely at what may very well have been antique treasures. She couldn't imagine why Miriam had put all those things in there; surely she wasn't going to try to burn them. But Justine also knew asking about it might lead to a long drawn-out conversation, so she said nothing and instead checked her cell phone for messages. Surprisingly there were none, as though she had stepped into an entirely different world once she'd crossed the boundaries of Miriam's property. She sniffed the phone before tucking it into her back pocket.

Miriam had gone into the kitchen, and now Justine found her sitting at the table with a half-drunk cup of tea and a new cell phone in front of her.

"Have a seat, dear," Miriam said. "I'm almost finished. Would you like some tea? Or something to eat? Look at you, so thin."

Justine declined the offer of tea and food. "Is that your phone, Grandma? A *cell* phone?"

"Yes, it is. I've decided it's high time I get with the program," Miriam said. "I hear you can do all sorts of things with phones nowadays. I'm tired of being attached to the wall with my old rotary. In fact, I'm tired of being attached to this old house." Her grandmother squinted at the owner's manual with miniscule print. "Now all I have to do is figure out how to use this darn thing."

Miriam may have had all the time in the world to figure out the phone, but Justine did not. She had so much to do and was anxious to get going. She took the phone, spent ten minutes setting it up and putting a few phone numbers in the address book, and handed it back to her grandmother. "All set, Grandma."

"You young people are so fast with all this technology. Can you show me how to text?"

"You want to *text*?" Justine could only imagine how often she'd now be hearing from Miriam. Probably at least as much as she heard from Charla who, come to think of it, had been awfully quiet so far today.

"I paid for a texting plan," Miriam said. "I might as well use it."

Sometimes Miriam was full of surprises. As her grandmother sipped the last drops of tea and studied her new device, Justine found herself surveying the kitchen just as she had the living room. Stacks of dishes on the counter, clean but not put away, and piles of folded dish towels, and baskets of handwritten notes that Miriam likely had written as reminders to herself, as well as greeting cards and junk mail. A rattling sound drew Justine's attention; it was the china cup vibrating on the saucer. Miriam's hand tremors were getting worse, along with the tremors of her entire head. Her body was failing her along with her house. Two old structures—a body and a building—racing to the inevitable end of time.

"Do you ever think about selling this place, Grandma? And moving somewhere that's easier for you?"

"Do you ever think about settling down and getting married?"

"Touché, Grandma." They volleyed the same two questions back and forth nearly every time they saw one another.

"I'd always imagined you living here and raising a family. I guess that's not going to happen," Miriam said without looking up from the phone's home screen. She sounded so dejected. Justine knew that her grandmother loved that old house as much as she loved life itself, and she felt guilty that she didn't share her grandmother's dream, but Justine simply could not imagine living way out in the middle of nowhere in a dilapidated old house. Even if she was married with children someday. But she just didn't know how to tell Miriam that sort of thing, that she didn't love what her grandmother loved.

After tea, Miriam puttered around upstairs for what seemed an eternity. Justine called up the stairs, asking if she could help, but the answer was as she'd expected: *no*. Sometimes her grandmother expected help, and other times she refused to give up her independence no matter what. Eventually, she made her way back downstairs, and the two of them then slowly made their way out to the car—a grueling process as Miriam shuffled step by step with her walker. It was a test of patience for Justine, but she had no other choice, really. Miriam needed her.

Once they got to the mall, Miriam insisted on getting lunch before they began to shop. Which really meant Miriam wanted Justine's undivided attention and time to reminisce. Which Justine didn't really want to do.

"This is a tough time of year for you, isn't it," Miriam said, dropping a Lipton's tea bag into a hot cup of water. "It sure is for me."

Justine stirred oyster crackers into a cup of tomato soup and nodded without looking up.

"I try to think of the good times we had in Decembers past," she went on." Christmas shopping, baking cookies, and all that—the three of us together. That's what your mother would want us to remember."

Justine kept nodding as she watched the crackers float. How could anyone know what her mother would have wanted? Other than to have survived the accident.

"It wasn't your fault, Justine. You don't still think it is, do you?"

Justine had been fifteen at the time, and although she wasn't getting along with her mother very well—they'd been having the usual arguments about boys, grades, and allowance—it should have been no big deal. Her friends weren't getting along with their parents either. The difference, though, was that her friends' mothers didn't go storming out the door after a fight and get behind the wheel on an icy night.

When Justine learned about her mother's accident—and death—she had blamed herself, and she'd run away. Eventually, a friend found her, and after one thing led to another Justine wound up moving in with Miriam. Over the next three years, she ran away three more times, but each time Miriam had taken her back lovingly, had accepted her for the fuck-up she'd been, had tried her best to finish the parenting job where Justine's mother had left off. Had even sent her to college, where Justine learned—in her first accounting class—that there was another whole world out there with rows and columns, debits and credits, structure and—to some extent—predictability.

There was one thing that hadn't sat quite right in the relationship between Justine and Miriam, however. Justine got the distinct impression—no matter what Miriam said—that there was blame in her grandmother's gaze whenever their eyes met. Over time, her guilt faded a little bit, like a painting that hangs in a bright window, where you can still see the subject even if the colors aren't quite as bright. Blame and guilt still hung between the two of them, and that was probably why Justine felt so committed to helping Miriam get along.

Now, she didn't know how to answer Miriam's question; there was nothing she could say that would change anything. The best she could do was chew and swallow her half of the BLT her grandmother had ordered—yet another experience they would share with one another, like shopping and death.

The conversation finally shifted to Christmas gifts, and Miriam fumbled with all her notes about what gifts to buy for whom.

"You want this coleslaw?" Justine asked.

Miriam waved at it as though smoke rose from the little bowl. "You eat it, dear."

Justine ate the slaw, and the waitress brought the bill, and Miriam paid in cash. Then she reached her liver-spotted hand across the table toward Justine's.

"Promise me that, no matter what happens, you won't leave me ever again."

Justine didn't know what to make of this request, and looking into her grandmother's cloudy old eyes didn't offer a clue. Miriam squeezed her hand.

"Of course I won't, Grandma. I'll always be here for you. I love you."

At Sears, Miriam suggested they start at the tools department. Justine asked if she was planning to buy someone a tool for Christmas.

"No, but there are always such good looking men milling about there."

"Oh, Grandma. We're not shopping for men." But Justine dutifully sauntered alongside Miriam, and as they approached the tools department she saw a group of shoppers crowding around the TVs in the electronics department, across the wide aisle.

"Hold on, Grandma," she said. "Let's see what everyone's watching over here."

She peered between a couple of bystanders and saw multiple images of the destroyed Lichtenstein factory and warehouse sprawled across the bank of TV screens. Her stomach did a flip-flop. She inched closer to the screens.

A reporter, standing in front of the building with a microphone, told the story.

"A three-alarm fire broke out mid-day yesterday at the Lichtenstein Chocolate Company's landmark warehouse on the near north side," the reporter said, his voice overflowing with worry and alarm. "The structure was located at the company's headquarters, where the original building survived the Great Chicago Fire in 1871. By now, authorities have been able to ascertain there were no injuries or casualties, and neighboring properties have suffered only minimal damage. But according to one company employee who asked not to be named, there seemed to be a malfunction of the automatic sprinkler system and, as a result, the building and its contents—including thousands of chocolate Easter candies and dozens of pallets of artisanal chocolates—are a total loss, estimated at over ten million dollars." The camera pulled back from the journalist and panned the singed landscape. Clumps of aluminum foil decorated the curbside. Melted bunnies.

The reporter touched his earpiece. "And this just in: The company is reported to have been delinquent on payment of payroll taxes and certain debt instruments, and a source close to the company has stated that the flames erupted just hours after the company's year-end inventory had been completed. Representatives of the company and its accounting firm, Hyde & Gold, are apparently not available for comment. Jeff, back to you."

"Oh my God," Justine said aloud to no one. She turned around and Miriam was nowhere in sight. "Grandma?"

Thankfully, she found Miriam browsing through the hammer aisle, just a few short shuffles away. Justine took hold of her grandmother's elbow. "Grandma, we need to shop as fast as we can. I need to get back home."

"Well, I'm going as fast I can," Miriam snapped back, although she didn't seem to be going very quickly at all.

Justine checked herself. She had no right to be so abrupt with her grandmother. "I'm sorry, Grandma. There's an urgent matter at work. I guess I'm a little stressed."

"All you do is work, work, work. It's not healthy for a young woman like you. You should be getting out and having fun. Some days I think it's my fault you haven't settled down yet, Justine. I'm too much of a bother for you." She shuffled down the aisle alone, grabbing ahold of her walker with white knuckles, mumbling as she went. Justine wasn't sure, but she thought she heard her grandmother say something about how she would soon not be needing so much help.

Justine's phone chirped.

Charla: *Where the hell are you?*

Justine felt like asking Charla where the hell *she'd* been all day, too. It wasn't like her not to text Justine as soon as she woke up.

Justine: *I'm in Lake of the Woods. With my grandmother, shopping. Why, what's up?*

Charla: *What's up? Have you lost your mind? It's all over the news. The fire! Call me!*

Justine checked on Miriam's stability, then excused herself and stepped over to the shoe department, out of Miriam's earshot, to call her friend.

"They're talking about it on all the radio stations," Charla said. "And they've even mentioned our firm's name. They're using words like suspicious and mysterious and convenient."

"Convenient?"

"And that's not all."

"What else?"

"You should hear the water cooler gossip in the office."

"We don't have a water cooler. Besides, it's Sunday. What are you doing in the office?"

"I've got work to do. Year-end, duh! Whatever. You know what I mean."

"No I don't. What? Don't keep me in such suspense."

"They've come up with a nickname for you around here."

"They? They who? What nickname?"

"They everyone. At the office. Torch."

"Torch? My nickname is Torch?"

"Yes! Isn't this exciting?" Charla was on the brink of hysteria.

"Exciting? How can you say that, Charla? How can they call me that? I didn't do anything. I didn't set the fire. Why are they blaming me?"

Justine was incensed. Even if it was a sick joke, it reminded her of being a child on the playground, getting blamed for hitting someone when she wasn't the one who'd done it. Or as a preteen, the time a little bonfire had gotten out of control and she, along with her friends, had been blamed when in fact it had been another group of kids who'd lit the fire and failed to tend it. Or later, when her mother lay dying. Is that the way the world worked everywhere? Problems happened, so blame needed to be assigned?

"Well, whatever," Charla continued. "The police are in BB's office right now. Yes, on Sunday. So you'd better hurry up and get in here."

Justine told Charla that she was several hours away from being able to make it in to the office. "Just tell them I'm not available."

"I can't do that. Don't you see? That would look highly suspicious. They'll think you've run away."

"Oh, please." If Charla or anyone else in the office knew that Justine had, at a younger point in her life, indeed been a runaway, it wouldn't be hard for them to come to the conclusion that she'd run again. But of course she hadn't. Still, Charla was right. Her absence would look suspicious, and Justine would have to figure something out. After hanging up, she fished through her purse for Barnes's business card and sent him a text. As soon as she got back to Miriam, now browsing the jewelry counter, her phone rang. She recognized the number immediately.

"Sorry, Grandma. I've got another phone call to take."

"My word," Miriam said after letting out a big sigh. "Go ahead and take it. I'll just keep shopping." She shuffled over to the next counter and started running her arthritic hands along several colorful silk scarves.

Justine turned away and whispered into the phone. "Hello?"

"I was hoping you'd ring me, Miss Davis."

Justine nearly swooned when she heard his voice, the lovely way he used the British word *ring* instead of the American *call*, and the way he said her name, too. Words got caught in her throat, the way big vitamin pills sometimes did, when she tried to reply. Maybe it would have been better if he'd just texted back.

"I'm sorry I bothered you on a Sunday," she said. "But I had to go out of town, and a friend said I'm looking suspicious for having done that, because of the fire and all, and I'm not sure what to do. I mean, I'm a little scared. I didn't know who else to contact."

Barnes told her not to worry about her absence; he would make a note in the files that she had contacted him. Then he asked if he could meet up with her and ask a few more questions in person.

"Not really. I'm downstate. At least two, maybe three, hours away from Chicago. Can't you just ask me the questions now, over the phone?"

How rude that must have sounded. What if he *did* want to drive all the way down there to interview her again? So what? It would be worth it just to see him. She recalled the way he looked at her the previous night. That starched white collar wrapping around his strong neck, that dark suit stretching across his broad shoulders, that mop of auburn hair. She was feeling overheated and took off her grandmother's old cardigan while trying not to drop the phone.

"I'd rather see you in person," he said. "Text me your downstate address. I'll leave right now. See you around four o'clock?"

Oh, the sound of his voice. Rich, deep, silky. "Oh." She felt a rush of warmth. What was happening to her? For a split second, Justine envisioned the two of them engaging in a carnal feast in front of Miriam's fireplace, but then she quickly came to her senses. She wasn't that type of woman. She was a nerdy little accountant. Besides, her grandmother's house was a wreck, especially with all that trash in the fireplace, whatever that was about. No, he couldn't come to Miriam's house. Justine would die of embarrassment.

Not to mention that she had nothing to wear. She took a peek into a mirror on the jewelry counter; she wasn't even wearing mascara, and her hair looked bipolar. No, he absolutely could not come.

"Um. Okay, yes, that sounds good." Her own voice had betrayed her. She hung up and texted Miriam's address to him. Then she texted Charla.

Justine: *Oh my God.*

She went into hyperdrive then, ignoring Charla's repeated reply texts. She hurried Miriam through the store, helping her pick out two pairs of elastic-waist slacks and a Christmas-themed sweater vest. Then she situated Miriam in the food court with another cup of tea, and she grabbed an extra hot triple latte for herself as she dashed back to Sears to look for something else to wear and some new mascara.

The sun, while low on the winter horizon, was still bright when they emerged from the mall, and the snow lingering in the nearby corn fields reflected the light right into Miriam's eyes. This was the first of Miriam's complaints on their way back to her house. Justine loaned her sunglasses to her grandmother, but then Miriam complained about Justine's driving speed. They were running behind schedule, and Justine didn't want to be late. But whenever she came even close to the speed limit, Miriam got upset. Way more so than usual. And then, after rummaging through her purse, Miriam announced that she'd lost her credit card.

"We have to go back to the mall," she said.

Justine told herself to keep calm and go along with the flow. Her grandmother had once been so smart, so knowledgeable about everything, so organized. But now she seemed like a small percentage of her former self, like an old savings account that had almost run dry. Even though she loved her grandmother dearly, and it was hard to watch Miriam growing old, Justine also found it more and more difficult to be patient. It was as though they were living in parallel universes moving through life at different speeds; the faster Justine's world spun, the slower Miriam's became.

Just when they got back to the mall and Justine had snagged a parking spot, her grandmother pulled a silver card out of her purse.

"Well look at this! Here it is. I've had my card all along. The darn thing must have been hiding at the bottom of my purse, beneath all this Kleenex."

Justine silently counted to ten. She saw, out of the corner of her eye, her grandmother holding up a clump of used tissue, then methodically settling the germ-laden trash back in her purse like a grocery store checkout clerk arranging eggs in a bag. Finally, after clasping the purse shut and checking the time on her old Timex watch, she suggested Justine head on back toward the house.

Justine let out a long, well-earned sigh.

When they were midway there, her phone chirped.

> Barnes: *Where are you?*
>
> Justine: *On way back to my grandmother's house. Sorry, running late. Why?*

"Should you be reading and typing on that thing while you're driving?" Miriam asked.

> Barnes: *What mile marker are you at?*
>
> Justine: *Not sure. Approaching Farmer City.*

"Justine, you're making me nervous. Please put that thing away or pull over."

> Barnes: *Get off at 159, wait for me there. I'm in a black MINI.*

Justine could not imagine why this abrupt need for a rendezvous; was it possible he'd been as attracted to her as she to him? Maybe his need to ask questions was just a ruse! Charla was right after all; this *was* rather exciting. And to think he drove a MINI Cooper, too. She loved those cute little cars.

> Justine: *Okay.*

She took the exit as instructed, then waited on the shoulder for him. Now Miriam had no complaints, as if she were enjoying this interruption. Probably because it gave her a little more time with Justine. That's the way grandmas are. Within minutes, Barnes came speeding along from the opposite direction, made an abrupt U-turn, and pulled up behind them. Justine checked her teeth in the mirror for wayward spinach or whatnot, then realized she was still wearing Miriam's old cardigan. Crap. She'd bought a new outfit but it was still in the bag in the backseat.

"What's going on?" Miriam asked. Then she held up her phone. She had typed a text, too, although she hadn't sent it.

Miriam: *Who is that maniac?*

Justine laughed. "He's not a maniac, Grandma. He's someone I know from…from work. His name is Barnes."

Miriam typed something else onto her phone, then held it up for Justine to read.

Miriam: *Odd name, Barnes. Boyfriend?*

She looked hopeful, her gray eyebrows lifted above the rim of the borrowed sunglasses.

If only that were true, Justine thought. If only Barnes were her boyfriend. "Oh Grandma, I need to teach you how to text."

The MINI's driver-side door opened, and Barnes stepped out. He was dashing in his classic black Ray-Bans and an argyle sweater. He headed for Justine's driver-side door straightaway. She rolled down her window and squinted up at him. Her car was in park, but her heart was still going the speed limit. Maybe faster.

"I came downstate to ask you some more questions about the Lichtenstein fire. But there's something you need to know. Something that has nothing to do with that."

"What?"

"You'd better just follow me the rest of the way."

"Why? Is something wrong?" She couldn't see his eyes through the sunglasses.

"I'm afraid there is. Follow me."

He sounded so official that it made her wonder if this was a trick. Maybe he was leading her to the police, and she was about to be arrested for the Lichtenstein fire, which of course she hadn't set. BB probably pinned it on her. He was probably in on some sort of conspiracy and threw her to the wolves to cover his ugly ass. Or maybe the police were calling her an accomplice because she didn't realize that stupid phone in the plant was an accelerant. Either way, there was probably a police blockade waiting for her in the direction Barnes was pointing.

But why Barnes? Unless he wasn't an insurance adjuster after all. Racing thoughts chased one another around in Justine's mind like rabid dogs.

"Okay," she said. "I'll follow you." What else was she to do?

As he returned to his car, Miriam said, "Mmmm-hmmm." Then she held up her phone for Justine to read. Another text.

> Miriam: *Handsome young man, that Barnes. Nice catch.* ☺

"Grandma, pleaaase." Justine couldn't believe Miriam sometimes. Was dementia setting in? This was certainly not the time for love.

"You could have at least introduced me to him," her grandmother said. "If you don't want him, maybe I'll take him."

"Grandma!"

They followed Barnes for the next fifteen miles.

"Why is he going so fast?" Miriam asked twice along the way. "What's the big rush?"

Finally, he took Miriam's exit and pulled over to the side of the road again. Justine followed him.

"Now what?" Miriam asked.

Justine parked behind Barnes, so close her front bumper nearly touched his rear. As she waited for him to make his way back to her from his MINI, she quickly sent a text to Charla.

> Justine: *Something weird happening down here with Barnes. And with my grandma, too. Life's getting really bizarre.*

Meanwhile, Miriam's mood had shifted yet again, the same way that winter weather patterns kept shifting by the hour in central Illinois. Maybe that was it. Maybe there was something wrong with the barometric pressure that was impacting her grandmother. Right now, Miriam was acting as though she hadn't a care in the world, or as though she hadn't a brain cell left in her head. A pleasant smile perched above her bony chin.

When Barnes came up to the driver's side window this time, Miriam asked outright for an introduction.

Justine sighed. "Grandma, this is Barnes. Barnes, meet Miriam, my grandmother."

Barnes reached into the car, his strong hand passing directly in front of Justine's face. He accepted Miriam's outstretched hand and said he was pleased to meet her.

"Nice to meet you, too, Barnes," Miriam said, removing Justine's sunglasses from her face. She was almost giggling. Justine made a mental note to start checking out Alzheimer's facilities next week. If she, herself, wasn't in jail by then.

Barnes smiled down at Justine, then nodded up the road. "See that?"

Justine followed his finger, pointing toward a plume of black smoke.

"You know where that's coming from?" he asked.

Justine had no idea. Truly. "No."

"How about you, Miss Miriam?"

"No idea, either," Miriam said, now grinning like she was high on something. Justine made another mental note, this time to check on her grandmother's medicine supply. "Why? Is there a problem?"

Barnes rested both forearms on the sill of Justine's rolled-down window. "Yes, there seems to be a big problem. That's your house, Ma'am," he said as he looked over at Miriam. "Or, what's left of it."

Justine felt her breath catch, the way her tangled hair sometimes got caught up in a comb. She wasn't quite sure she understood what he had said. Grandma's house was burning? But how? Why? What in God's name was going on with all these fires?

She was afraid to look over at Miriam, who'd lived a lifetime in that house. Who had raised a family there, including her daughter—Justine's own now-deceased mother. Miriam had accumulated more memories there than Justine could possibly fathom and would be devastated if that house burned down.

And so would Justine. Not because she loved the house—she didn't—but because she knew it wasn't only Miriam's life that would be destroyed. As if being on the verge of arrest for the chocolate factory's destruction wasn't enough, Justine would probably be blamed for this, too. She knew how suspicious it all looked, especially with both fires happening the same weekend. She'd be sent off to prison, even though she did nothing at all, and her crazy, old grandmother, for whom Justine was the only remaining family member who seemed to care, would become homeless and destitute. It was a nightmare, and Justine wanted to wake up. She kept her gaze on Barnes, who was studying Miriam, who was keeping her own attention fixed on Justine. A three-way standoff.

Eventually Justine mustered the strength to turn and look at the quiet old woman beside her. "Grandma? Did you hear what he said?"

Miriam's face was still set with that pleasant, Sunday-afternoon-drive expression. She seemed oblivious, unfazed by the thick black cloud up ahead. Had she not heard? Did she not understand? Could dementia kick in just like that? Maybe Miriam had a stroke, Justine thought. But then, for a flicker of a second, Justine thought she saw the corners of her grandmother's mouth stretch a little bit wider.

Justine may have been the last one to leave the warehouse, but she'd had no idea what the others had been doing while she'd been counting chocolates, packing up her stuff, and going to the bathroom. And she might have been the one to close Miriam's front door when they'd left earlier that day for the mall, but it had been Miriam puttering around upstairs for quite a while before they left. She had never been one to believe in coincidence, and she still wasn't sure she did.

And then she remembered all that stuff in her grandmother's fireplace. Old paper, photographs, film. Perfect accelerants, things that make a flame burn hotter.

Miriam had set her own fire.

She gripped the wheel at ten and two, even though her car was in park, and stared through the windshield. The smoke rose higher into the sky, filled with vapors and winged scraps of memories. Of history, family history. She felt Barnes looking at her, and she also felt another rush of heat in her cheeks, as though she were sitting right in front of the blaze. Her phone chirped.

Miriam: *Don't be angry with me. I did it for you.*

Justine felt blank in her brain and horribly sick to her stomach, and she knew these feelings had nothing to do with the alcohol last night or the way-too-strong latte at the mall.

"Let me know when you're ready to talk," Barnes said.

Talk?

She couldn't begin to talk right now. There were too many thoughts to sort through. First was the question of guilt. Justine may not have been responsible for the warehouse fire, but she was absolutely guilty of this one. She had talked too many times to her grandmother about selling the house and moving into assisted living. She had not spent enough time with Miriam. She'd made it clear she didn't want her grandmother's old house. And she hadn't bothered to ask about all that stuff in the fireplace.

And then, beyond trying to process her guilt, Justine knew she'd have to think about what this meant for Miriam's future, and for her own. She had no idea where to begin that unwelcome journey. She was not ready for that yet, either.

So, no. Talking was the last thing she wanted to do.

She gripped the steering wheel even tighter as a deluge of emotion stormed through her entire body. What most confused her was Miriam, looking happier than she had in a long time, sitting there bundled in her old cardigan, smiling either because she was completely lost in her own world, or because she knew everything there was to know, or because she had gotten all she'd ever wanted out of life and now was able to sit there satisfied, nodding from Parkinson's as though in peaceful complicity.

Smoke drifted toward them now, bringing along with it the charred smell of burning debris. Justine had worked hard to bring order to her life, order over chaos. And now this. Her eyes began to sting, although possibly not from the smoke.

"I didn't do it," Justine said to Barnes. "That's all I can say right now. I didn't do any of it."

"You didn't do what?" Miriam asked.

"The Lichtenstein fire."

"Well of course you didn't. They probably set that fire themselves," she said. Justine and Barnes both turned to look at Miriam, who shrugged and held up her hands, a look of either innocence or ignorance forming on her face. "Just sayin'."

Maybe Miriam was right; maybe the Lichtenstein family did set its own factory ablaze to create space for a new future. Miriam basically did the same thing. And look at what Justine's mother did, even if the outcome wasn't what she'd intended. Yes, destruction forces change, but that's not the right answer, Justine told herself. Chaos only breeds chaos. You're supposed to plan out your future, not escape into it, which was why she'd stopped running away, finished high school, and earned her college degree. Wasn't that the right thing to have done?

She looked out at the double yellow lines in the center of the road, painted there ostensibly to guide you forward, to keep you from straying into the path of those going in the opposite direction. But then she looked back at Miriam, who was happier, and more relaxed, than she'd been for a long time.

Justine inhaled deeply, then exhaled as slowly as she could. "Come on, Grandma. We've got work to do. I think we'd better start looking for a new place for you to live."

"No." Miriam said. "I've got a different idea."

Justine knew what her grandmother was about to say. Something about Barnes, or finding a good man, and now was not the time for that. But Justine was wrong.

"I think that's the last thing we should start doing right now," Miriam said. "And it's definitely the last thing *you* should start doing, that's for sure. The work we've got to do is to get you to start thinking more about yourself instead of me and everyone else," Miriam said. "Stop being so responsible. And stop worrying about everything and who's to blame for what. Relax, my dear. Let go. Live a little."

By now Barnes looked quite perplexed; after all, he didn't know Miriam set her own fire. And maybe he didn't need to know. Maybe, just this once, it *would* be okay to stretch the definition of accountability, Justine thought. A laugh unexpectedly burst out from her mouth, like a surprise burp; she hadn't even felt it coming. But there it was. She put on her left turn signal, then pulled the car off the shoulder and spun it around, now heading in that opposite direction, and as she did, she held her hand up to the side of her face, her thumb and pinky fingers extended, and nodded at him.

"Call me."

# GIRLS AGAINST
# PERFECTION

# Outer Edges

—ALEXA MERGEN

Against a storm door, snow piles
heavily on boards. This is the monotony

of winter, the bitter slog of January.
Sealed against the greyed sky a woman

is in utter darkness until solitude's tenacity
primes her pupils, widens creased eyes.

A green-tipped wooden kitchen match
scratched on a table's stainless edge

at first only deepens each shadow.
Five fingers tangle in sticky cobwebs

and withdraw,
unlearning the haste of reaching.

Still. Be
still. Wait.

Light will leak in like love among imperfections.
Not enough to see clearly, but enough to see ahead.

Upstairs, hot coffee, wool socks on chilly planks,
crystal drifts outside the windows glistening possibility.

**ONCE AGAIN,** nobody bothered to pick up the newspaper from our driveway or open our living room drapes all day, the same way many of my students didn't bother to turn in their homework, or put their names on it if they did turn something in. It was as though the world didn't care anymore—it had given up—and I was coming to that point, too. My life was becoming as pathetic and dreary and interminable as the weather, and I wanted a break from it. No, I *needed* a break. Not just a chance to run away to somewhere sunny and warm, like all the wealthy families did over the holidays. I needed a break from everything, probably even from myself. But that wasn't going to happen, at least not on this day.

It was a Friday afternoon. I trudged up to the door with several plastic bags of groceries draining circulation from my fingers.

"Anyone home?" I called into the house as I propped the front door open with my foot.

No one came to my rescue, of course. My husband Walt was out looking for a job, hopefully, and who knew where Sissy was. I didn't think she'd run away again. As a senior in high school, she had recently decided she no longer had to report in to us, no matter what we thought. I'm not sure when the powers shifted in our house, but obviously she was now in charge.

Along with the dog, who tore out the door before I could stop him.

I made my way into the kitchen and hefted the bags onto the counter between the stack of dirty breakfast dishes and the pile of yesterday's mail that I'd been too tired to deal with after work the night before. My cell phone rang before I'd even gotten the milk into the fridge.

It was Kayla. "We're at the Starbucks across from the school, Mrs. Berg, and we're wondering if you're still planning to meet us."

I had totally forgotten about this new student group I was supposed to be advising.

I didn't recall having given her my number, but the first few weeks after Christmas were always a whirlwind, so who knows what I did or didn't do. I'd been focused on trying to get the students back under control, revising lesson plans to make up for whatever we didn't accomplish before the break, and responding to the principal's requests. Not to mention the concerned parents' e-mails—which have become more and more frequent, and cumbersome, over the last ten or fifteen years. They should have restrictions about how often you can contact your child's teacher, and word length requirements, too. Something like Teacher Twitter: state your concern about your child in 140 characters or less. But then I'd have to learn how to tweet.

I heard myself saying I'd be there right away, even though the last thing I wanted to do was spend my Friday afternoon with four perky girls who had an idealistic notion about how to stop bullying and save the world. But they needed me, and apparently my family didn't. Twenty minutes later, there I was, coaxing my old Corolla into a parking spot, pretending not to notice the Lexus that had been waiting for the spot from the other direction. I hurried into the coffeehouse. Before I had a chance to scan the crowd, I heard the high-pitched squeal of young teenage girls.

There they were, in the far corner. Clustered around a cell phone and sticking their tongues out at it. What is it with 9th graders and their tongues? As I made my way toward them, one of the girls spotted me and snapped a photo of me, too. I'm sure I looked a fright; I hadn't even checked my lipstick in the rear view mirror. I hoped they weren't going to post it on some social media site—although I was pretty sure they would.

Kayla was a plain girl who barely stretched to five feet tall on good days. But it wasn't her height or her unremarkable looks that made her the target of bullying. Once she came out, last year in the eighth grade, she became known as Kayla the Kitty Licker.

Madison had a drop-dead-gorgeous china-doll face, and she was scary-smart, having scored in the 99th percentile on all her standardized tests over the years. I'd heard she had taken the SAT for the first time in 8th grade, scoring 750 on the math test. (If only my daughter Sissy could have scored half that high on her real SAT.) But life wasn't all rosy for Madison. She was already over 200 pounds at fourteen years of age, and she was known among her heartless contemporaries as Fatty Maddy. I don't know why she attended a public high school given her gifts; she would have fit in far better at a specialized school. (But who am I to judge? I probably should have sent Sissy to a convent.)

And Gabriela: vivacious and funny as hell. She was the cheerleader for this group. Given that her absentee father was ostensibly a big wig in a Mexican drug cartel, you wouldn't think anyone would make her the butt of a joke. But they did, precisely because of her background.

Finally, there was Fatemah with her phenomenally dark eyes, a wisp of black hair peeking out from a black headscarf, and skin so smooth even a baby would be jealous. She was gorgeous, except for a wicked scar running down the center of her neck. I didn't know her story, except that she was relentlessly teased because she didn't talk—ever. She smiled at me, and I saw she had a pad of paper in front of her with an elaborate sketch of something in black ink and a few calligraphied words.

Kayla sipped her frothy drink, fragrant with peppermint, and Madison nibbled on a scone. The aroma of coffee all around us, and the sound of milk steaming at the barista bar, was tantalizing. Gabriela offered to buy me a coffee, and I would have loved a latte, but I didn't want to accept handouts from these girls. So I did without.

"So, let's get down to business," I said as I scraped a chair back from the table and sat down. "You girls came up with the idea for this club just before the break, and I gave you some things to think about over the holiday. How'd you do?"

"Well, for starters, we came up with a name for our group. Which was really hard," Madison said, between bites. "We wanted to call ourselves I-GAP, for Indiana Girls Against Perfection, but it sounded like an Apple product."

"And I came up with HOOGAP," Gabriela said.

"Which was supposed to stand for Hoosier Girls Against Perfection," Kayla explained, "but we knew the Evil Queens would do something bad with that name."

The Evil Queens, also known as the EQs. Everyone knew who they were. The trio of beautiful cheerleaders from the rich side of town who would undoubtedly get BMWs on their sixteenth birthdays. Big boobs, Christy Brinkley smiles. The girls boys lusted after and other girls hated.

"Maybe you shouldn't worry about those girls. Rise above them," I said, although I knew exactly how difficult it could be to rise above people who had it all.

They had settled on NEWGAP, for New Quarry Girls Against Perfection, named after our little town. I was surprised they didn't think how *quarry* could be turned into *quarrel*—or *queer*—but I didn't mention that. Instead, I asked why they chose to use the word *perfection* in the name. I thought they were all about anti-bullying. And supporting those who are different.

Madison said there was too much talk about bullying that wasn't getting anybody anywhere. The girls wanted a different slant. "We're not just opposed to bullying, Mrs. Berg. We're declaring a war on perfection."

Kayla jumped in. "We've decided that you can't solve a problem like bullying until you solve the bigger problem: the idea that there's perfection out there, and that we should all be striving for it. There's no such thing as perfection."

I liked their ideas. There *is* no such thing as perfection, really. And bullies certainly tend to zero in on the so-called imperfections of others. This train of thought had some merit.

Madison chimed in next, asserting that perfection is simply an illusion. "Look at the Evil Queens, acting so rich," she said, "They think they're so perfect, traipsing around in their Michael Kors sweaters and Lululemon yoga pants and pink Uggs. Would they think they were so perfect if their parents worked at the gas station or the taco stand or the Laundromat?"

Or manufactured and sold drugs? I didn't say that of course. I loved that word *traipsing*, especially coming from a girl for whom English was a second language. I also liked her point about affluence not being equivalent to perfection. My sister Gillian, way out in Seattle, was rich by my calculations. But I never thought of her as perfect.

"We want to change the way the world thinks about perfection," Gabriela said, nodding at the others. "If the world learns to blur the lines between perfection and imperfection, then there won't be any reason to bully anymore."

Although I wasn't convinced their line of logic was calibrated quite right, I said I understood. Which I sort of did. At least I got their teenage idealism. But what I didn't get was what exactly they were going to do about bullying and perfection, or how they were going to justify making this an authorized school club. The mission had to be realistic. And time was ticking on. All of the other clubs were up and running by now, and one of the vice-principals kept asking me about the status of this one. I was embarrassed I didn't have more to tell him. And frankly I was worried that, when this didn't get off the ground, my little group of self-proclaimed misfits would become the laughing stock of the school while I became the laughing stock of the faculty for having gone along with their far-fetched ideas. Adults aren't necessarily any more understanding than kids.

I pulled a file out of my bag, handed them paperwork to fill out, and started to adjourn our meeting, hoping we could all leave before the EQs showed up. They came here every Friday after practice. I didn't know why my girls wanted to hold their own meeting then and there, under these circumstances; you'd think they'd want to stay as far away as possible. But there we were, across the street from the school, awaiting the enemy.

The coffeehouse door swung open. And there they were.

The notorious girls strode in like royalty cloaked in a collective confidence. Blond heads held high over salon-tanned faces, unzipped North Face parkas revealing low-cut tank tops, and short shorts underneath—despite January's bitter temperatures. I couldn't help it: I was thirty years older than they were but still hugely jealous. The EQs scanned the coffeehouse, settled their harmonious gaze on my NEWGAP girls, and burst out laughing. Clearly a choreographed assault, for no reason whatsoever. It stung.

"Let it go," I encouraged my group. "Come on, it's time to leave." I told them what they needed to work on during the next week—especially some specific goals and some ideas, at least, for how they might work toward achieving the goals. I also suggested we meet at the school next time.

But our next Friday afternoon meeting was again held at Starbucks, despite my suggestion to meet elsewhere. That's what the girls wanted. When I got there, the four of them bombarded me with a stack of paperwork, including a few official-looking forms and a lot of college-ruled paper with pink and purple handwriting. They also had some very big, rather vague ideas about how they were going to change the world through Facebook, Snapchat, and several other social media platforms, a few of which I'd never heard of. Their exuberance was so remarkable it was exhausting.

"Okay, slow down," I said. "How, exactly, are you going to change the world?"

Kayla laughed. "That's the million dollar question, isn't it? What did Martin Luther King Jr. do about civil rights? What did Elizabeth Birch do for gays and lesbians?"

"We're going to do what Gloria Steinem did for women," Gabriela said. "She said there's no such thing as reform. It has to be a *revolution*. She said the only way to change the way people behave is to make them *unlearn what they've learned*. She talked about exploring the outer edge of possibility. That's where we're going, Mrs. Berg." Gabriela cocked her head to the side and raised an eyebrow, ever so slightly. "To the outer edge."

I had been listening earnestly to all of the girls, but Gabriela's last words made my heart skid to a halt. A few months ago, when Sissy had run away, she'd left a note saying *she* was going to "the outer edge." Was this some new terminology the kids were using? One of those nondescript phrases like *I can't even* or *it's all good*? When Sissy had written that, I spent two long days imagining her dangling from a cliff—literally an outer edge. Thankfully, she was gone for only a couple of days, and the edge, I presumed, was just a metaphor, but those two days were the longest of my life. I was worried sick about her, and I was also pretty hard on myself, certain she'd run away because of seventeen years of my parenting mistakes.

But what made those two days even more hellish was a voice in my head that kept saying how cool it was that Sissy had taken that risk! Some part of me was *proud* of her for being so courageous and independent, something I'd never been. What sort of mother envies her daughter's runaway adventures?

Certainly not a perfect one.

"Mrs. Berg?"

I returned to the present and reiterated that the girls needed to come up with a specific plan for what they wanted to accomplish with their club.

"Don't get me wrong," I said. "You don't need to save the entire world in order to start a high school club. But you do need to have a plan about what possible benefit your efforts might bring, whether only to members of your group, or to others on the outside. Like, specifically, how you're going to stop bullying. I'd be careful about using words like revolution. Oh, and keep in mind the school requires a minimum of ten members for this to be an official club."

"Oh, don't worry about that," Kayla said. Madison and Gabriela exchanged knowing glances. "Membership will definitely not be a problem."

The self-confidence, and the verve, among these four was so amazing it was hard to comprehend. Their collective energy was also contagious, and I was becoming excited about their plans, not only for the benefit they might bring to others but, selfishly, for myself, too. Was that so wrong to hope their successes might help me? Maybe I could get a raise, I thought, until I realized how unlikely that would be with union contracts and all those rules. But maybe I could get a transfer to a newer school. Maybe I could even write a book and get it published. I could ride on the pink and purple coattails of these girls.

Kayla saved me from my ridiculous fantasies by opening her file and leaning forward with her own file, one leg curled under the other on her wooden chair. The other girls leaned in to listen above the ambient din, too.

"Like we said last week, our plan is to empower the imperfect, the victims. If there are no victims, there can be no bullies, Mrs. Berg. We're going to equalize society."

An intriguing and lofty goal, vague as it still was. And I loved the language they chose. In all my teaching years, I'd never met any other fourteen-year-olds who thought or spoke this way.

"We're going to create a new paradigm for the imperfect," Madison said, nodding at Fatemah. "Give them a voice."

*Paradigm.* Such a grown-up word. I loved these ideas. I loved these girls.

"I'm tired of how girls are always getting depressed reading magazines or watching movies anymore because they don't look like Angelina Jolie," she said.

"Ew, she's old and anorexic," Kayla said. "I don't even want to look like her. I want to look like Jennifer Lawrence."

"Or Jasmine Villegas," Gabriela said.

"But we'll show," Madison said, "that even celebrities like them aren't perfect. Did you know some famous actors and singers have extra nipples?"

I certainly didn't, and I held up my hand to protest any more information about that.

"Girls," I said, "this all sounds good, but it's still too abstract. We need to tease out more substance. But, unfortunately, time's up for today." I had to get home and shovel snow and take down the Christmas decorations before the next blizzard hit. "You've got some real conversation starters here, though."

"But we're not just starting conversations," Gabriela said. "Remember, we're starting a revolution!"

Oh, to be so young, so naïve. "We'll meet again next Friday, but by then I want you to have finished all the paperwork for me to sign off, and have some concrete steps in mind to accomplish your objectives. How exactly are you going to use Facebook and all your other social media platforms? Where are you going to get your content? And I don't want to be a naysayer, but I do want you to put on your devil's advocate caps for a minute and ask yourselves why? Why now? Why should you be the ones? What if you fail? You need to give me ideas that are both specific and realistic. Or else I just don't see this as a viable school club."

I started to put on my jacket.

"To answer your question of why now," Kayla said, "just look at the twelve-year-old girl in Florida who killed herself when she was bullied by her peers. The suicides happening at colleges across the country. The teen suicide earlier this month across the river in Louisville. Didn't you read about it? A girl with learning differences was mocked on the Internet and now she's dead. See? Even the word *differences* doesn't solve the problem. We can't afford to wait till we're older. We can't wait another month. We need to act now."

"And we're the right ones," Gabriela said, pointing at herself, "because *we're* what everyone thinks of as imperfect. Look at us: fat, gay, multi-cultural. We're the right ones to do this because we're smart, and we've got the conviction...and the money...to go somewhere with this."

"Failure isn't in our vocabulary, Mrs. Berg," Madison said. "Can we please meet before next Friday? It's really important."

"I'm sorry, Madison. I understand your enthusiasm, but I'm swamped. I've got essays to grade, exams to score, and a household to run, too. Take the full week to work over your ideas thoroughly and then we'll meet next Friday. A couple of extra days won't make that much of a difference. Trust me."

The girls exchanged disappointed looks. People with great visions don't want to be put on hold, especially when they're fourteen years old.

And when they are made to wait, they tend to take things into their own hands.

Sunday morning. I rolled over to check the time. 9:45. Shit. I drank too much wine.

On my way downstairs, I tried to piece together what happened last night. Walt had called around 8:00 to say he was going to play a few rounds of poker, watch a NASCAR race, and spend the night at Bill's since I had the car and he knew I wouldn't want to drive out in the snow to get him late at night. Sissy had texted me around 8:30, saying she was at a girlfriend's house and heading for a party. Obviously I told her to be home by curfew, or before the snow was two inches deep, whichever came first. I remember that much. But then the night became a blur. Must have been around 9:00 when I discovered all that spilled rice on the pantry floor—who knew how long it had been there?—and then, behind that, the bottle of wine.

I had no idea how it got there, but it didn't matter. I'd just spent a couple of hours grading papers, and I was hungry. I was also home on Saturday night all by myself. I remember thinking there was a song about that as I opened the bottle. Billy Joel?

Just a small glass, I'd told myself.

Right.

Now there it was, the bottle lying on its side next to the sofa, completely empty. It had been a long time since I'd drunk so much.

I bumped my way around the kitchen trying to capture and make sense of the random words and images bouncing from one brain cell to the next, like a game of hangover pinball. And then Sissy came into view.

She hadn't come home the night before. And it had been snowing hard. I was worried about her. On top of that, she had recently informed me that she was failing all her classes, including English, even though I'd been drilling it into her for years that she had to go to college after high school. There was no choice, I'd been telling her, if you want to survive in life. I'd pressured her about grades. I'd criticized her poor study habits. I'd warned her that her future would be difficult, perhaps even bleak, if she didn't hurry up and get her act together.

I knew I couldn't force her to do her schoolwork or even to want to go to college any more than I could force her to come home at night. In fact, the more I pressured her, the worse her grades got and the more often she stayed out all night. I knew all this, and yet I became even more obsessed about Sissy's academic performance after the Christmas break had ended. Maybe it was because college application deadlines were about to pass her by. Or maybe it was because I was comparing her to my go-getter NEWGAP girls.

I went back to bed thinking about her, and also about Madison and Gabriela and Kayla and Fatemah, and all their talk about perfection. Was that what I'd done to Sissy? Tried to make her perfect? At the very least, I had spent these past few precious years pointing out her imperfections—poor choices, poor study habits, and so on—rather than focusing on, and appreciating, her natural gifts—whatever those were, and her supposed imperfections, when taken together, had wound up becoming a breeding ground for inertia.

I was to blame!

I pulled my pillow over my head. It wasn't just Sissy. I had stood in the front of my classroom, day in and day out, for years trying to boost the morale and motivation of high school students, and notifying their parents when grades were slipping, trying to help them all attain some level closer to perfection. And all along I'd been oblivious to the possibility that the kids were underachieving not because they were inherently imperfect, and not even because of the weaknesses of our media or our greater society, but because *they'd been made to feel imperfect* by those closest to them, even if it was done in subtle or well-meaning ways. These kids were struggling at the hands of the very people who'd brought them into the world and raised and nurtured them. Men and women who'd coddled them in their younger years. People who'd told these kids they were loved unconditionally.

Sissy, and some of her peers, were failing because of hyper-well-meaning parents like me who judged them too critically.

Sadly, this all made sense in spite of the hangover haze and explained, at least in part, what had made the NEWGAP girls so successful. Maybe, in a bizarre sort of way, society had done them a favor. By calling out their differences in size or sexual orientation or whatever as imperfections, society had alerted their parents to the absolute necessity of really loving and accepting these girls no matter what. Maybe their parents had not taken it upon themselves to point to the flaws, as I had done with Sissy. Maybe those parents understood the need for acceptance, and tolerance, and bona fide sincere support that well-meaning parents of seemingly normal kids had inadvertently overlooked. Maybe that's how the NEWGAP girls were able to find their way to rebellion.

We ran out of groceries mid-week. I gathered up the jewelry I'd inherited from my mother and sold it at a pawn shop for $332. Walt hadn't had any luck in his job hunt, and was becoming increasingly depressed, and absent. One day he actually had the gall to suggest I call my sister and ask for a loan.

"No way. I'd rather starve," I told him. "I'll get another job. And I'll see about applying for food stamps."

When Friday came along, I drove across the street to Starbucks. I didn't look forward to what was about to happen—informing the girls I could no longer be their advisor. Even though I didn't spend much time with them, I needed to eliminate all unnecessary obligations from my schedule so I could get a second job. Actually, since I hadn't signed any paperwork, I wasn't officially their advisor yet, so I could resign without much fanfare. Still, I'd have to let them down gently, and let them know I believed in their vision no matter what.

I waited for an hour. They didn't show. And neither did the EQs. For a moment I thought maybe I had the day wrong.

And then my cell phone rang. The screen said the call was from a private number.

"I need you to come back to school. Immediately."

It was Chuck, the principal.

"Is it Sissy?" I asked. I hadn't seen her for a couple of days but hadn't been worried about her absence; I'd assumed she'd been staying at a friend's house.

"No, it's not about your daughter. I'll fill you in when you get here."

As I raced from the Starbucks parking lot back to the school's, I tried to imagine what the problem might be, but I came up empty. Chuck's secretary was waiting by the front door when I got there, her expression as cold as the air outside. She escorted me inside.

I'd always hated the layout of the new school office. The conference room was situated in the middle of everything, fishbowl-style with interior windows all around. It was surrounded by the administrators' offices and the secretaries' cubicles. Anyone and everyone could see into it.

The two vice-principals, the school resource officer, the Spanish teacher, and the school's psychologist were seated around the oval table with Chuck. The computer science teacher was also there.

"Hello, Veronica," Chuck said. "Please sit down."

I pulled a chair out from the table. It felt exceedingly heavy. As I sat, I glanced out the window and saw the EQs sitting in the principal's office, surrounded by a huddle of attractive tennis-type mothers. The girls had obviously all been crying. And not those beauty-pageant tears. The girls looked awful.

Chuck slid a two-page document across the table to me. "You're the advisor for this group, correct?"

It was the Application for School Club paperwork that I'd given to my NEWGAP girls to fill out. I flipped to page two and found my signature there. My forged signature? Or had I signed it in all the chaos of these first few weeks back to school? I was quite sure I hadn't. But then again, students are always racing up to my desk, in between classes, asking me to sign excused absence slips or what-have-you. It was possible I had signed it, but I didn't think so.

"Yes. And no," I said. "I have been advising them about starting a club, yes. But I...don't think I signed that form." I glanced around at the sullen faces at the table. "Are the girls okay? Are they in trouble?"

He took back the form, circled the signature, then set it aside and folded his hands. "We don't know if they're all right. None of them came to school today. And yes, you could say they're in trouble."

I felt clammy and sweaty at once. Those were not the types of girls to skip school or get into trouble. Not like Sissy.

Chuck slid a laptop across the table to me. "I presume you've seen this?"

I stared at the 13-inch screen, on which a Facebook page revealed a cover photo of a map of Indiana, across which the words A PERFECT REVOLUTION had been penned in black ink. Fatemah's calligraphy, I assumed.

The small profile picture to the left showed my four NEWGAP girls squeezed together; it may have been the very one I'd seen them taking at Starbucks a couple of weeks back.

The name of the Facebook page was NEWGAP.

"No, I haven't seen this."

From the looks of it, the page had just been opened that day. But somehow the girls had already acquired 492 friends. How could that be? I felt a smile breaking out. The idea that these *imperfect* girls could acquire so many friends, so suddenly, fascinated me.

Chuck tapped his pen on the table, his eyebrows doing that frown thing, and I figured I'd better read on.

The top post was Kayla's, and only now did I recall that she hadn't been in my Freshman English class that day. I hadn't given much thought to her absence, as Kayla always seemed to be suffering from some sort of vague GI problem.

Greetings from the land of the imperfect, my friends! We invite you to join us for what is sure to become the most famous crusade of the century. We are NEWGAP: New Quarry Girls Against Perfection. But you don't have to be from Southern Indiana, and you don't have to be a girl to join our cause. Are you sick and tired of the way the media focuses on the rich and beautiful? Are you fed up with the nasty names your peers bestow upon you because you're a little different? Then join with us. Rise up with us. Shout out with us! Together we'll deliver the demise, the downfall, the annihilation of The Perfect Ones!

There was a link to a video and 58 comments beneath the post. Before clicking on the video, I scrolled down to the next post, this one from Gabriela.

Hola, compadres! So you think I'm some sort of badass madre, eh? Just because my family comes from Mexico, you think you gotta right to pick on me. ¿Cuál es tu pinche pedo? Well I tell you what. I got friends in the right places, you know? Friends who can help you learn how to be a little nicer to me. If that's what it's gonna take. So I got a recommendation for you, burros. Shut up. No more babosada from you. Or else.

I didn't know Spanish, but it sounded ominous. Gabriela had also posted a link to the YouTube video, and she'd garnered 96 comments so far. I was feeling very confused right about then, and confused about how I was feeling, too, when I began to read what Madison had written.

Here are some math riddles for you morons. Does fat equal stupid? Am I just a minus sign for you? When does enough equal enough? How many fat cells do I need to subtract to be as perfect as you? What percentage of fat girls (and boys) are depressed? If everyone who was overweight committed suicide, how many kids would be left at our school?

And here's the bonus question: What's the ratio between famous fat people like John Candy or John Belushi or Louis CK or Jolene Purdy or Delores Price or Homer Simpson or Elvis Presley or Aunt Jemima or Sir John Falstaff or John Goodman or Chubby or Philip Seymour Hoffman or Jens Jonsson or Santa Claus or Neville Longbottom or Israel Kamakawiwo'ole or Aretha Franklin or Miss Piggy or Queen Latifah or Eric Cartman or Peter Griffin or Notorius BIG or Kathy Bates or Mama Cass or King Henry VIII or Teddy Roosevelt or Oliver Hardy or Rosie O'Donnell or Charles Barkley or Shaq O'Neil or John Daly or Drew Carey or Konishiki Yasokichi to world happiness?

It was rather clever, I thought, and no surprise coming from Madison, but I detected a tone of rage that I had never seen her display in person. It could have been just my imagination, but it worried me more than anything she'd actually written.

Another link to the video. 148 comments, the first of which suggested that people who criticize fatties are the ones who shouldn't be allowed to live. Were my girls rallying for violence? That hangover from last weekend was nothing compared to how I felt now: not just nauseated, but dizzy and unsteady. My NEWGAP girls were becoming the new Evil Queens. I placed my hands flat on the table as though that would somehow stabilize the roller coaster I was on.

The school psychologist, seated next to me, reached out and touched my arm. "Are you all right?"

"No. Yes. I don't know. Let me keep reading." Finally, Fatemah.

My voice is weak because of a sarcoma that was discovered on my larynx, and the surgery I needed to remove it. I choose not to speak aloud.

I am thankful for my three sisters who are giving me power. Praise Allah.

"Oh Lord," I said.

"Go ahead," Chuck said. "Watch the video."

I clicked on the link.

The four girls came on the screen. Three of them stood in front of a blank wall, lined up with a row of microphones. Fatemah sat to the left, at a keyboard. All of them were dressed quite stylishly and wore make-up, looking not at all like the girls I'd been meeting at Starbucks. They actually looked like rock stars. They looked awesome.

And then an image appeared on the wall behind them. It was a drawing that Fatemah had been working on during our meetings, a caricature of the three Evil Queens.

As the music started, Troy, the computer teacher, handed me a transcript to help me follow along.

> Just 'cause you got good looks, you might think you
>         got it all
> But let us tell you bitches that you're heading for a fall.
>
> We got shit on you, y'know, that you can't hide so well
> And now the world will know that your perfect
>         lives are hell.
>
> Those pills you take, Alana, might make you look all
>         sane
> But we know that you're bipolar and got problems
>         with your brain.
>
> Yo Carly, those big stretch marks on your tummy and
>         your butt
> Are cuz you got knocked up by cousin Joe—you're
>         such a slut.
>
> And Sophie you're all crazy cuz of your daddy's suicide
> And we got intel you're so dumb you botched it when
>         you tried.
>
> And all of you got problems in the classroom, so we've
>         learned.
> You cheat and suck your way through school but
>         pretty soon you'll burn.

At least that's how we see it and the world now knows
            what's true
You bitches are just witches stirring up a toxic brew.

I wanted to crawl under the table about then.

"So you don't know anything about this?"

The rhythm and the lyrics were stuck in my head like bad glue. I wanted to watch the video again. It was both horrible and remarkable. Horrible: all those things they said to the EQs. Remarkable: it was a high-quality video and had already garnered a couple of thousand hits, or views, or whatever you call them. These girls were getting fans. It was a full moment before I realized Chuck had said something to me.

"Um, no. Why would I?"

The resource officer turned his laptop screen toward me, then reached around it to click on another link from the Facebook page. When he did, my picture popped up with a caption: *Our fearless leader, Mrs. Berg!*

Oh God. Oh dear God God God. No, this was not good. Not at all.

No matter how much the imperfect me wanted to root for these girls, and no matter how much the young teenager me, still lingering somewhere in my bones, admired these girls for speaking out, the teacher me and the grown-up me absolutely knew what they did was wrong. Reprehensibly wrong. And this reference to me was a big problem, too. I could not be associated with this. I reiterated that I knew nothing about it. Maybe I should have known something. But I didn't. I asked if the girls' parents had been contacted.

"Actually, their parents contacted the school, and the police as well, to report that the girls had sneaked out of their houses last night. Eventually we all put two and two together. We've called their parents in. They're down the hall in the teacher's lounge. The police chief is on his way, too."

The NEWGAP parents, who I had just last week decided were probably the most perfect parents on earth, were now waiting down the hall. The Evil Queens and their mothers were here. And the police. In other words, a veritable lynch mob awaited me.

"Why did the girls call you their leader?" the school psychologist asked. I never liked her. She always acted so poised and knowing whenever she called Sissy into her office. Like she knew how to raise a child better than you did. Like she could read your mind.

"I don't know!"

The words shot out. I shouldn't have appeared so defensive, but I felt trapped. I was experiencing what that prissy psychologist would call cognitive dissonance: I was still, inexplicably, proud of the girls for having a vision, and for getting all those Facebook friends, and for creating a video. I was also proud of them for standing up to the EQs. But not the way they did it. I was deeply chagrined that they'd used social media to humiliate the girls like that. They'd taken the coward's way out and gone public with the EQs' very personal secrets. They'd gone way beyond their stated mission of promoting anti-perfectionism and instead had acted out in revenge.

"Revenge doesn't solve anything," I said aloud to no one. And then I realized that revenge is the first step most rebels have taken in the past when starting a revolution, so it made sense. But still, it was so harsh. So wrong.

My head was pounding. I asked for a glass of water. I wondered if I should be asking for an attorney.

As I drank, I felt the eyes of everyone at the table on me. I tried to replay my meetings with the girls over the past few weeks, tried to figure out if I was complicit in any way. The only thing I may have done wrong was to push them too hard, too fast. Or not ask enough questions.

"I don't know," I said again, this time more calmly, "why they called me their leader. I knew about none of this."

The computer science teacher said the video had been linked to posts on Twitter and all sorts of other social media pages. It had gone viral.

"And the girls have gone missing," Chuck said. "According to their parents, it looks like they've run away. Taken their laptops, their backpacks, and some of their clothes."

They'd done it. My girls had actually started a revolution. But like other revolutions of the past, it wasn't pretty, and they had to disappear. In the middle of winter.

Over the next couple of hours, I was deluged with more questions by school officials and the police. They became convinced, I think, that I wasn't to blame for the cyberbullying. The techies had figured out the girls had made the posts from personal IP addresses, and a school faculty member couldn't be held accountable for things students do from outside the school. Also, the faculty knew me well enough, I hoped, to know I wouldn't support any type of bullying, not to mention the fact technology isn't my deal. I could barely figure out how to use smart boards in my classroom. In theory, I was vindicated.

But I don't think I'll ever forget the glares I got from the NEWGAP parents, or the EQs and their mothers, when I was finally told I could leave. I walked like a zombie past a blur of faces as I headed for the main doors. Once outside, the brisk winter air slapped me in the face. I needed that.

I sat in my car for a long time with the heater running, my mind both overloaded and blank. When I finally thought to pull out my cell phone, I found a single text.

> Sissy: *Mom! I heard you got called back to school. Are*
> *you okay? Call me! I'm worried about you.*

She ended her text with a string of those funny emoticons, including a smiley face and a heart. And then my phone battery died.

Snow began to fall, big wet flakes on the windshield. I hunched in my cold, dark car for a while longer, replaying the last few days and weeks. Madison's comment that perfection is an illusion. How desperately the Evil Queens had hidden their secrets, how naked they must now feel. And Sissy's text.

Sissy had never done anything so bold as what the NEWGAP girls did. And she'd never done anything so mean. I was grateful, as I thought about the NEWGAP girls out there on this sub-freezing night, that Sissy had only run away for a couple of days, early in the school year when the weather was calm. She'd had the sense to know that life can't be perfect, no matter where you are. I hoped my other girls would come to the same conclusion. I worried about them out there. Yet, although my heart ached for their parents, there was nothing I could do for them now.

I flipped on the wipers. Maybe Madison was right. Maybe perfection is an illusion. Or maybe she got it all wrong, and perfection is very real in fact. Maybe it's actually all around us and we're just not seeing it, recognizing it. Maybe perfection is individually defined, and everyone, by definition, is perfect in his or her or their own way.

I backed out of my parking spot, and I slowly made my way on the slippery streets to what I used to think of as my imperfect little life, where snow would be piling up on the driveway. And dirty dishes would be cluttering the sink. And a stack of overdue bills would still be waiting for me on the counter even when my husband and daughter would likely not be waiting for me at all. When I got home, I'd turn on the evening news to find out what they were saying, if anything, about the NEWGAP girls. And I'd sit down on the sofa, amid the chaos, where I'd probably find a phone buried in the sofa cushions, and I would call Sissy. I would tell her how much I loved and admired her. I would tell her how perfect she was.

# SPRING

# FREEING THE
GORILLA

# Spoiler Alert

—ABBY E. MURRAY

Tom has driven to Providence alone to see *Ex Machina,*
a movie he says is good enough but too sexy,
its smartish plot watered down with boobs.
And why is the robot a woman, he wants to know.
She murders her maker and locks up her lover,
both men, before she beats feet, a killer on the loose
with bright blue synapses blooming in her skull
and a torso filled with wires.

I want to know what it was like to see a movie by
       himself.
Did people stare? He didn't notice. I've seen men
alone in theatres and assumed they were killing time
while their wives packed t-shirts and fly rods
into copy boxes at home, their yards filling with ugly
       lamps
and underpants she never loved while her boyfriend,
his boss maybe, made hummus in his kitchen.
Tom says if people were staring he can't remember.
I remember the look a boy gave me after I knocked
       him on his ass
in third grade, on the playground where he'd thrown
       my frog
over the fence and I pinned his shoulder to the asphalt
       with my foot.
He screamed *you're just a girl* and I put more weight
       down.

I want to know why I've never seen a movie by myself,
the judgment of other moviegoers looming over me
like black and red explosions: Poor girl can't get a date!
I want them to notice every cat hair on my shorts,
the mute face of my phone, my child-size popcorn and
          coke.
My whole childhood I wanted to be Bruce Willis,
my dad dragging me into *Die Hard* sequels while my
          mom
packed his things in her head, and we drove home
          singing
*yippee-ki-yay motherfucker* into invisible walkie-talkies.
Bruce Willis couldn't afford to rely on backup.
Bonnie Bedelia forgave the one who saved her.
Tom says I should go out alone sometime, I might like it.


Did I tell you he called from the Cheesecake Factory bar
where he ordered mussels and gin after the movie?
What did the waiter say? Flying solo tonight? Need a
          drink?
If I took myself to a movie I'd pretend I was a robot on
          the lam,
wear Tom's ski hat so nobody saw the wires in my ears.
I'd get cheesecake afterward and when the waiter said
*Just one tonight?* I'd say *You know how it is* all quiet like
          Bruce.
Why a woman? Tom still wants to know.
Because nobody wants to watch a male robot
take over the world before elections, I say,
or at least I think I say, because Tom asks if he can spoil
the rest of the movie for me and I'm certain I say he can.

## *April 12*

**TONIGHT WAS** one of those evenings when I didn't really want to journal. I almost got away without writing a word, but every time I walked into my bedroom, a voice cried out from the top nightstand drawer, like a forgotten babe that needed feeding. So here I am, letting my thoughts flow instead of my milk. Of course, I don't have any milk to flow.

I knew the day wasn't going to go well. It starts out with me pulling down my niece's diaper and finding the green slime. It is so gross! What makes it worse is that, the entire time I'm cleaning her up, Miley's screeching from her crib across the room. Hers is a penetrating and piercing cry, the kind that makes you want to throw yourself off a roof. Thank God my sister-in-law, Melissa, chose a one-story house. I don't know how she can handle it all. Twins are hard. And twin diarrhea is the worst. (*Note to self: beware the fertility drugs.*)

What was I thinking when I agreed to babysit for our nieces so that my husband's spoiled little sister could go off and have a nice career? Then again, I didn't exactly *agree* to the job. More like I was coerced after we moved here and I didn't have a job of my own.

(I know, I know. This isn't what journaling is supposed to be about. Here I am defacing these pretty pages with all this whining. *Whining.* You're supposed to *process your feelings* with your writing; that's what the how-to-journal books say. Whatever. My *feelings* say my life sucks right now.)

The rest of my day was pretty shitty, too—pun absolutely intended. One of the girls pulls herself up when my back is turned and the next thing I know a lamp is on the floor next to her, split in two. Then Tess calls when I'm back at the changing table again, where I spend most of my life. This time I'm with Miley, so of course I miss the freaking call, and later, when I finally get the babies down for a nap and make myself a cuppa from Melissa's la-ti-dah latte machine, I plop down on the living room sofa, where no one ever sits and I'm probably not supposed to be either, and I hoist my gorilla legs off the floor and listen to Tess's voicemail.

Here is pretty much verbatim what she said:

*Jen! Guess what? I got the job! I'm moving to D.C. next month! Can you believe it? I'm going to work for Senator Royce! I'm so stoked. I'll message you with more deets later, but talk to Boyd about the two of you coming out to visit me after I get settled, okay? Gotta go now. Love ya!*

"Fuck," I say out loud, which Melissa would be pissed about if she knew. I'm sure she wouldn't want the twins' first word to be *fuck*. Neither would I, I guess.

But shit. Tess is moving. Not just thousands of miles away from Seattle (that was the one good thing about moving to Seattle with Boyd...being close to my best college friend again), but she is also, apparently, moving way up the ladder, too. Just like everyone else. Way up the ladder of life. Last year, April got a six-figure advance for her historical novel, and now she's embarking on an exciting book tour around the country. Melissa, my psychic-turned-psychotherapist sister-in-law, apparently has people lining up to talk about their problems in her fancy downtown office. My sweet husband is poised to save the world, especially now that he's been lured away from Microsoft by that big-deal biotech firm to work on inflammation-resistant genes. Or something like that. Even Cherie, who I admit I never thought would amount to much of anything, has a zillion saps following her blog about how happy she is as a stay-at-home mom, back home in Indiana, with her three rug rats who she claims are gifted and talented or whatever. My point is that the world keeps spinning around me, and everyone seems to be getting exactly what they want. Except for me. (Wah-wah.)

So here I am at home now, feeling like I'm starving from professional malnourishment in this quaint little suburb called *Snoqualmie*. Instead of saving the earth's animals from disappearing, which is what I'd planned to do when I went to graduate school, it's me who's on the verge of extinction at the ripe old age of twenty-eight.

(This is what I hate about journaling. Yeah, it's reflective all right. Too reflective. Worse than a mirror on a bad hair day, it reminds you how bad your life is.)

Oh, one more thing. The irony of all this is that Boyd and I are working so hard to have our own babies while I'm taking care of other kids and complaining about it all the while. Makes you wonder. I need to talk to him.

(Break time.)

I'm back. So I sent him a text, which in hindsight was probably not a good idea, given my frame of mind. Here's how well that went.

> Me: *What time will you be home tonight?*
>
> Him: *Late. Prospective investor taking me to John Howie's for dinner. Don't wait up.*

Really? John Howie's? Boyd is being wined and dined by all sorts of investors, clients, and probably God himself these days in five-star restaurants, and I'm cleaning baby butts.

> Me: *Well, I certainly hope you enjoy your filet mignon. I had organic macaroni and cheese with the twins for lunch today.*

No reply. I probably shouldn't call my husband a fuckwad, even in my own head, but that's the first word that comes to mind when I realize he isn't going to text back.

(*Note to self: Do not journal about food when you're alone and hungry, especially if there's a lifetime supply of Snackimals in the house.*)

I don't know why we have Snackimals in our house. Binge City.


## *April 17*

A week gone by, and I still haven't had the talk with Boyd. I also haven't gotten any vajayjay love from him. It's exactly the right time of the month, but after all those other failed months, we've both gotten pretty burned out on basal temperature charts, *prescribed positions*, fertility *injectables,* and all that crap. And, anyway, he seems so distant these days. And so busy. Maybe he's just stressed at work. Or maybe he's reconsidering the whole idea of having kids, too. Point being: I think he's avoiding me and the whole topic.

I hope not, since I've practically made a second career out of trying to get pregnant. Not that I'm exactly looking forward to more body fat or maternity clothes or sagging breasts. Or diarrhea diapers. But there is a part of me that wants to hear someone call, "Mommy!" and have them mean me. Either that or I want to go back to my real work, helping the Mountain gorillas in Rwanda. I wouldn't be wiping their butts and they wouldn't be calling out for me in English, but we'd still have a relationship of some sort. They'd know I was there for them.

So I've decided (again) that tonight is The Night. We will have The Talk when Boyd comes home. It's going to be the first time he'll be here in time for dinner in a long time. I've got everything laid out for chicken marsala, and have already assembled a big healthy salad. I even made gluten-free garlic bread for him. And there's an expensive bottle of Pinot Gris chilling in the fridge.

(Break time.)

This is how it went down, more or less.

We sit down at the table and toast one another. He takes a big bite of chicken, and as he chews, I get the conversation going, sort of midstream.

"So about our kids," I say.

No sense dallying around with some sort of opener that might alert him to the idea that we are about to have a deep talk. Just go right for it, his sister-shrink had advised a day or so earlier when I'd asked her for advice. "When his plate and mouth are full of food," she said.

The problem was that I really wanted to have *two* Talks. One about my unhappiness. The other about the possibility of adopting kids. They may sound unrelated, but I'd been thinking that adoption might lead to greater happiness. At least we'd be happier than dealing with all this unsuccessful—and expensive—fertility stuff. Not that adoption isn't expensive, too.

Anyway, here's how the rest of the convo went.

"The thing is," I say, "I think I could make a really good mother, Boyd. But I'm not getting any younger. Maybe we should consider adoption."

He keeps chewing, swallows hard, and takes a long drink of wine. He takes another mouthful of chicken, and as he chews for a near eternity, I wonder if the chicken is really that tough. I thought I'd cooked it perfectly. Then he shakes his head.

"I don't want to give up on having our own kids, Jen. I want someone with our own genes. You don't know what you're getting when you adopt. It's like getting a kid on Craig's List."

Seriously?

"Craig's List? Come on, already. That's ridiculous."

*What was his problem?* A human baby is a human baby. But recently Boyd has become obsessed with genes. So I say, "Animals in the wild adopt orphaned babies all the time, sometimes even babies outside of their own species. They don't worry about genes. I could have suggested we adopt a different primate, say a baby gorilla, which would share 98.3% of our DNA. But I figured you wouldn't go for that. But now you say even a human baby, who shares 100% of our DNA, isn't good enough for you? Boyd, I've done some research on adoption."

I try to gauge how open he's going to be by the size of mouthfuls of food he's shoving in. Big mouthfuls = not very receptive. His were huge.

"Did you know you get to find out a lot of stuff about the baby's birthparents before you even agree to an adoption? You want a baby with brown eyes like yours? We can ask for brown-eyed birthparents. You want a baby with Spanish origin? We can probably arrange for that. If that's what you want to do: custom-design our kid the same way you can custom-design a car. Although I'm a bit concerned with our designer-baby, narcissistic society these days. And you know, even if we have our own kids, you won't really know what you're getting. Just because they'd be from our genes doesn't mean they'd be perfect."

I end my diatribe with a long drink of wine.

At first he doesn't reply. I hope he doesn't ask me to repeat what I said because I'm not sure I could. But finally he takes a long drink of wine to match mine, and then he says he heard me loud and clear.

"You're right," he says. "You never know what kind of baby you're going to get, but it's even more of a crapshoot with an adopted kid. And this is a lifelong commitment, Jen. Not just some car you can trade-in if it's a lemon."

Did he think I was an idiot of some sort? And worse than that, was he *really* suggesting that a kid could be a *lemon*, like a car? Kids are people! I wanted to shout back at him. Then that famous Dian Fossey quote came to mind, sort of. It was something about how the more she knew about gorillas, the more she wanted to avoid mankind. Yeah.

"You remember when Melissa told us about that client of hers—Miss Fortune?" I had pictured some sort of gypsy fortune teller when I first heard her name, until I heard the rest of the story. Of course, Melissa shouldn't have been talking about her clients. It was totally unprofessional. But that didn't keep me from listening.

Boyd says he remembers, but then he has to correct me. "Her name was Fortunae. What's your point?"

"My point is that she had this totally out-of-control son, who was always stealing and skipping school and all that, and Melissa was worried this poor woman was going to have a nervous breakdown. Or worse. And remember? This was her *biological* son, Boyd. Not an adopted kid. This boy carried her own genes and still drove her nuts. There are no guarantees in life."

I obviously didn't like the way the conversation was going and I hadn't even gotten to the unhappiness part. It wasn't just that I wasn't getting my way about him being open to adoption; it was the fact that he was so adamant and controlling about something that should be a decision made by both of us. As equal partners.

He finishes his dinner while I sort of pick at my plate. Then he says he just doesn't want to enter into any permanent situation that he isn't 100% sure of.

At this point I stab a chunk of chicken, which is in fact overcooked after all, and I say, "You married me." A dangerous assertion, I later realized.

He half-smiles, then scrapes some mushrooms and sauce from my plate onto a slice of garlic bread and stuffs it into his mouth.

Maybe he doesn't think of our marriage as permanent.

He wipes his mouth with a napkin and tells me the dinner was really good. "New recipe?" And then he points his index finger at me. "And you've made my point exactly. I knew what I was doing when I married you. I knew what I was getting."

I wondered if he really did.

"But I won't accept a child I don't know," he says, "unless it's one of my own."

He finishes his glass of wine, stands, and carries his plate and silverware to the kitchen sink.

So much for The Talks.

*(Note to self: consider using journal to plan difficult talks in advance rather than to record the disasters after the fact.)*

## *April 18*

I had to nanny not only for the twins but also for Lily, Melissa's best friend's daughter, today. A little prima donna about four years old. And I wasn't babysitting for them at Melissa's house because she was having her carpets cleaned. So I had to haul all the kids over to our house. Man, the shit was really getting piled on me. And it got worse.

When I finally get them all down for an afternoon nap in our guest/junk room that also serves as Boyd's home office, I collapse across our bed. I don't mean to fall asleep, but I quickly do, and I drop into this deep sleep and dream that I had kidnapped the twins, thinking how happy Boyd will be because he'll be getting exactly what he wants: children with at least some of his genes; children he already knows.

But then I wake up to the sound of a loud crash, and a child's cry.

I jump up from the bed. I am so disoriented I don't even cuss. I have forgotten about both Lily and the carpets, and I run out of the bedroom, ever-so-slowly realizing I'm in my own house and making my way to the kitchen, which I somehow know is the epicenter of the escalating cries.

There's Lily, lying on our hard tile floor, surrounded by shards of blue. There are so many pieces that I don't, at first, realize what they are. I rush over to her, to make sure she's okay, and scoop her up. There don't appear to be any cuts, or any blood, miraculously.

"Lily! What happened? Are you okay, sweetie?"

Then I see my stepstool, which last I knew had been in the pantry, now set up in front of the cook's desk, which makes no sense to me. I've never put it there.

By now Lily has pulled herself together a bit, although her lower lip is quivering and her eyes still watery, but rather than explain herself she decides to bury her wet, warm little face into my neck. And then it dawns on me what the blue shards are. My gorilla. The six-inch tall, one-of-a-kind, handmade ceramic gorilla. I feel the muscles in my arms tighten, my jaw clench. A torrent of heat rushes through my body and I shut my eyes for a moment to keep myself from completely losing it. Then, as gently as I can, I draw her head away from me so I can see her face.

"Lily? What happened here? Oh Jesus, Lily. Dear God, no. Were you playing with Jen's gorilla? Answer me, Lily!"

I put her down on the floor the moment I realize I understand why people sometimes shake their children.

Lily answers through staccato sniffles. "I just wanted to look at the monkey."

I stare first at her, then at the fragments scattered on the floor. And then I yell *no, no, no* as I pound one of my fists so hard on the black granite countertop that I'm surprised I didn't break the bones in my hand. Lily starts crying hysterically, all-out bawling, and she runs down the hall to the guest room, and obviously this wakes up the twins, thank you very much, Lily.

I am not proud of how I handled Lily here. I am also in no condition to take care of her, or the twins, or anyone else at the moment.

The only person I can think about now is Peter.

I carefully kneel down amidst the wreckage and gently cradle a stump of blue in the palm of my hand. A gorilla's arm. This had been the only remaining memento I had of Peter. And now the gorilla, and it seems my entire former self, is destroyed for good.

(Break time.)

Some things are hard to write about, and this is one of those things. So here goes. After all the hysteria settled down this afternoon, I called Melissa and told her I'd had an emergency. She would need to cancel her appointments or whatever for the rest of the afternoon and come pick up the twins and Lily immediately. I refused to answer any of her questions, other than to assure her the girls were all okay, even if I wasn't.

Once they were gone, I fell back on the bed and thought about Peter.

First of all, he was super hot. Amazing, actually, with a killer South African accent. He also happened to be my fieldwork advisor back in the day, when I weighed at least thirty pounds less than I do now and had an outlook on life that was disgustingly Cover Girl fresh.

But Peter was about so much more than sex. He was dedicated to all things Africa, and pretty much all things wild, which was also a total turn on for me. I was just beginning to dedicate my life, or so I thought, to wildlife conservation, and I was doing my primate fieldwork with him as my supervisor. We were a perfect match, IMHO, and I had a huge crush on him, even if he was at least fifteen years older than I was. But he was ultra professional and our relationship remained excruciatingly platonic at first. Until that day I saw my first Mountain gorilla family.

This is where journal writing gets a little dicey. You want to believe that no one will ever read your journal. It's one of those unwritten laws, right? But I once knew a woman whose husband read all fourteen of her journals and then filed for a divorce. I'm not looking for trouble. But I've never written about Peter before and the urge is hitting hard. So here goes. If you're reading this without my permission, please stop here.

Peter and I are in the Virunga Mountains, on the Rwanda side. It's springtime and raining hard, and we've been hiking for hours in search of the elusive creatures I have yet to see up close and personal. I feel, and probably look, like a drowned rat. I'm thirsty. Hungry. I have blisters on my heels the size of my eyeballs and I know I stink from sweat. I am not exactly a sex kitten. I want to turn back to camp and give up, another day without a sighting, but I can't let on that I'm being a wimp.

And then Peter spots them! They're up ahead not more than fifty feet, camouflaged amidst the trees. He wraps his arm around my shoulder, and we stand together that way, immobilized, and I am fascinated not only by those beautiful giant gorillas but also by the strength of Peter's arm and the harmonic rhythm of our breath. I am not sure which is more exciting. And then, right about the time that a lactating gorilla mother comes into our view, and her baby latches onto that huge black nipple, I feel so weak that I need to sit down.

I find a nearby fallen log, and as I hold my head between my knees, trying to remain conscious, Peter makes some comment about it being hard to ignore that maternal twinge when you see the little darlings. His comment startles me, kind of comes out of nowhere, and when I lift my eyes toward his I think I see a hidden message in his gaze. There is definitely a twinge in my body at this point, but it isn't what I'd call a maternal one. It's more of a pre-maternal twinge, right there between my legs. Peter must be feeling it, too, and later that night our primal tryst begins. For three months we tuck ourselves into his tent when each day's work is over…and let's just say our lovemaking isn't anything bordering on professional. Definitely not, except I do wonder if he learned some of his seemingly untamed moves from observations in the field.

When it was time for me to return to the States, I had these delusional ideas that we'd keep up with one another and maintain a very, very long-distance relationship, but that was just my inner school girl thinking that, and of course it was before I met Boyd.

The truth was I never heard from Peter again, even though I wrote him several times. I was broken-hearted, of course, but then I got so involved in my thesis, and then I met Boyd, and here I am. I stopped writing Peter…I'm not insane. But I do periodically keep trying to find him on the Internet. I've never really stopped loving him, I guess. And Boyd has no idea. Not that I hide anything from him on purpose. I never erase my search history, for example. I think he's just too distracted with his own work and life to even think about checking up on me. Which I'm not sure is altogether a good thing.

Anyway, all Boyd knows is that the blue gorilla was really important to me because it had something to do with the time I spent in Africa. He thinks it's some sort of souvenir I picked up in a little shop, I guess. It was actually way more than a souvenir. It was a ceramic sculpture that a local artist made one day, especially for Peter and me. My high school ceramics teacher once said that a sculptor's job is to make the invisible visible, and that's exactly what that African artist had done that day for us.

*(Note to self: Document as much as possible about Africa experience in separate journal before details, emotions, etc. are forgotten. Should've done this long ago.)*

## *April 23*

Over the last few days, I've been spiraling into a vortex of depression. I finally quit babysitting for Melissa (okay, it was a mutual decision after the gorilla incident) and I've sequestered myself from the rest of life. I stopped trying to reach Tess, partly because I got tired of hearing her voicemail greeting and partly because I didn't want to hear how fabulous things were going for her. I also stopped reading April's blogs. Sometimes you have to take care of your own needs and stop celebrating for your friends.

I mostly stare out at the gloomy Seattle rain now, like those children in The Cat in the Hat book, which Lily left behind on that fateful day and which I've actually read by myself at least a dozen times. Talk about depressed. I've been eating too much chocolate during the day, drinking far too much wine at night. And I've still been trying to find Peter on the Internet, but to no avail. I'm such a loser I can't even stalk somebody.

Boyd hasn't exactly been helping my mood either. It's not like he's been mean or anything. He's just either been out at fancy restaurants or working crazy long hours. And when he has been home, he's been playing a lot of video games, which I know helps alleviate his stress. Or helps protect him from me. He didn't exactly get what happened that day, and why I was so upset about the gorilla, or why I screwed up his sister's life by quitting, so he's been staying clear of me for the most part.

But I need to talk to him! I need to connect with him even though I'm not at all sure about what since connection implies some sort of mutual attraction or a force of some sort that draws people together, which doesn't seem to be at all in place lately.

I tried yesterday morning, while he was in the shower.

"Boyd?" I call through the shower curtain. "Do you have a few minutes to talk before you head into the office?"

He pops his head, lathered with shampoo, around the edge of the curtain. He asks if it can wait until the evening, and then he promises he'll even take me out to dinner. "Anywhere you'd like," he says.

I tell him okay and spend the rest of the day feeling sorry for myself. It isn't that I'm ungrateful about going out to dinner, but I'd worked up all that courage to talk to him—it's not easy admitting your vulnerability to someone who thinks life is swell—and now I have to wait again. I spend the day watching *Gorillas in the Mist* (twice), even though I've already seen it a zillion times. I eat an entire twelve-ounce bag of chocolate mints, too. And then Boyd calls late in the day to say that his boss needs him to work late again and could it wait until tomorrow night.

This is why I didn't journal last night. When I got that phone call from him, I felt like the ground had opened up and swallowed me, like one of those sinkholes you read about on the news and wonder if those things are for real. Sure, life is full of disappointments. And it wasn't like this was a huge surprise; it had happened so many times before. But yesterday I was already operating at such a low level of energy, as though I'd been circling the base of a mountain trying to muster the will to climb even a little bit higher, and now my hopes, slightly elevated since his dinner offer, were dashed once again.

I went to bed early, after finishing an entire bottle of wine. I woke up later to pee and found Boyd had fallen asleep on the living room couch, his right hand shoved down in the front of his jeans. Why do guys always need to do that? Maybe that's my problem: I don't have a penis to hang onto for security.

When I couldn't fall back asleep (*note to self: a half-bottle of wine is plenty*), I pulled the shoebox out from under my side of the bed where I'd saved the blue gorilla remains. Some of the pieces were so jagged it was a miracle Lily hadn't hurt herself. I picked up that gorilla arm again; its edge was also sharp, and I traced it along the blue vein on the inside of my wrist. How easy it would be. And how fitting, too. Not being killed by a gorilla. Being killed by a shattered dream. Not that I seriously considered it. Just a thought.

So this morning, as I lay in bed, I told my beloved husband that he couldn't leave for work until we talked. No more putting me off. One thing I've noticed is that, the more depressed I get, the more forceful I become about certain things. Like not working for Melissa anymore. And making Boyd listen to me.

He's playing a game on his iPad while still lying there on his side of the bed, and when I tell him we need to talk, he gives me this startled look. Then he scratches his chest and sets the iPad face-up on the nightstand.

"Okay. What's up?"

I think I detect reluctance in his voice, or maybe it's anticipation. I didn't think this at the time, but looking back I wonder if he thought I was about to tell him I was pregnant. Whatever, it doesn't matter now. What I remember thinking at the time was *at least he's turned toward me*.

He props himself up on an elbow. He sweeps a fallen wisp of hair away from my eyes with his free hand.

He says, "You're so beautiful, Jen."

It's not that I didn't want to hear compliments from him, but right at that moment I found it out of place, like he was trying to throw me off the scent of a trail. It was irritating.

"Boyd," I say, "I don't know quite how to say this, and I don't want you to think I'm ungrateful for everything you do for me. But, as you may have noticed, I haven't been happy lately."

"Is it something I've done?" he asks.

Although there are a lot of ways I can answer this, I tell him, "No. It's not you. It's me."

Which isn't exactly true. There are plenty of things he's done, or not done, that have accumulated together like ingredients for a bad recipe that result in intestinal upset. In this case, it's not my intestines but my emotions that are twisted, even constipated. One of those things that still bugs me is that whole conversation we had about Craig's List kids.

Then, his iPad chirps, and I see the temptation on his face. He is struggling to maintain his focus on me rather than attend to his electronic device, as though he is more married to it than to me. Is this a problem in other species? Not the electronic part, but in general: do female *beringei beringei* gorillas, for instance, need to do nearly as much to keep the attention of their males? Sure, they have to attract them in the first place. But then, once they've won them? We're not even talking about him getting distracted by another female. I am competing with a *thing*, for God's sake.

What a pair we are. When he does return his attention to me, he begins to tickle my breast through my nightgown, which I know is basically just another tactic of distraction. I push his hand away.

"I'll just come right out and say it. I'm depressed. I think it's partly because we haven't gotten pregnant. But also—"

"If you're going to bring up adoption again—"

"No. I'm not." I wasn't that stupid. "I don't think that baby thing is the whole problem. I think the bigger issue is that I'm bored."

"Bored? You live a complete life of leisure. What's there to complain about?"

"That's the problem, Boyd. Exactly! It's *too much* leisure. I'm not doing anything important with my life. Not following my passion. You and my friends are all having the times of your lives changing the world, and I'm changing somebody else's kids' diapers. Well I was, anyway. That's not what I was meant to do. It's not who I am. Or who I was before I left everyone I knew back east and followed you out west. To do nothing."

He looks hurt, which I knew would happen. It's like he thinks *he's* the failure if I'm not living in 100% bliss. Like he thinks it's *his* job to make me happy. Which is insane. I know it's not his problem. I just want to talk it over with him. *Process my feelings* with him instead of this stupid journal for once.

So what does he do? He tells me nobody *made* me marry him and move out West with him. Then he rolls over, gets up, walks into the bathroom, and shuts the door. The next thing I hear is the shower running.

Fuck! Game over.

I wasn't trying to hurt him. I do love Boyd. And I know I didn't *have* to follow him out here. But if I hadn't, I would have been back at the speed dating tables yet again, and I sure as hell didn't want to do that.

While Boyd takes the world's longest shower, I go into the kitchen and switch on my computer. I know it's a dangerous thing to do, but I open up iPhoto anyway and go to my Rwanda album.

Photos of gorillas. Photos of Peter. One with Peter and his team of researchers and assistants, all wearing t-shirts that read *A Wild Gorilla is a Happy Gorilla*. And a photo of the hospital Peter had taken me to one day, when I'd clumsily fallen and cut my arm on something. I don't even remember what. The facility was settled on a parched hillside, a cluster of single-story buildings that I remember thinking seemed to serve not only as a place for healing but also for hope and love. Especially with that magnificent courtyard garden where bald children with cancer squealed with laughter. Ugh. I was such a sap for romance back then. That was the day I told him I loved him. And it was the day he told me I was destined for greatness, that I would surely contribute *joy to the world*, whether in the animal kingdom or among humans, which was probably his way of letting me down gently since he wasn't going to profess his love for me, but I believed his words anyway, even if they were abstract and as hollow as my days have since become.

A mistake to believe Peter then? A mistake to reminisce now? Maybe yes, on both accounts.

I hear Boyd turn off the shower, close my laptop, and race back under the covers trying to calm my breathing. Boyd comes back into the bedroom naked, toothbrush in mouth. He is drooling suds, and now I begin to wonder if I love him anymore, or whether I ever did. Or if so, why I ever did. He's handsome, successful, has a good personality. He's honest and hard-working. The sort of guy your mother hopes you marry. But one thing he's not: my cheerleader. And neither was Peter, really, although at least Peter was able to recognize my passion and encourage me to move forward in that direction. Unlike Boyd, who simply wants me to follow him on his way to greatness.

*(Note to self: in next life, remember that true love means being a cheerleader.)*

Boyd comes over to the bed. "I feel like you're blaming me for your unhappiness," he says.

I appreciated his willingness to revive the conversation, but starting it up again with him acting so defensive was not an ideal entry point, because his assertion that I was blaming him in turn made me feel defensive. One of those infinite loops you can get into in a relationship that you can't find a way out of. Besides, it was a bit hard having a serious conversation with a man whose penis was dangling at my eye level.

I say, "Jesus, Boyd, that's not what I'm trying to accomplish here."

"Well what are you trying to accomplish? What do you want, Jen?"

Some *homemakers* have affairs. Some drink wine during the day (I don't permit myself to start till 6:00). Some gamble, smoke weed, use Oxycodone. There's one mom down the street who I'm pretty sure dabbles with heroin. I don't do anything wrong at all, and I sure as hell don't deserve that terse tone in his voice.

"Can you at least try to understand what I'm saying?"

"I am trying. I don't know what the answer is. Maybe you should get a job in the zoo."

The zoo.

Well, at least he was on the right track, finally. By mentioning a job in the zoo, he must have (at some level) understood the emptiness I'm feeling without a career, and my love of animals. But a job in the zoo wasn't even quite right. This was complicated, so complicated. Trying to explain this to someone like Boyd, for whom everything had come so easily (and who, maybe, was just someone who could find happiness and fulfillment more easily than me), was like trying to explain a kaleidoscopic dream you've had. Pretty much impossible.

He returns to the bathroom but I am not done. I call out to him as he spits into the sink.

"The problem is that I'm not sure what I want to do. It's not just a job in the zoo that I want. I need to find something to do to use my mind and my training. To release my passion."

"You used to be pretty good releasing your passion with me."

His use of the past tense stings a little bit—even if it is true.

"Boyd, I'm serious. That's not what I'm talking about. And you know it."

There was a small part of me that wished, right then, he'd jump me in bed. Instead, he leans his muscular, still naked body over me and kisses me with his toothpaste-flavored lips. Then he pulls a too-tight Power Rangers t-shirt over his head and steps into Avenger boxers. I could never figure out how he could be a child and an executive at the same time. Maybe that's what I loved about him, if I ever loved him. While at the same time I resented the fact that he was living the life he wanted. And I wasn't.

*(Note to self: watch the whining. It's getting annoying, even for me. And it can't be healthy.)*

## *April 29*

For the next several days, while Boyd has been at work, I have been on my computer. I don't know what motivated me; probably that note to self I wrote in my last entry. Either that or the fact that at least I'd been able to vent a little bit to Boyd, which created some space in my psyche. Who knows why I think and do what I think and do.

Anyway, I've updated my resume, such as it was, which was pretty tough since I haven't worked anywhere meaningful since I got my graduate degree; being a nanny certainly doesn't count. I've searched for wildlife conservation jobs here in the Pacific Northwest. I know it wouldn't be the same as being in Africa, but I'm not so sure I want to go back there anyway. Politically speaking, things have gotten worse over there. And as far as my marriage is concerned, I figure as long as I stay within a few hours of Seattle, there's a chance it could work, if we want it to.

I've written to my former professors. I even sent a long text to Tess, thinking that maybe she could make some connections for me given her high profile job.

And I've gone to every website I can think of looking for Peter.

I'm not sure why I've spent so much time looking for him. It's not that I think there is hope for the two of us, or that I even remotely think I could get a job from him. I just want to reconnect with him, if only in the virtual world. I guess I figure you sometimes need to go back to the past, to find the part of you that you've lost, in order to move on into the future. Or maybe I figure life is like one of Boyd's vintage video games:

you need to collect all the prizes on one level before you can move on to the next one. If you skip one along the way, you need to go back and get it.

I ran across dozens of articles and papers Peter wrote long before I ever met him, and I found, and ordered, the book he was writing, about the mountain gorilla, when we were in Rwanda together. But I couldn't find anything he's written since then and in fact his Internet presence seemed to have vanished. On one crazed afternoon, I found nothing current about him at all, and I worried that he'd died from pancreatic cancer or something. But you'd think if that were the case I'd at least have found an obituary.

And then, finally! This morning! Yes…I found him!

He wasn't mentioned in any fieldwork reports or other places I expected. Instead, I discovered a small event blurb from the D.C. area indicating he'd be speaking at a fund-raiser for African wildlife conservation. The event was called *Our Destiny Is in Your Hands* and it showed an old picture of Peter holding a very cute baby mountain gorilla.

My first thought was this: is this what he's doing now? Speaking engagements to raise money? On the one hand, it made sense; he *is* getting older (now in his mid-to-late forties, I presume), and he is also so good-looking and well-spoken that he could probably be quite powerful asking for money from rich benefactors. But at the same time, this whole idea depressed me further because Peter didn't belong behind a lectern any more than a gorilla belonged in a zoo. Or any more than I belonged at home all day by myself. It was like hearing that Dian Fossey gave up her gorillas to live on a golf course. It just wasn't right for either of us.

For the first time in weeks, I went for a run. The sun had come out, thankfully, but I could barely make it up the hill to the end of our block without dying from overexertion. It wasn't until the road leveled out that I caught my rhythm, and I headed for a trail in the nearby woods. The breeze in my face, and the soft dirt beneath my feet—and the image of Peter standing at a lectern—awakened something in me that had been sleeping for a long, long time. I didn't belong inside with my laptop or even my journal. (Sorry!) I belonged outside in the natural world.

When I got a cramp, I had to stop, which allowed me to notice all the birds singing overhead. And then I came upon a fallen bird. It had only recently died, I knew, because it hadn't been ravaged by scavengers yet. One minute it had been alive, perhaps even singing. The next minute: dead.

The lesson for me: time's a-wasting. While I've been eating junk food and trying to make babies and taking care of other kids, or just feeling terribly sorry for myself, I've been ignoring what's always been important to me. Not that Boyd, or having a family, isn't important. But Boyd is just one man, who happens to be getting along just fine in life with or without me, and who can satisfy a purely physical passion of mine but not the larger, cerebral one which (for me, anyway) seems to be the more important one. And babies, whether genetically ours or adopted, can wait too. I'm not *that* old.

I sprinted back to the house, and as my lungs filled with air, I felt freer than I had for a long time. Free and mobile. That was the good news about being a human primate. We might have things screwed up in our relationships with one another, and we might be absolute morons when it comes to believing we can design the perfect babies and shrug off those who don't meet our standards or needs. But we also have the opportunity to change our habitats. To leave behind that which is unhealthy for us. And to help those around the world who are less fortunate than we are (whether they're human or not).

I downed a glass of cold water when I got back into the kitchen, peeled off my outer layer of running clothes and threw them in the corner of the room, which Boyd always did and which I never would have done before, and switched on my computer, sweat happily streaming down each side of my face.

Peter's speaking engagement was scheduled to take place in two days, and I was going to be there.

There would not be enough time to lose weight or get a job. Not really enough time to shop for a new outfit or even explain to Boyd what in the world I was planning to do or why I decided to buy a first class ticket. Or even to figure out for myself exactly what I was about to do. I had no delusions about hooking up with Peter. And I didn't think I was planning to leave Boyd for good, although I wasn't sure about that. I only knew that this was going to be the first step in changing my own habitat, and that the only thing I had time for right now was to quickly pack a suitcase, take a shower, and race to the airport to catch a plane, direct from Seattle to Washington, D.C.

# FORTUNAE'S
# LETTERS

# Baby Teeth

—TEE ISEMINGER

Little one, mouth opening, closing,
opening again, and our eyes heavy
with the pull of the thing each of us
wants from this moment: I, sleep. You,
a large thing I can't name but can only
curl inside of. I rest you to me, your
cresting teeth scrape away what little
is left of the things I was before you.
And I let them go—ashy husks caught
on a whirl of warm air on its way out,
still neither of us yet with an inkling
of who we will turn each other into,
or, dumbly, that we will change at all.
In the half-sleep I think myself into your
future, and dream that I catch some
small whiff of you, ghost-boy at 5,
at 12,
at 20,
reach out for a faint blur of the harbinger
I don't yet recognize. But those teeth,
they never let me go far from this want
of now-you, this anchor only you can pull
up. Naively, I settle in to wait for the slack.

**A STORM WAS** kicking up. The wind blew; Doug fir branches scraped across the townhouse's rooftop. Normally Fortunae felt safer up on the top floor, where derelicts wouldn't be able to break in as easily. But on these dark, dark nights, she felt more exposed in her isolation, with her ex-husband Luke gone for good and her son Yuri never home anymore. Nobody would hear her scream.

It didn't help that she'd stayed up late watching another slasher movie.

Now it was 2:00 a.m. Since sleep wasn't an option, she did what she always did when scared or stressed. Or depressed. Or lonely. She wrote letters.

They were old-fashioned, hand-written letters. A lost art. Nobody under the age of fifty ever sent letters anymore, just texts and tweets and posts. Maybe nobody over fifty, either; her mother certainly didn't write very often. But that didn't stop Fortunae from using the ancient form of communication to let others know she was thinking of them. Just because something was gone from other people's lives didn't mean it had to disappear from hers.

First, her sister.

March 12

Dear Margee,

I hope this letter finds you well. I can't believe we live only twenty miles from one another (I'm so bummed you'll be leaving Seattle soon), but we still haven't seen each other since Christmas. I know you must be busy with those two boys of yours, but I wish we at least talked on the phone once in a while. I miss hearing your voice.

I saw that picture of Manny in the Seattle Times, snowboarding over some big mogul at Crystal Mountain. I bet he's pretty good on those jumps. And I'll bet little Ray is looking forward to Little League. Maybe practice has even started by now; I wouldn't know. Yuri's never been into sports. Hard to believe he's got our genes.

Not much happening around here. Luke is getting ready to move, also. He's heading to Tampa with his soon-to-be new wife, Danielle. Despite all that he and I have been through together (or maybe because of it), I'll sure miss him. I suspect you feel differently; I know you and Vern never really liked him. (Maybe, if our two husbands had gotten along better, you and I would have seen more of each other over the years and things would have turned out better for both of us. And maybe Manny and Yuri would have grown up as friends. Manny would have been a good influence on Yuri.) Anyway, Luke will be leaving town within a month or two, and I'll be on my own with that seventeen-year-old hunk of testosterone, energy, and defiance.

You may recall that school's been tough for Yuri, and junior year is the worst yet. He's just not cut out to be a student, it seems. I'll never understand why, given how Luke and I both have tried to instill the value of a good education in him from an early age. One thing's for sure: he's looking forward to spring break. I guess I am, too; I could use a break from trying to haul him out of bed every morning.

That wasn't entirely true. Yuri was home so infrequently these days that she rarely had the chance to haul him out of bed. But she didn't want to admit the whole story to Margee about him skipping school and everything else. This just sounded better.

Well, give a hug to those boys of yours for me. And please call or write when you can. I miss you.

With much love,
Your sister

She got up from her writing desk and went to Yuri's room. The lights were off, the door shut and locked, just as he'd left it a few days ago when he'd last been there. Why did he have to go off and disappear like this so often? And why did he insist on locking that door? She had asked him time and again not to do so. She'd promised never to go into his room without his permission. And she'd been keeping that promise, even though she believed a parent had the right to enter a child's room without permission, at least until that child became an adult. She didn't really know why she'd made that promise in the first place. Probably just to keep the peace, which seemed to be her primary role in the household and had been for as long as she could remember. Luke had once given her the title of Domestic Mediator. It was spot on.

March 12

Hey Luke,

I know you're really busy right now, what with your upcoming wedding and impending move. I just wanted to let you know a couple of things about Yuri, since you haven't been able to be on the scene much lately.

She looked at the fresh burn on the back of her hand. No, she wouldn't tell Luke about that. It would just make him mad, not so much that Yuri had burned her—he'd insisted it had been an accident—but that she hadn't been able to get Yuri to quit smoking. As if it was her fault their son smoked.

He hasn't been to school for two weeks, and it's not because he's sick. <u>And it's also not for lack of my trying to get him to go</u>, so please don't jump to that conclusion. Up until a couple of days ago, he was refusing to get out of bed. He said he doesn't care about school anymore. I've asked him if he's depressed and said we could get him a counselor, but he says it's not that. He says he just doesn't see the point of school. (Actually what he said was peppered with stronger language, but I don't feel like writing down what he did say). But each morning after I've gone to work, he's gotten up and left the townhouse. I have no idea where he's gone, but it certainly hasn't been to school.

And now, for the last couple of days, he's been gone 24/7. I've been checking his attendance records and grades online every day. (You can, too. Please let me know if you need me to send the login and password again.)

I'm not sure what to do about all this. I know this isn't the first time he's cut classes or stayed away for a couple of days, but this time seems far worse. It's his demeanor: sullen, angry, withdrawn. The school's been calling me for an explanation of his absences, for which, of course, I have none to give.

Meanwhile, I keep getting e-mails from the college counseling office about how he's supposed to be visiting colleges, taking entrance exams, and whatnot. The guidance counselor made it all sound so simple:

*You just need to let him know what your expectations are. Discuss your family values. And assign consequences when he doesn't follow through.*

As you know, Luke, we've been through countless sessions like that. Coming up with consequences has practically been a full-time career for me. And still no one knows what to do with Yuri, including me.

Your thoughts?
Fort

Her fingers had gripped the pen so hard as she wrote, especially as she came to the closing. How she wished she could have signed off with at least a simple "love." Not that she loved Luke all the time; he'd committed his share of transgressions throughout their marriage. But this was the man she'd shared a bed with for so many years, and she still loved him on a certain level. Yet she couldn't profess any sort of loving thought to him now. It would be socially incorrect. Life sometimes made no sense.

Now she rubbed her fingers. Her doctor had told Fortunae, back when Yuri was only six or seven, that stress would make the rheumatoid arthritis worse as she got older, and he was right about that. But what could she possibly do about stress so long as Yuri lived with her? Nada. And yet she didn't think she could kick her own son out.

And now the phone rang. Fortunae retrieved it from the kitchen counter.

"Hello?"

"Hello. This is Officer Scott from the Seattle Police Department calling. Is this the mother of Yuri Levkin-Monroe to whom I'm speaking?"

Fortunae's heart jumped into her throat, the same way it did when she watched edge-of-your-seat movies. She struggled to get out any words.

"Yes, this is she." She sank into a chair at the kitchen table.

Yuri was all right. But he'd been caught smoking weed behind the convenience store down the street. When she went down to the station to retrieve him (having given brief thought to the idea, or fantasy, of just leaving him there to rot in jail for a while), a female police officer pulled her aside. Fortunae knew she was in for yet another lecture by someone who just didn't understand.

But that wasn't what happened. The officer actually put her arm around Fortunae's shoulder. Fortunae began to weep. As they walked down a polished hallway, Fortunae fished through her purse for a crumpled tissue.

"He seems like an angry young man," the officer said. "Are you getting help?"

Tears were still flowing, and all Fortunae could do was to shake her head no.

"Is his father on the scene?" the officer asked.

"No," Fortunae said, her nose stuffy and her voice nasal. She blew her nose—a loud squeak—and took a deep breath. "Luke and I have been divorced for two and a half years. He had been seeing Yuri weekly for a while, but his visits have dwindled off. Understandably. Yuri's not an easy boy to be with. And Luke got on with his life: a new job, a new woman, even a couple of little girls about to become his new stepdaughters. He's going to move cross country soon."

The police officer gave Fortunae a shoulder-squeeze, then pulled back. Fortunae was tempted to assure her that being the single mother of a difficult teen wasn't contagious. But the officer didn't act like Fortunae had cooties, like some of her friends actually had when they learned about Yuri's shenanigans—beginning way back when he was a toddler with a tendency to break porcelain knick knacks and rip up recipe cards.

"It's too bad," the officer said, "that his father won't be around. Boys need men in their lives."

She led Fortunae into a break room and poured two cups of coffee. "So you're the primary adult in Yuri's life?" She handed a cup to Fortunae. Its aroma was rich, much better than you'd expect at a police station. "It must be really tough on you."

It was rare that anyone expressed this type of concern for the mother of a troublemaker.

"What about teachers, coaches, uncles, clergy from whom he receives guidance?"

Fortunae looked at the officer's badge. Officer Randee. She'd have to remember the name, write a letter to the chief.

"I'm pretty much the *only* adult in Yuri's life. He's not into sports. We don't go to church. His only uncle doesn't like him, probably because Yuri doesn't show him any respect. And most of my friends don't like Yuri either. As for teachers, he's pretty much pissed off every last one of them. Yuri has a good heart, but he's always been a handful."

"Has anyone ever told you about the at-risk youth program, administered by King County? It might be just what you need. A youth like your son can be held accountable to the court when he refuses to be accountable to his parents."

"The court?" It sounded awful. It also sounded too good to be true, and Fortunae wondered why, as a legal secretary, she'd never heard of this possibility. "How can I sign up?"

Officer Randee smiled. "You don't exactly sign up. You file a petition that requires your son to appear in court."

"I take my son to court...like a plaintiff? And he's the defendant?"

She nodded. "Yes, that's pretty much it."

Wow. Fortunae let out a long breath, as though she'd been holding all her stress in her lungs for the last seventeen years and was finally able to exhale relief.

And then the shadow of guilt started to surface. What parent takes her child to court?

But then again, why should she feel guilty doing this? It was certainly clear that Yuri was *not* accountable to his parents; Fortunae couldn't remember a time when he *had* been accountable to them or to any adult. When he was a toddler, in addition to being as destructive as the Tasmanian Devil, he'd had a bad habit of stealing money and lipstick from purses of visiting friends. When he went off to preschool, he took his disruptive and dishonest habits with him, as though Fortunae had packed them in his little-boy backpack right along with extra clothes and a bag of Goldfish crackers. He threw toys and blocks, stole snacks from other children, and shredded coloring books. He even pantsed little boys and girls. Fortunae was at a loss, when called into the director's office, to explain why a young boy would even think of pantsing another student. How do you explain why someone else has thoughts you don't understand?

And that was just the beginning of Yuri's career as a defiant, troublesome boy who couldn't care less about accountability. Fortunae could easily have slid through that mental trapdoor to the place where you store memories you'd rather suppress, but thankfully Officer Randee interrupted her thoughts by handing her a yellow Post-it note.

"Here's the phone number and website link for the at-risk youth program."

Fortunae felt a little lighter when she walked back into her townhouse that evening, as if she'd just started a cleanse diet. For once Yuri wasn't weighing her down.

March 20

Dear Mom,

How are you? I've been thinking of you a lot lately. I imagine you're getting in as much golf as you can before the hot temperatures come to the desert! Are the cacti blooming yet? I still enjoy looking at the painting you gave me of the ocotillo and saguaro last Christmas. I hung it above my bed, so I see it every day when I walk into my bedroom, and think of you.

Now for the hard part. Despite her best efforts, Fortunae was still feeling guilty about her plans to take Yuri to court. But that guilt was nothing like the emotional weight she'd be packing once she told her mother the other disappointing news.

As you know, Mom, I had really been looking forward to bringing Yuri down for spring break this year, and meeting your new beau. But it looks like I'll have to cancel our plane reservations. Yuri's been quite uncooperative lately, and frankly I don't know if he'd even get out of bed to go to the airport with me. Also, do you remember how he used to try to sneak pocketknives onto the airplane when he was younger, just to see if he could get away with it? Well, I don't want to think about what he might try to slip onto the plane now.

She debated whether to take that last comment out. It sounded so whiny, so needy. And it was practically begging for a reaction from her mother about how in the world Yuri could get anything inappropriate to the airport without Fortunae knowing, or why on earth Yuri would have any sort of weapon or illegal substance at all. Her mother had no idea what teens were like these days. Or at least what Yuri was like. And then of course her mother would worry, worry, worry. Which would make Fortunae feel guilty again. Sometimes she was caught up in a reel of guilt, one that kept playing over and over in her mind, an old Twilight-Zone sort of nightmare.

And damn it! She was tired of feeling guilty. She was also tired of hiding so much about her life, and her troubles, from the world, including from her own mother. Far too many people had looked down their long, judgmental noses at her for having such a difficult child. And far too many had offered unsolicited parenting advice, even though she had probably read more parenting articles and books, and sought help from more specialists, than all the other parents she knew combined. Fortunae had essentially gone into hiding in order to survive, and she wasn't sure how much longer she could stay there. For now, though, she would continue to understate the truth.

Things have been, shall we say, a bit difficult. Yuri's been sneaking out at night after I go to bed to "hang out" with his friends, and I'm afraid he'd do the same sort of thing if we came to visit you in the desert. I don't want to subject you to any unnecessary worry and drama. So stay home again, this year, we shall. I'll try to find a time when I can slip away and visit you without Yuri.

Fat chance of that. She didn't have any friends who would agree to look after him, and she certainly couldn't leave him home unsupervised. Actually, she didn't really have any friends to speak of at all anymore, anyway.

By now you're probably thinking *I told you so*. I know you always questioned our parenting decisions. You thought Luke and I were too lax in his upbringing. Trust me, we weren't. I just didn't share everything with you.

Was she going on too much here? Why was she on the defensive with her mother before she even finished the letter?

Yuri is just one of those extremely <u>spirited</u> kids. Well, enough of that already.

The good news (I hope) is that he's been dating a girl for these past few weeks, which is another reason why I'm sure he'd put up a stink about having to go down to the desert for an entire week.

Fortunae didn't really believe the word "dating" was the right word. It wasn't like he was taking the girl out for dinner and a movie or buying her flowers; he didn't have a car, and he'd lost his allowance privileges. All Fortunae knew was that he and the girl were spending a lot of time together, although not at her townhouse, and she had a sneaking suspicion they were doing more than just making out. She'd found packets of condoms in Yuri's pockets in the laundry basket. And he seemed to have a new hickey every day. What worried her was that he'd said the girl was only fourteen, at least three years younger than he was, and when she'd tried to discourage him from taking the relationship any further, because of their age differences, Yuri had walked out the door. She needed to meet with the girl's parents; maybe invite them out to dinner some evening.

I haven't met her or her parents. I'll let you know what becomes of that!

She dreaded the thought of what might become of that.

So, I'll keep you posted on what happens around here. As for me, I'm just going to work, doing the laundry, paying the bills, and working out when I have the energy.

Take care, Mom. Call when you have a spare minute!

Love,
Fortunae

PS I'm sorry I won't get to meet your new boyfriend.
Please send a picture!

A couple of weeks later, Fortunae took the afternoon off from work to attend an intake meeting at the courthouse. After entering through the metal detector and finding her way to the old elevator, she waited on an extremely uncomfortable wooden pew in a cold hallway. As she waited, well past the appointed time, for her name to be called, she reviewed a three-page list of Yuri's recent behavior problems that she'd typed up the night before. She'd categorized his transgressions: School Tardies and Absences, Curfew Violations, Other Rules Broken at Home, Parental Disrespect, Lies, Suspected Thefts, and Other.

Finally, a brusque woman with no makeup and a curt tone in her voice called Fortunae's name.

Fortunae followed the woman through an unmarked door. She had to work hard to keep up with the caseworker's long stride, feeling a little like a child trying to keep up with an adult. She felt a little like a child, too; although she was the one who would be filing a petition against her own son, she had the same feeling she frequently did that it was all her fault, that she had been the one to do something wrong. That she was an inadequate parent, maybe an inadequate person. That's the sort of thing that can happen when you feel like a failure day in, day out, at anything.

She sat on a plastic chair on the opposite side of a metal desk from the caseworker. There was a nameplate on the desk that indicated the caseworker's name was Mary.

"ARY or Chin?" Mary asked.

"Excuse me?"

"Are you here for an ARY petition or a Chin petition?"

"I don't know. ARY, I guess. I don't know what a Chin is"

Mary didn't explain what a Chin was. She simply pulled out a form and dated it. Fortunae saw the words, upside-down to her, across the top of the page: *At Risk Youth Petition Worksheet.*

"I brought some notes. I thought they'd help." She tried to hand a copy of her notes to Mary.

Mary waved the packet of notes away. "I'll take my own."

Fortunae shifted in her seat. "Okay."

"Name?"

"Fortunae Monroe."

"Is that your name, or the name of the youth?"

"That's my name."

Mary began to write Fortunae's name on the second line.

"That's F-o-r-t-u-n-a-e. No, there's an *a* before the *e*."

Mary sighed as she squeezed an extra letter into the name she'd written. Fortunae now felt guilty for having an unusual name.

"Youth's name?

"Yuri. Y-u-r-i." Fortunae watched as Mary misspelled Yuri's name at first, crossed it out, then corrected it. "Right. He's named after my side of the family. Russian."

"Address?"

Mary took down a few other pertinent bits of information: Yuri's birthdate, Fortunae's phone and email, and so on.

"Ever been in trouble with the law?"

"Who me?" Fortunae asked.

Mary peered up through her forehead, sighed again.

"I'm sorry. I've never done this before. I guess I'm a little nervous. Anyway, Yes," Fortunae said. "Yuri has. He was caught stealing a video game from Fred Meyer once. And he was with a group of teens who vandalized the mall on Halloween last year. And he just got caught smoking marijuana. I guess even though it's legal in Washington, since he's under eighteen—."

"Yes, I get it. That's why he's considered an at risk *youth*."

Duh. "What I meant was that the pot wouldn't have been a problem if he'd been over twenty-one." She felt the heat of Mary's stare. "But you already knew that, didn't you."

Was it possible to feel any smaller?

"What floors me," Fortunae went on, "is how everyone has been incomprehensively forgiving." She heard the quiver in her voice and worried that she sounded as nervous as she felt. "Aside from school suspensions and a couple of warnings or citations by the police, he hasn't been held accountable for most of his transgressions beyond the threshold of our front door—"

Mary held up her hand. "That's enough. What about school? Truant?"

"Um, yes. He's been skipping a lot of classes." Fortunae handed Mary a printout of his recent attendance records at school. Mary glanced over it, then shoved it back across her desk and made a couple of cryptic notes.

"Wouldn't you like to attach a copy of this to your report?"

"Not necessary. Tell me about Yuri at home. You've held him accountable for things at home? Doing chores, being respectful?"

Fortunae laughed, thinking *here we go again. Another person who just doesn't understand.* "I've tried. Luke, his father, and I both tried. But really to no avail. He disregards our requests...or demands...and does whatever he wants. Whenever he's disobeyed, we've given him every consequence we could think of. So it's not like we're being easy on him. But it seemed like the more we tried to rein him in, the worse he got."

"I assume your relationship with Yuri isn't very strong right now."

"How could it be?" Fortunae rubbed her right thumb over the burn on the back of her left hand. It was not an accident, despite what Yuri had said. "He's called us every horrible name you could think of. He's stolen money from our wallets. He even once threatened Luke with a knife. But he was only ten then. We didn't report it. We figured...we hoped...that was an isolated incident."

Mary circled a few tiny-font numbers on the second page, signed the paper with a bureaucratic flourish, rubber stamped an official-looking logo on the bottom of the second page, and stood up with a huff more suitable for an old dog than a human social worker. She walked away. Fortunae wasn't sure if she should stay or go, too. But a minute later, Mary returned with a copy of the form she'd completed and handed it to Fortunae.

"You'll be hearing from us about your court date. You can leave through that door." She pointed down the hall.

"That's it? That's all you need to know?"

"Pretty much. You can tell the rest to the Commissioner. At the hearing."

"I...I've never done this before. What shall I expect? Do I need an attorney?"

She could have asked one of the lawyers at her firm to help. But she didn't want them to know about her personal problems. Better to keep the office separate from home.

"Once you're notified of a hearing date, you'll need to come to the courthouse to pick up the service papers. You'll need to have an adult—not a parent—serve Yuri those papers. You won't need an attorney. The court will assign one for Yuri, free of charge. If you have more questions, please check the website." She handed Fortunae a business card with the same website address that Fortunae had already studied. "Now, our time is up and I must ask you to leave." When Fortunae had learned she'd be meeting with a caseworker, she'd envisioned a kindly, grandmotherly social worker who would have plenty of time to listen, perhaps even broad shoulders for clients who liked to shed tears. She hadn't expected a drill sergeant.

As she made her way back to the elevator, Fortunae's spirits started to slide as though dropping down one of those big chutes in the Chutes and Ladders game she used to play with Yuri, so long ago, before he'd scribbled all over the board with a permanent marker. For some reason she'd come into this ARY petition thing with the hopeful notion that the court would be supportive of her—and firm with Yuri. She now realized the court wouldn't be offering any warm fuzzies to her. And they would be offering an attorney for him, whom Fortunae couldn't possibly stand up to in court. Was this just a big set-up for another parenting failure? Another reason for Yuri to scoff at her?

And what about this whole bit about finding someone to serve him papers? He'd go ballistic once he found out she was dragging him to court. He'd certainly unleash a barrage of verbal assaults at her and whoever served him. And there was a part of her, a part she didn't want to even acknowledge, that worried he might become violent. She pressed the elevator button and wondered what had she gotten herself into, and why Luke couldn't have been there by her side. She had half a mind to turn around and tell Mary never mind. The only thing that kept her from doing so was Mary. Fortunae didn't ever want to face that woman again.

Two weeks later, after being notified of the hearing date, she encountered Yuri. She had just come home from the office, and he was walking from the bathroom to his bedroom, naked except for a red towel wrapped around his hips. She couldn't help but notice how strong he looked, how manly. What happened to the little boy who loved to play in the bathtub? Somewhere in her photo albums she had a picture of him in the tub, his full head of hair wet and smoothed back, his face decorated with a mustache and beard made from soap bubbles. She had included that photograph with all of her Christmas letters that year. Now there was nothing endearing about his face. He looked angry that she stood there, in her own hallway, as though her mere existence was a profound annoyance for him.

"Yuri, I have something important to discuss with you," she said. "I need to know when you and I can spend a few minutes together."

It was crazy thinking that a seventeen-year-old would dictate when the papers could be served, but that's the only way she knew how to deal with him. If she had simply told him to be home at a certain day at a certain time, she could be assured only that he wouldn't.

"I got a minute now."

The minute she'd said anything to him, she realized this was the one answer she didn't want. She didn't have the court papers yet, and she obviously didn't have someone lurking outside the door to hand him the papers, given that she hadn't even known he'd be home then.

"Not now. I'm thinking tomorrow or the next day. I'm bringing this up now because you're here so seldom."

"Why not now? I've got time now. I don't know what I'll be doing tomorrow."

"I'm not prepared now."

"What's it about?" He crossed his arms over his muscular chest.

Fortunae had desperately hoped he wouldn't ask this question. She also desperately hoped the towel would stay where it was now that he wasn't holding it up anymore. Thankfully, it did.

"I'm not getting into it now. I've got an appointment to get to." The second part was a lie, and she didn't like the idea of lying to him. But she couldn't afford to let him wheedle the topic out of her now or else she might never see him again to have the papers served.

Grabbing her purse to head out the door, with no destination in mind, she told him to meet her at home at 5:00 on Wednesday.

He shrugged. "We'll see."

That evening, after she'd gone to Chipotle for a quick meal—just long enough for Yuri to leave the townhouse, she hoped—she sat down to write him a letter, which she planned to give to him, to set the mood, right before the papers would be served. She'd read online that it's a good idea to write an *impact letter* to difficult children like Yuri because often they aren't even aware of how much others have done for them, or how their actions affect others.

She knew it was a risky idea—he could totally disregard it, or worse—but she did want him to start thinking about who he was becoming, who they both had become, and what impact—positive or otherwise—they each had had upon the other.

April 5

Dear Yuri,

Thank you for coming home to meet with me. I will soon explain what this is all about, but first I want you to read this letter.

I will start by saying that, when you were born, I finally felt complete as a person. That sounds so trite, I know, but it's the truth. I loved you like I'd loved no one else, and I continue to love you to this day. A friend of mine recently said that nobody will ever love you unconditionally in your life except for your parents, and once they're gone you'll miss that.

I plan to be around for a long, long time…this isn't a letter to tell you about a cancer diagnosis or anything like that. I mostly want to tell you some of the things I've loved about our time together over the years, but also to explain to you how some of your behaviors have impacted me over the years, too. Please bear with me.

I read stories to you over and over until we both knew them forwards and backwards, from *Goodnight Moon* to the *Goosebumps* series.

I wiped your salty tears when you fell off your bike, when your pet turtle died, whenever you were feeling sad.

I listened to your sweet voice, day and night, even as you yelled at me for things you didn't like…too much peanut butter on the bread, parmesan cheese on the broiled tomato halves. I loved your voice, no matter your mood.

I wrapped you up in a blanket like a burrito each evening and rocked you back and forth, rubbing your back through the fabric. Do you remember that?

I built elaborate sand castles with you on the Oregon coast. I took you on haunted house and ghost tours, at your request. I sat outside in the rain with you, watching cloud formations morph into monsters in the sky. I cut out thousands of construction paper shapes for your teachers at school. I carved creepy pumpkins with you, and I taught you how to build eggplant towers with tomato sauce and mozzarella cheese.

I turned down my music in the car so you could listen to yours.

There were hundreds of other things I did with, and for, you. I won't bore or burden you with all the memories I have of our good times. But then there were the tough times.

I responded to your teacher's cries for help, usually beginning by the third week of school each year.

I tried to defend you from bullies when school administrators wouldn't step in.

I moved you from school to school, even negotiated expulsions and suspensions, to try to keep you on track academically.

I took you to meet with many, many specialists who wanted to help you learn to behave better and to fit in with our world.

As your parent, I devoted many, many hours to helping you with your behavioral issues, and I've spent a lot of energy. All the battles at home. The weight gains, the lost friends. Lost sleep, too; some days I am literally drained.

And then there was my marriage to your father. Over time, I lost the ability to tend to his needs, to pay attention to him. I was so focused on trying to steer you on the right path, and so drained from all the school and therapy meetings and what not, that at the end of the day I couldn't give another ounce to anyone else. Your father and I grew increasingly cross with, and distant from, one another.

As a human being living in the same house as you, I've had to build walls around myself. Literally, I've had to lock up my wallet. And I've also had to build an emotional vault around my heart so that I can't feel as much pain when you scream at me, call me names, threaten me. And especially when you lie to me. Deception is one of the greatest toxins in this world.

She knew she'd just lied to him about having an appointment, and here she was chastising him for lying to her. She thought about taking this line out. But his deceit was so hurtful. He needed to know.

Yuri, I am so sad about all this. I love you very much, and I know I haven't always made the best decisions, although I did my best along the way. But now, here we are, and we can't go on like we have been. Our life together could be so different, so much better, if you would just follow basic rules of society: go to school, be respectful, be honest, don't steal. I'm not trying to impose a guilt trip on you, or make you feel bad about yourself. I just want you to understand why I'm taking this next step toward helping you make good choices in your life, for your sake and for mine.

Love,
Mom

Yuri didn't come home that night or the next, and when 5:00 p.m. Wednesday came and went, after Fortunae had rushed downtown that morning for the service papers, it felt like a final cloud of hope had drifted away. She and the townhouse complex property manager had been waiting in the kitchen, drinking tea and talking about the weather. She didn't explain to the property manager why she needed him to serve papers to Yuri on her behalf, and he didn't ask. She just hoped this whole thing wouldn't jeopardize her ownership here, like if there were HOA rules that said delinquent teens were prohibited or something like that. As she was asking when the exterior of the building would be repainted, the front door swung open.

"Who's that?" Yuri walked into the kitchen casting his thumb in the property manager's direction.

"Oh hi, Yuri. This is Mike, the property manager." Fortunae met the man's eyes briefly. "We're just visiting. Thanks for coming home so we can talk."

"With him here?" Yuri asked.

"No, he'll be leaving shortly. Here's a plate of cookies." She passed a platter to him. The cookies were store bought, but it was the best she could do. "And first I'd like you to read this, Yuri. It's from me."

She handed the letter to him, as well. Four folded pages of pink stationery.

Yuri looked at her inquisitively, then took the letter. He set the cookie platter down, shook the folds of paper open, and sat down on the edge of the ottoman in the living room, as if he was only planning to stay for a moment. Fortunae thought about moving to the doorway, to block him if he decided to bolt, but she knew that would be fruitless. If Yuri wanted to plow past her, he easily could. Still, she got up from her seat at the kitchen table, lowered the window shades, and turned on some lamps, one by one, so she was at least on her feet in case something happened. She felt Mike watching her every move and hoped this wouldn't turn into an embarrassing scene. On the other hand, it was comforting to know there was someone else with her, just in case.

Yuri studied the letter more closely than any homework assignment she'd seen in as far back as she could remember, and now she wondered if the letter had been a good idea after all. Maybe he did care more than he let on. Maybe she was too harsh, too honest, with her words. But no, she told herself. This had to be done.

Breathe, she reminded herself, as she stood by a window and watched him read. Breathe.

The apartment was silent, except for the pages crackling as Yuri moved from one page to the next. Even Mike sat motionless, the tea in his cup having long since grown cold.

Finally, when Yuri finished the letter, he looked up at her. His eyes were moist, and again she felt like a fool—or worse, like an evil mother—for having written all that to her son, until she moved closer to him and smelled that skunky aroma. He'd been smoking dope. That was why his eyes were red and moist. It wasn't that he cared.

He stood. "Now what?"

She quickly glanced at Mike and nodded. He pulled a thin packet of papers out from under a placemat on the table and walked toward Yuri.

"Yuri Levkin-Monroe?"

"Yeah?"

"These are court papers. You're being served."

Yuri looked thoroughly confused, which again upset Fortunae. She bit her lip and tried to hold it together when she really felt like she was about to collapse into a messy blob on the kitchen floor. Her son's expression reminded her of the day Luke informed them both that he was moving out of the townhouse and Yuri had acted so confounded, as though Luke had been speaking in gibberish. Both then and now Fortunae felt a stinging at the tip of her nose as tears accumulated in her eyes. What a horrible mother she must be to be doing this to her son.

The property manager stepped closer to Yuri, extending his arm and holding out the papers, and Yuri snatched them from him. Mike took a step back, and Yuri's hands shook as he read the very official-looking first page. Then he looked up, first at Mike, and then at Fortunae, with narrowing eyes. It was eerie, almost as if he was about to transform into a werewolf or some other monster, and Fortunae felt a chill run down her spine. She'd seen that look before, but only on the screen of B-rated horror movies. Never in person, never from Yuri.

"You fucking bitch," he said. It was almost a growl. "You'll be sorry. *Really* sorry."

Mike and Fortunae glanced at one another. The property manager looked like he was about to run out the door, but before he had the chance to, Yuri ripped the service papers into shreds as he glared at Fortunae. He threw them onto the floor, pushed Mike out of his way, and stormed out the front door.

"Are you all right?" Mike asked.

Fortunae nodded and said she was.

He signed a document indicating he'd been the server, then left.

Fortunae tried to convince herself she was all right. So was Yuri, she insisted. She went back to the living room. Her letter to Yuri lay scattered on the floor, next to the ottoman where he'd been sitting, and there was still an indentation on the cushion from his butt. She stared at the indentation, wondering if that might have been the last time she'd ever see him. And in some ways she hoped it would be, because there was no telling what he might do next.

After a week of sleepless nights behind a locked bedroom door, Fortunae sat at the front of a dreary, windowless courtroom feeling strangled by her peach and teal silk scarf and her nerves. To her right was Adriana, Yuri's court-appointed attorney, and to Adriana's right was Yuri.

It felt to Fortunae as though Adriana was serving not only as an attorney but also as a wall. She was tall, big-boned, and very stiff. And for that Fortunae was grateful. Both frightened of her son and remorseful that it had come to this, she appreciated a barrier between the two of them.

Of course, it had been a surprise to Fortunae that Yuri had gotten out of bed, taken a shower, and ridden the bus downtown with her. She hadn't expected that in a million years, given that he hadn't even grunted at her since the papers had been served. But now Yuri sat there looking very smart and handsome in a black dress shirt, pink and red striped tie, and pressed slacks. His hair was combed neatly, he was clean-shaven, and his eyes were white and clear. If you had looked into the courtroom through the window at him, you'd have never suspected he was the type of boy to misbehave so much that his own mother would file a petition against him. But indeed she had. Maybe, she thought, this would be his awakening. Maybe now, finally, he'd take her seriously and they could live happily ever after.

The three sat lined up in the front of the courtroom, and Fortunae couldn't help but feel like she was on *Law & Order*. They rose when the clerk instructed them to do so, and then a woman introduced as Commissioner Santiago strode into the courtroom, robed in judicial black. Fortunae didn't know why she was referred to as a commissioner rather than a judge, but that didn't really matter. Although the commissioner was a diminutive woman, Fortunae felt small and powerless under her honorable glare from behind the elevated bench. Fortunae also felt like she was the defendant, the one on trial for failing to properly raise her son. She glanced around Adriana at Yuri, who didn't look the least bit frightened or nervous. Instead, he wore an expression of humility and respect that she'd never seen before.

Which made Fortunate again, for the thousandth time, question her decision to bring him to court, just as she'd questioned so many of her other parenting decisions over the years.

The commissioner asked Adriana how the youth responded to the motion. Fortunae's throat tightened. It dawned on her, suddenly, that Yuri might refute her allegations or, even worse, blatantly lie to the commissioner about what type of mother she had been. She wouldn't put it past him to even make up stories about neglect or abuse, as he'd done numerous times over the years at school. In a matter of minutes, she could be the one standing behind bars awaiting legal representation. She held her breath as the attorney and Yuri stood. Adriana buttoned her blazer; Yuri straightened his tie.

"Your honor, my client does not contest the petition."

Fortunae was both flabbergasted and relieved. She had won? This easily?

She nearly broke down then, from relief. The court was on her side! Yuri had seen the light! But before she could revel any more in this pronouncement, the commissioner asked Fortunae if she had anything she wanted to say. Tucking her two pages of talking notes—summarizing Yuri's various behavioral issues—into her purse, and feeling almost foolish at having thought she'd need them in the first place, Fortunae stood to address the court. She cleared her throat. And then she reconsidered.

"No, your honor."

At that point, the commissioner turned to Yuri and lectured him on his need to attend school, obey curfew, and otherwise follow rules imposed by teachers and parents. If he didn't, he would have to face consequences of the court. "And they won't be pretty," Commissioner Santiago said.

Yuri nodded, deferentially. Fortunae felt her heart skip, as though it was a carefree little girl on a playground. She also felt vindicated.

Until the commissioner turned her cold gaze on Fortunae.

"This is a serious matter, Ms. Levkin-Monroe. You have decided to bring your son into this court to encourage him to obey rules and laws. And the court has ruled. What that means, now, is that you are required to report back to the court if your son refuses to obey these court orders."

This was new information to Fortunae. Mary, the unfriendly social worker, hadn't bothered to mention this.

The commissioner went on. "In the event that your son disobeys court orders, you will need to file a motion for contempt. The burden will be on *you* to prove this. Yet, if you do not report his violations, you could be held in contempt as well."

This was new information, too, and suddenly Fortunae felt queasy. It was one thing to tattle on her son once or twice. But what if she failed to mention something, and he tattled on her? This whole thing could backfire on her, when all she'd wanted was to find something that would motivate Yuri to go to school and obey the law. The notion that she would now be accountable to the court also was unsettling, to say the least, and she briefly wondered if this would affect her job as a legal secretary. On top of that, she didn't appreciate being lectured by a perfect stranger—the commissioner— in such a harsh tone in front of her son.

She caught a glimpse of Yuri's face. It was cold, his glare smug. He was going to retaliate, she knew.

Fortunae had to file numerous reports over the next few months. For the remainder of the school year, she accumulated printouts of attendance records which revealed that Yuri had skipped 82 percent of his classes. She kept a running log of when he came home at night, if at all. He missed curfew by over an hour for six out of seven nights a week, on average. And even though the court didn't ask her to document his attitude and abusive tone with her, she kept records of how many times he called her a *fucking bitch*, or worse. Over the course of four months, she recorded 122 instances where he called her a foul name. Twice he even used the c-word.

Had she been a fool to think this whole petition process would change his behavior? Now, school was out for the summer, so the truancy component of the court's ruling was irrelevant, not that the court had impacted him anyway. All the court made Yuri do, as a consequence for his truancy, was four hours of community service picking up roadside trash and a half-day seminar on the importance of education, during which, Fortunae was later told by the proctor, he flirted extensively with the girl sitting beside him.

At her fourth court appearance to file another motion for contempt—without Yuri, who hadn't bothered to show up after that first proceeding—Fortunae had to once again endure the commissioner's lectures and deep sighs. This whole At-Risk Petition thing was going nowhere, it seemed, and Yuri's attorney, who did show up for the hearings, pulled Fortunae aside afterward.

"This petition stuff almost never works," Adriana said.

"It doesn't?"

"Sadly, no," Adriana said.

"Why didn't anyone tell me this in the first place? If this is the case, why does the court even offer ARY petitions? Is this just the government's way of making a parent feel hopeful for a few months?"

Adriana shrugged. "Good questions. I don't have the answers. I guess ARY is offered because, once in a while, these proceedings do work." She checked her watch. "You might want to think hard about whether you want to continue this. Think about what's in your best interests, Mrs. Monroe."

"Thank you," Fortunae said, although she wasn't sure what she was grateful for. In fact, she was so deflated with this new bit of information that she didn't even bother to correct the attorney about her last name.

On her way home, Fortunae made a mental note to find out what would happen with this whole petition business once Yuri turned eighteen. And then she got off the bus two stops early and headed for the mall. Shopping always made her feel better. Poorer, maybe, but better.

Having picked up a couple of presents for Yuri, even though she wasn't sure she wanted to give him anything, Fortunae found herself in the lingerie store holding up a pair of panties imprinted with cute little angels. She was trying to decide if she should bother trying them on when she had that feeling you get when someone's looking at you. Lifting her eyes, she saw a petite woman standing on the other side of the panty table. She looked familiar. Brunette pixie haircut, big brown eyes.

"Officer Randee," the woman said. "You probably don't recognize me out of uniform."

Fortunae set the panties down and studied the woman wearing a tank top and tight, low-rise jeans. Yes, it was the police officer, and immediately Fortunae felt her shoulders relax. Seeing this police officer, who had been so kind, was kind of like seeing an angel in real life.

"Would you by any chance have time for a cup of coffee or tea?" Fortunae asked, absentmindedly running her fingers across the silk merchandise. "I've had a rough day."

"As a matter of fact, I would."

The women smiled at one another, then left the lingerie store and walked side by side toward the food court, talking as they went about the price of lingerie, the unusually hot weather, and other ordinary conversational fodder. After they got their drinks, they went to sit down.

Officer Randee asked how Yuri was doing, and Fortunae was impressed that the officer had taken such an interest in him that she even remembered his name. Fortunae told her that she'd been back and forth to the courthouse several times and that little had changed.

"You can't blame yourself, you know," the officer said. "You're a good mom, I can tell."

"You have no idea how welcome those words are."

"I had a brother like Yuri," Officer Randee said. "He drove my mom nuts. Like a wild horse that could never be broken."

"I never wanted to break Yuri," Fortunae said. "Just tame him a little."

"I know. I get it."

"He was a good boy, you know. When he was little, he always wanted to hold my hand, and he was good to our cats, and he liked to hunt for pretty leaves and stones for me. He wasn't a demon child. Just hard to understand, and hard to teach. As though he'd come from another planet with another set of cultural rules." She took a sip of coffee and looked around the mall with a soft, reminiscing gaze. "And in case you're wondering, he was never abused."

Officer Randee tilted her head to the side.

"I've been asked that many times by the specialists we've seen."

"I hadn't even thought to ask that," the policewoman said. "My brother wasn't abused either."

They sipped their drinks in unison. The warm beverage coated Fortunae's throat with what felt like medicinal peace. Once again tears sprang from her eyes without warning, and she wiped at them with the little square napkin the barista had given her. She had to stop crying all the time.

"I'm sorry," she said with a shallow laugh. "Living with Yuri has been like living with a slow drip that can't be fixed, and over time the drip grows louder and faster and you know one day the pipe will burst. The energy I've spent trying to help him has taken a very great toll on me."

Officer Randee set her hand on Fortunae's forearm. "It's hard to take care of yourself when you're focusing all your attention on your child."

"Yes, it is." Fortunae thought back to all the help she and Luke had sought for Yuri: psychologists, social workers, educators, clergymen. They'd even taken Yuri to a hypnotist. They all had different theories, but no matter what they said, she lay awake many a night wondering what she was doing wrong, what she could do differently. "You're right. In fact, it's hard not to constantly bash yourself. And forget about friendships and relationships." Maybe that was why Margee hadn't written back for a long time. Maybe even her sister was sick of hearing about Yuri's antics and Fortunae's despair.

"I'm sorry," she said again. "I didn't mean to go on like this. You just seem to understand. And I guess I needed a listening ear."

"Of course. I'm glad I could be of help," the police officer said. But she also checked the time on her cell phone.

They both looked out at the crowd of shoppers again, not speaking, just holding their empty cups in their hands.

"How's your mom now?" Fortunae asked.

"She's good. She's *really* good."

There was hope for Fortunae after all.

"And your brother?"

Officer Randee shook her head. "We don't know. Haven't heard from him since he turned eighteen. That was eight years ago."

The police officer's words echoed in Fortunae's mind for the rest of the day and all through the night. And now that day was here: Yuri's eighteenth birthday.

She'd had mixed feelings over the years about the idea of Yuri growing up. When he was little, and so needy of her love, his palm fitting inside hers so perfectly, she'd wished he would stay young forever. She'd had this strange feeling they were destined to be soul mates, not as lovers, but as two humans navigating their way through life's hard climbs, although she never admitted this to anyone else. She knew she couldn't keep him from growing up, but she took comfort in the certainty that she would never let go of him, nor he of her.

But, as the years went by, Yuri began to sport his true spirited colors the way a peacock shows off its plumage, with no misgivings about who he was or what he did. In fact, he showed little remorse for the trouble he caused. And little love, or concern, for his mother. And so, as his eighteenth birthday had drawn nearer, it began to look more like a beacon of freedom for Fortunae than an impending loss.

The freedom may have come earlier than expected, as it turned out. Fortunae hadn't seen, or heard from, Yuri in over a week. She had asked him last month how he'd like to celebrate his birthday, and he'd snort-laughed at her. So she dropped the subject. But then she started to feel like a bad mother for ignoring his eighteenth birthday. She was always hearing women in the grocery store or in yoga class talking about throwing elaborate parties for their kids when they turned eighteen. She worried that she'd regret letting the big day go by unnoticed. And there was a small part of her that still held out hope that a party might be just the thing. He would see, through her efforts, how much she really loved him.

"I know you're too old for a party, per se, but I'd love to have you bring some of your friends over," she had said a couple of weeks after she first broached the subject. He was busy playing a violent video game at the time and didn't respond. "Maybe you could invite your girlfriend, or some of the guys you hang out with. I'd like to meet them. We could order pizza, rent a movie. Or I could hire one of those poker party packs. Wouldn't that be fun? You know, bring a dealer in and a few game tables?" She moved closer to the screen where the game was playing, careful not to step in the way. "Or if you'd rather go out somewhere, I don't know, to go bowling or even a concert, we could arrange that."

He glanced at her only briefly, his expression one you might expect if she'd suggested drowning puppies, and she felt just about as guilty, or at least as stupid, as if she had. She never used to feel like a weak person. Was it possible a woman's natural demeanor could change at the hands of her own child?

"Mom, there's no fucking way I'm bringing my friends over here for a *party*."

He emphasized the last word with vehement sarcasm. Sometimes Fortunae felt saddened about the type of young man her son had become. Sometimes she felt afraid of him. And lots of times, like now, she just didn't like him. At all.

"Please don't talk to me that way, Yuri."

He shrugged.

"Okay," she said. "We can keep your birthday low key. I'd just figured this is an important day to celebrate."

He paused the game. "Why? What's the big deal? So I'll be a day older than the day before. So I can get drafted. Oh yeah, I can vote. As if I care who runs this lame-ass government. It's not like I can drink or smoke weed or anything just because I'll be eighteen."

He went back to killing aliens, and she wanted to reply by saying life isn't all about drugs and alcohol. Or violent games. But she didn't.

"Well, *I'd* like to celebrate it," she said. "You've been an important part of my life. How about if you and I go out to a nice restaurant somewhere, and afterward you can hang out with your friends."

The first sound that uttered out from his mouth was a cross between a choke, a cough, and a sigh. And then he said, "I don't know."

All she was asking for was one stinking hour at a restaurant. In his honor. His ungrateful honor. But she knew what his response meant. *I don't know* meant *no*.

Now she sat on the floor of Yuri's room, all by herself, on that *special day*. This sure had turned into a fine celebration.

She checked the clock on her cell phone. 5:30 p.m. She shook her head and laughed at herself. Just in case he decided to show up after all, she'd made a 6:00 reservation at Ruth's Chris. And she'd bought him that iPod and an Italian leather wallet at the mall. Not that she could afford a restaurant like that or those presents; things had been tight ever since the divorce. But she wanted to make him happy somehow, to show she still cared. To maintain, or rebuild, the relationship. Especially after that letter she'd written to him and the court fiasco. She just didn't know how anymore.

By 9:00, Fortunae had drunk two glasses of chardonnay and read, in reverse order, most of the letters she'd written to her son on each of his birthdays for the last eighteen years. They were unsent letters that she kept in an old shoebox, tucked away in the corner of her closet. She wasn't sure when she was ever going to show them to Yuri. Maybe when he turned twenty-one, maybe when he had his first child. Maybe when she lay on her deathbed.

Now, after pouring another glass of wine, she opened the letter from his first birthday. She'd written it on pastel paper and had affixed stickers of teddy bears and trains all over the envelope. What had she been thinking? Obviously as an adult, when he finally read the letters, he wouldn't care one bit about such juvenile decorations. The funny thing was that she wasn't even the crafty, sticker type. But something happens when you become a mother. The new role brings out an entirely different person that you never knew was hidden inside you. What you don't realize, at the time, is that this new, other you is really just visiting. One day that person is going to disappear, voluntarily or otherwise.

> My dear, Baby Yuri,
> I have waited all my life for you. And now here you are, bringing such joy into my world that I can't imagine how I lived all these years without you.
> I love the way you look at me with your eyes, gray and clear, as though you know me through and through. I love the way you squeeze my hand. And the sound of your voice, sweet and gentle as a bird. I love how your energy keeps me going, bringing a fullness to my life that I've never known until now.

And maybe more than anything else, I love watching you sleep at night, and listening to your rhythmic breath, and knowing that you have such peace in your little soul, a peace that is heartwarmingly contagious.

Your forever mother,
Fortunae

She shook her head.

It wasn't the cliché, shallow words that she'd written that goaded her now. It was the obvious fact that she'd so misread her baby, been so wrong about her future, about who he—or she—would become. To think he had once brought her peace.

How could she have been so naïve? And to what degree was she culpable?

She wanted to call a girlfriend, to cry into the phone. But she had no one to call. All those friends from long ago had slowly backed away and turned in other directions. Friends do that, Fortunae had learned. They disappear when you, or your family, don't turn out to be as perfect as they are.

And sometimes family members do, too. There was no way she could cry on her mother's shoulders now. She wouldn't understand. And neither would her sister Margee, with those two perfect boys. Margee, her sister who never bothered to reply to Fortunae's last letter months ago.

Being the mother of a kid who gets in trouble is a lonely job. You wind up crying on the shoulders of cops.

What the hell, Fortunae thought as she made her way back to the kitchen. There wasn't that much wine left in the bottle. Might as well finish it off.

When the final glass of wine was empty, she sat back on the sofa, unbuttoned her blouse, and pressed Luke's icon on her cell phone.

"Hey, Luke," she slurred into the phone when he answered. She slipped her hand down into her jeans. "Wanna fool around?"

"Fortunae?" There was a hollow space at the other end of the phone line. "Everything all right?" He sounded sleepy. Sexy sleepy.

"Mm-hmm. Everything's just fine. Fine and dandy." She hiccupped. "I just wondered if you'd like to come over and play."

"Fort? Are you okay? You don't sound like yourself."

"Well it's definitely me here."

"Do you have any idea what time it is?"

"Time?" Fortunae turned around to look at the microwave clock. "Mm-hmm. Ten o'clock." She lowered her voice, trying to sound like a news anchor. "It's 10 p.m. Do you know where your children are?"

He didn't reply, which triggered a pissed-off feeling in her gut. She pulled her hand out from her jeans. Déjà vu.

"Jesus, Luke. Answer me. Don't you remember that? They used to say it on the news all the time. Where did that come from, anyway Luke?"

"I don't know. I think it was before our time, Fortunae. But it's not 10 p.m. where I am. It's 1:00 in the morning here in Tampa."

Tampa. Fortunae heard a woman's voice, whispering something in the background. And then she realized what Luke had said. And what the woman's voice meant. She had totally forgotten.

"Tampa? Oh shit, Luke. I forgot. I forgot you moved. I even forgot you got married to Darnelle."

"Danielle."

"Whatever her name is. I'm sorry. I'm so, so sorry. And never mind about the…the fooling around part. I was just kidding."

She knew he knew she was lying about that.

"Fort, are you're drunk?"

She hiccuped again, then giggled. "Yep, I guess I am. A little. But here's a riddle for you: can you be a little drunk? Like being a little pregnant? There you go, Luke. I know you remember that one. We used to tell people I was a little pregnant right after we found out. Remember that?"

There was another long silence on the other end of the phone, long enough for her to hear her own breathing, and to think about what that long pause might have meant. Long enough to feel even more stupid, if that was possible.

"I'm sorry, Luke. It's just that Yuri didn't come home for his birthday."

"I know."

"You know?" There was an echo inside her head.

"We had a text exchange. I wished him a happy birthday."

"He exchanged texts with you, and not me? And he told you he wasn't coming home to celebrate with me? And nobody bothered to let me in on it? I made a reservation, Luke. And I bought presents."

"I didn't know he didn't tell you, Fort."

She didn't know what to say. She didn't even know what to feel. The easiest thing to do, right now, was to just check out of life for a while. She hung up without even saying goodbye.

She wandered back into her room and picked up the letters she'd left scattered across the floor. After tucking them back into the shoebox, she looked up at the top shelf of the closet, at the shoeboxes that contained letters that had been sent to her over the years from Luke, from her mother, and even from Margee. There weren't that many. People didn't write to her like she wrote to them. When Luke had once asked why she saved all those letters, she'd had no good reply. But now she understood exactly why she'd saved them. For a night like tonight, when she had to find a way to remind herself about a time when she was once happy.

On her way home from work the next day, Fortunae made a mental note to find out what to do about the ARY petition now that Yuri was eighteen. She then began to write an apology letter to Luke in her head. She had been such an idiot last night. And it wasn't just that she'd made a fool of herself to him. She'd made some poor choices for herself, too, including staying up late watching a vampire movie after she called him, so that today she walked around feeling like she was the one whose blood had been drained from her body.

Now, as she walked up to her front door anxious to lie down for a brief pre-dinner nap, she saw a dashing, middle-aged man standing in her way. Salt-and-pepper hair, naturally. A suit that had to be Armani, although she wasn't quite sure what Armani really looked like. He was polished all the way down to his shoes. He could have been a gift from heaven, except for the sour expression on his face.

"Ms. Monroe?" the man asked.

"Yes, that's me. Levkin-Monroe," she said, although after her performance last night she wondered who *me* really was anymore.

She heard footsteps coming up behind her and turned.

"Hello, Fortunae." It was Officer Randee. Her face was lined with worry.

"Is your son home?" the man asked.

"I don't know. I'm just now coming home from work." Fortunae was reluctant to ask the next question but knew it was in order. "Is there some sort of problem?"

Officer Randee took a step closer. "Mr. Hayes would like to talk to your son about his daughter," she said.

Fortunae had a sick feeling then. She wanted to find a reason to get away. Any excuse possible to turn around and leave. She simply didn't have the energy to deal with a new Yuri matter today, perhaps in part because of the lingering hangover from last night's wine, but also because of the chronic hangover she'd been burdened with for the last eighteen years, waking up day after day to face more of Yuri's problems. A hangover not from alcohol but from something far stronger and more toxic.

She put her key in the lock. "Well, let's see if he's home."

She stepped inside and called for him. No answer. For once, she was grateful for this.

"No, I guess he's not here." She stood in her doorway. Mr. Hayes remained outside on the front step, but was obviously trying to peer around her into the townhouse. She turned and glanced quickly around the kitchen. Nothing looked out of place, other than her cereal bowl and coffee mug that she hadn't washed that morning.

"Now what?" she asked Officer Randee, ignoring the tall man who stood uncomfortably close to her.

Before Officer Randee could respond, Mr. Hayes did. "I'm going to file charges against your son, Ms. Monroe. For statutory rape."

Fortunae's lungs seemed to collapse right then. Rape? Yuri had done a lot of bad things, but Fortunae had never thought it possible he'd commit rape. But then again, if he was still hanging out with that fourteen-year-old...it could be statutory rape. "Can he do that?" she asked Officer Randee.

"He can do whatever he wants," the officer said. "Whether or not his charges will stick is another matter."

Mr. Hayes sneered down at the police officer as though she were an irritating fly. "Oh, they'll stick. In fact, I'd suggest you get yourself a good lawyer." He handed her a business card. "This is my attorney. Have yours contact mine."

Fortunae immediately thought of the attorneys at her firm. She certainly didn't want to tell them about this. "Officer?" She looked to Officer Randee.

"I can't give you legal advice here, Fortunae."

At some point, Fortunae's lungs started breathing again, but now her heart was going into overdrive. Lately, it wasn't just the rheumatoid arthritis that worried her. What about her heart, her lungs? Which did she need most? An attorney—or a doctor?

And what if Yuri did rape this girl? She felt faint, and wanted to sit down, but she didn't want to leave her doorway until Mr. Hayes left. She rested her arm against the doorjamb for support and watched him, and his police escort, walk away.

After setting her purse down on the kitchen counter, she went upstairs to her bedroom. Maybe now she could take that nap. Or maybe a long, hot bath would help. And some wine. Her knees were really starting to throb. But as soon as she crossed the threshold into her room, she froze.

A nail was protruding from the wall above her bed. A lone nail, without a painting.

The desert painting from her mother was gone.

The Tiffany alarm clock that Luke had extravagantly given her on their first wedding anniversary was missing from her nightstand. As was her iPad.

Her jewelry box gaped open on her dresser. It had been raided of everything.

Oh God. Dear, sweet Jesus. She'd been robbed.

She hurried downstairs to the front door, quickly thinking she could call out for Officer Randee. But before she turned the doorknob, she thought again. A thought she didn't want to admit having surfaced. She couldn't shake it free any more than you can shake a cobweb off your fingers.

What if Yuri had done this?

No, she would not accept that idea.

But just in case, she wasn't ready to talk to the police about it. Not even Officer Randee.

There was only one way to know for sure, and that was to check her secret stash of really fine jewelry, which she kept in the pocket of that old raincoat she never wore. Nobody, besides Yuri, would think to look there. She'd made the mistake of showing him the antique alexandrite brooch her grandfather had brought back from Russia for her grandmother, which had later been bequeathed down the line to her. The gem changed colors depending on the time of day, like Yuri's eyes, and she'd always hidden it in in a silk pouch in the pocket of the old coat. Since that day when she showed it to Yuri, she'd added to her precious collection a diamond and pearl pendant which her father had given to her mother, only months before he died, and the gold necklace and bracelets which Luke had given her on their wedding day.

Her knees creaked as she lowered herself to kneeling position; although she'd have a hard time standing back up, she felt she needed to get close to the floor now. Her heart raced with irregular beats, irregular as her thoughts had been lately about Yuri: strong, weak, good, bad. She slowly forced her hand toward the coat pocket, tentatively, as though a poisonous spider or some other vicious creature might jump out and bite her.

Finally, she reached down into the left pocket. It was empty. That was all right, though. She'd thought the jewelry would be in the other one.

She reached down into the right pocket.

It was empty, too.

Panic latched onto Fortunae like a baby to a breast. It felt like it was sucking the life out of her. She lowered herself all the way to the floor.

No. The jewelry couldn't be missing. No, no, no. She must have been mistaken. She pulled up onto her knees and reached into each pocket again.

Still empty.

Her heart began thumping harder, faster, like a sprinter on the track. Maybe there was a hole in the pocket and the pouch of jewels had fallen to the floor. She pulled out all the shoe and boot boxes on the floor of the closet and ran her hands around the dusty baseboard of the closet. Still nothing.

Maybe she was wrong, maybe the jewels weren't in the pockets. She'd probably moved them somewhere else a while ago and forgotten. She had been feeling scatterbrained lately. Yes, that was probably it. She told herself to breathe and tried to think, to remember where she had hidden the jewelry. Yuri would not have stolen her most precious belongings. Of course he wouldn't.

Déjà vu. She'd felt this same panic on the night Luke had told her he was leaving. She had had trouble breathing that night, too and had thought she was having a heart attack. *There must be some mistake, some misunderstanding. This can't be happening. You can't do this to me, Luke.*

She had not been able to imagine living without Luke. And now she could not imagine not having that jewelry. Not because she wore it, because she didn't. Not because of its financial value, either, although the jewelry could be a last-ditch back up if she ever became destitute. It wasn't even the sentimental meaning that was the worst part of all this. It was the idea that her own son had stolen something so precious from her.

She began to open up shoeboxes. Boot boxes. She shook them upside down, scattering footwear all over the bedroom floor. She pulled out her dresser drawers, flinging underwear and socks and scarves across the bed. She ran to the bathroom and emptied the drawers and the cabinet underneath the bathroom sink. She dumped all of her worldly possessions out all over the place. She knew the jewelry had to be there, somewhere.

By now her knees were killing her and she could barely stand. But she didn't care. She needed to find the jewelry. She needed to prove, to herself, that Yuri didn't do this. She returned to the closet and reached up to the shoeboxes on the shelf above her hanging clothes. The boxes of letters, including the birthday letters to Yuri, that she'd just read through the previous night. She lifted them down to the floor and sat down. She started with the box of letters to Yuri, lifting the lid.

The letters were gone.

Yuri *had* stolen from her. Not just coins from the coin jar or cash from her wallet, which he'd done countless times in the past. Not even just precious jewelry. Yuri had stolen her letters. Her love.

He'd stolen her life. He'd even taken Luke. She knew this to be true, although she'd never allowed herself to think that way before. If Yuri had not been so difficult, she and Luke wouldn't have fought so much. They wouldn't have split up. Luke would have been with her this very minute if not for Yuri. It was terrible to think, but it was the truth. Her son had stolen everything from her. As this truth slowly came into focus, a range of emotions dispersed through her body like rancid fumes from a forgotten package of raw meat. The emotion that eventually rose higher than the others, even overtaking panic, was anger.

She opened up the other boxes of letters—the ones from Margee, and from her mother, and from Luke. She let out a long sigh.

These letters, surprisingly, were all there.

But then she noticed black marker bleeding through the envelopes, stains that hadn't been there when she'd read through the letters in her drunken state the night before. She pulled some letters out at random and saw that it was Yuri's name that had been crossed out. Everywhere. The only letters that hadn't been tainted were the ones written before he was born.

Yuri had redacted himself.

He had been there today, the day after his eighteenth birthday, and while his mother was at work, making money to support the two of them, he had removed himself from her life.

Furious now and frightened, too, Fortunae couldn't think straight. She went into the bathroom and looked in the mirror, then out to the kitchen where she looked around as though lost. She went to Yuri's room; the door was locked as usual but that would not stop her. She took one swift kick and broke it open, not sure what to do next.

She turned, then stomped outside and down into the storage area of the building's basement, and she brought two large suitcases back up to the townhouse and all the way upstairs to her bedroom. She swept the chaos of clothing off her bed and laid the suitcases out.

She still had no idea why she was doing this or where she would go. She only knew she had to get out of there. She didn't know if he was done retaliating. Moreover, her home had become hazardous to her health. Emotionally toxic. She could not return until somehow its evil aura had been cleansed or otherwise dissipated. She stuffed as many of her clothes and toiletries into the suitcases that would fit and dragged them down the stairs to the front door.

But she was damned sure not going to leave the townhouse—her home—to Yuri. She got a few Hefty garbage bags from the pantry and went back into his room. She tore clothes off of hangers and dumped them into the bags. She pulled out dresser drawers and dumped the contents into the bags. She gathered loose coins, unused packets of condoms, a flashlight, and other random things off his desk and stashed the whole lot into the bags. Finally, she went into his bathroom and scooped up his toiletries and dropped all that stuff in, too, not carrying one iota whether shampoo leaked all over his belongings. She bumped each of the bags downs the stairs, then out to the front porch, and taped a sign on one of them with Yuri's name. Written in black permanent marker.

She called a locksmith and said she urgently needed to change the locks.

She left a message for Mike, telling him she had to go away suddenly—family emergency—and asking if he'd please water her outdoor plants until she returned. She did not know when that would be.

And then she sat down at the kitchen table with a box of stationery.

She did not write that apology letter to Luke that she'd been planning on her way home earlier in the day. She didn't write to Margee, who hadn't bothered to reply for so long. She couldn't write to her mother just yet; it would be too hard to explain everything to her. And she sure as hell wasn't going to write another letter to Yuri. Damn him. She wasn't going to write to him ever again. Even if he was her son. Even if she loved him on some level and possibly, inexplicably, always would.

So to whom could she write? Who was left? She had all this pent up rage, and she knew she had to get it out somehow so she could breathe again.

But she had no one to vent to.

She studied the luggage in the hallway, by the front door. Where was she going to go?

It wasn't only her bedroom upstairs that looked like a disaster had struck. It was her whole life, and she had nowhere to go, and no one to turn to, for relief.

She thought about the impact letter she'd written to Yuri. It hadn't worked out so well. Maybe there was a different impact letter she needed to write now.

> Dear Fortunae,
> How are you?

She had been asking that question of complete strangers for practically her entire life, but how often did she check in on herself?

How *was* she? Physically speaking, she was a mess. She mentally scanned her body: her knees were killing her from the RA; her breathing had become so shallow from all the stress that she could barely climb the stairs without huffing and puffing; she always felt, lately, as though she was coming down with something—a sore throat, a cold, even stomach flu. And she kept putting on weight even though she rarely ate. Her body, it seemed, had forsaken her.

But worse than that: she was emotionally, and mentally, a wreck. She couldn't sleep through the night, and when she did finally succumb to rest she had horrible nightmares. She was chronically anxious and easily upset. She was absent-minded, missing meetings at work and forgetting to pay bills. She was often cross with others, but she was especially cross with herself.

Funny, she thought. She'd studied and studied how to raise a happy, responsible child, all these years, but she hadn't read a single book on how to make herself happy. She'd tried to teach Yuri to be kind to others, but she hadn't been very kind to perhaps the only person who would matter until the end of her days. The life that was most sacred—her own. She had been too busy focusing on his needs—however she defined them—to focus on her own. She had relied on Yuri, and Luke, and Margee, and everyone else, to take care of her.

They had all failed. But then again, maybe it had never really been their job.

And that's why she couldn't write to them, or turn to them, now for help. She had to do this on her own. She just didn't know how.

There was a knock at the door; she startled, and her heart, which had slowed to a leisurely half-marathon pace, now kicked up a couple of notches. But when she called out to ask who it was, a man identified himself as the locksmith. She let him in, and as he started to work on changing the lock, she ripped up the beginning of the letter to herself. She had nothing to say, really. She went into the living room, sat down on the sofa, and turned on the TV. That movie with Hugh Grant and Sarah Jessica Parker about an estranged couple going into a witness protection program came on.

As the locksmith worked, Fortunae started to fantasize about running away. Really disappearing, starting over. Did it have to be only a fantasy? Yuri was eighteen; she had no legal obligation to support him, and there was certainly no emotional connection—as awful as that sounded. She had no lover, and no real friends. She didn't think Margee would care one way or the other if they ever spoke again. And although it would hurt to never see her mother again, she knew that her mother was happy. She was that type of woman who always, somehow, found happiness. Fortunae didn't inherit that gene.

It was a preposterous idea, to disappear.

And she loved it.

All these years she had been hiding the full truth of her life from others, and now what she really needed was to go into hiding so she could rejoin life. Besides, it would probably be good for her RA. Less stress and all.

She watched the movie for a few more minutes, then looked online for the Seattle address of the US Marshals office.

She sat down at the kitchen table one more time and began to write.

A few minutes later, the locksmith finished, and he came to stand at the edge of the living room, laughing at something on the TV screen. Fortunae looked up from her work at him.

"Hilarious movie," he said. "Preposterous, but funny as hell."

She nodded. Preposterous, indeed. She paid him; he left. She finished the letter and discovered that she hadn't felt this good in years. She folded it into an envelope. She addressed it. She affixed a stamp.

She smiled.

They probably don't get many letters like this, Fortunae thought. Not these days, anyway. Nobody sends letters anymore.

# SUMMER

# WRITING THERAPY

# Regeneration

—AUTUMN STEPHENS

Who supervises our visits to the personal
past, makes us jot regrets on skims of sea and sky?
Now everything looks like the measles, even
the beaches we used to stroll, searching for radiant
stones in the sand. A mistake, what's that—a beat
you lost, a wave you didn't catch? Starfish grow
new limbs from their wounds; squid send clouds
of ink to baffle old demons when they come scrabbling
over the rocks. Shall we blame the skin for itching,
the tide for turning, the hermit for outgrowing
its home? Each empty shell tells the story of desire
that pointed in two opposite directions, a life
turned inside out. Let a two-faced goddess take us
in her ten blue arms and teach us to amputate
what no longer serves. Let us find words to crack
the chambered heart of dis-aster, linked by ear
to fracture, but also a flower named for the stars.

**RAINA HAD RESISTED** seeing the bitch-ass therapist, the same way she'd resisted seeing that asshole principal when she was a school-aged girl, or that sleazebag truant officer when she was a young teen, or all those social workers and judges once she became a single mother and, to use *their* word, a junkie. She'd also resisted going back to her father's swanky condominium in the heart of Chicago, her hometown. Back to this place where memories of homelessness and death reached out to her from darkened alleys like panhandlers, where wild animals howled from claustrophobic cages in Lincoln Park Zoo, just north on Lake Shore Drive. But her thirteen-year-old daughter Frankie had run away, and Raina knew both why and what she had to do if she ever wanted to see her daughter again.

She had to get with the goddamned program. She just wasn't sure she could.

Her father had arranged for her to stay with him so she could see the "best therapist in Chicago," a woman who also happened to have been a friend of the family. Now Raina slouched into a corner of a purple faux-suede loveseat. As she adjusted her thick black hair so that it splayed across the furniture, she felt as ugly as that Greek monster Medusa, with the snakes growing from her head. She waited for the inevitable interrogation from Beatrice LaCroix.

"I'm so happy to see you again, Raina," Beatrice said, sitting in a mahogany chair facing Raina, in front of her desk rather than behind it. She wore a silk dress, and her silver hair was swept up in a chignon, and a peach-tinted smile had been painted on her face. Like some sort of china doll.

Raina didn't remember ever meeting Beatrice and wondered just how much her mother had told the shrink over the years.

"I've heard so much about you over the years."

Well there you have it. This was practically like having to face her mother all over again, and she sure as shit didn't want to relive those times.

"I still remember the day I received your mother's announcement, more than thirty years ago. She was so happy when she and Jack adopted you as a newborn baby," Beatrice said. Her voice was soft, her face kind. But there was a cool aura surrounding her. Her words sounded plastic. And that one word, *adopted*, scorched like bad crack, fueling a memory dating back to when Raina was a teen, when she began to first think about what it meant to be adopted: she'd come out from some other woman's vagina and had been handed off the way people recycle presents they don't want.

"Did I say something that upset you?" Beatrice asked.

Man, she was sharp. Sharp as a needle poke. Raina set her jaw tight. A crystal bowl filled with peanut M&Ms had been planted on a glass-top table at the end of the loveseat before she'd arrived. Without skipping a beat, Raina picked it up and dumped the entire collection of candies into her purse.

The therapist made a quick note on a lavender legal pad, the pen scraping briefly across the paper. Raina craned to see what Beatrice had written.

"I'm guessing it was my mention of your *mother*."

"My mother?" Raina scratched one of her arms. "Which one? The bitch that raised me? Or the real one who got it on one night without a condom and then dumped me?" She stood and walked to the window. It overlooked the choppy blue waves of Lake Michigan. She was eleven floors above the lake as she stood with her back to the therapist, and she felt anxious, like that water down there. Nauseated. She turned around, circled the room behind Beatrice, and looked over the therapist's shoulder. It was a heady feeling, standing there above the shrink. Although thin, Raina had always been tall and naturally strong. Beatrice was small. And old. For once Raina felt like she was in charge. Like she had power.

Until she saw a word on Beatrice's notes that was underlined twice.

"What's that mean?" Raina pointed to the purple pad.

Beatrice twisted around to look at Raina standing behind her, then back at the page. "Attachment? It's quite literal, about how attached a person is to someone else. In your case, your parents. I'm wondering how you feel about your relationship with your mother in particular. Your adoptive mother."

"It was fucked up. Our relationship was fucked up."

"Why do you think that was the case? That your relationship was so poor?"

Raina scratched her head now, hoping she didn't have fleas. Or lice. She hadn't taken the time to wash her hair before coming to this appointment, and she knew she must look like a wild woman straight out of the bush. She certainly felt like one, unable to find the right words to say how she felt. How the hell do you explain to a complete stranger why your relationship with your mother was fucked up?

"Well for one thing, she died. Now if that's not fucked up I don't know what is."

"What about when she was alive?" Beatrice kept a poker face here, showing no emotion at the mention that her so-called friend was dead.

"Man, I don't know. Why do most people hate their mothers? She was strict. She wasn't cool. She was white."

"You're white, Raina."

"Are you blind? My skin ain't white."

"I agree, your skin has a beautiful golden hue. According to what your mother told me, you have a mixed ethnic background. But what I'd like to understand is what your mother's race had to do with your feelings about her. Do you feel that way about all white people?"

"Who doesn't hate white people? They go around shooting blacks." Some of Raina's johns were white, and even they hated the white cops, after Ferguson and Baltimore and all the shit that went down in so many other cities. "But what's this got to do with anything, *Bea*?"

God damn it. What *did* this have to do with anything? Raina wanted to get the hell out of there. She knew just what she'd do, too. There was a bar right around the corner.

"Your relationship with your mother has everything to do with anything that's important. Like you getting clean and sober. And getting Frankie to agree to come back home."

Raina knew she was being played with, a rat tormented by a cat. This shrink was way different from other social workers Raina had dealt with over the past umpteen years. They wanted to lecture her about what she needed to change, or offer her rehab resources, or threaten her with jail or even with losing Frankie. This bitch wanted to get inside Raina's head. And Raina resented that, especially how Beatrice acted, all high and mighty, like she had something stiff shoved up her ass. Like she looked down on Raina, the mixed breed, the high school dropout, the *junkie*. The broke ho. Even if it was all true.

Again, she walked to the windows and looked down to Lake Shore Drive below. Hundreds of cars passed by as she watched, heading in one direction or another. At least they knew where they were going.

"Anyone ever try to jump out this window?" She heard Beatrice's hesitation, as though the air just got sucked out of the room.

"No, nobody that I know of. Do you think about suicide, Raina?"

Raina was taken aback that Beatrice would ask this so directly. But then she grinned into her faint reflection in the window when she heard the therapist's scribbling pen yet again. An idea came to her. She didn't need to be the rat. She could be the cat. She didn't have to tell the truth.

"Have I thought about suicide? Hell, yeah. 'Course I have. I've thought about homicide, too."

She waited for a reaction from Beatrice but, to her dismay, got nothing this time. Back to square one. "Robbery, grand larceny. Bombs. You name it." The part about bombs wasn't true, but it could've been.

"Let's go back to your mother," Beatrice said, as though the bitch hadn't even heard what Raina had said. "Come back here and have a seat, please."

Raina waited a moment; whether it was because she wanted to show Beatrice who was in charge or because she was half-afraid to talk about her mother, she wasn't sure. She crossed the room, sat next to the empty M&M bowl, and wrapped her arms around her knees. She wondered if Beatrice noticed the needle scars.

Beatrice handed Raina a piece of paper and held another one just like it on her lap.

"This is a poem I'd like to have us read, together," Beatrice said.

What the fuck? What was this, English class?

"Sometimes we learn about ourselves, and our world, by reading poetry. And sometimes poems can evoke feelings inside that help us sort out our thoughts, process our emotions. This one is an easy one. I'm going to read it aloud, and all I ask of you, Raina, is that you follow along."

It was a stupid poem by Linda somebody or other about a daughter leaving home. It didn't make much sense to Raina. But for some reason it made her feel like crap. Beatrice asked Raina what she thought about it.

"I don't like poems. I don't get what they mean," Raina said, now crossing her arms across her chest and wrapping one of her legs tightly around the other.

Without skipping a beat, Beatrice said that was okay. She handed Raina another one. This was a short one about clothes. Raina read it, then crumpled up the page. "I don't really want to think about my mother's clothes."

Beatrice sighed. "Okay, let's do this instead. Rather than reading about what someone else has written, I'm going to give you a paper and pen, and let you do some writing. Just for three minutes. I'd like you to brainstorm whatever comes to mind about your mother. There is no right or wrong answer. Whatever comes to mind is right."

Was this some sort of trick? Like a schoolgirl, she'd have to *write down* her thoughts? She hadn't written anything important since high school, if you call that important. What about just lying back on the couch and letting the shrink do all the work?

"This is bullshit," Raina said. Of course she could just write down a bunch of lies.

"Just write whatever comes to mind," Beatrice said. "No judgment, no pressure, Raina."

Raina conjured an image of her mother. Tall, always dressed beautifully. Well spoken.

White. Rich bitch. Controlling. Perfect. Fucking therapy. Silk pillows ~ fire. Homework. Rules. No allowance. Grounded. Didn't understand me.

She looked up at Beatrice, who sat patiently in her chair looking at her watch, that peachy tight-lipped smile still frozen in place.

Hated her. Cancer. Dead.

"Here," she said, ripping the paper from the pad. She handed it over to Beatrice with that same sinking feeling she'd had way back in high school, knowing that after handing in her essays she'd be asked to stay after class to explain the *disturbing thoughts* she'd revealed.

Now she sat there waiting while Beatrice read her words. Behind Beatrice hung a painting of a beach somewhere, a sandy beach where the waters were turquoise, the same shade as those blue pillows her mother had once brought home from India. A white sailboat drifted on the horizon. Raina was surprised at how that stupid writing exercise made her feel now. Her fingers ached, but worse than that, she felt exhausted.

She should have just lied; it would have been easier. She didn't want to think any more.

Beatrice glanced at Raina's foot, and when Raina looked down she saw her foot wiggling as though it were on speed. Then Beatrice studied her watch. "There are a few observations I'd like to share with you during our remaining time today."

Shit, Raina couldn't believe time was almost up. She wasn't so sure she was ready to hear these *observations*.

"Yeah?"

"These are things for you to think about between now and the next time we meet," Beatrice said.

Raina shifted in her seat, glanced at the empty crystal bowl, thought about ripping that off, too, when she left. She reached into her purse and popped a green M&M into her mouth.

"First, I want to assure you that your parents loved you very much," the therapist said. "I know that from what your mother told me over the years."

"Well they sure as shit had an odd way of showing it."

"It might be, Raina, that you simply didn't recognize it as love, the way many children would. I'd like to come back to that word *attachment*...but before I do, I want to clarify how this is all going to work. First, I'm not what you might expect from a typical therapist."

Damn straight.

"As one of your mother's closest friends, I've had the privilege of insight into your life for many years. I know a lot about you, which means I might be biased. You and I will have to learn to deal with that if we're going to work together."

That bar around the corner was only a few minutes away.

"And one of the things I know is that your stakes are pretty high right now. You want to get your daughter back, and I want to help you. And that means I'm not going to go easy on you, Raina. I'm going to call you on the carpet when I think it's warranted. Fair enough?"

Beatrice's gaze was hard but not necessarily cold. It wasn't quite as bad here as being under a bright light at the police station, but almost.

"One other thing," Beatrice went on. "Since your mother is now deceased, I am not going to worry about patient confidentiality. If anything, I think your mother would appreciate it if I made sure our conversations here were straightforward. She would want the best for you and Frankie if she were still living."

Raina now felt the same way she'd felt at the cemetery on the rainy day they'd buried her mother: like an umbrella turned inside out.

"Let's go back to the idea of attachment," Beatrice said. "It's what I think might have been undermining your relationship with your parents, and thus what might have led you, in part, to where you are today. Many adopted children don't ever completely attach to their parents. It's not for lack of love, and it's nobody's fault."

Beatrice set her purple pad of paper down on the table, and her pen, too.

"Raina, a parent's love is sometimes hard to understand." Beatrice had also lowered her voice a notch, and now it came out softer, and more inviting, like the pillows on the loveseat. Something Raina could almost lean into. "All the rules, all the lectures...even all the broccoli and carrots when you were young were really just signs of their love for you. Your mother and father cared so much for you, and they were in such pain when they saw you doing things they considered mistakes. Trust me, I know. I spent hours with your mother, who was often in tears." She paused. "And, unfortunately, they weren't bottomless wells of energy. At some point, although they still loved you and always would, they just didn't have any more energy to show it to you. They couldn't give any more."

Beatrice came and sat at the other end of the loveseat. She turned toward Raina, which was unnerving. She was getting too close. Raina didn't like the way all this talk was making her feel. What if this bitch was right? Raina leaned away, but she couldn't lean away from what Beatrice had said.

"Can I go to the bathroom?" Raina asked. "I feel sick."

"You do look a bit pale. Sure, Raina. Right through that door." Beatrice pointed to a door off to the side. A private bathroom.

Raina kneeled before the toilet and stuck her finger down her throat. It was the first thing that came to mind, and she wasn't sure if she did it because she wanted to punish herself for being such a rotten daughter, or whether it was because she might feel better if she vomited. Regardless, nothing came up. She splashed hot water on her face, then cold. She scrubbed her hands so hard that a scab broke open and started to bleed. And of course there were only pretty little hand towels there, no ordinary paper towels, so she had to press toilet paper against the wound until it stopped. When she went back out, she wondered how much time was left in the session now. She couldn't take much more of this.

"I'm going to ask you a difficult question," Beatrice said after Raina sat back down on the loveseat. "And I want you to be honest, not for my sake but for your own. Ready?"

Raina wasn't sure she was, but she nodded anyway.

"Do you think you ever loved your mother?"

At least it wasn't a question about Frankie. Still, it rankled. She had come in today expecting to talk about drugs and staying clean, or being a hooker. She had never in a million years expected to be made to feel so bad about herself as a daughter. She'd certainly never expected *this* question. It was something she'd never even asked herself.

Beatrice's eyes were penetrating, glacier blue with black pinpoint pupils, eyes that could probably see right into your thoughts. Raina closed her own eyes. She could lie and say she loved her mother, but this woman sitting beside her would see right through that. The truth, however, was too hard to say. Even the pimps and dealers she knew loved and respected their mothers. But she didn't, and never had, and right then she thought that was quite possibly the worst flaw any human could have, and her nose started to sting as tears threatened to surface.

She opened her eyes and gave Beatrice the best dagger glare she could muster.

"Why the hell do you care? It sure as shit doesn't matter now that she's dead."

Beatrice actually stiffened at that remark. "Raina, let me come right out and say something to you. I've noticed today how your attitude and vernacular don't match what I know to be true about your upbringing. Your parents raised you in an educated and value-based environment. Your mother frequently told me how smart you were. So if you want to cut all this tough chick crap with me, and lose the street talk, we'll get a lot more accomplished in future sessions. Something for you to consider."

Raina was back to hating this bitch.

"Now, about my question. Do you think you ever loved your mother?"

Raina wasn't sure how to respond. "I'd like to write down my answer."

"That's fine." Beatrice handed the pad and pen to Raina, who pressed the pen hard onto the paper.

<u>NO! I NEVER LOVED MY MOTHER.</u>

Raina handed the pad back, and then the pen. "There. Satisfied?"

The therapist took the confession, then reached over and set her hand softly on Raina's knee. "Are you satisfied? How do you feel now that you've written that?"

Raina shrugged. "I don't know."

Beatrice nodded. This bitch was too understanding.

"Thank you for your honesty, Raina. Being honest with yourself is an important first step to staying clean. I know this is a lot to think about, and we'll explore this more next week. Good work today, Raina. Very good work. And now our time is up."

Beatrice stood and walked to the door. When Raina stood, she felt chilled. Naked. Exposed and rejected. As though she'd been ripped open and also handed a heavy load of guilt and shame. A load she would now have to carry all by herself throughout the next week.

As she walked through the doorway, the image of Frankie came to mind, and she realized that her own daughter probably didn't love her any more than she had loved her own mother. Which was not at all. She rode the elevator down to the building's lobby, exited through the revolving door, and headed straight for the bar.

After the torture of that first therapy session, it was hard for Raina to drag herself back for more the next week. She wanted so badly to smoke a bowl to help her get through it. Instead, she looked at herself in the gold-leaf hallway mirror before leaving her father's condo and reminded herself to be strong. That bitch had gone too deep into Raina's memories and feelings last time. That sure as shit wasn't going to happen again. This time, Raina would keep the power.

"Therapy is hard work," Beatrice said, picking up her lavender legal pad and pen as Raina sat down on the loveseat. "How are you feeling today?"

"Lousy."

"I'm sorry to hear that. Would you care to elaborate?"

"No."

Beatrice hesitated. "All right, then. I'm going to do my best to make today as simple, and enjoyable, as I can. Today I'd like to delve deeper into your childhood."

Shit. Raina picked up one of the throw pillows on the loveseat and hugged it against her stomach.

"Let's start with another poem. This time we'll read something by George Ella Lyon. It's called 'Where I'm From.'"

Beatrice read it aloud, and Raina followed along. She didn't understand some of it, but she did like the part about the girl eating dirt that tasted like beets. Raina remembered eating dirt, too, when she was little. When Beatrice finished reading, she pointed out some specific words the writer had used. Once again, Raina felt like she was back in school. If this was what therapy was supposed to be about, it sucked. Who cares about fudge and clothespins and whatever other words were in that lame poem?

"It's important to spend some time thinking about the past," Beatrice said. "Your past is your foundation. And sometimes it's your launching pad to the future."

Whatever that meant.

"Take a few minutes to think back to your own youth, Raina. Then I'll ask you to give me three words that describe who you were as a child. You'll give me an adjective, meaning a one-word description of yourself, a verb that shows a memorable activity from your younger days, and an emotion—just one word to describe how you commonly felt as a child."

Raina closed her eyes and let images of her youth fast forward through her mind. Fighting with other little girls in the sandbox, stealing shiny coins from a bowl on top of her father's chest of drawers, unraveling threads from her mother's silk dresses when her mother was in the kitchen on the phone. Soon, she settled onto one scene that was particularly vivid, when she was around seven years old.

"I'm ready," she said, opening her eyes. "My adjective is blue. My verb is scorch. My emotion is thrill."

She waited for Beatrice to ask questions, impatient to tell about how she'd set fire to her parents' house, before the family moved into the condo on the lake. But, to Raina's disappointment, Beatrice didn't ask for an explanation. Instead, she wrote each of the three words across the top of three separate pages. Then she handed the pad to Raina.

"I want you to write down what blue means to you."

What? "It's a color, obviously." This was bullshit, although there was a part of her that felt a surprising twinge of delight, reminding her of magazines for children with puzzles and quizzes that her father would buy for her at the store now and then when she was little.

"Yes, blue is a color. But let your mind go with it. See where *blue* takes you."

Raina wasn't sure what Beatrice meant. Whatever, she looked up at that painting on Beatrice's wall and thought about those blue silk pillows again. They had caught fire right away. She began to write.

Pillows. Fire. Destruction.

"Remember to focus on the adjective," Beatrice said although she hadn't even seen what Raina had written. "Try to keep your thoughts directed to *blue*."

Smooth. Cool. Sad.

This was a bunch of crap.

Veins. Bruises.

She remembered a condom that a recent john had used. It was blue.

Sex. Hot.

Raina glanced at the therapist, who was making notes on a separate pad of paper. She didn't even know what Raina was writing; what could she possibly be making notes about?

She handed the first page to Beatrice, then began thinking about her verb, *scorch*. She recalled the heat of the flames, the whooshing sound they made as they moved from the pillows to the draperies.

Fast.

Which made her think of sex again. She hadn't had an orgasm in a long time; it wasn't something she let happen when she was with the johns.

Skin. Sex.

"You seem to be focusing a great deal on sex," Beatrice said after Raina handed her the second page.

She was still an ice queen, but at least she'd reacted somehow.

"Raina, the purpose of this exercise is to help you recall your childhood. Shall I infer that you had sex when you were a young girl, or that you were somehow sexually abused as a child?"

"No," Raina said, which was the truth. She may not have loved her parents, but she had no reason to accuse them of anything like that. What about the fact that Beatrice allegedly knew so much about Raina's parents? She should have known they didn't abuse their only daughter.

"I have an idea about what's happening here," Beatrice said. "Could it be that you're hiding behind sex?"

Raina thought Beatrice seemed smug now. But she wasn't sure. Maybe Beatrice just didn't like sex.

"So let's try to stick with the plan for today of working on your childhood and removing sex from the discussion, since it's irrelevant for the time being. All right?"

"Yeah. Whatever."

"Now, let's move on to the third word, the emotion. Write down your experiences, when you were a child, in relation to your emotion word."

*Thrill.* Raina had felt a thrill whenever she did something wrong as a child. Stealing. Setting fires. Even lifting up her skirt in public. She still got that thrill when she did something wrong in a place where she was expected to behave properly. Like here. Like at the last session, Raina had felt thrilled when she'd poured the M&Ms from the candy bowl into her purse, right in front of the bitch. Anything to get a rise. Now she picked up the bowl and prepared to empty it into her purse again.

"Hold on," Beatrice said. She walked over to her desk, opened a drawer, and pulled out a box of Ziploc bags. "Pour them into this." She handed a bag to Raina. "They'll stay clean that way."

The Ziplocs automatically deflated the thrill. Raina set the bowl back on the table and left the candy alone.

"Go ahead," Beatrice prodded. "Write down what comes to mind when you think of the word thrill, as it pertains to your younger days."

Wild. Trouble. Hidden.
Illegal. Power. Rebel.
Danger. Break. Different. Rush. Steal.
Escape.

"I see," the therapist said, glancing at the words when Raina turned in the page.

"Don't you want me to tell you about some of my *thrilling* childhood experiences?" Raina asked. "How I set fire to the house? How I stole things at school? How I got in trouble in the neighborhood, or at my parents' church? The lies I told? When I smoked my first cigarette? I was only eight, you know." Raina was dying to talk about all the trouble she'd been in as a child. If she couldn't talk about it, then how could Beatrice know who she was? Or help her? Wasn't that the point?

"Sometimes, Raina, you find more meaning in your past experiences when you revisit them privately than when you tell someone else about them. And when you write the words down, they reflect back to you like a mirror. That's what we're doing here. What I'm hoping for, Raina, is that *you'll* gain insight into who you are as a person—your authentic self. Did you ever read Robinson Crusoe when you were young? The author, Daniel Defoe, said the soul is like a rough diamond, and must be polished, or its luster will never appear. That's where we're working on here, Raina. We're looking for that diamond, and then we're going to polish it."

Just like the first time she was here, Raina got up and went over to the window. Today the lake was charcoal gray, complicated.

"I'm done for today," she told Beatrice.

The therapist encouraged Raina to sit back down and talk some more, or write some more, but Raina refused.

"Writing is hard," Beatrice said. "And healing is hard, too. It's fine with me if you end this session early, if that's what you really want to do."

Raina had no idea what she really wanted. So the easiest thing to do was to leave, which she did.

The third session focused on Raina's days on the streets. After the opening question of how Raina was feeling, which Raina blew off with a shrug and an *okay*, Beatrice asked her to write a letter to her former self, to the teenage girl who ran away from home at seventeen. At least they weren't going to read any idiotic poems this time.

"This time, it's a private letter to yourself, Raina. No one will see it but you."

"You're not going to read it?"

"No, I'm not. The value in this exercise isn't turning in your paper. The value is in recognizing the differences between your younger self and your older, wiser self. You were still young, still a child, Raina, when Frankie was born and when you became a prostitute. That inner child never had the opportunity to grow up in safety. That young girl is still inside you, vulnerable, keeping her memories and experiences locked up in a little vault. What I want you to do is to write a letter to her. Tell her what you've learned."

This therapy shit was getting weirder. Write a letter to her former self? What for? Talking about her past was one thing. Writing to a person that no longer existed was another. It wasn't like she could mail it at the post office.

"What if I don't want to do this?"

"I can't make you do it," Beatrice said. "But I think, once you get started, you'll decide it's useful. Remember, we're here to help you understand yourself better so you can make wiser choices from now on."

"How long does the letter have to be?"

Beatrice's smile seemed warmer today than on that first day. "It's your choice. It depends on how much you have to say."

"How much time do I have?"

"As much as you need. I'll be sitting over here at my desk, working on my computer."

"No talking today?" Raina asked.

"I'm completely available if you want to talk. But I think, for today's purposes, the most important conversation you need to have is with yourself. I'm just here to facilitate that."

Raina set the pen to the paper.

> Dear Raina,
> How are you?

"This is bullshit." What was this, some sort of time travel? Where should she begin? What should she say? She let out a long, annoyed sigh.

> This is weird, but I'm writing this letter to you because my therapist told me to do it. Yes, I/you (we?) are seeing a therapist now. She told me to think back to when you got pregnant.
> You don't want to remember this, do you? You came back from that school trip to the Mediterranean, and you

had all those horrible fights with Mother and Dad. About stupid shit, like curfew, because you couldn't tell them what you really wanted to tell them. Instead of going to them for help, you treated them like crap.

And then, when your period stopped, and you took a pregnancy test, and you knew for sure, you started getting high all the time. And you dropped out of school and went to live with that new boy you met.

Luis.

He was so handsome, so cool and funny, right? He treated you well. And even he said you were pretty shitty to Mother and Dad. Do you remember calling Mother a whore? It's all coming back to me now. I wonder if that's when she started getting sick.

Luis was going to solve all your problems. Yeah, he even promised to help you with the baby after she was born.

Frankie.

And you were so young you believed him. Love conquers all, you thought.

And then along came winter. The rats in the slum. The snow blowing in through the roof. You could have moved home with Mother and Dad. But you were so proud. So stupid.

Raina put the pen down. She hated this. Hated what she'd written. Her hand hurt. But she liked the feeling that was coming over her. A sort of painful freedom.

She glanced over at the woman who had been her mother's friend. Raina knew little about Beatrice. There was probably a lot about her mother's life that she didn't know, and now never would.

You were an idiot, not telling Mother about the baby. Yeah, she would have been pissed off, but she loved you, and she would have helped. You never knew how to accept help, did you?

"Should I keep going?" Raina asked Beatrice.
"Yes, if you'd like. There's still time."

Raina held her pen over the page as she tried to capture her thoughts, flitting around like gnats in the late afternoon sun.

> Of course, you didn't know then what was going to happen to Luis, or how that image of him lying there cold and blue, a needle still stuck in his arm, was going to haunt you for the rest of your shitty-assed life. You didn't know you were going to become a whore and a horrible mother for Frankie. What the hell were you thinking? What the hell were you so afraid of?

Raina wiped her wrist beneath her running nose. Beatrice quietly brought a box of tissues to her.

More thoughts fought against one other inside Raina's mind like rival gang members. Was this what therapy did to everyone? Make them feel like shit? Guilty? Ashamed? She saw Luis's dead body, and, later, Frankie as an infant wrapped in ratty old blankets as they lived in a slum with other prostitutes and their kids. She hated that girl to whom she'd just written a letter. She wanted to purge that person from her past. Disown her. Exorcise her, like in that old movie. She wanted to go running out of Beatrice's office and get high right now. She wanted to pass out and, maybe, never wake up.

She ripped the pages from the pad, then ripped them into shreds which she flung into the room. "Fuck this shit. I can't do it. I'm outta here."

Before Beatrice could say anything, Raina stormed out the door.

Raina didn't go home to her father's condo that afternoon. Once again, she headed for the bar, and after that she went out into the streets, wandering north along the lake until she found someone selling. She got strung out before falling asleep under a park bench and avoided her father and his condo for two more days and nights.

When she came to on the third morning, she found herself lying behind a dumpster in an alley. She was sore all over. A woman was sitting nearby, huddled in a filthy brown blanket. When the woman saw that Raina was awake, she came closer with a torn and dirty shopping bag.

Dark tangled hair, green eyes, ripped denim jacket: Raina wondered if this was another street bitch who would rip her off, or worse. She might have been somewhere around Raina's age, but it was hard to tell.

"Here," the woman said, reaching a hand out to Raina, who recoiled. She didn't want any help from this filthy woman. She didn't really want any help from anyone. She didn't deserve it.

The woman took her hand back. "Looks like you took quite a beating." She gently helped Raina sit upright, then set down the bag. Raina recognized the Lord & Taylor logo; it was a store where her mother used to shop. The woman took the dirty blanket from her shoulders and, sitting down beside Raina, wrapped half of it around Raina and half around herself. The woman stank.

Raina drew her chin in and dropped her head toward her chest. The blanket was disgusting, but it still felt comforting.

After reaching into the shopping bag and pulling out a half-eaten chewy granola bar, the woman handed it over. "Here," she said again.

Raina stared at the bar, then took it, not sure what she would do with it. They sat together for a while without talking.

"I totally fucked up," Raina finally said. At first the woman didn't respond, but then she laid her hand on Raina's arm. Her nails were dirty, ragged.

"We all fuck up," she said. "We're human. Some of us get past it, some of us don't. Those of us who don't, well, we wind up here." She laughed, then coughed. Brown sputum splattered into her palm.

Raina turned away.

"I started to get clean," Raina said when the woman stopped coughing. "I'm trying to get my daughter back. She's only thirteen."

The woman nodded. "I've got two sons. Haven't seen them for a long time." She closed her eyes, started to hum a tune Raina didn't recognize. "Probably won't ever see them again. They wouldn't want a mama like me."

An image of Frankie, running away, flashed before Raina's eyes. She wasn't sure if it was a memory or a nightmare. But she knew one thing for sure.

"I've got to go," she said.

The woman shook her head. "Not just yet? Stay and talk a while with me. I could use the company."

Raina sat huddled with the woman for a few minutes, then insisted she really needed to go. She handed back the granola bar.

"You be careful out there," the woman said. "And don't look too hard in the mirror, girlfriend. It's dangerous."

Raina shivered, wondering how bad she really looked. She unwrapped herself from the blanket and tucked it tightly around the woman. As she stood, her body screaming from three days of hunger, drugs, and abuse at the hands of God-knows-who, she thanked the woman and wished her good luck, knowing she would need just as much herself.

As she rode the elevator up to her father's condo an hour later, she felt like she had to puke. The withdrawals would be hell all over again, not to mention the litany of lectures she expected to hear when she walked through her father's front door.

But he did not lecture her; he didn't even acknowledge her at first. He simply sat in his leather recliner in the living room, dressed sportily in a navy V-neck sweater and khaki pants, reading a book.

"Dad?" she said.

He paused, then placed an index finger on the page and gently closed the book over it. When he looked up at her, his half-smile, and his nod, told her he was resigned to accept whatever she threw at him. Like Beatrice had said, he was worn out.

"Welcome back," he said, without any hint of judgment. "How about a cup of jasmine tea?" He rose from his chair and headed for the kitchen.

Raina followed.

They sat at the table in silence as they waited first for the water to boil and then for the tea to steep and cool, a ghostly silence reminiscent of the day her mother had died. They sat in further silence as they drank, avoiding each other's gaze and instead studying the porcelain cups. Finally, when hers was empty, Raina asked him if he'd let her stay on, even though she'd totally fucked up yet again.

"A deal's a deal," he said. His eyes now slowly rose to meet hers. Raina didn't remember him looking so old and tired. "Sometimes, Raina, we have to work hard for the things we want most. And we make mistakes along the way. That applies to both of us. I said you could stay here as long as you tried. And I know you're trying. So, yes, you can stay here. In fact, I'm glad you are here. With me."

When Raina told Beatrice, at the next appointment, what she'd done, the therapist reiterated that therapy is hard work. "You've been unearthing feelings that have been buried a long time. It's difficult, but in the long run it's better to let these emotions out than to keep them stifled. Today I invite you to take off your mask."

Raina touched her face. It was still bruised.

"I'm talking about a metaphorical mask, Raina. The thing is, it's become such a part of you that you don't recognize it as a mask anymore. We all wear masks, to some extent, because they hide our fears and vulnerabilities. But they also hide our ability to see. Like those masks you probably wore on Halloween when you were a small child."

Raina felt uncomfortable, in a different way than before. It wasn't this lecture that bothered her. It wasn't this perfect, sophisticated woman sitting across from her and telling her stuff that Raina should already have figured out at a much younger age. It was something else.

"Raina, I know a mask when I see one. There's still something that's serving as a division between you and Frankie. I know you say you love her, but I'm not feeling that love when you talk about her. This might sound harsh, but I don't see your eyes light up. Is there something you want to tell me? Or something you want to write down?"

"No."

"Okay, then we'll go exploring together. Consider this personal archaeology. I thought about this a great deal over the past week. We're missing something and we need to dig deeper. I'd like to go back to sex and see what's there. Unpeel the onion, as they say. Sometimes we hide our most frightening vulnerabilities in plain sight."

"You said sex is irrelevant."

"I may have been wrong."

Beatrice asked Raina to start by writing about her experience as a prostitute, anything that came to mind, and Raina wrote about it matter-of-factly. She was taken in by a pimp, after Luis died, who offered to take care of her so long as she agreed to start turning tricks only three months after Frankie was born. She handed the paper to Beatrice when she'd finished describing that time of her life.

"That must have been extremely difficult for you," Beatrice said after reading what Raina had written.

"It sucked."

"Who took care of Frankie?"

Raina explained that she traded childcare with the other young mothers in the stable of whores. "That was how it worked. And once you got in, you couldn't get out. I've told you everything. I'm not hiding anything here."

"What about other relationships?" Beatrice asked. "Other boyfriends?"

Raina laughed. "I haven't had time for that kind of shit for a long time," Raina said. "And no pimp would allow it anyway. I haven't had a real boyfriend since Luis."

Beatrice made some notes. "What about when you were younger, before Luis? Is there someone from that time period you can write about?"

Raina picked up her pen and listed everyone she could think of, from her youth, with whom she'd had some sort of intimate relationship. The first time she kissed a boy was fifth grade. First oral sex, seventh grade. First time going all the way, eighth grade. First girl she made out with, freshman year. Raina had had three or four somewhat steady boyfriends in high school, but dozens of one-night stands—so many she couldn't remember them all.

"Anything else?" Beatrice asked. "Any other memories about sex you'd like to share?"

There was a memory trying to make itself known. It had been pounding on a door to come out ever since Raina started coming to see Beatrice, and today the pounding was fierce, but she didn't know exactly what it was.

Raina picked up the pen, then set it back down.

"I went on a trip with a bunch of geeks and nerds during the summer between my junior and senior year. I was totally pissed off when my parents made me go. It was a tour of the Mediterranean, a school-sponsored trip. I hated it, and I snuck away from the group whenever I could. The chaperones hated me as much as I hated them."

The memory was coming into focus. It made her feel both itchy and warm all over, the way the homeless woman's blanket had felt comforting. She started to write.

> One night, when we were in Italy, I snuck out and met
> a boy from Sudan. He was handsome, with big hands and
> long legs and a kind voice. We talked all night long, about
> everything. Our parents, our friends. Our governments.

Raina thought back to that night as though it were a dream. A lovely dream, before everything really turned to shit.

> We made out. But...we didn't have sex. I wanted to,
> badly. He was so hot. But he was too polite. He told me he
> respected me, which I'd never heard from a boy before.

As the sun began to rise, and I had to go back to my group,
he took my hand and said one day we'd meet up again.

Raina stared out the window. She was on a beach at dawn with a Sudanese boy, a boy whose name she could no longer remember. She showed her writing to Beatrice.

"And then you came home and met Luis?" Beatrice asked.

"Yes. I met him right after I got back from the trip."

Now Raina thought back to an image of Luis, not as tall as the Sudanese boy but with equally dark eyes and a heart just as big. He had a huge dick, too.

"So let's go a bit farther back in time," Beatrice said. When was your last sexual relationship prior to that trip, prior to meeting the Sudanese boy?"

"I think it was with a boy named James. Jamie, everyone called him."

"And when, exactly, were you with him?"

"A few months before I went to Italy. I remember because he'd invited me to prom and then he uninvited me. I didn't go out with anyone after him." She felt a chill, then tucked her feet under her legs on the loveseat as she noticed Beatrice gazing at her intently. "What?"

"Hmm." Beatrice slipped her silver reading glasses on. "Let's take a break from that and read a poem together. I think you'll like this one. It's by Maya Angelou."

At least Raina had heard of this poet.

It was the one about a bird in a cage that sings all day long.

"Now let's go back to what we were talking about," Beatrice said. "There's something missing from your timeline. You said there was no one between Jamie and Luis. But based on when Frankie was born, you've omitted a very important person. Her father."

Raina's whole body tensed. She gripped the legal pad tightly.

"Raina?"

This time, instead of going to the window, she curled herself deeper into the loveseat cushions.

"What aren't you telling me? What aren't you facing?" Beatrice asked.

Raina's eyes began to burn.

"Raina. What is it? Were you assaulted? Were you…raped?"

Raina heard the therapist's words but couldn't quite process them. She sat immobilized, feeling as though she was made of stone, paralyzed the same way she sometimes was right after shooting a speedball. She had never told anyone, except for Luis, that her daughter Frankie was the product of a rape. But now Beatrice LaCroix, damn her, had figured it out.

Which meant Raina would be forced to reconsider her entire fucked up world of tangled truth and lies.

"You were raped," she heard Beatrice saying again, not as a question nor as an accusation, but with a voice far more tender than anything she'd heard from the woman until now. She wanted to melt into Beatrice's warmth right then, but the murky haze cleared and she saw the image.

"I have to write it down," Raina said.

> I can still see his dark curly hair, his shiny black eyes. I can feel his weight on my body. His sweaty skin. His rough hands pressing down on my shoulders. I can smell his breath, rotten as the dead fish at the local market down the street. I can see his dark erection.

She handed the page to Beatrice. "It was the night after I'd met the Sudanese boy, and I'd gone out looking for him after the chaperones had gone to bed. This Italian guy came up to me and struck up a conversation. I had a bad feeling about him. But before I could make it back to my hotel, he was on me."

Now, even though she was sitting in the safety of Beatrice's office, and sixteen or so years had passed, Raina could still feel the cramping in her stomach and the tearing in her vagina from his forceful thrusting. Even now she could feel a hot tear trickling down her cheek.

Beatrice quietly sat down beside Raina, setting her hand gently on Raina's arm. She asked if Raina had ever told the field trip chaperones about what happened.

"No," Raina said. "I was too ashamed. And I knew I'd get in trouble. I'd get sent home."

"Did you tell your parents?"

"No. They would never have believed I wasn't to blame. They were always pissed off about everything I did, and they always said I was loose. They wouldn't have understood. They would've just said I asked for it, and they would have punished me. So I left home. I ran away.

"And when I met Luis, he didn't think of me as damaged goods. He said he loved me no matter what. He said he'd help me with my baby. And then he died."

"And still you didn't go home to your parents," Beatrice said, her forehead now creased with what Raina assumed, and hoped, was sympathy.

"No, I didn't."

"I see. That must have been a frightening time for you," Beatrice said. And then a light blinked on the wall next to the door. "Excuse me, my next client is waiting in the lobby. I'm going to ask her to come back later."

Once she'd stepped out of the room, Raina's tears began to flow. She wept for Luis, for Frankie. For herself. And for her mother, whom she'd so completely cut out of her life. Maybe that was her biggest mistake. Maybe she hadn't given her mother enough credit.

"Rape is never your fault," Beatrice said, a box of tissues in her hand when she returned and sat beside Raina again. "I can't say this for a fact, but I want to believe your mother and father would have known that."

Raina's tears kicked up a notch.

"But I'm not saying this to make you feel bad about not telling them what happened. You did what you thought you had to do. That's what life is all about, right?"

Raina was hunched over like an old woman now, her shoulders shuddering. She nodded as she wiped her nose with a tissue.

"You can stop running now," Beatrice said.

They sat for the next while as Raina continued to cry, clumps of used tissue piling up on the loveseat between them. Her sinuses grew stuffy and she could barely breathe through her nose anymore. Finally, she mustered the energy to ask the question that had been hovering.

"Are you saying I've been running away from Frankie all this time because of the rape?"

"Perhaps," Beatrice said, taking both of Raina's hands into hers. Her eyes were moist, too. "And that's understandable, Raina. She's the embodiment of your wound. She's the tangible reminder of what happened. Every time you see her, a part of you remembers, even if only on a subconscious level."

Raina leaned back and closed her eyes. "So I've been doing the same thing to Frankie that my biological mom did to me? I've been abandoning her?" She pressed the heels of her hands into her eyes. "It's a fucking never-ending cycle, isn't it? First I get abandoned, and in return I hate my adoptive mother, who didn't deserve my anger, and basically kick her out of my life. Then I abandon my own daughter, who didn't deserve that, and now she detests me. What next, Beatrice? How many more lives do I have to fuck up?"

"Raina," Beatrice said. "Your past is done, but how you hold those memories, how you choose to incorporate them into your future narrative, is up to you. Abandonment is a heavy word, and we should probably spend some more time exploring what really happened with your birthmother. From what I know, she placed you with your mother and father as an act of love, not abandonment. But right now I want you to be gentler with yourself."

She picked up the candy bowl.

"You're like this crystal bowl, Raina: strong and beautiful. And multi-faceted."

Raina looked at the bowl, remembering the first time she was here and stole the M&Ms.

"You obviously love Frankie," Beatrice said.

"Yeah, well if I loved her so much, why would I have turned into who I am now? A fucked up whore?"

"You're not alone," Beatrice said. "There are a lot of girls and women who won't admit to being raped because they don't want to worsen the trauma. Who are afraid of not being believed, or of being blamed for the assault. And then they wind up doing the unthinkable: they wind up living promiscuous lives. Freud called this repetition compulsion, an unconscious attempt to take charge of your life and extinguish the pain. In your case, you turned to prostitution, and as you said, once you get into that world, it's hard to get out. I'm not saying this happens to all rape victims, but it's not an unusual development, either."

Beatrice placed each of her hands on Raina's shoulders. "You can handle this, Raina. I know you can. You will. You'll get clean, and you'll get your daughter back."

"I don't know," Raina said, her voice weak. "I don't even know where Frankie is right now."

"We'll find her," Beatrice said, her voice now also a whisper. "When you're ready."

Raina went into the private bathroom. She ran cold water from the tap and cupped her hands under it, then lowered her face to her hands. She felt like she'd been on fire and then doused in ice water. Pain to soothe the pain, but not at all healed. Worse in fact. She dried her face with one of Beatrice's pretty hand towels, and when she was done, she avoided looking in the mirror. Beatrice had said that written words reflect back to you like a mirror. But the homeless woman told Raina that a mirror is a dangerous thing. Truth was: Raina knew, if she looked, she'd scare herself shitless. There would be a madwoman leering at her. A woman with wild hair. Frightened, bloodshot eyes. Scarring inside and out.

The imagined reflection ignited so much anger and self-hatred that Raina felt as though she was going to explode. Go up in flames like those silk draperies all those years ago. She needed to get out of there.

"Are you going to sit down again?" Beatrice asked when Raina came out. "What's wrong, Raina? You look anxious. Would you like a glass of ice water?"

Raina didn't know what she wanted. Not water. Not booze. Not even drugs right now. She had never felt this way before, this mounting of anxiety. She paced back and forth behind Beatrice's chair. She picked up the crystal bowl and tried to imagine why Beatrice said she was like the bowl. Strong? Beautiful?

Hardly.

She hated that bowl almost as much as she hated herself. She just wanted to heave it at Beatrice's head. Or at least throw the fucking thing toward the lake view window. How good it would feel to fling her arm wide and watch the goddamn thing sail across the room into an explosion of fireworks. Red and blue and green and yellow candies scattered everywhere. The bowl and the window both shattering, with hundreds of pieces of glass falling to the carpet. Glittering like lethal snowflakes.

She cradled the bowl in her hands. It was heavy. Heavy with toxic lead like the crystal bowls her mother had collected. If she threw it, it might not even break. Perhaps a chip here, a hairline crack there. But, for the most part, it would probably remain intact. It probably couldn't be broken, no matter how hard she tried.

Let someone write a poem about that.

She carried the bowl to the window, where she looked first south, and then north, along the lake. Lincoln Park Zoo was just a few blocks north. Like some of those animals, Raina had not been born in captivity but had somehow become trapped in a world where she didn't belong. Whoever came up with the idea of caging wolves and seals and lions in the middle of a big city? She thought of how she used to hear their howls and barks and roars, back when she lived with her parents at their fancy condo. She had wanted to run down to the zoo at night and set them all free. Let them all run away, to wherever it was they belonged. As it turned out, it was Raina who had run, and then Frankie. But now Raina was back, and as she pressed her ear to the cold window, holding the bowl to her chest, she listened for the animals and the sound of all their sorrows.

# RUNNING WITH
# GHOSTS

# Her Defiance

—ANN TEPLICK

is a barbed wire tetnused with rust is the crust
of a canker the lunge of a panther
when you tell her you've had it with suffering
enough is enough, when you tell her
she needs to screw her head onto her neck
not backwards or sidewards but forwards
is the scar in the swath of cotton is the venom's steam
is the cream with the maraschino cherry is the Rainier,
Royal Ann, and Gold is preserved in brine is the sulfur
dioxide, calcium chloride is the FD&C Red 40
is the cocktail the Molotov is the petrol bomb the poor
man's grenade is the urban gorilla. Just wants to be loved.

**"I CAN'T TAKE IT** any longer. She's turning into a slut."

Sixteen-year-old Sierra sat upstairs in her room, eavesdropping on the landline phone conversation between Dawn, her evil stepmother, and Dawn's own grandmother, Great-Grandma Josephine.

Did Dawn really call her a *slut?*

"This isn't what I signed up for," her stepmother continued, and a hint of pride swept over Sierra. At least she was making Dawn miserable in return. "Why did she turn out this way? What am I doing wrong?"

"You mustn't blame yourself, Dawn," G-G Jo said. "You've done everything you can over the last ten years; she's just taken a few wrong turns along the way. You need a break, that's all. And so does she."

"What she needs is a break from her vagabond friends," Dawn said.

But the truth was just the opposite: Sierra needed a break from meddling grown-ups. Especially Dawn.

"Don't worry," G-G Jo said. "Send her down to me for the summer. I'll straighten her out."

*What?*

When Dawn agreed, Sierra clicked the phone off and threw it on the bed. No way would she be sent to live with her ancient step-great-grandmother in Northern California for the whole freaking summer! Especially because G-G Jo didn't have any claim on Sierra whatsoever. This wasn't fair! Just because she didn't get a summer job or run track or play some namby-pamby flute like those kids who went to Dawn's church, she was being sent away? And because she stole a little makeup and beer? Maybe if Dawn gave her a bigger allowance she wouldn't have to steal.

And she couldn't believe her own stepmother would call her a slut. So she wasn't a virgin anymore. Big deal. She couldn't help it that she was hot, that boys liked her, and that she liked orgasms, which Dawn had probably never had. But still, Sierra didn't deserve to be called a slut. Especially because Dawn had no idea what she was talking about—no idea how often Sierra did have sex or with whom.

The problem with being a teenager is that you don't get any respect. And you don't have any control over your life. And you're treated like dog shit. This was what Sierra was still thinking when she and Dawn checked in at the airport for a flight to Camp Punishment, and still thinking when they pulled up in a taxicab at G-G Jo's, where she'd be trapped like a cat in a cage.

G-G Jo showed Sierra to the guest room. It was about the size of her bathroom at home, decorated with lace and other frilly stuff and lined with shelves that displayed hundreds of porcelain figurines. (Probably a set-up for Sierra to get in trouble, if she accidentally broke one or whatever.) But the bed was super soft, and just as she lay back on it thinking she could handle this for a couple of days (not a whole summer, obviously), Dawn called her out to the backyard. *Fuck.* Sierra hauled herself off the bed and obeyed the call, not even quite sure why she did, only to find a hoe, a shovel, and a pair of god-awful floral gardening gloves waiting for her. It was her first day here and already she was being forced to work under the hot sun like a West Coast Cinderella, digging little holes for new plants and pulling out weeds while her step-great-grandmother and stepmother sat in the backyard under an awning with a couple of tall glasses of lemonade that were decorated with froufrou sprigs of fresh mint. A dog that looked nearly as old as G-G Jo panted at their feet.

*Wasn't slavery outlawed like a long time ago?*

But Sierra, having no choice apparently, began to slam the hoe into the soil, feeling as pissed as that caged cat with every stroke. At least Dawn was going to be leaving soon (hopefully within the hour, hallelujah) to fly back to Oregon. And the other good news was that Sierra heard G-G Jo tell Dawn that, if Sierra's chores were completed on time and without griping by the end of the afternoon, she'd be *granted the freedom* to explore the redwood forest, out there beyond the vegetable garden and through the white picket gate.

"There's no place for her to get into trouble out there," G-G Jo said.

*Oh yeah? Watch me.*

Sierra stopped for a minute and rested her arm on the shovel, wiping sweat from her forehead with her other hand as she looked out into the forest. Dense and dark, it stretched on forever. A girl could get lost in a place like that.

So she worked hard, barely stopping to say goodbye to Dawn, and when her step-great-grandmother said it was okay, she headed for the gate. The dog sniffed at her when she passed by, as if it would have wanted to come along in its younger years. (Sorry, sucker!)

The redwood grove grew denser as she padded along the soft trails. She forgot about her sore digging muscles and blistered hands once she started to imagine she was hiking with her uncle, a major nature commando sort of dude who was always hiking through forests or exploring jungles or climbing mountains or diving oceans. He and her father were both mountaineers, but her uncle was way cooler than her dad, and he'd once promised to take Sierra climbing on the big mountains when she officially became a teenager. Which meant he should have started taking her along with him three years ago, but because she got in a little trouble over the past few years, Dawn had decided she couldn't go with Uncle Jay. *It wasn't safe for a girl like Sierra to go exploring with Uncle Jay. He takes too many risks. He's not a good example for a girl like her.*

As if Dawn actually cared about Sierra. As if Dawn was an expert on everything. And there was one thing she didn't know anything about, that was for sure: how to *live*. Dawn didn't know the meaning of fun. Her main claim to fame was *control*, as in controlling other people.

And her other specialty was punishment. When Sierra's friends got in trouble, they didn't get detention or suspension like she did. Their parents came to their rescue. But not Dawn. She refused to help Sierra one bit, saying she needed to be accountable for her own actions and deal with the *consequences*. And because Dawn controlled Sierra's father like a puppet, he was of no help at all either. The only *help* Dawn offered was constantly praying for guidance or whatever, which was ironic because Dawn certainly didn't practice the forgiveness she preached.

So anyway here she was, wandering through a forest by herself, thinking about her uncle who at this very minute was up in Alaska on another expedition. Without her. (Which totally sucked.)

Uncle Jay was awesome. He was like fifty years old but he had the body of a twenty-something-year-old: tanned, strong biceps, no flab. He wasn't very tall, so his eyes were at Sierra's level, and whenever he looked at her she felt like he was looking into her, like he really understood what she was saying, and even thinking. She could open up to him about boys and other things that she could never talk with Dawn or her own father about. If he wasn't her uncle, and if he was a bit younger, she would've had a major crush on him.

A breeze startled Sierra back to reality, and she became aware of shadows that seemed to be moving alongside her through the forest. She knew she should turn back. G-G Jo would be expecting her soon for dinner (Pot roast and Jell-O? Yeah, right.)

But she couldn't turn back. There was this thing building inside her, a feeling that took hold of her periodically, something she could control no more than she could control her monthly period. Just as headaches and cramps foreshadowed her periods, this sensation of restlessness tingled in her bones for a day, sometimes two, like an alien slithering through her bones, and then suddenly, *kapow*! She'd find herself doing something forbidden and gnarly and totally awesome.

Plus, the idea of doing something that would piss off Dawn was pretty sweet.

So she kept going, and veered to the east, trying to take mental notes of landmarks so she could find her way home, the way Uncle Jay had taught her. Situational awareness, he'd called it. A bent trunk here, a huge spider web there. Three saplings standing only inches from one another and a fallen bird nest on the ground between them. She had it under control.

Until she heard something.

The sounds weren't discernable at first, some sort of rumble, or a whirring of the wind. But then as she drew closer she figured it out. Her heart inched higher in her chest. Just beyond the last line of redwoods sat a row of small homes with unkempt yards. In front of one of the houses: a group of teenage boys.

And not just any boys. These were dressed in black leather and denim. Bandanas hung round their necks. Cigarettes dangled from their lips. And shiny black motorcycles were lined up in the driveway. The sound of heavy metal music and the smell of weed and trouble drew her closer yet. This was exactly the sort of scene her pseudo-Buddhist-vegan-hippie father disliked and her ultra-Christian stepmother abhorred. Her stomach growled, but there was no freaking way she was turning back now. She crept forward.

Finally, Sierra couldn't handle the temptation any longer. She ripped off the ugly blouse Dawn had made her wear that day before leaving home, revealing a black halter top she'd smuggled underneath (along with a couple of condoms in her jeans pocket). She tossed the blouse over a branch, then combed her fingers through her hair and used her pinky fingernail to check for any makeup clumps in the corner of her eyes. Her imagination ran wild.

One of the boys smiled at her right away when she stepped out from the trees. He had long, straggly blonde hair that hung well below his eyes and a blond scruff beard. A tight black t-shirt and equally tight jeans looked as though they'd been molded onto his body like clay from Sierra's high school ceramics class. His hands were as big as dinner plates.

He walked over to her and asked if she wanted to party. She said yes. He pulled a small pipe from his back pocket and lit it. She smoked a bowl, and then he did, too. Sierra liked the idea that his mouth was right there on the pipe where hers had been, their saliva and germs already comingling. They grinned at each other quietly for a couple of minutes, and then he asked if he could show her something in the woods.

Before she knew it, they were in the forest making out, and the danger of it all thrilled her, especially with the way his hips pressed against hers and the rough tree bark dug into her back. The smoky smell of his breath blended with the woodsy forest aroma and she could barely tell where he ended and the rest of the world began. It must have been fifteen minutes before they came up for air and he introduced himself as Dougie.

"Let's slow down," she said to him, taking him by the hand and trying to lead him out from the trees, toward the light.

"I don't know slow," he said, pulling her back. Her heart lit up like a flashing signal alerting her to sharp curves ahead. For an instant, she saw Dawn's face, and then, pulling away from Dougie, she headed toward his friends. She knew full well he'd follow. (Boys didn't *not* follow her.) She adjusted her halter top.

"Hey assholes, this is Sierra," Dougie said from behind her. His friends all nodded and laughed and gave him a thumbs-up. Sierra wondered what gestures he might have been making back there. She turned around and caught his eyes.

Deep and blue, they reminded her of Uncle Jay's. They were remarkable. Reckless. Relentless.

"Take me for a ride?"

Now his eyes brightened; it was as though she'd asked a mountain lion if it wanted a slab of fresh meat. He nodded his head sideways toward what seemed to be the biggest Harley there.

"Anyone got an extra brain bucket?" he called to his friends. No one answered, so he handed her his helmet.

"Here, put this on. We're gonna hit some twisties."

She put on the helmet, climbed onto the bike, and held onto Dougie tightly, excitement heating in her veins. At first they rode through town, with the sound system turned up super loud and the engine roaring like a ginormous monster. Old ladies and mothers with small children stared at them as they whizzed by. If only her friends, if only her father and Dawn, if only Uncle Jay could see her now.

Soon they were heading north through the curves of Highway 1. The twisties. The wind blew Sierra's brunette mane wildly where it hung below the helmet. As Dougie accelerated, Sierra gripped tighter around his waist. The world blurred past. On the left: the inky Pacific Ocean dotted with whitecaps, the sun threatening to drop below the horizon. On the right: slopes teeming with waving grass and chaparral. They didn't have scenery like this back home in Central Oregon, where the land was as brown and dry and boring as a recycled-paper grocery bag. (And they sure as shit didn't have boys like this, either. Or at least she hadn't found them.) The bike sped up.

When Dougie pulled off to a viewing area, Sierra was relieved for the break. She took a deep breath. But then he turned his head to the side to peer at her.

"You okay if we take it up a notch?" he asked.

"You mean faster? Yeah!"

He studied her, then said maybe they should rest there a few minutes first.

She was confused about his intentions, but this complexity actually drew her deeper in. She got off the bike to stretch, legs wobbly. She took the helmet off and the wind blew her hair across her face and into her mouth. He reached up and pulled a few strands from her lips.

"You okay?" Dougie asked.

"Yeah," she said. "I'm fine." And it was then she realized she felt something different about Dougie than she had for all the other boys she'd been with. He was the first to make sure she was okay.

She turned to face the ocean, which was churning against rough rocks far below. Her heart was still racing, as though it was still on the bike. On the one hand, Sierra wanted him to come to her, to kiss her. But, on the other hand, she didn't. This was partly because she was a long way from G-G Jo's house, without a cell phone (because Dawn had confiscated it from her before they left home), and she could practically hear Dawn's voice saying Sierra was *asking for trouble*. But that wasn't the only reason she wanted to hold off. She turned back around, expecting—and hoping—to see Dougie looking hungrily at her. Instead, she found him gazing across the road and taking a drag from a joint.

She wondered how high he was going to get.

"What's over there?" she asked, reaching for the joint. (The more she smoked, the less he could.) "Do you see something?"

"The Miwok Indians called that the Mountain by the Bay," Dougie said, the wind stealing his voice and tossing it behind them, out into the salty air. He told her about the tribe that used to live in these lands. *How weird*, she thought. *One minute he's a badass biker boy, the next he's some sort of historian.* She studied his face, his eyes, thinking she could fall in love with him. And then his expression hardened.

"They were hostile son-of-a-bitches, those Miwoks. Especially toward white women." His look gave her a shiver. "They murdered some of my ancestors, you know. Sometimes I think I can see their ghosts, in the shadows up there." He pointed to the hills. "The men being murdered, the women being raped. One of these days—"

She shivered again, thinking of the shadows she'd seen in the forest. She didn't like his hostile tone or the image of his ancestors' ghosts. "What? What's going to happen one of these days?"

"One of these days, there'll be payback."

He reached for the joint, and she considered tossing it away, out of his reach, but was afraid to. (How can you be both afraid of, and falling in love with, someone at the same time?) She relented and gave him the joint and, after he took another toke, he smiled that luscious smile again and lowered his face toward hers so gently she couldn't imagine him doing anything hostile to anyone, not even the Miwoks. He was so tough, yet so tender, same as Uncle Jay.

He took her chin between his index finger and his thumb and held it delicately, as if she might break if he pressed too hard, and he kissed her softly, tauntingly, until she couldn't take it any longer. The wind and waves were roaring all around her, and she pulled in closer to him and lifted one of her legs up high around his hips. When he ran his tongue down her bare neck, the combination of his wet tongue and the Pacific breeze and his hint of revenge brought goose bumps out along her neck and pretty much everywhere else.

And then, just when she was ready to completely open herself to him, thinking *what the hell—let's do this*, he surprised her once again by putting out the joint and saying it was time to get back on the bike. He had one more thing to show her, he said, and his abrupt stop to their groping made her kind of crazy but it also kind of made her love him even more. She put on the helmet.

They were back on the bike then, heading further away from where she was supposed to be. The wind and the weed prevented her from thinking about pretty much anything except that her crotch was right behind Dougie. She held him tight around his waist and tried to anticipate what his next surprise might be. So she didn't really notice the sharp curve in the road.

Apparently neither did he.

Sierra didn't remember flying through the air, or landing on a slope and rolling downhill where prickly brush raked at her back. And she certainly had no recollection of the sound a Harley makes when part of it smashes into a eucalyptus tree.

Later that evening, she awoke. Irritating tubes were sticking up her nose. Her right arm felt heavy, and she saw, when she opened one eye, that it was in a cast. An IV needle was stuck into the top of her left hand. A TV was mounted on the wall opposite her. Something was beeping behind her. She realized she was in a hospital but didn't know why.

Then someone placed a hand on her shoulder.

It was her father, looking weary, with baggy circles under his eyes. Dawn sat beside him, looking like her usual bitchy self: eyes cold, mouth turned up on one side only, the way she always looked whenever she was inconvenienced.

"Dad?" It hurt to speak.

He leaned over Sierra's hospital bed. "Shh. Don't talk. Just rest. We're here now."

Dawn stood up beside him. She was the last person in the world Sierra wanted to see. "Do you remember anything?" Dawn asked.

Sierra closed her eye, in part to shut out the image of her evil stepmother, and in part to try to remember something. Anything. She was foggy, like she sometimes got when partying. (There had been mornings when she'd awakened and not even known who she was, let alone where she was or what day it was.) Was this a school day? No, she was on summer break.

She remembered G-G Jo's house. And the old dog. The grueling garden work. The white picket gate. The forest. Her mind went blank then, until she recalled standing along a highway looking over the Pacific Ocean. She was with someone. Who was it? She saw a boy, a superhot boy with a motorcycle. (Or was that a dream? She couldn't tell.) She looked up at her father, whose forehead was crinkled, like it always got whenever he'd have to pick her up from the police station or detention at school.

"What, Dad? What's wrong?"

When he began to weep, Sierra glanced down at the sheet over her body. Was she all there? She had a splitting headache. She'd seen movies where people had lost their legs and didn't even know it. *Oh my god.*

"I'm sorry," her father blubbered out. He turned his back and walked across the room, looking out the door as he blew his nose into a handkerchief (which Sierra had always thought totally gross that he didn't use a tissue). Then Dawn stepped into her line of sight.

"You gave us a good scare, honey."

Sierra didn't want to hear that *honey* shit. What she wanted was for Dawn to stop talking to her like she was a child. Or to just disappear completely. But of course Dawn wouldn't do either of those things. She started in on the old lecture about how Sierra had better learn to make *wiser choices.* About how Sierra's lifestyle was causing *too much stress* for her father and the entire family. About how it was time Sierra grow up and *show some responsibility,* blah blah blah. Sierra's mind, mercifully, wandered off.

(Dougie. That was his name. The boy with the bike. She remembered kissing him. And smoking a joint with him. Something about Indians.)

"I'm sorry, Dad," Sierra said, looking past Dawn at her father's back.

He turned around, his eyes now so red they looked like zombie eyes.

"I'm sorry if I'm causing you so much pain."

"Oh, Sierra, I know you don't mean to. I'm just grateful you're all right."

She didn't believe him. "If I'm all right then why are you crying?"

"There's something else that's happened. I didn't want to tell you like this. But you need to know."

She glanced down at her legs again. She wiggled her toes. "What?"

"Ironically, you aren't the only one who's had an accident."

Sierra tried to recall an accident. But her brain wasn't cooperating. Same as whenever she had to take a test at school. Sometimes her brain just checked out, like a traveler checking out from a motel room. No forwarding address.

And then she thought about the motorcycle boy. "You mean Dougie? Is he all right?" She heard a machine start to beep faster.

"Who's Dougie?" Dawn asked.

"A boy. A boy I think I met."

Her parents gave each another one of those parental exchanges that Sierra had seen so many times, the *what-are-we-going-to-do-with-her* look.

"We don't know anything about that...that boy," Dawn said. "Although I'm sure we'd like to know who he was and how you already met a boy on your first day here. You were supposed to be with G-G Jo. She's been worried sick."

*God, she was soooo annoying.*

"In fact," Dawn went on, "I'd like to know more about how you landed in this hospital."

"Dawn," Sierra's father said, using his stern parental voice for his wife, which was the first good thing Sierra had heard so far since waking up. Dawn was the one getting in trouble now. (Totally awesome.)

The beeping on the monitor slowed down.

"Well then who are you talking about? Who else had an accident? Is G-G Jo all right?"

Again, Dawn and Sierra's father exchanged knowing looks, *Mr. and Mrs. Know-it-all*, and Sierra felt as she had several years earlier as a naïve child.

"Your Uncle Jay," her father blurted out, now breaking down again. Although he was referring to his wife's brother, it was he who had been close to Sierra's uncle for many years and, in fact, it was through Uncle Jay that Sierra's father had met Dawn.

"Uncle Jay?"

What were they talking about? Sierra tried to clear her foggy mind. She remembered she'd been thinking about him when she was walking through the forest, but she couldn't remember what she'd been thinking about. All she knew for sure was that she loved Uncle Jay, and now her parents were acting like something was wrong. Very, very wrong.

Her father wiped at his stream of tears. "His plane went down, sweetheart. In Alaska."

Sierra felt a new roaring in her head. Her dad was saying something but she couldn't focus on the words; all she could think about was Uncle Jay and all she could see was his face, and the way it lit up whenever he talked about his adventures. She'd just talked to him the night before he left on his trip. He'd told her about the Alaskan climb he was heading out for, and how he'd be gone for a few weeks. She'd heard the joy in his voice and wished so much she could have gone with him. If she had, she wouldn't have been sent to G-G Jo's.

"What do you mean his plane went down? When? But he's okay, right, Dad? Uncle Jay's okay?"

Her father didn't answer. He didn't need to.

There had to be some mistake. But now that she thought about it, she hadn't heard from her uncle since he'd left on his trip, and normally he would send her a text or something.

"We just got the call today," her dad said. "The plane went down a few days ago in a remote area. They're still trying to get to the wreckage."

This had to be a lie, something Dawn made up to upset Sierra. That was the only explanation. Either that or Sierra was having a really bad nightmare.

"Please leave," Sierra said, pressing her eyes shut. "I want to be alone."

Her father and stepmother continued to sit there for a while, ignoring her request, disrespecting her need for privacy the same way they barged into her room at home whenever they felt like it. Her father tried to console her with some lame words; her evil stepmother babbled about something Sierra refused to even hear. Finally, they left the room. Only after she heard Dawn's little heels click clack down the hospital linoleum floor, and the elevator button ding, did her brain clear up enough to think.

But she didn't like where her thoughts were going. She knew this wasn't a story Dawn made up. And that it wasn't a nightmare. Her brain kept forcing her to see a little plane crashed into a mountainside and her uncle's bloody body sprawled across the snow. Her brain kept telling her that, if she hadn't been such a fuck-up, she might have been in Alaska with Uncle Jay. Or maybe they would have gone somewhere else entirely. Sierra got so mad at the way she was thinking that she picked up the pink plastic pitcher of water by her bedside and threw it across the room.

Now she was able to think other thoughts. Now she thought about the motorcycle ride, and Dougie, and she remembered how his lips had felt, and how gently he had held her chin, and how he had asked if she was okay. She remembered the wind blowing his hair, and how strong his shoulders had felt. She remembered a funny little mole on his ear lobe and a tattoo of Chinese symbols on his neck. She remembered feeling something she'd never felt before, and she wondered if that was love.

She needed to find out where Dougie was. She pressed the call button for a nurse and asked for more water. When the nurse came in and asked what happened to the pitcher and why there was water everywhere, Sierra said she had a little accident.

"Speaking of accidents, can you tell me if the boy who was driving the motorcycle I was on came to the hospital too?"

The nurse's strict expression softened, and just as her father hadn't needed to reply to her question about Uncle Jay, the nurse didn't need to answer either.

The next evening, Sierra was discharged from the hospital and had to wear an ugly lavender velour sweatshirt and matching velour pants that Dawn had brought for her, compliments of G-G Jo. When she got back to G-G Jo's house, Sierra retreated directly to the guest room, refusing to speak to anyone. There was no point in it anymore. There was no point in much of anything. Including love.

Yes, she had fallen in love with Dougie. And he with her. She was sure of it. That explained why they had taken it slower than either of them wanted to. They hadn't wanted to fuck. They had wanted something more. They'd gotten back on the motorcycle, she now remembered, because Dougie wanted to show her something else. Maybe it was a special place. A cabin in the woods. A secluded beach. Maybe it was a place they would share with one another, just the two of them. Now she would never find out what it was.

There was a slight knock on the door, and G-G Jo came in with a cup of chicken noodle soup and some saltines. Sierra pretended to be asleep and left the food on the nightstand untouched. Her father came in later with her pain medicine, which she only pretended to swallow. Dawn tentatively brought in a pile of magazines and the local newspaper, acting as though Sierra had stashed a sawed-off shotgun beneath her covers and was planning to blow the evil stepmother away (which Sierra would have considered if she'd had such a weapon). Even the old dog tiptoed around her.

It wasn't long before Sierra grew tired of people waiting on her, treating her like she was one of those fragile porcelain figures lined up on G-G Jo's shelves. She was sore from lying around in that hospital bed and from the crash, too. She was already sick of her cast. She wanted to sleep but couldn't, maybe because she was afraid of where her dreams might lead.

She picked up the newspaper that Dawn had delivered, trying to get her mind off all the unwelcome thoughts bouncing around in her head. She only skimmed the pictures and headlines, not looking for anything in particular, and she was certainly not interested in boring shit about the economy or the Middle East. She was about to wad the whole damn paper up into a giant ball and heave it across the room when a headline on page eight caught her eye.

### GIRL SURVIVES FATAL MOTORCYCLE CRASH

A hospital spokesman said a teenage girl involved in a fatal motorcycle crash along Highway 1 last night was "remarkable, having extracted herself from the twisted metal of the motorcycle and removing herself to a safe distance to await emergency personnel." The unidentified girl, who wore a helmet, suffered only minor injuries, but the driver of the motorcycle was killed.

Dougie *was* dead.

She had known him for less than one day, and he had given her his helmet, and now he was gone forever.

Why did the newspaper call her *remarkable*? Sierra didn't feel the least bit remarkable. If she had been so remarkable, able to remove herself from the bike and move to a safe distance, why couldn't she help Dougie? If she had been so remarkable, why hadn't she insisted he wear a helmet too?

Sierra wasn't remarkable. She was guilty. Guilty as sin. She ripped the newspaper into shreds with such vehemence that the pain nearly brought her, and the dog cowering by the door, to tears.

She had to get out of there.

She climbed out of bed and raised the window, careful not to bump her broken arm on the casement and hoping the dog wouldn't rat her out. She crept alongside the house to the patio, where it was dark, the yard lit only by the incandescent light shining through the kitchen and family room windows. She heard the clinking of dishes coming from the kitchen sink, and the sound of the dog now lapping water from a bowl, its tags clanging against a metal bowl. She heard her father's new age music through another screen window.

Over all the other sounds, she heard Dawn's condescending voice, coming from high up on that pedestal of perfection, the sound of a persistent wasp. Dawn, the woman who lived a monotonous and risk-free life with her organic produce and hybrid car and obsession with fitness and yoga, who looked down upon her own brother and her only stepdaughter. A woman whom, for some unknown reason, Sierra's father had chosen to marry.

"This is what happens to people who take risks," Dawn said, her voice dropping when she said the word *risk*, as though it were a swear word she shouldn't be saying. "She's just like my brother was, making poor choices all the time. We have to do something about this, you know. We can't allow her to go on like this. Something else will happen."

Sierra stepped back from the window, practically falling over a planter filled with petunias. And then came that tingling restlessness again, a rushing force that started way down in the soles of her feet, then rising upward like a geyser through every vein or nerve or whatever in her body. She needed to run. She needed to scream. She sprinted to the back of the yard and hurtled herself over the fence, not bothering with the gate and not worrying about her arm, which now seared with pain after she landed on the ground. She got up; she kept on going. She crashed through the forest with Dawn's voice close on her heels. She tripped over a fallen log in the dark, and twisted her ankle upon landing, but she got up yet again and kept running as fast as she could, so fast that wind whirred past her as she cut through the air, so fast that she busted through dozens of silky but tenacious spider webs strung from tree to tree without flinching.

Finally, when she could barely breathe anymore, when her ankle had started to swell, and when her throat was stinging from dehydration, Sierra stopped. She rested her hands on her knees. Blood rushed to her head; her pulse throbbed in her ears.

Damn Dawn! Tomorrow, Sierra knew, they would take her back home to Oregon, the experiment of Camp Punishment having failed. She would be hauled off like some sort of juvenile delinquent, and once back home, *changes would be made.* (She'd heard that line countless times.) *Rules would be enforced.* The evil stepmother would ruin Sierra's life yet again.

Sensing her way deeper into the woods slowly now, like a nocturnal animal hunting in the filtered moonlight, she headed east, wishing that Uncle Jay was there with her, guiding her along. He'd know what to do. She stopped for an instant to sniff the air, full with redwood sap, bay leaves, and pungent mushrooms. Once again she saw shadows in the moonlight, making her think of Dougie's story and the Miwok spirits, making her think of what he had said about payback. This led her, again, to think about Dawn.

That bitch thought the whole world revolved around her like she was a sun goddess or something. Maybe if she was a nicer person, Uncle Jay wouldn't have felt like he had to go off and explore the world all the time, getting as far away from his sister as humanly possible. Maybe if Dawn was a little more understanding, and a little less demanding, she and Sierra could have had a better relationship. And if that were the case, who knows? Maybe Sierra wouldn't have gotten in so much trouble. Maybe life would have turned out differently.

But that wasn't the case. She looked up toward the forest's ceiling, the giant redwoods encircling her, like a tribe embracing a newcomer, their needled tops pointing toward the heavens. Her neck began to hurt, but she held her stance, inhaling the forest's fragrance.

And when she righted herself, she knew what she needed to do. She would not allow Dawn to hurt her by calling her names, or to control her with her unreasonable rules, ever again. Maybe that wasn't exactly the payback Dougie had been referring to with the Miwoks, but it was one way Sierra could get back at Dawn. She could take the power away. Yes. Sierra would take her precious memories of Uncle Jay and Dougie and keep going. She'd take their very ghosts right alongside, if they wanted to come. The Miwok victims, too. And whatever guilty shadows wanted to follow her. She didn't know where she would go, or how she would get there, or who she'd find when she got to wherever that was. These uncertainties scared the shit out of her, but the alternative was worse. Maybe she couldn't run from her past, or from mistakes that she or others had made, but at least she could try to make sure her future was *hers*. God damn it, at least she could be true to her self.

Whoever that might turn out to be.

# COCO PALMS

# The Moon

—KIERSTIN BRIDGER

Just when you thought you needed a quiet night,
for there to be soft waves tilting back and forth,
a somber lullaby sung only for you.
When rustling palapas above warm saltillos and
            coconut air
seem the only solution to soothe the blister
of your particular heartbreak—
look a little closer out of the portal of your tired heart.
The moon has her nose pressed against the glass.
She is the return of night-swimming,
and just hatched turtles wading out to sea.
She is the same round-faced witness
that watched as your mother gave birth to you,
saw her stumble in the night and protect you from the fall.
She is the white glow that made your first kiss radiate
            through your cells,
She is breathing-in the miracle of you,
your salty pillow, the quiver of your chin.
Crawl out from under your blanket, child,
she is here beaming at you. She is fortune's wheel
spinning a new tale with her starry ink.

**THEY SIT OPPOSITE** one another at the kitchen table, and when Margee looks across at him, he reminds her, now that he's started to shave his head bald, of a *Periplaneta americanas*, the American cockroach. His scalp is tanned and shiny. His eyes are dark. His demeanor hard. He is not the man he used to be. *The chips in the glass tabletop are evidence of that*, Margee thinks. *Like chips in my heart.*

She sets down the macramé sling she's been making for her orchid and reaches her foot under the table to his. She touches her bare toes to the tip of his loafer. Searching, hoping, one last time. The leather is soft and inviting. But he jerks his foot away as though he's been bitten.

"Vern," she says, picking up a cloth napkin and fanning herself. Her voice is gentle because a calm approach is the best way to tame an angry beast. "The boys are having such a hard time settling in here. With school out of session, there's no way they can possibly make new friends if they're working all day in the back yard. Must you push them so hard?"

He slams the teacup down. It was her Great Aunt Margaret's, and now there's a crack in the ivory china. Her calm approach hadn't worked. But then, when he pushes back from the table and charges into the kitchen, reaching into a drawer for scissors, she realizes it wasn't her fault this time. She realizes what he's doing. She hears the scissors snip.

"Gotcha," he says.

Vern always insists that the best way to kill these six-inch centipedes is by cutting them in half. Margee tried to convince him, once, to spare a centipede's life and just relocate it outdoors. But he'd scoffed at her. Now, she fingers the pearls around her neck as she tunes in to the scrape of her sons' shovels digging into dirt, the clang of metal against rock, the occasional grunt. And as she waits for Vern to return to the table, victorious. She has always worn these pearls every day, to please Vern. One of these days, she won't. Soon.

The toilet flushes. Vern returns to the table.

"I hate those blasted creatures." The glint in his eyes from murdering the little thing rivals the pang in her soul. It was a senseless killing. Unnecessary.

"Now, as for your question about our sons working so hard, I'm trying to teach those boys a lesson or two. I won't have them growing up entitled like the rest of the brats in their generation."

"They've been digging for two days," she says. "They'll be exhausted when they finally get to sailing camp."

"There won't be any sailing camp if they don't get their job done. Damn it, we moved all the way to Hawaii and bought this fucking big-ass house with a gargantuan back yard and we don't even have a single palm tree. It's like we're not even in the tropics."

She doesn't know why he's so angry about all this. Moving here had been his idea. Actually, it had been his demand.

"I know, sweetheart, I know. But can't we take it one step at a time? We're only talking about a couple of silly coconut trees."

His jaw sets, and Margee knows she's pushing him nearer the edge. This whole charade of a conversation is a waste of breath, like so many others lately. She picks up her lemon wedge, and instead of squirting into the teacup, the juice sprays sideways into her eye.

"Jesus." The scorn in his voice is more acidic than the juice itself. He tosses his cloth napkin at her. "Clean yourself up. And fix that bra strap." He gets up and storms outside.

As Margee reaches for her strap, she recalls a time he loved seeing her in lingerie. How gently he would take down the strap, unclasp the bra. But over the years he has changed. His diminishing interest in her, she had first assumed, was because she was aging and gaining weight. But at the same time he is becoming more opinionated, more old-fashioned—even more restrictive—about so many matters in life. It might be because he has two boys about whom he's worried, boys who will soon be facing a complicated world on their own. But it also feels like there's even more to it than that, especially now that they have moved across the ocean, and away from all their old friends and relatives. His temper is shorter, his moods darker.

She could have worn a full t-shirt today, not a tank. Then the bra strap wouldn't be a problem. But it's so hot. She could have begun to cry when he spoke to her that way, but she didn't. Her eyes are as dry and her heart is as hard as the earth in which the boys are digging.

She should never have let him coerce her into this move. She's no better off than the caged animals at the zoo where she worked which she has now left behind. She thinks of Norma the tiger and runs her fingers along the four parallel scars on her neck, then heads outside to see how the boys are doing.

There are two holes in the yard for the palm trees. Manny, the fifteen-year-old, has dug a crater three feet wide and two feet deep. He leans his sweaty, muscular body—naked from the waist up—against his shovel and waits for his father's approval. Ray's hole, several feet away, is noticeably smaller. Ray is also noticeably smaller, especially with his shirt off. Still a skinny twelve-year-old, he is stretched out flat on his back on the Bermuda grass, eyes closed.

"Stand up!" Vern says to Ray when Margee steps out on the lanai, as though performing for her. "Man up. Look alive."

Ray rolls to one side, then pushes off the ground with the fervor of an old man lying beside his grave. His face is red.

Vern circles the perimeter of Ray's hole, his arms crossed against his chest, his nose scrunched as though Kilauea's volcanic sulfur was venting directly from his son's hole. He wipes his forehead against a sleeve, then circles Manny's hole.

"If you were my employee," Vern says to Manny, "you'd be fired."

Manny throws his shovel down, mutters something under his breath, and walks to the edge of the yard overlooking the Pacific, where shades of blue run crosswise, parallel to the horizon. He combs his fingers through his black hair, stretches his arms above his head, and twists his torso from side to side. Margee studies his smooth, tanned skin and strong physique. It won't be long before the island girls are after him, she thinks. If Vern ever lets Manny out of his sight.

"And yours," Vern says to Ray, "is pathetic." Ray slumps back to the ground.

"Come on, Vern. Don't you think these holes are big enough by now?" Margee asks. "You don't want them to be too big for the root balls, do you?"

"What, you think I don't know what I'm doing?"

"No, sweetheart, I'm not suggesting that at all." Although of course that is exactly what she thinks. It's just that sometimes it's easier to agree than to disagree.

Ray squints up, first at his mother and then his father. He reaches for a water bottle on the ground and shakes the last couple of drops into his mouth. Then he stands, slowly, one muscle at a time, and tosses the bottle down. Vern kicks the bottle into Manny's hole.

"Look, just because you were once some sort of animal guru with a la-di-da degree," he says to Margee, "doesn't mean you know everything. I've done the research and I know what I'm doing. So why don't you go dust the furniture or mop the floors, or whatever it is you do, and let me do my job."

Margee opens her mouth, then snaps it shut and looks away. Her husband's shadow and ego loom over her. It's bad enough when he speaks to her this way in private. But when he humiliates her in front of the boys, it's far worse. On days like this, she has to remind herself there are only two reasons she stays with Vern: Manny and Ray.

"Manny!" Vern's voice is a loud bark that reminds Margee of a *Zalophus californianus*, a sea lion. "Get that garbage out of your hole."

Manny turns around, the sapphire water and clear sky a surrealistic backdrop for his dark features and glistening skin.

"What garbage?"

Vern motions, and Manny walks back to take a look at the bottle his father had kicked into his hole. "I didn't do that."

Vern clenches both fists and tightens his jaw. "Are you back-talking me? It's your hole, young man. Your responsibility. Just like the kitchen sink is your mother's. Now get that water bottle out of there."

Manny looks at Margee; she nods at him. "Go on, do what you're told." Again she says this to keep the peace, but also because she wants the boys to go to sailing camp. Manny jumps into his hole, and two yellow birds—finches, she thinks—dart out from a scraggly keawe tree just beyond it. Just like that, they flutter away.

Manny climbs back out with the bottle and walks past Vern, bumping his shoulder and angst against his father before disappearing into the house. Vern clenches his fists again.

"Relax, Vern. Let him go."

He storms into the house after Manny. Margee listens to be sure there's no more arguing or fighting, then flops down on a chaise lounge in the shade, throwing her forearm over her eyes. She can no longer make her husband happy. She isn't even sure if that's her job anymore, or if it ever was. She recalls a conversation from the past. She'd been with her girlfriends on a Florida beach, and with her sister, too, late into the night. They sat beneath the stars and the moon drinking tequila sunrises and reminiscing about their first kisses and deciding how many children they'd have and sharing ideas about how they would, someday, make their future husbands happy.

How naïve they had been.

How she misses those friends. How she misses those times. If only Vern didn't control the credit cards and all the spending, she could go back to visit.

If only she could go back in time.

What is that song about the past? It lurks at the edges of her memory. She can't quite name it yet, but she can hear the rhythm. Yes, it was an old Don Henley song. The first few notes are becoming clearer now, and then the words begin to take shape: something about a Deadhead sticker, a Cadillac. Oh yes, she remembers it now. *A little voice inside my head said don't look back, you can never look back.*

The boys dig for two more days, and Margee can hardly sleep at night, restless in the heat as she lies beside Vern and his staccato snores. She dreams erratically about her sons digging their way to hell, and about the girlfriends she misses back home, and about those birds flying away. She dreams about a tiger's claws just centimeters from her face. She dreams the boys miss their sailboat launch. When she startles herself awake at one point, she's lying in a pool of sweat. Surely another way to earn her husband's scorn: early onset of menopause.

On the third morning, while changing the sheets, Margee takes a look at the stack of books on Vern's nightstand. He has changed his reading habits from history to mystery. She understands neither genre; poetry is her preferred escape. She puts his books back exactly how she found them, feeling as though she's being watched. She quickly turns, but no one is there.

Later in the day, while resting on the lanai, she hears Vern tell the boys to take a break from digging and to start packing for camp while he inspects their work. They are supposed to be down at the marina by 5:00 p.m., in less than two hours. She hurries into the house to help them, then refreshes her makeup and puts on the white top and skirt that compliment her figure so nicely. She wants the boys to remember her as being pretty while they're sailing away.

The boys are sitting in the truck bed, surrounded by their gear, when she heads out the front door.

Ray sees her coming and waves. His smile runs practically the width of the truck. Then Vern comes out from the garage.

"What the hell do you think you're doing?" he says to her.

"Going with you, to the marina."

"Oh no you're not. None of us are going anywhere. Those holes aren't finished." He heads for the back of the truck, reaches in, and heaves one of the boys' duffel bags into the garden. It lands atop the old orchid Margee has been nursing back to health. The one she's been making the macramé sling for. Now the poor thing's stem is broken. Vern reaches in for the other duffel bag.

"Are you joking?" She stands with one leg in the truck, on the passenger side, her purse slung on her shoulder. It is one thing to let him treat her poorly. It is altogether another thing for him to take out his bad moods, or personality disorders, on the boys.

"Those boys have been working like mules," she says. "Let them go to camp."

She peers through the truck's cab window to the boys in the back. Ray had looked so happy a moment ago, and she had felt a rush of something she couldn't quite name. Perhaps the thrill of knowing her beloved son was about to have the time of his life. Or perhaps it was a wallop of envy. Now she feels the electrical charge of rebellion, a sensation she hasn't felt in years.

Vern drops the second duffel bag onto the ground. "The trees are being delivered tomorrow and the holes aren't ready."

The boys look at Margee, who is still standing half-in and half-out of the truck. She swears Ray is now going to cry. She will not let that happen.

"I'll finish for them," she says. "*After* we get back from the marina."

Vern crosses his arms. "No you won't. I know you well enough to know there's no way in hell you'll go down in the holes. You're too claustrophobic."

She ponders this idea. He is right about that silly phobia, and it has gotten worse over the years. But she is not about to let the boys lose this trip just for his stupid palm trees.

"I'll be fine."

"Prove it."

Margee stares at this man, an imposter for the person she once thought she loved. The corner of her mouth twitches. She'd learned, in her former life at the zoo, how to face down terror. A baboon with serious PMS. A brown bear, having a bad GI reaction to some medicine. And then there was Norma the tiger. Margee had even survived Norma. The key, she knows, is to let the animal know who's in charge. With a tiger, you maintain eye contact—that's how she got away after only a single swipe of the claw that nearly fateful day. With a bear, you avoid the eyes. You have to understand each species to know what to do.

But now, with Vern, she isn't sure what to do.

He has locked his eyes onto hers, and he begins to slip the strap of her purse from her shoulder—slowly, not breaking eye contact. Daring her.

"Are you coming, Mom?" Ray asks from the back of the truck. "Come on, Dad. We need to get going."

Neither Margee nor Vern turn to look at their son. They are still staring each other down.

"No," Vern says. "Your mother's decided to get some things done around the house."

"Aww, Mom."

Odd, that he didn't tell the kids that she's going to finish *their* work. Odd, that he didn't blame them for her sacrifice. He has been blaming the boys readily for all sorts of things lately, but not today, and for this alone, Margee is thankful.

"We're going to miss the boat launch," Manny says. She hears the panic in his voice, remembers her dream. She will give up this battle about going to the marina, but she will win the one that lets them go to camp. Everything for the boys. She narrows her eyes at Vern as she climbs out of the truck.

"I knew you'd see it my way," he says. He pats her on the head as though she is a pet. "Guess it's just us guys after all. But as you can see, boys, your mother loves you very much." His words turn her stomach. He has no right to tell them she loves them, not after what just happened, after how he treated her. He has no right to intercede whatsoever between Margee and the boys. But he does it anyway. He has to have ultimate control.

"Oh, and I'll bring home a nice fillet of ono from the fish market," he says to her, after he's thrown the duffels back into the truck. "So we can have a romantic dinner, just the two of us, tonight."

The idea of this both repulses and frightens her.

"But please clean that disgusting barbecue before I get home. And refill those goddamn soap bottles. Jesus, you can't even wash your hands properly when you want to around here."

She glares at him, and thoughts dart around her mind like rabid monkeys in a cage. After he turns the ignition, and revs the engine, and shifts into gear, and peels away, and after she fervently waves and blows kisses to her two sons riding in the back of the truck, she spits where the truck had been parked.

She heads for the backyard but makes a detour into the house. She's not quite ready to face the task of climbing down into those big holes. She calls her sister, and then her two best girlfriends on the mainland, but nobody picks up. She thinks about calling her mother, but she'd hear the same refrain. "You made your bed, now lie in it." She doesn't see how she'll ever be able to lie in that bed anymore.

She resorts to housework for solace—making the boys' beds, sweeping floors, wiping down toilets, folding laundry—all the while luxuriating in the defiance of working so hard in her nice outfit.

She sprays the air with lemon-scented Lysol as she's done for years, ever since Vern had said it was like an aphrodisiac for him, but again the image of lying naked in bed with him is clouded by disgust as thick as volcanic fog.

As she's sponging off the kitchen table for the second time that day, she discovers Vern's beard comb on the seat of his chair, along with a clump of beard hair. She hates when he grooms himself at the table. She mindlessly stuffs the comb and trimmings into the pocket of her skirt for now and goes outside.

Even after all that housework, which is normally therapeutic for her, Margee is nervous about climbing down into those holes. She sits at the lip of Ray's hole, dangling her legs into the empty space, and thinks about how hard Vern has been on the boys, especially little Ray. She recalls how red her son's face was when he flung himself on the ground, how worried she's been about heatstroke. And how blistered his hands were getting. She looks into the hole and estimates it to be about seven feet down to the bottom. There's no way it needs to be so deep for a stupid palm tree. But Vern still insisted it's not big enough. Seven feet down. How bad could it be?

Just as she is ready to jump in, Margee realizes that she is still wearing nice clothes. And all white. She knows she should go back into the house and change into something old and worn. But, yet again, the pulse of rebellion charges through her. It even energizes her. She takes a deep breath, squeezes her eyes shut, and pushes off.

She lands with a thud. After catching her breath, she begins to dig with the shovel Ray had left behind. It's hard work, trying to chip away at the notoriously hard blue rock. The unforgiving sun, even this late in the day, zeroes in on Margee as though she's a target for its rays. Sweat runs down her face and neck and pools between her breasts. She's already thirsty after only fifteen minutes and decides to go get some water.

That's when she realizes her grave mistake. There's no ladder to climb out.

She is stranded.

And it's only seconds until she can't breathe. Her pulse begins to throb in her ears like a tribal drum. The dirt walls start to close in. Her heart races, her breathing shallows. She can't get enough oxygen. She's suffocating. It will be hours before Vern comes home.

Margee's throat grows drier as each minute passes.

*Calm down,* she tells herself. She tries to visualize how Ray had climbed out. He had skittered up the wall like a spider. She tries to replicate his moves. But there's no way; she can't get a finger's grip into these rocky walls.

She tries to use the shovel to create little handholds, but it's too unwieldy; either that or she's too clumsy. She reaches into her pocket for something—anything—that could help her dig some indentations in the rock wall to help her climb out. All she finds is that plastic comb and the disgusting clump of Vern's beard hair. She flicks the hair out of her fingers and down to the ground.

The comb breaks immediately when she tries to use it to dig.

Discouraged, Margee sits down and listens for the occasional car driving by. Whenever one does, slowing for the curve near her driveway, she hollers for help. But no one hears, or at least no one stops.

She will just have to wait for Vern. She tries not to think about how thirsty she is. She curls into a ball at the bottom of the hole. At least it's a little cooler there. But immediately the reddish dirt begins to stain her white clothes, and her rebellious high becomes replaced by fear.

Vern will be furious.

How ironic. Sixteen years ago, he'd been the one trapped in a moat—a zoo moat, and she'd been the one to rescue him. Vern had been the zoo's exterminator, and his insecticide tank had rolled down into the moat. He had climbed down after it and gotten stuck down there. The zookeeper in charge of big cats on that day had made a grave error and assumed the exterminator was gone. He had released Norma, the 300-pound *Panthera tigris altaica* from her indoors cage. Norma had immediately sprinted to the edge of the moat. Margee had been called on the radio when the error was discovered, and she got to the exhibit just as Norma leapt down from her perch. Margee still remembers her own fear as she scrambled down into the moat, much deeper than this measly seven-foot hole. It was an intuitive, albeit foolish, reaction; she had simply known she could not leave the exterminator down there alone with Norma.

Once down in the moat, Margee had approached Norma bravely, cautiously moving into the space between the tiger and the handsome man in a yellow uniform who would later adorn her with gratitude and praise, lift her up onto a pedestal, and become her husband. She had no idea that pedestal would become so shaky over the years.

Now in the hole, Margee traces her fingers along the scars on her neck again and wonders *what if?*

Something catches her eye at the base of the dirt wall to her right. It's a tunnel, about twelve inches in diameter, which she hadn't noticed before. She crouches down, rests the side of her face on the cool soil, and peers through. Sure enough, it leads into Manny's hole, which from this perspective looks bigger, brighter, and far more hospitable. The tunnel is lined with metal, a culvert of sorts. For irrigation? A spider crawls toward her; she picks it up and gently turns it over. It looks like *Theridian grallator*, with red and black smiley face markings on its yellow abdomen. The Hawaiian happy face spider. She sets it down and it hurries through the tunnel.

Margee wonders if it will be easier to climb out from Manny's hold. There's just one problem. There is no way she can fit her hips through the tunnel as it is. She will have to make it bigger. She begins to dig around its edges, careful not to cut herself on the sharp edge of the metal. As long as she keeps moving, she's able to maintain her composure and forget about how frightened she is. Yes, she has to keep digging, or else. Or else what, she doesn't know. But she doesn't want to find out.

Finally, after several hours and a protracted sunset, but also after very little progress with the culvert tunnel, she hears a truck pulling into the driveway. At last. She tries to wipe dirt from her face but suspects she has made it worse. She glances down; her white outfit is filthy.

Soon, a light shines down at her. Vern appears above Ray's hole, holding a flashlight.

"Margee? Are you down there?"

"Thank God," she says, trying to smile up at him when in fact she wants to scream at him and ask what took him so long. He had said he'd be back in time for dinner, but it was just as well that he hadn't followed through on that promise, as she'd forgotten to clean the grill. She reaches her arms up toward him. "Get me out of here, Vern. Please."

He glances around. "How'd you get down there?"

"You'd be proud of me, Vern. I jumped down. But I didn't realize there wasn't a way to climb back out. Silly me."

"What, did you think there was an elevator or something?" He shakes his head, and his tone unsettles her. Now he crosses his arms and the light shines away.

"No, I didn't. Now, can you please give me a hand?" She reaches up further, and rises up on her tiptoes, but he doesn't extend a hand down to her.

"I'll get a ladder," he says.

"Vern!" she calls, but he is gone. When he returns, he has a bottle of sparkling wine and two paper cups instead of a ladder.

"What's this all about?" Margee asks. Her neck aches from looking way up there at him.

Vern pours the wine into the cups, lies on his belly, and reaches one of them down to her. "Here's to our new Hawaiian home," he says. "I'm finally getting what I wanted."

Margee, confused as all hell, takes the cup and, eventually, sips. But something's not right, and she begins to feel sick to her stomach. She doesn't know what he means by that. From her point of view, he'd gotten plenty of what he wanted over the years. Again, she suggests that maybe now would be a good time to get a ladder.

"Not yet," he says. He pours himself another cup—he's on his third, and she hasn't even finished her first. She wants to get out of there. And then he startles and drops his cup. He slaps at his arm, then flicks whatever it was away. It sails through the air and lands in the hole near her foot.

"Shine your light here," she says.

It's the Hawaiian happy face. She reaches down for it, but it isn't moving. Her husband killed the little guy.

"Vern! You didn't need to be so rough! It was harmless. Completely harmless."

He doesn't show the merest sign of remorse. In fact, he looks happier than he had all day. A memory shakes loose in Margee's mind. When he was younger, he'd always looked happiest when he was on the job. As the exterminator.

"Vern, please get me out of here now. I've had enough. Get the ladder."

He nods and walks away. After a few minutes—longer than he needed simply to get a ladder—she calls for him. "Hey, Vern!" She stands with the shovel in one hand, blade up. "Hello? You forgetting something?" She listens, waits. "Vern? Very funny!" She calls louder. "Where are you? Please get me out of here!"

She calls again, and again, but there is no answer, just the clacking of some nocturnal creature. Her heart starts to race, and her breathing immediately shallows once again. She feels light-headed. Her mouth is dry, despite the small sip of wine, and she still feels sick—a heavy, queasy, feeling. A sinking feeling, like this time she's really going to puke. She shouldn't have had that sparkling wine on an empty stomach. As before, she searches for something to use to climb out. She tries to wedge the shovel into the wall to help boost herself out. But it doesn't work. It's useless.

The walls close in, tighter than before. And then, when jazz begins to emanate from the house, along with the smell of barbecue sauce, she knows everything has changed. Everything. Vern has become some sort of monster, and now it's getting late, and everything around her has gone black except for a few stars in the sky. The moon is blocked by clouds, and soon the stars are, too. She curls up at the bottom of the hole and waits, afraid to fall asleep.

But sleep does come, and the next morning Margee awakens to find two plastic bottles of water, a protein bar, and an orange next to her at the bottom of Ray's hole, like the offerings that islanders bring to the volcano to appease the angry goddess Pele.

She knows by now that Vern has clearly gone mad, although she doesn't understand why. She knows she must get out of here, although she doesn't know how. She cries out for help, but her parched voice gets caught in her throat, and the nearest neighbor is several acres away. With such a vast sky overhead and the ocean roaring beneath it, no one can hear her call. Her voice dissipates like mist.

Starving, she eats the fruit after sniffing it, hoping Vern hasn't somehow poisoned it. She drinks half of a bottle of water. And then she starts digging at the walls of the hole again with her fingers. She digs frenetically, as though she is trying to carve out an answer to what is happening as much as she's trying to carve out fingerholds in the dirt wall so she can climb out. But the more she digs, the less progress she makes. Dirt keeps collapsing down to the bottom of the hole, so the hole gets wider but not deeper, and the indentations where her fingers are meant to dig in for purchase won't hold in place. When her fingernails start to bleed, she uses a plastic bottle cap, and when the bottle cap breaks, she takes off her wedding band. It works as a miniature shovel, but the progress she makes with the ring is so slow that Margee worries it will take a lifetime to work her way out.

And that thought frightens her more than any other so far. She doesn't know how much of her life remains.

While taking a break on that first afternoon, she thinks again about her friends, her sister, her mother. Her past. Maybe she should have listened to her mother, who had begged Margee not to marry Vern. *How can you, an animal lover, marry a man who takes such great joy in killing?* Margee had thought her mother had it all wrong, that Vern was just doing his job to protect the wellbeing of the zoo animals, keeping their cages and food free from roaches, rodents, even ants. That's what he'd told her anyway. He'd said he was really an animal lover. And she had believed him. She had also been incensed that her mother had basically called him a killer.

Now, she sees her mother may have been right all along. Not that Vern is necessarily a killer. Margee still can't believe that he is. He is punishing her for some reason, she concludes. But no matter what he has become, he is clearly someone different than the man she married. Is this what happens to all married couples, this drastic change of character and diverging paths, this waking up to a discovery one day that there's an ocean of differences between the two of you? And then, of course, there is the question of whether she is somehow to blame for his metamorphosis.

No, she tells herself, now turning to work on the culvert again. The sun is now hot overhead and she tries to wiggle the edge of the metal back and forth, taking periodic breaks for sips of water as she works. Her fingers slip off the edges from her blood and sweat, but she keeps trying. Finally, after the sharp edge has given her several cuts on her hand, a piece of metal loosens, and Margee feels her adrenaline crank up. She works on the metal edge with renewed enthusiasm. Back and forth, back and forth; eventually, a piece falls off into her hand. Like a cave woman, she has created a new tool. To celebrate, she rests and finishes her water.

She spends the rest of that evening using the piece of metal to dig better finger- and toeholds. She can dig deeper into the rock now, and the indentations she creates are holding strong. But it is still slow going, and her blood and sweat make everything slippery. At the bottom of the hole, the dirt has turned into mud.

On the second morning, Margee awakens to find two more plastic bottles and a papaya. She eats the fruit, then digs all day. For the most part, she does not allow herself to stop for more than a minute or two at a time because, as she discovered on the first day, this gives her too much time to think about how frightened she is, and how dirty she is, and how much she misses her boys. At one point on the second day, however, she allows herself to take a longer break and, wishing she had a book to read, she recalls the books she'd found on Vern's nightstand. She'd read the back covers; one of the books had been about a housewife buried in her own backyard.

Despite the heat, Margee shivers.

And then she starts asking herself how she let this happen. Somehow, she hadn't seen the warning signs. Or the signs that he needs help. Yes, that's it, she begins to think. He'd been the one who had been frightened when he noticed her pulling away from him, and he must have felt like he was losing control. She has somehow driven him to this; it's all been a misunderstanding. If only she can get out of this hole she can help him.

These are some of the thoughts that replay over and over and that, for too long, keep her from going back to work. But there are others, too—thoughts that are less compassionate toward him and also less compassionate toward Margee. *You let him do this to you. This is all your fault. You let him have too much control over the family. You should never have agreed to move here. You should never have married him in the first place. Or saved him from the tiger.*

By the end of the second day, Margee knows she is becoming severely dehydrated. Her tongue feels swollen and she feels dizzy and confused. She is nearly done digging her finger- and toeholds. But she is not ready to climb out. She needs a plan of what to do once she escapes: a plan for survival. She works late into the night and throughout the next day.

Now it is the evening of the third day, and Margee has grown both weak and strong. She is almost ready to execute her plan, which is good because there was no fruit for her this morning when she awoke, and only one water bottle. By now her head hurts nonstop and her legs keep cramping from dehydration. Her stomach feels permanently knotted from lack of food. Her back aches.

Overhead, the sky is purple. A papaya-tinged wisp of cloud floats overhead. She can hear waves lapping at the rocky shoreline in the distance; she imagines the cool, blue water and the ocean whitecaps. She tries to replace her unanswerable questions about what went wrong in the past, and about what Vern might be planning to do tomorrow—or even tonight—and about the mysterious palm trees that were never delivered, with visions of her sons' sailboat on the open sea.

And now, finally, she glimpses what she needs for her plan to be complete, only inches from her bare left foot. *Scolopendra subspinipes*—a centipede, nearly six inches long. She is not afraid; she knows that centipedes avoid humans and will only attack if disturbed or threatened, but she also knows about their bites. She knows how they sink their poisonous fangs into their victims. She knows that a centipede bite hurts like a hot branding iron. And she also knows that, although the bites are rarely fatal, it's possible to have an allergic reaction to the venom. Once, years ago, Vern had an anaphylactic reaction to a wasp sting.

While Margee waits for the centipede to make its next move, she retraces the last three days in her memory, and the last sixteen years, trying one last time to understand what happened, wondering one last time if somehow she brought this on herself, if she has been an unintentional contributor to Vern's madness. One can never know for sure what motivates another being, or what influence we have upon others.

And then she lets her memory focus on that one day—that first day, and she lets herself ask that question one more time: What if she hadn't saved him from the tiger in the moat? If the tiger had killed him, the animal would have been destroyed. She'd had no choice then, but now she does. Soon, she will no longer be trapped. Margee wonders how many other women have found themselves like this, one way or the other, desperate for a way out, and a feeling of sisterhood washes over her like a great, warm wave. The idea that she is not alone strengthens and invigorates her.

The centipede skitters up the dirt wall, paying no attention to her as it heads toward the opening, toward freedom. It's now just inches from her face. Slowly, and carefully, she presses the back of her hand against the wall and waits. The centipede freezes. They are each both predator and prey. She identifies the ocelli on each side of its head but realizes she's never before made eye contact with a creature this small, and she doesn't know what impact eye contact would have on this species. Threaten or calm? The centipede begins to move forward. It goes straight for her hand. She braces herself. But when it sets its first pairs of feet on her palm, it tickles, like a butterfly kiss. She holds her breath until the centipede is completely in her palm, trusting her, and then she cups her hand to an empty water bottle, tipping it slightly so the centipede will slide off her skin and into the plastic. Once it's trapped, with its little legs kicking in unison like paddlers on an outrigger canoe, she screws the bottle cap on.

*This is it*, she thinks.

In addition to the centipede, Margee has collected a menagerie of other creatures in her empty water bottles as they have crawled into and around her hole. One German cockroach and a three-inch American one. Three scorpions. A few spiders and ants. And finally the centipede. It's amazing how many creatures can be found in the Hawaiian earth, she thinks. And what allies they can be. She has adorned the inside of each bottle a bit of dirt, some fruit scraps, droplets of water, and strands from that disgusting clump of Vern's beard hairs. The creatures have been able to survive in the bottles until now, but Margee can tell time is running out for them, too.

She has also been crafting a rope by braiding together threads she's pulled from her filthy white skirt and top, and now she knots the rope around each of the six plastic water bottles. She hangs the rope around her neck like a scarf, and she positions herself in front of the finger- and toeholds she diligently excavated over the last three days.

The sky is completely clear now, and the moon beams down at her, watching. A warm breeze blows the hair back from her face, and kisses her skin, when her head rises above the edge of the hole.

Waves crash louder now. She turns to the water, where lights flicker from a lone boat. Margee tries to remember how long Manny and Ray were supposed to be out on the water with sailing camp. Five days, she thinks. They are still out there, safe for now.

She is ready. With the sliver of culvert metal between her teeth and her scarf of nervous allies, she takes a deep breath and muscles herself up, hoisting her belly and hips over the lip of the hole. Then one knee, and then the other, and finally she climbs out, dirty and barefoot like an angry and determined native from long ago.

She fixes her attention on the house.

The kitchen light is on; the TV's bluish fluorescent light shimmers against the living room wall.

Vern is in there.

Margee belly-crawls like a mercenary across the Bermuda grass to the side of the house, then prowls along the stucco walls and creeps around to the front door, careful to keep the bottles from making any noise. She peeks in through one of the sidelight windows. Yes, there he is. Vern is on the sofa watching TV, his back to her, his fingers interlaced behind his head. His bare feet are propped on the coffee table; his cocktail glass sweats on the table at his side.

She checks the doorknob. Good, it's unlocked. He hasn't taken his final walk of the evening, down the long driveway in the moonlight, with his cigar and without her. She silently opens the door.

One of the plastic bottles taps against another. She freezes, waits. Vern doesn't move. She slowly slips the rope down from around her neck. Her little zoo waits, the animals anxious. She opens the door an inch further, stopping just before it creaks, and reaches in for his loafers. They are still soft and inviting.

Working quickly, she opens the bottles and lets the little arthropods tumble and scurry into his shoes. They won't all stay put there, she knows. Some will make their new homes on the sofa, or between the sheets, or perhaps near Vern's toilet. They will all be her accomplices, no matter where they go. They will do their jobs.

She sets the loafers back in place and places the sharp piece of metal inside the right shoe. She hangs her pearl necklace—that anniversary gift—over the doorknob, as a farewell message to him. But then she reconsiders and removes it.

It's a long walk down the driveway to the road, longer than she remembers. Margee listens to the clacking geckos and a lone cow. She hears the incessant pounding of waves that have separated her from her friends, her mother and sister, her past and her future.

A lump forms in her throat when she pictures Manny and Ray. She will be there when their boat comes back. She can already see their tanned faces, the wind blowing through their unruly hair.

The tropical breeze feels so good on her face now, already blasting away the questions and the fear and the dirt. She breathes deeply as she walks, feeling more alive now, from the roots of her filthy hair to the blisters on her bare feet, than she has in years. And then she hears her husband's piercing cry, shattering the night. She's tempted to turn in that direction, tempted to second guess what she's just done. But she doesn't. She rips the pearl necklace from her neck and tosses it, along with the empty plastic bottle, into an open field. After that purging, she looks straight ahead and keeps on going down the road, replaying Don Henley's song in her head one more time.

# TASTING
# FREEDOM

# Our Circles

—NESSA MCCASEY

Parent cares for the child,
For better or poorer
And finally, the child gets to do the same.

Why are we so undone about the final step,
as they prepare to leave this world?
Look at the possibilities:
Knowing we cannot fail for they love us.
Knowing that our best will always be enough
Though it ends in death, of course.
And then it begins all over again.

The circle is amazing geometry.
There now, breathe and realize
There is much to admire
In our bumbling about.

**LYNN SET HER BACKPACK** on the gravel parking lot surface and breathed in the morning's still-dark but eager air. She needed to be out here in the mountains. She needed this hike today. It had been a long week at the Portland bookstore where she worked; she'd practically been a servant to two best-selling, prima donna authors who'd held signing events there in the last few days. And then she had indeed *been* a servant to her elderly mother, Penelope, all week long, who insisted on living independently even though she really couldn't manage on her own very well anymore. Now it was all behind Lynn, and she looked forward to clearing her mind while hiking Central Oregon's South Sister, a non-technical climb which guidebooks called *arduous* but which she relished.

Even if she was going to be climbing with a bunch of old climbing colleagues.

It was rare for her to agree to climb with a large group; unlike her mother, Lynn had always been a bit of a loner. But it was a sort of fiftieth birthday party for Ethan, one of her colleagues, and rumor was that he'd come down with an unnamed terminal illness. She knew she had to go.

They started early in the morning, headlamps illuminating the trail as the wind moaned through the Douglas firs and dark blue lakes materialized beneath the creeping daylight. It was going to be one of those perfect days when you just put one foot in front of the other and let your mind completely zone out. She had spent the entire preceding afternoon and most of the evening at her mother's house, trimming bushes and cleaning toilets and vacuuming stairs, like every other visit at Penelope's. Always a list of chores. And Lynn, for some reason, couldn't say no to her mother. Penelope was the only person in the world who yielded such power over Lynn, and one of these days Lynn was going to have to put her foot down. But the older her mother got, the harder that became. When the chores were done yesterday, the final request came in, just as it always did. "Stay. Have a glass of wine with me."

It was the same conflict every week. It was as though her mother had developed a very selective memory, one whose purpose was solely to serve her own needs and desires.

"I don't drink, Mom."

"You don't know what you're missing." Penelope wore her normal half-smile at times like these, when she was upset—the sort of smile you see on politicians' wives.

"Sure I do. I'm around it plenty. Greg drinks all the time, you know. Too much." It wasn't that her on-and-off partner was a lush; he handled his liquor fine most of the time. It was just that it was unhealthy for him.

"I just have no interest in consuming unhealthy substances. They'll ruin my mind, my body, my entire game."

"Game? That's what you call that mountain climbing business? A game?" Her mother had of course, by then, poured herself a glass of Sauvignon Blanc. She swirled her wine, sniffed it with her eyes closed, and took a long, slow drink—all dramatic effect for Lynn, no doubt.

"It's just an expression, Mom."

"Well. I'll never understand why you won't drink a single glass of wine with your own mother now and then, for heaven's sake."

Lynn hadn't wanted to leave her mother on that tense note, but she had to catch a few hours of sleep before driving three hours over the pass to the High Desert and setting out on the hike before dawn. Now, she could just relax. And enjoy Ethan's company. He was a kick to be around, and infamous for initiating random philosophical discussions. Just as the group was crossing the sandy plateau at the Moraine Lake junction, he—who had been in the lead—stopped and turned around.

"So tell me," he said to the group, "where do you all think the best place to die might be?

The sun had just begun to rise over the tree line, and the sky was in the process of transforming into lapis lazuli, and although no one had yet answered Ethan, Lynn thought that this spot, right here, might very well be the best place to check out for good.

The group hesitantly bounced ideas back and forth about where they might like to die; it was an uncomfortable conversation given Ethan's prognosis. Because this was a group of climbers, most of them voted for Nepal or Mt. Rainier or some such mountain setting, but Ethan said he wanted to be in Cabo san Lucas. On a golf course. They all laughed; this was so *not* Ethan.

Lynn was about to say her choice would be to die right here when her phone chirped. She looked down at it, surprised to see a signal. It was a text from Greg.

Greg: *w/Penelope.*

Poor Greg. Penelope's list of needs had become so lengthy that now, if Lynn wasn't available, she'd contact Greg for help. But what could her mother have possibly needed so early in the day? It had been less than twelve hours since Lynn had left her, and her mother was notorious for sleeping in late.

Lynn's first thought was that Penelope had a medical emergency, but her mother was *fit as a fiddle,* as she frequently liked to say. And then Lynn remembered her mother having told Greg, not too long ago, how she'd love to go golfing some time. Maybe he had taken her out to his country club; this would be a perfect day for that since Lynn—who hated golf—was out of town. What a guy.

Dying on a golf course, maybe even in Cabo, would be Greg's choice, Lynn imagined. She pictured him with Penelope on a course right now, Penelope dressed in a silk suit and heels, riding in a golf cart. Hanging on for dear life with one hand, hanging onto her hat with another, and Greg driving wildly around the lakes and sand bunkers. He was the type of guy who would do that for her, and given that he was the head pro, he could get away with it if no one else was around. What a pair they would be. Then another text came in, and Lynn shielded her eyes from the sun so she could read her cell phone's screen.

Greg: *at hospital* ☹

Oh. Shit. They weren't golfing.

She texted back to ask what was going on but got that frustrating red exclamation point indicating her text didn't go through. Now was not the time to lose the signal.

She stopped for a moment as the others kept on hiking. She tried to convince herself it was probably nothing serious. Penelope had a flair for the dramatic; once, she'd insisted on rushing to the ER when a rash began to surface on her forearms, certain it was some third world disease she'd picked up while traveling. Lynn had to cancel a trip to Smith Rock that day. As it turned out, it was only a reaction to a few flea bites she had sustained while visiting a friend and her toy poodle. All she needed was some Benadryl.

This was also probably nothing—or at least nothing more than Penelope's need for somebody's attention—so Lynn told herself not to overreact. She caught up with the group and rejoined the debate about best places to die. But she couldn't completely shut off worries about her mother any more than she could completely ignore the irony of Ethan's question. When the group stopped to admire a view of the ancient Broken Top volcano, and to hydrate before beginning the ascent toward the Lewis Glacier saddle, her phone buzzed again. Another text had made it deep into the Cascades.

Greg: *Lynn, please call ASAP.*

"Shit," she said to the group. "I might have a problem. With my mom."

The others gathered around.

"Apparently she's at the hospital."

"How old is she?" One of them asked.

"Eighty-something. I can't remember exactly; she's always lied so much about her age that I can never keep track. Regardless, she was fine yesterday. And she just went in for a physical and her doctor told her, and I quote, 'Penelope, Death isn't ready for you.'"

"It's probably something minor," Ethan said. "But still. You should turn back. I told my dad not to worry when he called me from Vegas to tell me about a headache—I figured he'd drunk too much the night before, as usual—and the next thing I know he's died from a brain tumor."

Once he said that, thoughts began to tumble over one another in Lynn's mind like rocks in a landslide. She pictured Ethan's father dying alone in Las Vegas, which she figured had to be the worst place in the world to die. Greg used to tease Lynn that once she turned fifty, all bets would be off. She'd reached fifty now. She didn't want Ethan to die. She didn't want to die. And she didn't want her mother to die, either. She definitely wasn't ready for that.

"You're right. I've got to go back. Sorry, Ethan." She gave him a hug and said her goodbyes to the others.

As she retreated back down toward the trailhead, she kept trying to get a hold of Greg. But the service was bad, and when the call did go through, he didn't answer. Then her phone died.

They always die when you need them most.

As she drove north along Highway 97, Lynn tried to convince herself that everything would be fine, but she couldn't help but think about the great *what-if*.

*Don't think like that*, she told herself. But the more she tried to rein in morbid thoughts, the stronger they became, and the fields of alfalfa and peppermint blurred past as she began to imagine how life would be so different—and, in all honesty, so much easier—if and when Penelope passed away. Lynn could stay in bed on Sunday mornings with Greg and not feel guilty about it. She wouldn't have to listen to Penelope's grandiose stories about worldwide excursions or her lectures about how Lynn needed to loosen up and live a little, and she wouldn't have to answer any more questions about why she and Greg weren't planning to marry—questions she didn't even know the answer to. She wouldn't have to trim all those bushes and run all those errands and shuttle her mother from doctor's appointment to doctor's appointment. Her heart pumped faster when she thought about the longer adventures she could sign up for without listening to her mother's warnings—worrying about something happening to Penelope while Lynn was gone. There wouldn't be any more worry. So many possibilities if her mother died.

But then, as she drove into the little town of Terrebonne and gazed out at the sheer cliffs of Smith Rock, where rock climbers from all over the world congregate, she pulled off the road. She, too, had spent a good amount of time there, climbing up chimneys and scaling four-pitch routes, and being the first woman to finish The Big R. As she gazed out at the cliffs, simultaneous conflicting thoughts bumped into one another, and Lynn suddenly felt more drained than if she'd just been clinging upside down to a crux on a rock wall. *What kind of monster am I, to think such things about my own mother? Do other daughters have such thoughts?*

Penelope did not die.

Lynn walked in to her mother's hospital room and was shocked at what she saw. Somehow she had anticipated that Penelope would be sitting up in bed wearing a silk kimono with fashion magazines spread about and several nurses catering to her every need. Instead she found her mother lying in the bed in a drab hospital gown with a drip line poked into the back of her hand and several bruises beneath her eyes, resembling the eye black that football players wear. This was not the look her mother normally wore: fine eye pencil, muted eye shadow, and lash-lengthening mascara, and a bit of rose-tinted blush on each cheek.

She had also, at least, assumed Greg would be sitting at Penelope's side. But there he was, passed out in a vinyl chair by the window, a half-eaten candy bar in his hand and a chunk of chocolate lying on his chest. Like a child getting away with something behind his mother's back, Greg often indulged in unhealthy eating when Lynn was gone.

"What took you so long?" Penelope asked when she opened her eyes and noticed Lynn had arrived.

"Sorry, Mom. I was hiking in Central Oregon when I got Greg's text. I got here as fast as I could. What happened?"

"Nothing happened, really. This is all so unnecessary. I took a little spill, that's all."

One minute Penelope is asking what took Lynn so long. The next she's saying this is all unnecessary. Typical Penelope.

"This doesn't look like nothing," Lynn said. She approached the bed and gently touched the bruises. "Tell me what happened."

Penelope explained that she'd been repotting some plants and hosing down her front porch and steps. "Somehow, the next thing I knew, I was here in the hospital."

Lynn studied the bruises on her mother's face, trying to envision the accident in her mind. "What time of day were you out on the porch? It must have been awfully early."

"Yes, I suppose it was. I guess I couldn't sleep."

This didn't sound like her mother.

"Did you fall? Were you knocked unconscious? Do you have a concussion?"

"I don't know, Lynn. We'll have to ask Greg."

Greg was still out cold.

"Did you break anything, Mom?"

"I'm not sure. I'm worried I might have broken that beautiful pot you gave me last year for Mother's Day."

"Mom. You know what I mean. Did you break any of your own body parts?"

"I don't think so. But why all these questions? I don't have any idea why they're keeping me here, except maybe to run up some hospital bills. I'm perfectly fine. I want to go home." She glanced over at Greg, who was now snoring. "There's no one to talk to here."

Lynn followed her mother's gaze. "I can see that."

"That candy bar sure looks good," Penelope said. "I could go for one of those."

"Haven't you had anything to eat, Mom?"

"No, they won't give me anything yet. They say they have to do more tests first, and I'm starving. And look at this ridiculous hospital gown they've put me in. Sweetheart, you've got to get me out of here."

As Penelope struggled to sit up straighter, unsuccessfully given the angle of the bed, Lynn stifled a laugh. It was true, her mother looked rather pathetic—a far cry from her usual stylish appearance.

"And the staff treats me like I'm senile. I swear. They talk to me like I'm a child. I can't take it here. Take me home, Lynn."

Penelope continued to prattle on about the poor service, which assured Lynn that perhaps her mother was going to be all right. At least she wasn't about to die.

Finally, Greg woke up. He yawned, stretched, and raised himself from the chair. When he saw Lynn, he smiled enthusiastically. "Welcome back, Birdie."

Lynn wished, for the thousandth time, that Greg would find a better pet name for her, one that didn't refer to golf.

"You must be famished," he said just before shoving the rest of the candy bar into his mouth.

"I am a little hungry," she said. She hadn't eaten anything all day, either.

"Good," he said. "Now that you've seen your mother, let's go down to the cafeteria to get some food." He came over to her and placed his hand on the small of her back, gently steering her toward the door.

"She just got here!" Penelope said. "For crying out loud, let her have a seat and visit with me. She can eat later."

He pointed to the clock on the wall. "The cafeteria will be closing soon, Penelope."

Lynn started to protest, too, but he gently pushed her even closer to the door and told Penelope they'd return soon, with something special from the cafeteria for her.

"We need to talk," he whispered once they were out in the hall. He waited until they had turned the corner and were out of Penelope's earshot before going on. "Your mother's situation isn't quite as simple as she's described. The social worker stopped by earlier to talk about next steps."

"What do you mean, next steps?"

"It's a long story." They rode the elevator down to the basement and hurried through the cafeteria line. Lynn loaded up a plate at the salad bar and Greg ordered a cheeseburger, fries and a Coke. They met up at the cashier's station.

"You know there's all these HIPPA rules about what they can and can't tell me," Greg said, "since I'm not the one with access to her health records. But the good news is that the ER doc and the neurologist assigned to her both belong to my club."

"Your...country club? They're your golf buddies?"

He took a long drink of Coke while nodding.

"That's the good news?" She stirred her salad dressing into the lettuce.

"Well, it's part of the good news. Here's what I've been able to piece together about what happened. First, it's probably true that your mother had been hosing down her front porch when she fell. What nobody knows is when or why she fell. It was just past sunrise when a neighbor saw her lying facedown on the steps, and he ran right over. Apparently she was breathing but unconscious. He called 911, then scrolled through her cell phone contacts—her cell phone was in her jacket pocket—and he found my number." Greg lowered his head. "I guess I was listed as ICE."

"She listed *you* as her emergency contact? Instead of me?"

He continued. "She didn't actually wake up for several hours."

"And then what? You fell asleep as soon as she woke up? You make a fine emergency contact." As she said this, she knew how ungrateful she sounded. "Sorry."

He held his hands up in mea culpa fashion. "I'm sorry, too, Lynn. It's been a long day for all of us. Anyway, the other good news was that there was no sign of any broken bones based on X-rays, except for one of her fingers, which they think she probably fell on. But the bad news is that the doctors are worried about a couple of things. First of all, they think she was probably out working on her flowers either late last evening or even during the night. I guess this sort of thing happens a lot with older people. They call it sundowning."

"I've heard of that, but never thought about it with my mom."

"They're also worried about traumatic brain injury, like the football players get. They're pretty sure she hit her face on the edge of one of the steps, which caused the hematoma beneath each eye. And they're worried it could be worse."

"Like a concussion?"

He ate a couple of French fries. "Or even more serious. Don't get yourself all caught up in your petticoat, not yet anyway, but they made it sound like it could be a big deal. No one knows what caused the fall—if she had some sort of seizure—"

"A seizure? Like epilepsy?"

"I don't know. They don't know. She's been complaining of nausea and a bad headache, and she's been confused since she woke up about what happened and about where she is."

"She seemed fine to me."

"I know, but she's been going in and out of it. At times she's had trouble finding the right words, and she asked not only for you and Aunt Miriam, but also for her mother."

"My grandmother's been dead for years."

"I know. But she said she saw her in the doorway."

"Jesus." Lynn put her fork down. She couldn't eat any more salad. "Oh God. Shit. I need to go back upstairs to be with her."

She started to stand, but he extended his arm toward hers.

"Not yet. We need to talk about a few more things."

Greg explained that they'd done some basic tests that day and would be running a number of additional tests the next day. The doctors also wanted to keep her there under close observation for any signs of physical, cognitive, or emotional trauma. If things went well, she could be moved to rehab after a couple of days. But, depending on how everything progressed, there might need to be a pow wow to talk about her future living arrangements.

"All from falling down the stairs," she said.

He nodded as he gulped down the rest of his cheeseburger. "And hitting her head," he said, ground meat still in his mouth.

"You'd better slow down and watch what you eat yourself," she said, "or you'll be the next one checking in here."

"Mom, we need to talk."

A week had passed since Penelope was admitted to the hospital, and Lynn had been running around trying to get as much information as she could from doctors and nurses while trying to hold down her job at the bookstore, read up on TBI, and take care of her mother's demands. Feed the cats. Pick up some dresses from the dry cleaners. Call the travel agent and confirm that Penelope had purchased travel insurance for her upcoming trip to Myanmar—just in case she had to cancel. And check on the cleaning lady to be sure she did a good job and didn't slack off in Penelope's absence.

Finally Lynn's mother was going to be moved to rehab. This was good news, although in part the move seemed to be driven by the fact that there was nothing more the hospital could do for her at this point. Medicare wouldn't pay for her to stay there anymore because tests had been inconclusive.

And there were still concerns about whether she'd be able to fully recover.

Lynn had noticed her mother had been having trouble paying attention, and she was still periodically confused about where she was and having difficulty finding the right words. Then again, she'd shown some of these symptoms before the fall, and Lynn had assumed it was just normal old-age stuff. But since coming into the hospital, Penelope's moods had been swinging erratically, too.

"There's nothing to talk about," Penelope said. "I want to go home."

"I know you do, Mom. And while the doctors agree you're stable enough to be released from the hospital, they want you to spend time in rehab for further evaluation. And to regain your strength, too."

"I'm *fine*. Why doesn't anyone believe me? It's just that we're in rough waters now. That's why I can't walk very well."

Lynn held her breath. She hadn't known her mother to talk in metaphor.

"Rough waters?"

"Yes, rough waters! This ship is rocking side to side, that's why I'm nauseated, too. Don't tell me you're not feeling it."

Penelope used to love to go on cruises. Was she living in the past?

"Mom, we're in the hospital now. We're not on a ship. You know that, don't you?"

Penelope stared at Lynn, blinked a couple of times. Then a new expression washed over her face as though she was waking from a dream and the world was coming into focus.

"Of course I know we're in a hospital. I'm not crazy."

"Of course you're not, Mom. But the doctors—and I—are a little worried about your cognitive well-being. And your emotions." The doctors had told Lynn her mother had been intermittently argumentative and weepy. "We need to keep a close eye on you for a while, that's all. In rehab."

"This is nonsense. There is nothing wrong with me. And the only emotional problem I have is when you get that look on your face and say we need to talk."

Penelope had always had a way of shushing Lynn, like a book being slammed shut.

"And the notion of rehab is ridiculous, too," Penelope continued. "It makes me sound like a drug addict. Going to rehab! All I did was fall down the stairs because they were a bit slippery. It could have happened to anyone. But here they're treating me like I'm a little old lady on the verge of her demise."

"It *could* have been your demise, Mom, at your age. You're lucky."

"Well, I'm not feeling so lucky right now. I think somebody stole my paintings."

Lynn was taken aback by that one. "Your paintings? You mean at home?"

It was Penelope from whom Lynn had inherited the wanderlust gene. Granted, Lynn traveled in order to climb mountains, while Penelope traveled to collect miniature paintings from every corner of the world. But the fact was they both were always going somewhere while never really appreciating the purpose of each other's travels. Then again, travel was only one of the many things Lynn and Penelope didn't understand about one another. And this allegation of theft also fell precisely into that category of communication breakdown.

"I don't understand what you mean, Mom. Are you worried that someone broke into your house and stole your artwork?"

"No!" Penelope shouted, her tone suggesting that Lynn was a moron. Penelope's hospital roommate, who liked to keep the curtain between them drawn shut, called out to ask if they could please keep their voices down.

"Oh, never mind," Penelope said. "Just help me into the bathroom."

Lynn did as she was told, and Penelope shut the door, hard. Lynn listened to the toilet flush and the faucet run, wondering if she should have left her mother in there all by herself. She could fall, but at least she had a walker in there. Besides, Penelope had been so upset about the paintings that Lynn didn't want to upset her any further by insisting on helping her use the toilet. She was always wondering which subjects were worth arguing about with her mother, and lately she'd been facing that dilemma more and more.

When the bathroom door opened, Penelope hobbled out with her walker, reached for the hospital bed's handrail, then sat down on the mattress out of breath.

Lynn sat beside her.

"I just want to go home," Penelope said.

"That's what we need to discuss, Mom. Going home."

"I know, I know. You're going to say I have to go to rehab first. For eight to ten days, that's what they told me. And then I'll go home."

Penelope told Lynn to hand her an empty cosmetic bag from the closet shelf, then pushed herself up from the bed and shuffled back into the hospital bathroom with it and with her walker. Again, she closed the door behind her. When she came out this time, the cosmetic bag was overflowing with makeup brushes, combs, and hair spray. Although she was no longer attached to tubes and hoses, she moved slowly, tentatively now, as though her battery was running low. She reminded Lynn of a mountain climber at high altitude suffering from oxygen deprivation.

"Mom, sit down. I'll pack up your stuff for you. Did you hear what I said a moment ago? Did you hear what I said we need to talk about?"

Penelope zipped her cosmetic bag shut with a flourish. "Of course I heard you. Now you think I'm deaf, too?"

A nurse came in with final discharge papers. Lynn appreciated the interruption, hoping it would allow the air between her and her mother to clear. Allow the conversation to reset.

"There's always someone coming in here," Penelope complained directly to the nurse. "You can't get any rest or privacy here. Another reason I need to go home." Still looking at the nurse, she pointed to Lynn. "Just go over all that boring stuff with *her*."

It was the same as always: so long as Lynn was there to do the work, Penelope didn't need to lift a finger or bother with life's administrative matters. Normally this irked Lynn, but today not so much. When the nurse left, Lynn patted the bed. Penelope sat down again, and Lynn took hold of one of her hands.

"Mom. You may not be going home. Even after rehab. We're thinking it may not be safe there anymore. We might need to find another place for you to live. A new place to call home." She couldn't believe she'd actually said those words to her own mother, especially since she wasn't yet convinced of the idea herself.

"Oh, that's nonsense." Again Penelope stood, this time with greater struggle, to go back into the bathroom.

But Lynn stretched her legs out, blocking Penelope's path. She reached for her mother's hand.

"Move your legs! I forgot to pack my toothbrush and toothpaste."

Sometimes Penelope could be downright obnoxious, and Lynn wished Greg were here to help. Her mother loved Greg.

When Penelope came back out of the bathroom for the third time, she pointed her toothbrush at Lynn like a bristled finger. "Have you allowed yourself to be brainwashed by those doctors, too? You don't think I know what everyone's been saying? You all think my fall was caused by some sort of brain snafu and that, in turn, has made it so I can't understand anything anymore. Well, you're all wrong. I know exactly what's going on. You're all against me, all of a sudden."

Lynn wondered if this was paranoia, or dementia, and—whatever it was—whether it was caused by the fall. The TBI.

"Where's Greg?" Penelope demanded. "He'd understand. He'll tell you my home is perfectly safe. Just let me prove it to you. To all of you. You, of all people, should understand how I feel, Lynn. Do you quit climbing mountains every time you have a little problem? No, you don't. I can just be more careful from now on. I won't hose down the front steps anymore."

"Mom. It's not just the steps outside. It's the steps up to your bedroom and down to the basement. And it's not just the steps. It's everything. Especially after this fall. The doctors don't know for sure what this fall may have done to you on the inside. To your brain. So you shouldn't live alone anymore. Just in case."

The space between mother and daughter seemed to have widened now, even though neither of them had moved a centimeter, and Lynn's suggestion of living elsewhere had permeated the entire room like spray from a clinical disinfectant.

"And you can't compare yourself to me, Mom. You're...older." Something caused her to twinge inside when she said this. A memory, perhaps, of a time when her mother was fifty and Lynn was in her teens, ready to take on the world. She had thought, back then, that her mother was an old woman, unable to understand how necessary it was for Lynn to live her life on her own terms. And now here they were, practically having the same conversation again, except in reverse.

"Fine then," her mother said. "I'll get someone to live with me. I'll find some handsome young gigolo. Will that satisfy you?"

"Oh, Mom."

It wasn't the gigolo remark that bothered Lynn. Penelope had always been a flirt, and there had been a lot of men in her life after Lynn's parents divorced. The problem was that a gigolo might not be able to offer the type of help that her mother needed.

"She may need help getting dressed," Greg had said just that morning when they were discussing, yet again, whether it was time for Penelope to get some real assistance. They had talked about the kind of help Penelope might need if she didn't get better in rehab. And even the types of help she might need as she grew older, regardless of what progress she made in rehab. They had discussed the various housing possibilities in bed that morning, and then in the shower, and then over oatmeal, when Greg had pored over Penelope's bank statements and checkbook. Lynn had made it clear that Penelope would want to stay in her own home. Who wouldn't?

"There's no way your mom can afford upwards of $6- or $7,000 a month for a qualified full-time caregiver," Greg said. "But she doesn't seem to qualify for any government help. We could try part-time, but then what if something happens when the helper isn't there?"

Lynn had no answer for that.

After breakfast, they made phone calls to various retirement facilities, but concluded that the nicer retirement homes were just as expensive as live-in care, especially when you start adding on various levels of assistance with dressing, meals, medications, and toileting.

"The most affordable alternative," Greg had said at lunchtime, as he stirred cheese into a bowl of chili, "would be to have your mother move into our spare bedroom."

Lynn had been mid-bite into an apple. "Into my writing room? Oh no, that's not happening."

"Elderly parents move in with their grown children all the time," he said.

"Not this elderly parent. And not this child. It would never work. You know that." She set the apple down and wanted to spit out the chewed pieces in her mouth. That little writing room, where Lynn kept all her books and wrote in her journals and even took naps now and then, was critical to her emotional well-being. The mere thought of losing that space, to her mother of all people, destroyed what little appetite she'd had. "There's no way my mother would accept living in that little room and disposing of all her fine furniture and belongings. She'd take over. Before you knew it, our furniture would be gone and our living room would evolve into a miniature Versailles. She'd be in the master bedroom and we'd be crammed into my writing room. And worse than that, we'd become her full-time servants. You have no idea how grueling it is to spend even a few hours with her."

"Sure I do. I see that look on your face whenever you come home from her place. But it would be different if she lived with us, in *our* house. She wouldn't be so demanding."

Seriously?

"She'd find *some*thing for me to do. All day, every day. It's who she is. I'll never understand how she can jet all over the world but can't change a light bulb. Besides, if she's really mentally disabled in some way, she'd need a lot of care. If Mom moved in with us, my life would be over. I'm not ready for that."

Greg contemplated as he chewed, like a Tibetan yak ruminating on grass. "Even with me here to help, you don't think it would work?"

Was he suddenly siding with Penelope? If her mother moved in with them, Lynn's freedom would be obliterated. She didn't want to have to climb a mountain every time she needed to find some space. Not to mention having to hire a caregiver for her mother when she went to work, or having to worry that her relationship with Greg would probably end forever if Penelope lived with them. She'd drive him crazy and out the door; either that or he'd spend every day on the golf course. *He* could do that; she wasn't his mother. But Lynn wouldn't be able to disappear so easily.

And there was also the very real possibility that Penelope and Lynn might kill each other.

"So the solution is…?" he asked.

"I don't know. I hate to say it, but maybe she could move in with Aunt Miriam, back in Illinois. At least it would be more affordable."

The conversation with Greg had been a necessary dress rehearsal for this conversation she was now having with her mother at the hospital. She studied Penelope's face. Could she do this? Could she say the words *retirement home* or *assisted living*? The doctors had said Penelope was likely to have lingering cognitive and emotional deficiencies from the fall, given that she hadn't shown much improvement this past week at the hospital. But to Lynn, Penelope seemed no less ornery or obstinate than usual. Maybe the doctors just didn't understand her mother. Maybe Penelope really would be capable of returning to her home.

While Lynn also knew that one day her mother *would* decline further, whether mentally or physically or both, and that this uphill climb toward adult-onset orphanhood would continue to be littered with conflict over difficult decisions, she just wasn't ready to make this one yet. Or at least not ready to tell her mother.

"Sure, yeah. Go for the gigolo," Lynn said. "Just tell me this: where are you going to find him?"

Lynn felt like a failure then, not having the strength to do what Greg and the doctors believed she needed to do, tell her mom the truth. She was about to speak up again, and tell her mother she'd changed her mind, that she *insisted* her mother move into assisted living, when the door opened and an orderly walked into the room with a transport chair. He was about twenty-five years old with a scruffy beard and long, blond hair pulled back in a ponytail. He had steely eyes, full smooth lips, and a lanky but muscular physique. He was a dead ringer for the actor Charlie Hunnam. The perfect gigolo. Lynn and her mother looked at each other and burst out laughing, driving away the tension between them. They laughed so hard that Lynn thought they'd both pee in their pants. It felt so good; she couldn't remember when the two of them had shared the same thought, or laughed so liberally. She was relieved she hadn't slammed the bad news down on her mother just yet.

"Are you ready to go?" the orderly asked Penelope.

She, having momentarily recovered from her laughing fit, gave him the once over. "Your place or mine?"

"Mother!" Lynn said, but she broke out laughing again, until Penelope adjusted the neckline of her zippered velour jacket to show a little wrinkled cleavage, and the flushed orderly abruptly left the room.

"Mom. Come on. That *was* a bit much."

"I was just playing with him."

"Like a cat plays with a little field mouse. Poor kid." As inappropriate as her mother's behavior had been, Lynn was grateful to see the spunk. But then, when two nurses and a brutish, older orderly came into the room and informed Penelope that she had to cooperate, she snapped and became an altogether different person.

"You know what I think?" Penelope's voice came out as a gritty whisper. "I think you're all just moving me around to get rid of me. Hot Potato Penelope. And I bet," she said directly to Lynn, "that the longer they keep me locked up as an inmate here—in the hospital or rehab or wherever—the happier *you'll* be."

Penelope's venom made Lynn shiver, the way a wicked witch frightens a child. But it also brought Lynn back to reality. The truth was that neither persona reflected the true woman who had been her mother. The doctors were right.

"Mom, you know that's not true," Lynn said. But, in a way, it was.

Penelope's days in rehab flew by. While her walking gait improved and her bruises began to heal, she continued to show signs of what the therapist called cognitive impairment. The doctors became less convinced Penelope would recover, especially given her advanced age. A social worker called Lynn into the hall one afternoon while Penelope was working with the occupational therapist.

"I know you want what's best for your mother," the social worker said. "And, on an emotional level, I know you think that letting her return to her house is the right thing to do."

Lynn held up her hand like a crossing guard. "I know what you're going to say. So save it. The only way for me to be sure that my mother is physically safe is if she's not alone."

That night, Lynn left the rehab facility and went to her mother's house to feed the cats. She entered through the front door and set her backpack down on the white carpet, next to the rosewood chiffonier, instinctively bracing for her mother's voice telling her to *get that filthy thing off the carpet*. But of course now she heard nothing but the quiet hum of the refrigerator, the whirring of cooled air flowing from the floor vents, and a harmonious feline mewing as both cats rubbed against her legs. It was odd being in her mother's house, alone.

She went into the kitchen, as she had every Sunday afternoon for all these years—except for those Sundays when either she or her mother were traveling, although never traveling together—and she half expected to see her mother standing at the counter pouring two glasses of sauvignon blanc, igniting the eternal debate about why Lynn wouldn't even have a sip. She fed the cats and then opened the fridge.

There were two raw chicken breasts and a salmon fillet that had been waiting to be roasted, or broiled, or whatever, before the whole hospital/rehab debacle—now well past the use-by date. A couple of artichokes, a bunch of asparagus, and a pint of fresh blueberries had also gone bad. And there, on the second shelf, were six chilled but unopened bottles of white wine lying on their sides. She inspected the labels: California, Chile, France, Italy, Australia, South Africa. No surprise, given that her mother was such a world traveler, having been to Reykjavik, Johannesburg, and Buenos

Aires in the last year alone. She packed the bottles into some empty shopping bags to take home to Greg.

She toured the rest of the house, with one cat leading the way and the other following. They went from front to back, and top to bottom, as Lynn let memories of her entire life wash through her mind and as she took inventory of what needed to be sold, what should be given away, and what would move.

She took the rest of the week off from work and did what needed to be done.

First, she called Penelope's sister, Miriam. Her aunt was delighted to learn Penelope would be moving to Illinois, and she insisted that they share a two-bedroom apartment in assisted living. After that call, Lynn felt a bit of relief, and called the facility's business manager to take care of specific arrangements. Next, she brought a moving company in to pack and ship Penelope's clothes, favorite furniture, and all those international paintings to the retirement home. She had them move the rest of her mother's stuff to a drop-off center for a local charity. Finally, she hired a realtor and put her mother's house on the market. She was able to do all this without discussing any of it with her mother because Penelope had signed power of attorney over to Lynn earlier in the year, ostensibly as part of her estate planning but more likely because she didn't want to be bothered with the paperwork of dying. Of course, Penelope would never have dreamed that her own daughter would sell her out, literally.

And Lynn had never thought she'd do such a thing, either. On the last day before Penelope's discharge from rehab, Lynn moved the cats to her own house, hired a cleaning service, and left several large bags of trash curbside, waiting to be taken away forever.

Now, as she and Greg sat in bed watching *The Bucket List* on TV, with Penelope's cats purring at the edge of the bed and Greg sneezing from allergies, Lynn began to second-guess herself once again. She thought back to that drive through Oregon and how she'd envisioned how free she'd feel upon her mother's death. She was, of course, thankful her mother had not died, but she now wondered if those demons had somehow tricked her into making this decision to force Penelope into a retirement home. Way back in the Midwest, of all places. She muted the sound.

"I feel evil, Greg. And sleazy and dirty for forcing this on my mom. I keep trying to convince myself I'm doing it for the right reasons, in Mom's best interests. But every day when I visit her at rehab and look her in the eye, withholding this information about what I've been up to, I feel ashamed for being so deceitful. How can you lie to a person you love?"

"You're not lying, exactly. You're just withholding information until the time is right."

He sneezed again.

"Are the cats bothering you? We can find a new home for them, you know."

He shook his head. "Hay fever, most likely."

She knew he was lying.

And now he poured himself a glass of wine. It was from one of Penelope's bottles, which he had brought into the bedroom before the movie started. A Pinot Gris. "Want a taste? This is mighty fine wine. Nothing but the best for your mother."

"The time will never be right," Lynn said.

"For the wine?"

"No. For telling her the truth. I'm not looking forward to tomorrow."

She reached for his glass.

Lynn had not let wine, or any alcohol, pass through her lips since she was a young woman dedicated to fitness—and to climbing mountains all over the world. Greg looked puzzled and reached his hand to her forehead as if checking for a fever. His fingers were gentle on her face.

She took a small sip, and wasn't prepared for the flavor—a crisp mixture of citrus and mineral, something that tasted earthy, natural, even elemental. She closed her eyes as she let it linger on her tongue before swallowing. When she opened them, she saw that he'd been watching her as though watching a miracle unfold. He reached out to reclaim his glass, but she held on to it and took another, longer drink—a gulp for a woman who'd been lost in a desert for a very long time.

Only when the glass was emptied did she hand it back to him. She rolled onto her stomach. He reached over and began to rub lotion onto her back—a bare expanse of skin except for a couple of small moles and six small tattoos—of the major mountains she'd summited over the years—inked across her upper back.

"You were right not to let her move in with us," he said. "Your mother would keel over and die if she ever saw these tattoos."

He kissed each of the inked images.

"Mom's also right," she said.

"Excuse me? Did you just say your mother is right about something? Must be the wine talking."

"No, I'm serious, Greg. She intimated that we were all moving her around so nobody would really have to take care of her. Isn't that exactly why I'm insisting she move into a retirement home with Aunt Miriam? So I don't have to do it? Aren't I shirking my responsibility? Running away from it?"

"No, Birdie, you're not." He brushed her hair back from one of her ears. "There's nothing wrong with what you're doing. Your mom needs help, and it makes sense you'd want her to be with her sister, rather than in a facility where she wouldn't know a soul."

"Of course there's something wrong with it." She flipped to her side to face him. "I'm being selfish. When I go to pick her up at rehab tomorrow, I'll essentially be kidnapping her. I won't be taking her to the home she's lived in for forty-seven years. Sure, I'll tell her where we're headed. And I'll let her stop by and say goodbye to the house if she wants to. But it won't be the same. It'll be the ghost of her house. And then I'll be stuffing her into my car and taking her on a 2,000-mile road trip to a place she doesn't want to be and dumping her off there like a bag of old clothes being donated to Goodwill."

"Don't you think you're being a bit melodramatic? A bit hard on yourself, too? First of all, you have broached the subject with her a couple of times before, so it's not entirely new news. And secondly, I'll go with you to pick her up. We'll sit her down together and tell her what the doctors and therapists have said. We'll show her pictures of where Miriam lives. She can call her sister if she'd like. We'll be very open about it with her, and you can tell her how lovingly you chose which furniture to send out there, and you can assure her that all her little paintings will be there waiting when she gets there."

"I don't know."

"You can promise to visit her often," he said. "And besides, this road trip could be the experience of a lifetime for a mother and daughter. You'll have plenty of time to talk about all this—about everything—along the way. And think of the scenery you'll pass through, the hills you'll climb. The golf courses you'll drive by." He traced one of her nipples with his thumb.

"Maybe. And it will be the first time we've traveled together. Ever."

"It'll be an adventure," he said.

She told him about Ethan's question. He leaned in, nibbled her ear, then whispered into it. "I know where I want to die. Right here, lying next to you. Even if you are evil, sleazy and dirty."

She pushed him away with her hand. "I know one thing. I don't want to die in some retirement home surrounded by a bunch of grumpy old people I barely know. And I don't want someone else forcing me to move there, either."

He laughed. "But you'll be one of those grumpy old ladies, too. You'll fit right in."

She hit him, lightly, on the shoulder.

"Seriously, Lynn, you're getting way ahead of yourself. Neither you nor your mother is about to die. What you've done is make a decision based on what you think she needs, what the doctors recommended, and what your mom could afford. You've selected a good retirement home. And Miriam is there, so right off the bat Penelope will have someone she knows. Someone who loves her. Sounds to me like you made this decision lovingly. Thoughtfully. As a good daughter would. And if she throws a fit tomorrow, or if she moves there and hates it, you can go to Plan B. Whatever that might be. For now you need to let it go and return to the present. Here with me."

This time she let him kiss her. As his hand trailed down her stomach, she began to let go of all the worries she had about the next day, about facing her mother with the news. And as Greg's hand slid between her legs and she tasted the wine on his breath, she started feeling something else, a growing awareness—emanating from somewhere deep inside, not too far from her heart—that freedom from the responsibility of caring for an aging parent was like her mother's fine wine: acidic and essential, yet deliciously addictive, too.

# BRIDGE OUT

# California Legal

—ANDREW LEVI WOOD

I pull out of the local truckstop
just north of Sack of Tomatoes. Getting on
the North I-5, heading toward Oregon

final destination Seattle,
I'm buttoned-up California legal, hauling
miscellaneous electronics close to max gross.

At the next scale I could be bitten
by a bear. Bubblegum machine lights flare
the air and I slow my roll,

pull toward the shoulder, but old Smokey speeds past,
sirens squealing, cutting through the exhaust. At mile-
          marker 415
a brake check causes my discs to shriek

when a mama coyote and her pups skirt across
the Interstate. I swerve to miss mama
and the zigzagging pup. Nine tires sing

a low moan across the drive-by-Braille grooves.
When the right drive blows and an alligator skin
rolls into the dust, I mix the stick, throw
the four-ways on and pull to the shoulder.

ROXANNE COULD HAVE had that fresh start she'd been working toward for years, finally walking out of that godforsaken cubicle in the heart of Louisville, Kentucky, and climbing into Peggy Sue—her shiny new Class 8 sleeper truck—and heading north by northwest into the teasing sun. She could have kept on hauling ass up straight-as-a-ledger-column I-5, with that azure sky overhead and Carrie Underwood on her upgraded sound system. If only she hadn't just hit the doggone bridge.

But now, where gray pavement and grazing pasture had been reflected in her side view mirror only moments ago, she saw her load of steel rods—extending askew over the edge of her flatbed—and, behind them, buckling steel and a tremendous cloud of dust.

Holy moly.

Turning down the music, she stepped hard on the brake, and Peggy Sue started to jackknife. Roxanne let go, glanced in the side mirror again. Her load appeared stable now, but that bridge back there was a heap of rubble. And there was no traffic behind her. Not anymore. All the northbound traffic that had been following her was stuck on the south side of the collapsed bridge. Or, Lord have mercy, sinking into the river.

She was going to be in a world of trouble. She started to sweat and gripped the wheel tight with both hands, her foot hovering mid-air as it waited for a command to either accelerate again or stop altogether. A voice told her to keep going. *No one will ever know it was your fault*, the voice said like a shadowy murmur. She tried to ignore it, the way you try to ignore flashing lights and sirens heading your direction. It only works until they catch up with you.

And now there were sirens for real, heading southbound on the other side of the interstate toward the disaster. Someone over there was bound to take note of her shiny pink cab and bed of disorderly steel rods and realize she was the last vehicle that made it across the bridge northbound. Yessiree, she'd be found out as the one who somehow caused that thing to implode, although Lord only knows how that could have even happened. And then? Her brand new trucker's license hot off the press would sure as pie get revoked, and she'd be spending her retirement years in jail, about as opposite as you could get from her plan to be out on the open road.

*Step on it! Head for the border! Canada's only a couple of hours away!*

There was that inner voice again. Roxanne hadn't slept well the night before, with all the excitement of starting her second career, and while she knew it was a lousy idea to drive while fatigued, she hadn't realized how being so tired could make you hear voices. Especially irrational ones. Canada? That was where Viet Nam draft dodgers went back when she was a little girl.

She could make a run for it, she supposed, if she wanted to give in to that craziness she was hearing. Maybe those folks on NPR were right; maybe a quarter of our population really was mentally ill, and she was one of them. But still, even if she were going nuts, she was still an honest woman. An accountant for nearly thirty years, for crying out loud, Roxanne had continuously implored her bosses to follow generally accepted accounting principles and make full disclosures to the SEC and all that jazz. She would not, could not, now run from her own mistake. She would have to quell that strange voice and deal with it later. Right now she needed to stop and think. And find a strong cup of coffee.

As her hand reached for the gearshift and her foot depressed the brake again, and as she heard the hissing of the Jake brakes and felt the shimmy in the cab, having not quite mastered the art of downshifting and smoothly stopping this behemoth of a vehicle, she also heard some sort of rustling coming from the sleeper bed behind her seat. Upon turning around, careful not to tweak the steering wheel, she discovered a young teenage girl. Skinny as a pencil. Climbing through Roxanne's curtain of pink and yellow beads that she'd hung to separate the seats from the sleeping compartment. The girl wore a cherry red bikini.

"Keep going!" the girl said. "Or they'll kill me. And probably you, too."

Roxanne lifted her foot off the brake and stared while Peggy Sue coasted along. She couldn't make sense of what she was seeing. Why was there a girl in her truck? And what could she possibly mean?

The girl was rather exotic looking by Roxanne's estimation: smooth skin the color of India Pale Ale with a dash of Woody's barbecue sauce stirred in. Amber eyes flecked with copper. Long black lashes.

"Get going, please," the girl said.

Despite all the questions bouncing around in Roxanne's mind, there was one thing she was pretty certain about. This girl was scared of something. Whether she was really being chased by bad guys or was just your run-of-the-mill runaway, she needed Roxanne's help. And it felt good to feel needed like that.

"What the dickens, you only live once," Roxanne said aloud. And then she laid down the hammer.

Peggy Sue practically sang as she sped back up to seventy miles per hour. Meanwhile, Roxanne sneaked glances at the girl who had made herself right at home in the passenger seat and was now gently touching everything in the cab—gauges, vents, the smooth surface of the dash—as though touching helped her see, or believe, or understand. Then she reached for Roxanne's iPod resting in the faux-fur-lined console.

Which irked Roxanne. It's one thing to hijack somebody's truck and entire life; it's another to have the audacity to take charge of somebody else's music. But soon, as the girl curled her bare feet under her legs on the gray leather seat, Willie Nelson began to sing "On the Road Again." Which was fine by Roxanne. In fact, there was something about that song that invoked an adventurous spirit in her—a spirit she'd kept in a cage all her life for a reason unbeknownst to her. She knew she should get off at the upcoming exit and find the nearest police station to get help for this girl, and she knew she should turn herself in, too, for destroying the bridge. She knew she should call company dispatch and tell them everything, too. But Willie, and this strange girl, were sabotaging Roxanne's good judgment like some sort of psychic hypnotists, destroying the integrity she'd been so proud of all her life. They were conspiring; it seemed, to turn her into a fugitive. And this thrilled her.

If only her old stick-in-the-mud friends back home could see her now. She recalled the looks on their faces when she told them she was going to become a truck driver out West upon retiring.

*You, a truck driver?*

She might as well have told them she was going to become a bank robber, given how they reacted. How they laughed.

*Oh, Roxanne. At your age?*

They didn't think she could do it. Didn't think she had the balls. But she did it, by gosh. She packed up her bags and moved to Oregon. She did her training and got her commercial license and bought Peggy Sue. And here she was on her first long haul from the Golden State almost all the way to the Canadian border. How proud they'd have been of her, she thought. *Impressed.* But now, to think she actually might be doing something illegal! She imagined the looks on their faces when they read the headline on the front page of the *Courier-Journal*: Kentucky Accountant Wanted for Theft and Kidnapping.

There was something delicious about making this 180-degree turnaround, from goody-goody accountant to wanted woman.

It wasn't just the fugitive aspect that Roxanne found so compelling. There was more to it than that. It was the possibility of camaraderie.

She'd never had a sister, a husband, or a child. And the friends she'd had, and the men who'd come and gone, well they were just as boring as she had always been. A wild night was going to the movies and getting a giant bucket of buttered popcorn, except for that one time she and some of the other gals went to see Billy Ray Cyrus in concert. Sure, they hooted and hollered at him as a chorus. But there was no real connection among them, no real purpose to their relationships with one another. And now, suddenly here was this notion, implausible though it may be, that somebody needed Roxanne. Things always happen for a reason, they say.

When Willie sang, "Like a band of gypsies we go down the highway/We're the best of friends," she stole another look at the girl. She was young enough to be Roxanne's granddaughter; did this mean she was too young to be Roxanne's friend? Lordy, lordy. But still.

"So what's your name?" she asked the girl who had been looking out the window. "Mine's Roxanne." She patted the dashboard. "And this here is Peggy Sue."

The girl said nothing, which didn't sit very well with Roxanne. Didn't she have any manners?

"Look here. You just told me someone's trying to kill you, and maybe me, too, and you told me to step on it and whisk you away to who-knows-where. I think you owe me the decency of at least telling me your name."

Mileposts blurred past.

"Okay, I'll give you a name," Roxanne said. "Let's see. Hannah. No, Lucy Mae. No, wait, let me think." She studied the girl, who shifted like a cat trying to get comfortable. "I got it. You look like an Angie. Or Angela. An angel."

"I do not. My name's Frankie. Francesca, that is. But everyone knows me as Frankie."

Ha. One fact down and a thousand to go.

The next song that came on was Golden Earring's "Radar Love." They passed another semi-trailer and then a Dodge pickup hauling a trailer full of horses. Roxanne had been around Frankie's age, she supposed, when she'd learned how to ride and jump on her aunt's horse farm. Funny how thoughts work that way. One minute she's on the highway and the next she's watching her uncle break in a new filly. He was so smug and satisfied when he finally got the bridle on the horse, the same way Roxanne felt when she extracted Frankie's name.

Frankie reached up to touch a peace pendant Roxanne had previously hung from the sun visor.

"Lynn has one like this," the girl said.

"Who's Lynn?"

"My grandmother."

Aha. Another fact.

"Does she live around here?"

"Not really."

Frankie didn't elaborate, but that was all right. Roxanne liked games. She'd get more out of the girl.

They listened to Chuck Berry, Tom Petty, Tom Cochrane. When Jerry Garcia started singing "Truckin,'" Frankie cranked up the volume liked she owned the place. And when she started to sing along at the top of her lungs, Roxanne joined in. They were horribly out of tune, but in some other, intangible way, they were in harmony, and when the song ended they laughed so hard that Roxanne needed to stop and pee, the thought of which slapped her back to reality. They couldn't stop if they were being chased. She checked her side view mirror. Nobody there, that she could tell anyway. This whole business about killers was surely a lot of bunk. She wondered how long till the next rest area.

Meanwhile, the theme song from *Thelma and Louise* came on. Imagine that, Roxanne thought. And when Glenn Frey sang, "Wherever we may travel/Whatever we go through," Roxanne belted out the words along with him, and Frankie looked up at her and smiled, and Roxanne pretty much melted like a pat of butter on a fresh-baked biscuit. Then Frankie shouted.

"Oh my God!"

Roxanne, startled from her reverie, jerked the wheel and nearly jackknifed her load.

"Oh my God," Frankie said again. She slid down in her seat, flipped herself over like a flapjack, and dove through the beads into the sleeper compartment.

"What? What's going on, Frankie?"

Roxanne scanned the road ahead but couldn't discern any trouble. She checked her mirrors, too. Meanwhile, she heard wire coat hangers scraping along the rod in the little sleeper compartment closet. She tried to see what was going on back there by looking in the little mirror on her sun visor, because gosh darn it trucks like hers didn't have rear view mirrors, but all she could see was Frankie's back.

A car horn brought her attention back to the road, where several cars were about to merge onto the highway. A gray pickup. Two white sedans. A red Prius, tailgated by a black Escalade. She heard a zipper. Was Frankie going through her purse? Gosh darn it. She moved into the left lane to make room for the merging traffic.

"Slow down!" Frankie said. "Please."

Roxanne checked the speedometer. Seventy-two. "Tell me what's going on and maybe I will."

Frankie poked her head through the beads, and now Roxanne had that feeling you sometimes get rubbing up and down the inside of your memory bank like a cat rubbing against your legs. She had seen this girl before, she now realized. But where?

Crouching down between the driver's seat and the passenger seat, Frankie reached for Roxanne's sunglasses in the console. She put them on, then pointed straight through the windshield. As she did, Roxanne noticed a ring of bruises around the girl's wrist and wondered how on earth she hadn't seen them before. There was also a gash on the inside of Frankie's arm.

"That's them," Frankie said.

"That's who?"

"In that car."

The Escalade was riding right alongside them now, trying to merge, and Roxanne saw a pale, elderly man in the driver's seat. He turned and looked up at her and smiled, friendly-like.

"That man? He's chasing you?"

Frankie ducked back into the sleeper compartment. "Just slow down. Get behind him."

Roxanne felt a bit of sweat forming on her upper lip and in her armpits. "Fetch me some water from the fridge back there, will you?"

Frankie handed a water bottle to Roxanne.

"Thank you kindly," Roxanne said. "Now don't you think it's about time you come clean with your story? You're either running from someone or making up a mighty tall tale."

"I can't tell you," Frankie said. "Or anyone."

"If our lives are in danger, then you absolutely can. And should."

"They told me not to tell. And they said nobody would believe me anyway."

Roxanne wondered if maybe Frankie was part of some sort of theft ring. She thought of her purse lying out on the bed. And then it dawned on her that she hadn't asked the obvious.

"Frankie, how did you get into my truck?"

"I snuck in."

"When?"

"At the truck stop. Right before that bridge."

Roxanne tried to recall the details. It seemed like a lifetime ago that she'd pulled into Truck City to gas up. Practically cost her entire monthly pension check. She'd thought she'd been so smart installing dual fuel tanks. But when she saw the damage—nearly $500—well she almost didn't go inside for lunch. But she did, splurging on a club sandwich—salad instead of fries. Surely she'd locked the cab when she did.

"You were checking your load," Frankie said. "I'd seen you walking from the truck stop to your truck, and I saw you toss your purse inside and then walk to the back of the truck, and I made a run for it when no one was looking and slipped in through the driver door and hid under your blankets."

Roxanne had trouble visualizing how this could have happened without her noticing, but it was true that she'd been preoccupied with her load. And the cost of that gosh darn gas.

"But why? Who—" And then she remembered. When she'd first pulled into the truck stop, she'd seen a group of young girls in bikinis and cowboy hats and cowboy boots in the parking lot, maybe twenty or thirty yards from her rig, surrounded by a semi-circle of other tractor-trailers, like wagons circling the women and children, out of sight from the truck stop building. There was also a photographer with a couple of those silver reflecting umbrellas and a horde of truckers standing around with their arms crossed and their tongues pretty much hanging out of their mouths. It was a photo shoot, she'd figured, even if it was an odd setting for one, but until this moment she hadn't given it a lick of a thought.

"Were you one of those swimsuit models?"

Frankie, still back behind the beads, didn't answer. Roxanne tried to remember more details. She recalled about seven girls, and about fifteen truckers watching. One photographer. And a couple of men dressed like Miami Vice standing off to the side.

"So just how dangerous is that old man?"

"I don't know. I've never seen him before."

"You said he was after you."

"No, not him."

"Then who on God's green earth are you afraid of?"

"The one in front of him."

That couldn't be right.

"We're afraid of a Prius?"

Frankie extended her feet through the beads. One of the feet waved.

Roxanne tried to piece it all together, to figure out what the dickens this all meant, and finally she came up with a theory. It made her sick to her stomach.

"Oh my God," she said. "Almighty God."

And then a new rush of adrenaline surged inside Roxanne. Now she was like the untamed horse, and she was mad, and there isn't anything meaner than a wild and crazy mare. She stepped on the accelerator, moved into the left lane and sped past the Escalade, and Frankie started yelling at her, asking her what she thought she was doing, but Roxanne paid no heed to what the girl was saying and switched back into the right lane directly behind the Prius, keeping her foot pressed firmly on the pedal, until good old Peggy Sue nearly kissed the red car's rear bumper.

"What are you doing?" Frankie said, her head now poking through the beads, her pitch having grown hysterical. "You're going to get us both killed."

"No, I'm not. I have a plan."

The truth was that she had no idea what she was doing. She had no plan except to somehow punish whoever was in that Prius for subjecting Frankie to what Roxanne concluded had been going on back at that truck stop.

She'd heard about this sort of thing, but she had never in a million years thought she'd run across it in real life.

For the next couple of miles, Roxanne kept a steady distance of twelve to eighteen inches behind the Prius and waited for her heart to settle down so she could think straight. She might not yet have all the tricks down about managing rear loads, but one thing she did know was precisely how many inches there were between her rig and the car. As long as the Prius didn't do anything stupid, they'd all be fine. They passed a green milepost sign: 240. Fifteen miles until her Bellingham exit, where she was supposed to deliver her load. She tried to think, think, think.

The more she thought about what Frankie had become involved in, and the more she thought about that Prius out to hunt the girl down, the more revved up she got.

"How old are you?" she asked.

"Fourteen."

"Christ the Lord." Now Roxanne was really pissed off. She switched to a playlist that a co-worker had compiled for her as a going-away gift. It was called "Road Rage". She knew, at the time, she'd never listen to songs filled with so much anger. But now everything had changed.

The first song, Metallica's "Battery," started calmly with gentle guitar plucks and chords—the same way she'd started her day so many long hours ago down in California—but soon it splayed open into dissonant chords and frenetic drumbeats. In another life she'd have found this music, if you could even call it music, horrible. It would have made her hair stand on end. It would have made her want to drive right off a cliff. But right now it matched her mood. Like the lyrics said, she was becoming a powerhouse of energy. Then came AC/DC's "Highway to Hell." She turned up the volume even higher.

Soon her exit would be coming. She clicked her left turn signal. With only inches between Peggy Sue and the Prius, she changed into the left lane and passed, and as she did she got a quick glimpse of the driver. A woman. A blonde. Roxanne didn't know how prostitution rings worked, but she knew enough to know that women could be bad guys, too. She'd teach that little bitch a thing or two. She swerved back into the right lane, now mere inches in front of the Prius. She liked being so precise. All those years as an accountant were paying off.

Next, Roxanne turned on her right signal and exited. No surprise. The red car followed. And then as if on cue, the sound of an engine starting up came through the speakers.

"What's this?" Frankie said.

"I don't know."

Frankie crawled into the front seat and checked the playlist. She was now wearing one of Roxanne's tank tops, although it was so long on Frankie that it worked out to be a mini-dress, and she'd wrapped a gold chain necklace of Roxanne's around her waist like a belt. Oh to be young and skinny again.

"It says 'Duel Soundtrack Suite.'"

Duel soundtrack, like two soundtracks? No, that didn't make sense. But then Roxanne figured it out, and she felt sinfully wicked. This was the soundtrack from that old thriller about a psychopathic truck driver. And it gave her an idea. She would need patience. And so would her customer, because she wouldn't be delivering her load on time after all. She had something far more important to do.

Instead of heading to her planned destination, Roxanne drove along the Mt. Baker Highway, through green hills east of Bellingham with views of Canada's coastal mountains to the left. She drove down into the Nooksack River Valley and made it over the bridge, safely this time. She cruised by a little white chapel on the left side of the highway and rolled past berry farms. In the tiny town of Deming, she came upon a fuel station. She didn't need gas but wondered when the last time was the Prius had filled up. She kept going, and so did her assailant.

Soon she veered south onto Highway 9, a two-lane highway, and then headed east on Highway 20, toward the northernmost pass over the Cascade Mountains.

"Where are we going?" Frankie asked.

"Well, honey, that's what we're about to figure out."

She handed Frankie her iPhone and coached her on how to look up some key information. Elevation of the passes along highway 20. Highway grade. Height and load restrictions. Fuel stations, rest stops—she still had to pee. And she had Frankie also check the distance to a remote Canadian border crossing.

As Frankie did her research, Roxanne noticed the firs and pines and telephone poles lining the two-lane road were already casting long shadows, and she knew sunset came early in the mountains. She also knew that, although the grade now was a gradual incline and the curves were soft, this would soon change. Before long she'd be testing Peggy Sue's resilience against centrifugal force.

Roxanne spotted a metal structure ahead. In the shadows, it was hard to tell what it was. Then she saw it was a narrow bridge, not more than a quarter mile up the road and getting closer by the second. There was no way Peggy Sue would clear it. She hit the brake pedal hard.

"I thought you checked all the height clearances, Frankie!"

"I did! Don't yell at me. I did exactly what you said."

The bridge was coming closer, fast. Roxanne scanned both sides of the road; there was no place to pull over. She downshifted. The engine roared. She lifted her foot from the gas to activate the Jake brake, trying to remember whether the progressive switch should be flipped to low or high. She took a guess, flipped to high. She glanced in her side view mirrors. She couldn't see the Prius, it was too close. The compressed air hissed. For the second time in one day, Peggy Sue was going to hit a bridge.

"Holy shit!" Frankie yelled.

But then, like a miracle, the road turned sharply to the left. Just in time. Roxanne hadn't seen that curve with all the shadows. They, and the bridge, would be safe, so long as she made the turn all right.

"Hang on, Frankie!"

She wheeled her rig around the curve, then stepped back on the gas once she'd made it around the bend. Sure enough, the red car was following right behind, like a colt following its runaway mother.

The mountains bulked up in the dimming light. The landscape, once fir green and granite gray, shifted to ominous hues of gunmetal and soot. There were fewer houses and towns out here now, with glimmers of incandescent light separated by lonely miles. Roxanne settled into the rhythm of the curves, twisting first to the left and then the right, but she didn't lose the intensity of her commitment to get Frankie to safety.

She started calculating.

She'd filled up with gas back before that fated bridge—200 gallons at the truck stop. In good conditions, having opted for every fuel economy gadget available for her rig, she could easily travel over 1,000 miles, and probably more, between stops if she didn't have to eat or pee. But there were a lot of factors to consider when estimating how far she could go now: vehicle load, grade, torque, auxiliary units. The grade at Newhalem was going to be upwards of 4 percent, and by the time she got to Washington Pass—if Frankie did her research correctly—she'd be looking at a 7 percent grade. That could lower her fuel economy an awful lot. As she turned off the air conditioning, she remembered a formula she'd learned before earning her commercial license, something about the position and speed and acceleration of the vehicle determined by Newton's second law of motion. Sigma $F_i$ = m · a, where $F_i$ are all forces acting on the chassis in a longitudinal direction, m is the mass, and a is the longitudinal acceleration of the chassis. Oh, drat. Shit! What she couldn't do was remember how to apply it. All she really knew was that she could go a long way. But she wasn't sure exactly how long. Could she make it all the way to Canada? Probably. Frankie had figured the border crossing she was aiming for was 238 long mountainous miles from Mt. Vern. But who knew where they were right this very minute?

And, maybe more importantly, would the Prius make it? On these roads, Peggy Sue certainly couldn't outrun the little shit, so the best Roxanne could hope for was that she'd outlast it. What was the gas mileage for those cars these days, anyway? Around 50mpg, she figured, in good conditions. How big were the tanks? Ten gallons? Fifteen? She asked Frankie to check with the iPhone, but by now there was no service. The Prius had entered the highway north of the bridge Roxanne hit, so it had traveled less distance than Peggy Sue. But there was no way of knowing when it had last been filled up. If it was right before getting on I-5, it could easily handle a trip to Canada.

If not, which Roxanne hoped was the case, then that little hussy back there would run out of gas in the middle of nowhere. The sky would soon be blacker than midnight; it would be obsidian, and the nighttime temperatures could easily plummet to below freezing. Nocturnal creatures would be on the prowl. Ha! Roxanne pictured the blonde sitting roadside, hungry and thirsty and afraid to get out of her car. If she ran out of gas out here, she could be waiting for help a long time.

The road rose higher in the mountains. After the Siskiyous, this was Roxanne's second foray driving a truck at elevation, and she knew the drop-offs here were pretty severe. Thankfully, she couldn't see much as night settled. Frankie had fallen asleep, which was a good thing. It gave Roxanne time to think.

For now, she was still thinking Canada was the answer. Of course, Frankie probably didn't have a passport, or any identification for that matter. And chances were good that Canada would have an extradition policy with the US. It wasn't a permanent solution, and at some point, Roxanne would be in big trouble. Before she got any crazier with this…what was *this*, anyway? A mad scheme? Well, before she got much further she would need more information from Frankie. And it had better be the truth. For now, though, she'd let the girl sleep.

They drove over passes and rolled down the other side of the mountains to join up with US 97 with that little red thing still on their tail like a boil on your butt until, finally, once they were well into cowboy country with sage-scented air. The Prius made a move to pass Peggy Sue—a strange move for a huntress.

Roxanne laughed. Like the psychopath in *Duel*, Roxanne tailed the Prius so closely that Peggy Sue could've licked the car's rear bumper if she'd had a tongue. The Prius sped up, and so did Peggy Sue. Then Roxanne slowed her down, way down, just to play with the little missy's head. Sure enough, the Prius hit the brakes, too. Back and forth they went, speeding up and slowing down; Roxanne had no idea what the blonde was up to but she was plenty satisfied to go along with it. She knew she could outsmart the other driver. That was a fact.

Finally the pair veered left, off the main highway, onto Loomis Oroville Road. Then right at Similkameen Road. They were less than a mile from the border crossing, which the driver of the Prius might not have even realized when she slowed way down, with her emergency lights flashing, and then came to a complete stop smack dab in the middle of the road.

Roxanne had no choice but to stop. She lifted her foot from the gas, engaged the Jake brake, then depressed the regular brake. *I've become pretty darn good at this*, she thought. *That stop was as smooth as beer pouring into a glass.*

Still, Frankie woke up.

"What are you doing?" She rubbed her eyes. "Where are we?" Then, when she saw the Prius, she shouted at Roxanne. "Oh, shit. Get going! You can't let her catch me!"

But Roxanne shifted into park. She turned off the engine and checked to be sure the cab's doors were locked. She checked the side mirrors. No other traffic was on this desolate road in the middle of the night, thank goodness.

"Listen, honey. I'm at least as worried, and maybe as confused, as you are. I think I know what your problem is, but I don't know what that Prius is up to. We're at the Canadian border and it's time you tell me what's going on. Everything. I need to know what we've gotten ourselves into here. So I know what to do." Of course, if the Prius driver was nearly as dangerous as Frankie had suggested hours earlier, stopping there and turning off the engine could have been the dumbest idea Roxanne ever had. She should have opted for the bulletproof windshield.

But before Frankie could answer, the blonde got out of her car and stood beside the driver's door. She was a small woman, and her thin arms hung by her side. She didn't seem to have a weapon and didn't appear the least bit dangerous as she looked back toward the truck. Roxanne flicked on the high beams and saw this was not exactly a woman. It was just another teenage girl.

"What the devil? She's just a child!"

"Yeah, I know. But she's older than me. And she's also the bottom bitch."

"The what?"

"The queen of the stable."

"I don't know what in the Sam Hill you're talking about."

"That's Sissy. Joey's new main girl. He probably sent her after me."

Roxanne tried to make sense of it, and all she knew right now was that she'd been playing nighttime highway chicken with a teenager and it made her feel sick and stupid and about as awful as she'd ever felt, especially to think what might have happened to the girl if there'd been any sort of accident. "Is Joey your pimp?"

Frankie didn't have to say a word. Her look gave it all away.

"How can you be afraid of Sissy? She looks as tiny as you."

"Because she can tell Joey whatever she wants about me. He'll listen to her."

Sissy now approached the truck.

"Oh my God," Frankie said, diving back through the beads. But as Sissy came closer, Roxanne saw how young and weak and scared she looked.

"She's crying. And she's holding up her cell phone, trying to show it to us."

"She's what?" Frankie asked. She looked out the windshield and saw Sissy, her phone in one hand and the back of her other hand wiping away tears. "Oh, no!"

Frankie flung the passenger door open, jumped over the two steps, ran out toward Sissy in her bare feet, and threw her arms around the crying girl. There, in the middle of the road, illuminated by the blazing headlights, they stood in a tight embrace, scantily clad and shivering.

"Well, I'll be," Roxanne declared.

What in the world was going on here? As she climbed down from her seat, Roxanne couldn't help but feel she'd been duped. All this time she'd been trying to protect this little brat and it had all been some sort of ruse? What was this, a prank? Roxanne had run from an accident. She'd hijacked her load. She'd believed every word Frankie had told her, gullible idiot that she was, and was about to bust into another country with a teenager in tow. She had half a mind to get back in the cab and drive off.

But, having half a heart still, and hungry with curiosity, Roxanne hiked up her jeans—now baggy after all those hours in the truck—and strode, weak-legged, over to the troublemakers, vowing to lay into that stowaway, let her really have it, and also vowing to herself not to believe another word that came out of that darn Frankie's mouth.

"Shhh," she heard Frankie whisper to Sissy. "It'll be all right."

"Frankie," Roxanne said. "What's going on?"

"Shhh. I'm all right."

"Frankie, I need answers. Now."

The two girls looked at her.

"Could somebody please tell me what's going on? One minute you're mortal enemies and the next your BFFs?"

This was like *The Twilight Zone*; either that or Roxanne had really lost her mind. She knew she had to get out of there before things got worse. But when Frankie and Sissy looked at one another, it wasn't the sort of look that two pranksters exchange. There were no giggles, no smug expressions. What they exchanged seemed to be dead serious, a promise of sisterhood, a shared vulnerability.

"He got to you?" Frankie asked Sissy.

The other girl nodded and held her phone for Frankie to see. A text message, Roxanne supposed.

"You can't go back."

Sissy shrugged. "I don't have much choice."

Roxanne heard the Hoosier twang in Sissy's voice. A girl from back home.

"Where're you from, honey?" Roxanne asked.

"Indiana," Sissy said.

"Does your mama know where you are?"

"Not really. She'd kill me if she knew what I've gotten myself in to."

"*He's* gonna kill you first," Frankie said. "Joey is. You've gotta come with us. In the truck."

"Now hold on just a cotton-pickin'-minute. What are you suggesting, Frankie?"

Sissy piped up. "She's right. If I go back with her, he'll beat the crap out of her. And if I don't, he'll beat the crap out of me."

"He'll do more than beat the crap out of either of us," Frankie said.

"So that's why you've been chasing us all this time?" Roxanne asked. "You either need to collect Frankie or run away yourself?"

Sissy hung her head. "I guess so."

"Just how old are you?"

"Eighteen."

"Holy Christ," Roxanne said. She recalled a story she'd seen recently on television about sex trafficking. What little these girls had said was matching what Roxanne remembered. Even right down to truck stops being used as places for setting up tricks. She figured if the girls answered her questions reasonably, they were probably telling the truth.

There were three questions she wanted to ask. How they got into this mess in the first place. How long they'd been doing it. And how she'd gotten roped into it all. She decided to start there.

"So how did Joey know I had Frankie with me?"

"I don't know much," Sissy said. "All I know is I was working at a different truck stop, I guess a few miles north of where Frankie was. Joey called me and told me someone saw Frankie climb into a pink truck that headed north. He told me to drop my john, get into the car he gave me, and track you down. I kept praying I'd find you because if I didn't Joey would have really flipped his shit."

"Guess this is your lucky day," Roxanne said. Before she went on to her other questions, she noticed shadows on Sissy's shoulders. She stepped a few feet to the side, and even with a different slant of light from Peggy Sue's high beams, the shadows were still there. Except they weren't shadows. They were bruises. She had a ring of them around each wrist, too.

There was no need to ask any more questions. Not yet, anyway.

"God. I have to pee," Frankie said.

"Me, too," Sissy said.

Roxanne threw her arms up. "Might as well."

The three women crouched and peed at the side of the road, and as her urine streamed out fast and warm as a mare's pee, Roxanne felt like maybe she was also letting go of whatever order and sanity she'd had left inside her body and was about to leave it pooled there on the side of a desolate road. She'd never encountered anything like this in her entire life. There were no generally accepted principles for life outside the world of debits and credits. No columns to add up or forms to fill out. No clean-cut answers. Sometimes you've just got to do what comes natural to you, what seems right at the time, and worry about tomorrow tomorrow.

"All right. Get in the truck," she said as she zipped up her jeans.

"What are we going to do?" Frankie said.

"Just get in."

Roxanne climbed up into the driver's seat and started the engine. The two girls climbed in through the passenger door and slammed it shut. Frankie sat on the floor between the two seats; Sissy rode shotgun. Roxanne checked her side mirror. Headlights were approaching from the rear.

The lights could belong to Joey, Roxanne speculated. Or the customer looking for their steel rods. Or the Department of Transportation could be coming after her for knocking down that old bridge, which had seemed like such a far-fetched thing a few hours ago. Or maybe it was the state police out to get her for kidnapping a youth. Or who knew? Maybe border control had detected her and somehow knew she was heading for the border without passports for these girls. All she knew for certain was that trouble was about to arrive. And that other thing she'd so desired—adventure after retirement—had sure enough come along, too.

She repositioned the trailer so that it cut diagonally across the road. She engaged the fifth wheel release switch. Peggy Sue shook as the flatbed of steel unhitched. It wasn't as eloquent as it would have been if she'd gotten out to put down the landing gear, but she didn't have time for finesse.

"Here we go," Roxanne said. She laid down the hammer one more time and headed for the border, leaving the weighty load behind. The security crossing gate would be down at this time of night. But that wouldn't stop Roxanne or the girls. Peggy Sue would just bust them right on through.

# FROM HERE TO CAFAYATE

# One Afternoon at Santa Lucia Station

—KAKE HUCK

Two calico sisters, all bone
with age, are sleeping near the narrow
causeway that connects Venice, The Most
Serene, to Europe (so that the latter isn't lonely)

when one cat (the larger - a bit
of orange beneath her oval chin)
is startled by the noon-time
train's hot rush and reaches
for her ancient box-mate,
who is now already stretching
into elsewhere,  leaning away
from the always forever
hunger of the other's need.

**MIRIAM SHUFFLED** across the retirement home's dining room, moving her walker forward inches at a time, toward the booth in the back corner where her sister Penelope was seated. Finally, she got there, and as her hands held fast to the walker, but before she could maneuver her old bones down onto the seat, she thought she heard Penelope say she was leaving.

"What's that you said?" she asked. "You're what?"

Penelope scanned the dining room, ignoring the question. Miriam squinted at the old Timex her parents had given her for Christmas long ago that, miraculously—and just like her self—had taken some lickings but still kept on ticking. Although she could no longer read the numerals, she knew she wasn't late for dinner. She had taken great care to get the laundry out of the dryer—the aide's job, but sometimes the aides didn't finish their work before going home—in plenty of time. Why on earth, she wondered, would her sister insist on leaving so soon?

A memory appeared in her mind, an apparition she'd been unable to dismiss for decades. There she sat at a long high school cafeteria table, alone, a skinny little freshman bookworm, a girl who had hoped to sit in the lunchroom with her big sister, the popular one, the student body president, only to discover—when she spotted Penelope on the other side of the cafeteria, laughing with a group of older students—that siblings had no responsibilities toward one another once outside the purview of their parents. That day had been just one of the countless times her big sister had rebuffed or even abandoned her, like the runt of a litter, over all those years.

"Why are you looking at me that way?" Penelope now asked, finally acknowledging Miriam's arrival. "Why do you always have that clueless look on your face?"

A server, the tall woman with very, very dark skin whose name Miriam could never remember, brought waters to the table, and Miriam was grateful for the time to pause. As she reached for her water—it was her turn now to avoid her sister's gaze—she was half tempted to throw the glass across the table. Why did Penelope always insist on putting her down? Miriam was not stupid, far from it. And Penelope, who had barely made it through two years of community college, knew that.

Besides, even if Miriam did *look* stupid, she certainly didn't look any worse than most everyone else here. Nearly all the residents wandered, and hobbled, and wheeled around in a daze half the time, their big, weepy eyes peering through humongous eyeglasses, trying to figure out who said what to whom. Which is what she was still trying to do, figure out what Penelope had said, or at least what she had meant, about leaving.

Of course, her sister was different from the others around this place. Slim and straight and terribly smart-looking in that stylish silk-tweed jacket. Shoulders erect, boobs still almost perky. She still had her own teeth, rarely wore cheater glasses, and never complained about arthritis. Her memory was intact, too. Aside from the list of wrinkles across her forehead, you'd never know Penelope was pushing ninety. She kept on go-go-going like...what was the name of that pink bunny marching with the drum? Miriam, who could once recall and recite 32 digits of pi, could no longer remember anymore the name of a silly rabbit on a battery commercial. She resented Penelope's health. She resented her sister's arrogance, too.

"I'm serious, Miri," Penelope said. She picked at the wedge of iceberg lettuce and French dressing the server had just set down. "I've had enough. Of everything. I'm checking out."

Miriam watched the server, whose belly was now showing her condition. She wondered who the father was, whether perhaps he worked here. And what was the girl's name? Alice? Alicia? She had such beautiful skin. Miriam imagined she was from somewhere in Africa, an exotic place she'd never seen in real life. And what did Penelope mean about checking out?

"Miri? Miri! See, this is exactly what I mean," Penelope said. "I move in here with you, at your urging, and all you or anyone does around here is sit in a chair and watch the world go by."

"Hmm?" Actually, although Miriam had agreed it would be nice if Penelope moved in with her, it was Penelope's daughter who had done the insisting. "Oh, I'm sorry, Pen. I admit it, I've been feeling a bit off lately." She lowered her voice. "I think they've changed my meds." She stabbed a chunk of lettuce and forked it into her mouth, but her lower dentures were loose. Her teeth threatened to slip right out of her mouth whenever she began to chew, and she felt a string of saliva tracing its way down her chin at the same time she felt the heat of Penelope's glare. "Now what were you saying?"

Just then, a gaggle of eight women came into the dining room like they owned the place, all chittering and chattering and making quite a scene. Two were driving those fancy electric wheelchairs, and a couple of them had walkers but moved at a much faster clip than Miriam could. The rest of them walked fairly well, like Penelope, although they were certainly far younger than she was—maybe in their seventies. They, too, always drew attention from others wherever they went, what with their fashionable clothes and salon hairdos and all the carrying on they did with each other. They called themselves the Golden Girls.

Joanne and Bette were part of that group now. They had been Miriam's two best friends at the retirement home, and the three had always dined together before Joanne and Bette were invited into the clique when a couple of other women died. Now they were part of the group of eight who ate, played Bunko, and had their nails done together, and Miriam was once again a nobody.

Today they sat at the table next to Miriam's.

"Oh, for heaven's sake," Penelope muttered. "Wipe your chin, Miri. And stop staring."

Miriam turned back toward her sister, but her thoughts were caught over at the Golden Girls' table. She wished she could be one of them, but then again was glad she wasn't; Bunko was a stupid game, and she considered herself far too intellectual for their gossip. She didn't even like most of them, and she certainly didn't approve of their middle school rules about who could sit with whom. So why did she feel so jealous?

She pressed her teeth into place, then swiped her fingers across her napkin until she noticed Penelope's expression.

"I'm leaving, Miri."

"But you've barely touched your salad."

Just then, the server returned with two plates of tilapia. One had creamed corn on the side, the other peas. The server smiled warmly at Miriam as she gave her the plate with the corn, but her expression neutralized when she gave Penelope her food, which gave Miriam a rare and unintentional jolt of superiority.

"I'm tired," Penelope said. "And I want to get the hell out of here. This whole scene."

Now Miriam began to understand. She wasn't talking about leaving the table. She was talking about leaving the home. "You've only been here a few weeks." Miriam recalled how much she had looked forward to sharing an apartment with her sister.

"Two weeks, and three days, to be exact. And I hate it."

It was hard not to take that sort of comment personally. But Penelope never had been known for her tact. Or her math skills. She was off by a week; it had been three weeks and three days. And four hours, give or take.

"Okay, whatever you say," Miriam said. "I know how hard it is to get acclimated here. It was hard for me, too." A bit of a lie. She had grown tired of being alone, and had craved camaraderie, and had found it rather easily—at first, anyway, until the *rules* became clearer. "But you have to give it some time. This is a big adjustment. Giving up your home, your independence, your freedom."

"Exactly my point!" Penelope pointed the tines of her fork at Miriam. "And ever since I got here I've felt totally confined. Same old food every day, same old activities. Same old people."

"Well, this *is* an old folks home. And you *are* old."

"Maybe so, but I'm not ready to give up my independence and my freedom. That's why I'm leaving."

"But where will you go? Your daughter sold your house."

Penelope scooped a pile of peas onto her fork, using her knife to steady them. Her frosty lavender nail polish was so pretty.

"And I can't imagine Lynn would let you move in with her," Miriam continued. It was a harsh thing to say, but true. Everyone knew Penelope didn't get along well with her daughter Lynn, which Miriam could never understand. She would have given anything to save her own daughter from that horrible automobile accident. Some people just don't recognize their blessings; for them, nothing is ever good enough.

"Well obviously I won't move in with Lynn. She made that perfectly clear when she forced me to move here. Besides, she's too busy climbing mountains all over the world to worry about little old me."

"May I remind you that Lynn inherited her travel genes from you?" As far as Miriam was concerned, her sister—having traveled the globe first as a stewardess and later as the co-owner of a travel agency—had no business sounding so self-righteous about Lynn. She spooned some creamed corn into her mouth, careful not to spill any down her chin this time, and then scooped a portion of fish onto her spoon.

"So where *are* you going?" Miriam asked.

"Well, first, let me ask you this. Do you have any idea what's going on out there?"

Penelope waved her fork mid-air in a wide swath toward the window, and a small bit of fish flew off. Miriam watched the fish sail toward the windowsill, then turned her attention to the dark clouds hovering over the rooftops of the adjacent neighborhood.

"No, what's going on out there? Do you mean that thunderstorm?"

Penelope rolled her eyes. "Really? You have no idea what I'm talking about? Haven't you been listening to the news lately? Haven't you heard what the government is doing to all of us?"

What a turn of the tides this was. Miriam had once loved studying world affairs and debating politics with their father, while Penelope was off gallivanting with friends. Even when she had been student body president, Penelope had had no idea what she was doing. Miriam had coached her through that year and even had to teach her big sister about *Robert's Rules of Order*. Now here sat Penelope, arranging her peas in a line on her plate and trying to sound like an expert on all things political. The mere notion entertained, Miriam, even while it exasperated her.

"What do you mean, Pen?"

Penelope harrumphed. "See what I mean? This is what happens when you live in a place like this watching *Wheel of Fortune* and *Jeopardy!* I'm not going to let that happen to me."

Miriam's hackles rose. Until her big sister had moved in with her, Miriam had spent much of each day reading the *New York Times* or listening to NPR or watching PBS specials. Granted, her attention span wasn't all it once was, but she was still deeply interested in life outside of this elderly ecosystem. In fact, it was only after the sisters began to live together, and Penelope was always complaining about one thing or another, that Miriam had switched on those game shows because she couldn't concentrate on the more serious matters with her sister around. She opened her mouth to defend against Penelope's assertion, but again felt that same sense of déjà vu, and she was just too old and tired to get into a snit with Pen, the same way she was too tired to discuss the world's problems anymore, as if she'd been born with a finite number of social debate cells, like ovarian eggs, and they were now all used up.

"Let's start with the spies," Penelope went on. "They're everywhere."
She poked at invisible spots in the air. "You know this, right? They're
watching our every move. Everything we say and do. They listen to our
phone calls. They read our tweets and posts—oh, I forgot, you *still* don't
use the computer."

This was true, but Miriam *did* have a cell phone, at least.

"And they have those teeny little things that fly around and peer into
our windows, like hummingbirds. Drones, they call them." Penelope's
chin was raised high.

None of this was news to Miriam.

"And that's not all. Did you know the government is dropping
chemicals into our atmosphere from the chem trails emitted by aircraft to
control population growth? Or that all the fluoride going into municipal
water systems is intended to dumb down our population? And you
haven't had a flu shot, have you, Miri? They're implanting chips in us
when we get our flu shots to track our whereabouts."

Had Penelope started taking a new medicine and was now having a
bad reaction? Would that explain all this sudden paranoia? Drones, NSA
allegations, and conspiracy theories of all sorts had been around for years.
Even if some of those things were true, Miriam really couldn't imagine the
government bothering anyone in an old folks' home. She did, however,
recall having read stories of old people in nursing homes being fed
medicines that made them crazy, and she started to think about where she'd
last seen Lynn's phone number. She needed to call her niece. Let her know
something was wrong with Penelope.

"Where are you getting all these ideas?" Miriam asked, because
Penelope had never been one to read the paper. Even way back in the
fourth grade, when Penelope had coerced Miriam into doing her current
event assignments for her.

"It's all over the news, Miri. Why, everyone's talking about how bad
it's become out there. The government is cracking down on all of us. The
IRS. The CIA. FBI. NSA. The TSA, and DEA, and NEA and PTA. They even
track what we buy at the grocery store. And decide what we can and cannot
eat, like raw milk, for instance. And they're taking our money, too."

Miriam reached for the pepper. The fish was bland. "But you don't
even drink raw milk."

"And that's not all," Penelope went on, ignoring Miriam. She had set
her utensils down and was gripping the edge of the table as though for

dear life. "They're going to raise taxes again, you can bet your bottom dollar on that. Even on little old ladies like us. And I read where they're going to eliminate Social Security."

"Oh, Penelope, my goodness. They're not going to eliminate Social Security for people our age. As for taxes, we're both on a fixed income so I'm not too worried about that. And the rest of all this? It's just rubbish. You don't really believe it all, do you? Are you getting all this off the Internet? See, that's why I stay away from that technology. It's not good for you."

Joanne leaned toward them now from the other table.

"Hi, girls. I couldn't help but overhear your conversation. You know what I heard? The State of Illinois made Martha leave here because she required more care than an assisted living place is supposed to provide. They forced her into a nursing home!"

"It gets worse!" Bette said. "I read about an AARP tour group planning to go to the French Open, and the United States wouldn't let those poor people out of our very own country! Can you imagine? They treated those senior citizens like war criminals trying to defect."

"See what I mean?" Penelope said.

Miriam suddenly felt trapped there in the booth. She couldn't believe Joanne and Bette's audacity, interjecting their stories into her private conversation with Penelope. How rude could they be? Worse yet, she saw a new alliance forming as Penelope and Joanne nodded at one another.

"Pen, you're getting yourself all worked up over nothing," Miriam said.

Penelope ignored Miriam. Again. "They're all crooks," she said, not only to Joanne and Bette but to the entire adjacent table. All the women were now devoting rapt attention to the discussion. "From the President right down to the post office clerks. Every last one of them is a crook. And forget about the media. They're owned by the CIA, you know."

Miriam didn't know what to do, other than eat. She mixed her peppered tilapia into the creamed corn—better for the loose teeth—and scooped a spoonful of the mush into her mouth.

"You know what?" Penelope slammed her fork down. "I'm actually glad they don't say the Pledge of Allegiance in the schools anymore. Because I certainly don't think our government deserves anyone's allegiance."

Oh Lord. This was sacrilege, Miriam thought, to talk about our country this way. The United States of America. The greatest nation on earth, a nation that had been so good to both of them when their generational counterparts had suffered at the hands of villains and dictators around the world. Of course the President and Congress had their flaws. But it could be a lot worse. Even today, they could be living in some third world country. Or worse, they could be six feet under. She glanced at the Golden Girls, whose eight sets of eyes were big and round.

"Penelope, you sound like a terrorist. Stop this."

"And then there are all these illegal citizens," Penelope said anyway, her voice rising higher. "They're taking over our country. All those Hispanics and Ethiopians and of course the Asians, too. Our freedoms and taxes are being robbed from us while all those foreigners are coming in and getting health care and driver's licenses. It's appalling, that's what it is."

Now Miriam wanted to slide under the table and die. Her sister sounded like a right wing zealot. Had she always had these views? Or was dementia setting in? Being on the high school debate team had taught Miriam when to speak and when to listen and how to plan her next remark. But right now, although she'd been listening, she couldn't fathom what kind of retort she should offer. Her mind felt about as mushy as the fish on her plate.

The server approached the table with a coffee pot, and Miriam hoped to hell her sister didn't spout off anymore about foreigners. Then, as the girl poured coffee into Miriam's cup with one hand, she rested her other hand on the tummy bump. Miriam guessed she was at least five months along, maybe six, and then she recalled her own bump before her daughter was born. And then Penelope's bump, which had been so huge they were certain there would be twins. And then she thought of Penelope's daughter's pregnancy. What chaos ensued after Lynn announced her own pregnancy. She remembered it like it was just yesterday.

Penelope had called Miriam in a complete dither. "He wears a turban! What am I going to do? I can't allow my daughter to marry a Muslim! I can't allow her to raise a foreigner."

Miriam had thought it thrilling that her niece was dating a man from the Middle East, something relatively unheard of back in those days—when was that, the 1970's? At least it was unheard of there in the Midwest. She'd tried to convince Penelope that it was up to Lynn to decide if she wanted to marry a Muslim, and that there was nothing whatsoever Penelope could or should do. Furthermore, as long as it was Lynn's baby, it wasn't exactly a foreign baby. Not to mention the fact that the entire country was made up of foreigners, except for the Native Americans. But Penelope wouldn't listen to a word Miriam said, and kept saying *foreigner* as though it was a dirty word. When Miriam heard that Penelope eventually persuaded Lynn to give the baby up for adoption, she was heartbroken. She had looked so forward to that baby. No wonder Penelope and Lynn's relationship became rocky.

And now, thirty years or so later, nothing had changed. After all these years, Penelope was still opposed to the idea of people coming into the country from other lands. Miriam had never understood why her sister, *the world traveler*, had these views; certainly it hadn't come from their parents. Maybe it was because she'd failed to appreciate her social studies classes. Maybe it was because she'd wanted to set herself apart from Miriam—the bookish, liberal daughter. Whatever the reason, all that mattered now was that Penelope was attracting the attention of even more retirement home residents, now gathering around and listening to her shallow proclamations as though they'd been brought down from the mountain by Moses himself, the same way the high school students listened to her pronouncements as a popular yet uninformed student body president all those years ago.

"So I tell you, I've had enough," Penelope was saying. "You all can stay behind, if that's what you want. But I'm leaving."

This was getting out of hand. Miriam reached across the table toward Penelope. "Let's go up to our apartment, Pen. We can have someone bring more coffee up to us."

Miriam started to push herself up from the seat—not an easy task—without waiting for her sister's reply, but that handsome man who lived down the hall, and whom half the women swooned over—was his name Martin?—came along, and without warning or invitation he scooted into the booth beside Penelope. He had never so much as said "boo" to Miriam, but now here he was *flirting* with her big sister. He had the bluest eyes and the same magazine-cover Germanic features as Penelope. The two could have been brother and sister. In fact, he looked more like Penelope than Miriam did.

Soon another man came over and stood next to Miriam's side of the booth. This was Tom, Martin's sidekick. The two men went everywhere together, like an aristocrat and his butler, like those characters on Downton Abbey. Miriam had exchanged short conversations with Tom now and then, ever since his wife Helen had passed. His ears were as big as the flowers on some of Miriam's old hats, and he only had about two strands of hair left on his head, both of them gray. But he had a nice smile.

He motioned to the booth's seat with rheumy, questioning eyes. Although Miriam really wanted to get out of there, she also didn't want to be rude, and she felt a flutter of excitement that a man would sit next to her. It had been oh, so long—decades—since her husband had died, so she scooted deeper into the booth, next to the wall, and he sat down, and now the four of them sat there in the booth as though they were on a double date. Yet Miriam felt rather trapped, and as it turned out Tom was far more interested in Penelope's passion, which glowed even brighter now that she had two men in her audience. Another familiar feeling from the past.

"I'm talking about the end of the world as we've known it," Penelope said, nodding with confidence, her cheeks flushed and her eyes shining brighter than the diamonds on her rings.

"The demise of our empire," Martin said, nodding in agreement, and Tom nodded, too, and then all the heads at Joanne's table wobbled in unison like dutiful constituents, although one could never be sure if they were agreeing or just suffering from Parkinson's disease. Martin asked Penelope a series of questions, as though Penelope were some sort of political expert, and soon more men and women from the retirement home were gathered around the booth and Joanne's table, too, and the server—bless her heart—tried to weave in and around the crowd serving coffee and tea and ice cream, including two more cups passed in to Miriam.

"We need a gold standard. I assume you're invested in gold?" somebody from the crowd asked, and Penelope and Martin exchanged looks, and she—ever so cleverly, Miriam assumed—demurred to him for a reply.

"Don't get me started on that!" Martin said.

"Whatever happened to our Constitution?" asked another, and Martin replied that it had gone the way of the Model T.

"What I worry most about is this police state," he added, and when a moan of agreement permeated the room, Miriam thought she felt her blood pressure spike. She was tired of all this societal criticism; back in the day she would have reveled in this sort of banter, but nowadays it took too much energy to keep track of, to comprehend. Martin asked Penelope if she'd gotten her second passport yet, his voice loud enough for all the TSA officers in the county—and pretty much the entire country—to hear. Second passport? Miriam was trying to recall whether she herself had ever even held a first passport, not having traveled out of the country in her entire lifetime, when she then heard Martin add something about Uruguay being the place to go if you want a second one. Uruguay? It sounded so...far away.

By then she had already finished three cups of coffee and a tall glass of water, and Miriam realized her bladder was perilously full. There she sat, tucked in the booth against the wall, and who knew where her walker had gone. Then, as the conversation drifted to a discussion of other exotic places like Nicaragua and Papua New Guinea, and just before she had the chance to nudge Tom to ask him to let her out of the booth, Penelope answered his question.

"Yes, as a matter of fact I have. And I am leaving...the country."

And that's exactly when Miriam lost all control.

She felt the warmth, and the blessed release of the sphincter, and once the flow started there was no stopping it. No one, of course, could see her peeing, but Tom glanced down at the seat between them, then grimaced and scooted away from her and out from the booth entirely. And then Penelope, across the table, scrunched up her nose and asked what that smell was. Martin asked what the devil and looked under the table, but so far it still wasn't too bad, until one of the women at Joanne's table stood up and loudly shouted out for some help over here, pointing directly at Miriam, the way a mean girl once did in kindergarten seventy-some-odd years ago when Miriam had peed in her pants, which was one of those memories you could never forget—even after the early stages of dementia have settled in.

"Oh, for heaven's sake," Penelope said, and Miriam didn't know if her big sister was more exasperated about the accident or about the fact that Miriam had inadvertently interrupted her sister's performance, but it didn't matter. What mattered was that Miriam thought she was going to die of shame.

Thankfully, Alice, or Alicia, matter-of-factly wheeled a vinyl-seated wheelchair to the table, already prepared with a towel for Miriam to sit on. Bless her heart.

After changing clothes and cleaning herself, Miriam settled on her sofa and pulled a crocheted afghan over her lap. A stack of newspapers waited for her on the side table, but she wasn't interested in reading about the world's problems right now. She wasn't interested in doing much of anything; Penelope's performance, and her own traitorous bladder, had seen to that. After making a note to order some of those disposable underpants, which she'd resisted until now because it seemed like yet another nail in her coffin, she was about to doze off into restful bliss. Until she heard a key in the door's lock.

In walked Penelope.

"We need to talk, Miri," she said.

Miriam scowled at her sister.

"Are you angry with me?" Penelope asked. "I don't know why you would be. I'm not the one who had the accident."

"Are you serious? You have no idea why I'm upset? Well, I have no idea how you can be so insensitive."

"What? Because I didn't help you clean up that mess?" Penelope reached for the TV remote, and that was all Miriam needed now, a bunch of irritating background noise and something else to interfere with their sister relationship. She tried to snatch the remote control back, but Penelope held on tight.

"No, Pen, that's not it. God forbid you should do something like that for me. It's everything else that upsets me. Did you listen to yourself down there? Did you hear what you said about our country?" She straightened the afghan on her lap.

"Well it's all true."

"That's a matter of opinion. And what about what you said to me? You called me stupid, Penelope. And ignored me and acted like the Miss Know-It-All Queen of Sheba with all those people, people who used to be my friends. It was embarrassing, but you don't care about me or what I think. Maybe I never should have agreed to let you move in here. Maybe I should have learned, a long time ago, to pretend you don't even exist."

She winced as she said this, not sure she really meant it, and Penelope looked stricken. Miriam had lost her husband, her daughter, and her parents years ago. More recently, she'd lost her house. She didn't want to lose her sister now, too, but then again maybe she'd never had her. The old grandfather clock chimed.

Penelope reached into her handbag. "Here, Miri. I thought you'd want to see this."

She shoved an envelope at Miriam, who simply looked at it.

"Take it. Open it."

"Not until you apologize."

"For what?"

Had Penelope not listened to a word Miriam had said? "For a lifetime of being hurtful toward me."

"Oh, Miri. You're acting like a child."

"So?"

"Maybe it's you that should apologize."

"For what?"

"Exactly. See, you've done things to me and you don't know it either. Just open the envelope and I'll get out of here," Penelope said.

"Not until you apologize. Or tell me what I've done that's so awful."

"Then you'll open the envelope?"

"Yes," Miriam said.

"Promise?"

They were both behaving like children, for goodness sake. "Pinky promise," Miriam finally said without even a hint of a smile. "Now tell me."

"Well," Penelope said. "Here goes nothing. To tell the truth, I've always resented you."

"What? You've resented me? And that's why you're so mean to me?"

"I've always been jealous of you."

"Why? You were always the popular one," Miriam said.

"You were the smart one. The one with straight A's."

"You were tall and slim."

"You didn't need braces or glasses."

"You were a free bird. Adventurous. Courageous, too. You got to travel all over the world," Miriam said.

"You were Mom and Dad's favorite," Penelope said.

"Was not."

"Yes you were. Goody two-shoes."

"Well maybe that's because I went to school and did my homework and obeyed their rules. And when they needed something I helped them. I showed them I loved them. Maybe I deserved being their favorite."

"Maybe. Now open the envelope."

"'Course, it's not like it matters anymore," Miriam said, ignoring Penelope's command. "They're gone, and you didn't even go to their funeral."

"I was out of the country. You didn't tell me they'd been in an accident."

"That was your problem, not mine, Pen. No one even knew where you were. And whether or not that was a valid excuse for missing their funeral, what was your reason for not coming to my daughter's funeral?"

Penelope reached for the back of a dining room chair. She pulled it out from the table and sat down, her face relaxing as she did. "Is that what this is all about, Miriam? Me missing your daughter's funeral? That was years ago."

"You know, Penelope? You're the one who's always calling me clueless, but that word really applies more to you. Of course I was upset you didn't come to her funeral. And to her wedding. And my fiftieth birthday party. And everything else, too. But most of all, I'm upset you missed the whole part about being a sister. We're supposed to belong to one another. But you've always been so full of yourself. And we don't have much time left."

Miriam scooted forward to the edge of the sofa and rocked back and forth three times before she was able to boost herself out of the seat. "I'm putting the kettle on. Would you like some chamomile tea?"

"Not until you open the envelope. You promised."

"I'm not sure I can see what it says without my reading glasses."

"You're wearing them," Penelope said. She pointed to the chain that hung from Miriam's neck.

"Oh, so I am."

She put them on and ripped the envelope open slowly. There was a glossy brochure inside. She pulled it out.

At first she looked at a colorful picture of people drinking wine in a vineyard, laughing—as models are prone to do—and another of men riding horses in polo outfits, and then one boasting acres of a lush golf course. She began to read the words, and as she did she felt like she was falling, like she was spiraling down into a dark hole. She had heard Penelope correctly.

"You're really leaving the country? You're moving to Argentina?"

Penelope, beaming, nodded.

Miriam's mind went blank for a moment, like fuzzy snow on her TV way back in the 1960's. Then she began to focus again, slowly. And instead of feeling like she was sinking, she felt something bubbling up inside. Emotional magma. She felt heat rushing through her body. A hot flash, like she'd had decades ago when going through menopause. But this wasn't a rush of hormones. This was the feeling of a raw wound, the torment of tender skin being ripped apart and the heat of blood gushing out. Her sister was leaving her again, this time once and for all.

If Penelope were abandoning her by dying, it would be forgivable. But no, she was moving halfway around the world as part of some cockamamie plan to get away from the greatest government in the world in order to live in a country with a notoriously bloody past, rather than spending her final years with the one person who'd loved her no matter what. All the anger and sorrow from the past seven or eight decades of disappointments came cascading back into Miriam's fragile memory, disrupting and scattering all the thoughts and feelings she'd spent years tending to and organizing and filing away.

"Argentina," Miriam said.

"Yes! There's so much to do there. The weather's lovely. The people are delightful. And it's cheap. You can live off the grid if you want. You've got absolute freedom."

Miriam found her mind wandering to *Evita* and then to history books, in which she'd read about corruption in South America, the Dirty War when thousands of Argentines disappeared, and the economic disaster surrounding the new millennium. Absolute freedom? Not likely. And besides, what kind of person runs away to a place like that?

"You're a traitor, Penelope. To your country. To your daughter. And to me. And what about your argument against foreigners coming into *this* country? Aren't you being a bit of a hypocrite?"

"You're being naïve, Miriam. The Argentines love us. We bring good things to them. You have no idea what we're in for in this country."

"And neither do you. As far as I'm concerned, let them spy on me here. I've got nothing to hide. This is our home, Pen. If you really have a problem, then you should take action to fix it the same way you'd fix a broken pipe in your kitchen. Running away doesn't solve a thing." She knew as she said this that, at their advanced age, there was really little they could do to change the world, and neither of them could fix a pipe these days either.

She also knew there was a tinge of resentment in her voice; maybe if Pen had invited her to come along she'd have been more willing to keep an open mind.

"I'm not running away, Miri. I'm choosing a new path. There's a difference, you know."

Miriam envisioned Penelope on a horse, galloping across the open pampas. She saw her sipping rich coffee at an outdoor café, where donkeys nibbled on grass in a town square. She imagined a handsome young man teaching Penelope how to speak Spanish.

But then she saw her sister at the border, trying to travel back into the States. Maybe it would be for Miriam's funeral that Penelope would come back, though not likely. Whatever the reason, would Argentina let her sister leave? Would the USA let her sister return? Miriam's heart began to beat fast. Palpitations, her doctor had called them. From her atrial fibrillation. She closed her eyes and tried to take some slow breaths, thinking she should probably also take another aspirin.

"Miri? Are you all right?"

Miriam tried not to imagine her final days alone. Her final day. Sitting on her loveseat, or perhaps lying in her bed. Her heart would race out of control. She would push the button to have an aide attend to her, but the aide would be slow to arrive, as they all were, and by then it would be too late. Penelope would be sipping wine somewhere far south of the equator, and Miriam would be gasping for her last breath in this very apartment, alone.

"I thought you'd be proud of me, Miri."

Miriam felt Penelope tugging on the brochure in her hands. She held onto it tight. "How long do you really plan to be gone?" Miriam asked, keeping her eyes closed against the answer she knew would come. But before her sister had a chance to answer, she saw a flash against her eyelids, and when she sat up and looked out the window, she heard a crescendo of percussion booms. The lamps flickered. The windows rattled.

"I guess the storm's arrived," Penelope said.

The two looked into one another.

"Has it ever occurred to you that maybe I'm not content to just sit here in my rocking chair, waiting to die?" Penelope asked.

Miriam held her hand to her heart. Stress was not good for people with heart trouble. And although she'd been the star on her high school and college debate teams all those years ago, she'd never learned how to keep her cool when dealing with her own sister. Waiting to die? Is that what Penelope thought she was doing?

"I think you're just a coward, hiding behind all that nonsense about this country's failings. You're afraid to grow old."

"A coward? Oh Miri, please." Penelope's words were strong but her lips twisted. "A coward wouldn't take this opportunity. It's the adventurous, courageous person—the type of person I am—who, even in old age, still wants to try something new. Reading books and newspapers isn't enough for me. I need to experience life and the world. Yes, it's the person with dreams and hopes who does this sort of thing, my dear sister. The person who never gives up believing in Shangri-La."

Miriam thought about that. Maybe Penelope was on to something. At least she was still following her dreams.

By now rain was pelting the window. Miriam turned the brochure over and looked at the word on the cover. "Is that the name of this place? Cafayate?"

Penelope cleared her throat. "Yes. It is. But you pronounce the *y* as *zh*. Ca-fa-zha-tay. It's named after an early tribe."

"My Lord, Pen, it is beautiful." She looked up and thought she saw a tear in her sister's eye, for the first time. Ever. "It does look a bit like Shangri-La. But you don't need to move there, do you? Can't you just visit, and then come home?"

Penelope shook her head. "Aw, Miri. You can't leave paradise once you finally find it. It's not humanly possible."

Miriam looked at the photos again, then tossed the pamphlet onto the coffee table and lifted her eyes to meet her sister's.

There was a knock at the door, and Penelope went to answer it. It was an aide, who had come to see if Miriam had changed her wet clothes yet.

"Yes, thank you, dear. I've changed," Miriam said. She had changed her clothes, anyway. But she was still the same person she'd been all along: stable, conscientious, agreeable. And Penelope was the same, too. Still wandering off to a new land about which she knew very little. Still courageous, and still selfish.

"I'd best get packing," Penelope said, moving toward her bedroom, the larger of the two.

Miriam tried to stand, too, but she was too weak and tired to get up from the soft sofa cushions. "Penelope. Come here."

In one way, she wanted to slap her big sister across the face for leaving her. But she also wanted to hug her and wish her farewell. Two opposing thoughts, aimed at one another like a couple of angry, hissing cats.

Penelope came to the sofa and sat down beside Miriam, and tentatively they reached for each other's hands. Once Miriam felt the strength of her sister's hands wrapped around her own, she decided this was exactly how she'd want to die, right here with her sister beside her. But today wasn't her day to go.

Penelope gave Miriam one of her half-smiles, and her eyes looked moist. Miriam wanted to think this meant they finally understood one another, which was all Miriam could really ask or hope for. And then Penelope glanced down at the watch on her wrist. Miriam followed Penelope's eyes and saw that her sister still wore her old Timex, too. The two sisters had different lives—always had, always would. But they still had matching watches, and no matter where they were, and no matter how many thousands of miles separated them, they would always keep time together.

Until the day came when time—or at least their Timex watches—would finally stop.

# Gratitude

I have been on the brink a number of times in my life, and while I have never actually gone over the edge or even run away for more than a couple of hours at a time, I confess I have thought, worried, and even fantasized about the possibilities many times. What keeps me tethered to my present life, and work, is the comfort in knowing there are people who care about me—people I would also miss terribly if I did, in fact, disappear one way or the other. I am grateful to all of them for their love.

With regard to this collection—which has also led me closer to the brink on more than one occasion—there are a great many people I need to thank. They showed me their interest, they kept me on track, they believed in me.

My fellow writers, who offered insightful critique along the way: JoAnn Heydron, Kim Kankiewicz, Bharti Kirchner, and Christine Z. Mason.

My phenomenal and very smart readers (some of whom are also accomplished writers), who each saw different strengths—and flaws—in the stories and thereby helped make me richer and fuller: Linda Allasia, Amy Byron, Tammy Dietz, Connie Druliner, Norma Dubois, Hilary Kretchmer Fulp, Lea Galanter, Barbara Farley, Erin Fielding, Nancy Horton, Kake Huck, Donna King, Glenys Loewen-Thomas, Kelleen Lum, Lauri McCulloch, Sue Moseley, Julie Russell, Lori Sollom, April Spiese, Sharon Spiese, and Sherie Weisenberg.

My poet contributors, who discerned meaning from each of my stories and re-expressed the meaning as only a poet can do: Ryan Bradley, Kierstin Bridger, Lea Galanter, Kake Huck, Tee Iseminger, Nessa McCasey, Alexa Mergen, Abby E. Murray, Elaine Nussbaum, Mary Salisbury, Patricia Reynolds Sørbye, Autumn Stephens, Ann Teplick, and Andrew Levi Wood.

My cover artist, who found a way to beautifully express how overwhelming some of life's most critical conundrums and most important decisions can be: Lindsey Surin.

My publishing team, who stuck with me along a sometimes bumpy road: Maria Aiello, Erin Curlett, and J.C. Wing.

My husband and three sons, who have supported this project, my writing career, and me: John, Dylan, Forrest, and Harrison Kretchmer.

And finally, my late mom, who constantly asked me if I still enjoyed writing and, in so doing, made me examine over and over again what I was trying to accomplish and whether my work was really expressing the things I wanted to say: Marge Spiese.

These stories are for all of you.

# About the Cover Artist

**LINDSEY SURIN** is an artist from Orland Park, Illinois who studied Studio Art at Saint Xavier University. She specializes in portraiture, and her medium of choice is graphite, but she also incorporates charcoal, colored pencil, oil paint, acrylic paint, and photography into her artwork. Her work has been featured on the cover of Saint Xavier University's art and literary magazine, *Opus*. Lindsey finds joy in creating photo realistic drawings with a huge attention to fine detail. For more information about Lindsey Surin, please visit her website: <u>surinl01.wix.com/lindseysurinart</u>.

# About the Poets

**RYAN BRADLEY** is the author of eight books including *The Waiting Tide*, a poetry collection, and the novella, *Winterswim*. He lives in Oregon with his wife and sons.

**KIERSTIN BRIDGER** earned her MFA at Pacific University and is a winner of the Mark Fischer Poetry Prize and the ACC Writer's Studio Prize. You can find her poetry in *Prime Number, Thrush Poetry Journal, Cactus Heart, Fugue,* and other publications. Please visit her website at http://thepoetryloft.net/kbridger/.

**LEA GALANTER** is a Seattle-area editor and writer with a background in history, journalism, and philosophy. After writing plays and performing onstage in Seattle for many years, she ventured into poetry and has studied with the poets Kelli Russell Agodon, Susan Rich, and Elizabeth Austin.

**KAKE HUCK** says she has made so little money writing poetry that the IRS considers her a "hobbyist." Her poems have appeared in *Women's Encounters with the Mental Health Establishment: Escaping the Yellow Wallpaper, Regrets Only: Contemporary Poets on the Theme of Regret, Beyond Forgetting: Poetry and Prose about Alzheimer's Disease* and a variety of small journals.

**TEE ISEMINGER** is an alumna of the Squaw Valley Writer's Workshops and was the recipient of the Sierra Arts Literary Award in 2013. Her work has appeared in *Sixfold* and *The Meadow*. She lives in Reno.

**NESSA MCCASEY**, PTP, CPT, Mentor, is the Director of the International Academy for Poetry Therapy, a credentialing organization for the field of poetry therapy. She shares what has helped her get through the hard parts of life through her work as a poetry therapist and mentor.

**ALEXA MERGEN** teaches yoga in Washington, D.C. and leads movement-based poetry workshops throughout the United States. Please visit Yoga

Stanza (www.yogastanza.org) for links to her published articles, essays, stories, and poems and for a list of upcoming events.

**ABBY E. MURRAY** is a Ph.D. candidate at Binghamton University and has an MFA from Pacific University. She teaches creative writing at the University of Washington-Tacoma. Her poems have appeared in *Rattle*, *River Styx*, *Cimarron Review* and *New Ohio Review*.

**ELAINE NUSSBAUM** has been writing poetry since 1962. She holds a Certificate in Poetics from the Naropa Institute (now Naropa University) and an MFA in Writing from Pacific University. She recently retired, after 20 years working as a Special Education teacher in Portland, Oregon. She published a chapbook of poems, *Poems in the Key of D Flat*, and is working on a poetry collection *Poems in the Key of Sea*.

**MARY SALISBURY** is the author of *Come What May*, a chapbook published by Finishing Line Press in 2014. She received an MFA in Writing from Pacific University and was a recipient of an Oregon Literary Arts Fellowship.

**PATRICIA REYNOLDS SØRBYE** is a native Californian, clinical hypnotherapist and poet. She lives in Oakland with her musician husband Lief Sørbye and her black and white cat, Miss Madeleine Jones.

**AUTUMN STEPHENS** is the author of the *Wild Women* book series, editor of two anthologies of women's essays, and the second-ever New York Times *Modern Love* columnist. A journalist, essayist, and poet, she leads workshops for cancer patients and last-minute memoirists, and teaches creative writing privately.

**ANN TEPLICK** is a Seattle poet, playwright, prose writer, and teaching artist who writes with youth at Child Study Treatment Center (Washington State psychiatric hospital) through Pongo Teen Writing; Seattle Children's Hospital, through Writers in the Schools; and Coyote Central, an after-school arts program.

**ANDREW LEVI WOOD** lives and writes in Golden Valley, Arizona. He is a graduate of Pacific University's Master of Fine Arts in Writing program and was once a truck driver delivering propane. He likes to spend time with his dachshund, Mr. Weenie.

# About the Author

**G. ELIZABETH KRETCHMER** holds an MFA in Writing from Pacific University. Her debut novel, *The Damnable Legacy*, was first published in 2014 and re-published in a second edition in 2015. Her short fiction, essays, and freelance work have appeared in the *New York Times*, *High Desert Journal*, *Silk Road Review*, *SLAB*, and other publications. When she's not writing, she's facilitating therapeutic and wellness writing workshops or exploring the Pacific Northwest with her husband and Lani the Labradoodle. You can learn more about her at www.gekretchmer.com.

# Also by
# G. Elizabeth Kretchmer

THE DAMNABLE LEGACY

Dear Reader,

Thanks for reading *Women on the Brink*!

I've always been fascinated by the idea of running away. Or, more specifically, the idea of *women* running away. Once, I pitched a novel to a male agent at a writing conference; the premise of the novel was that a mother took a two-week sabbatical from her difficult family, and during that time some things happened that made her reexamine her life more closely and question whether she wanted to return home. The agent looked at me when I'd finished my pitch as though I were out of my mind.

"No woman would ever do that," he said. "So the premise of your novel is faulty from the start."

He was wrong, of course. While I didn't personally know any wife and mother who'd permanently run away, I knew quite a few who periodically took breaks from their families. I also knew a number of women who regularly fantasized about what their lives might be like if they did run away. Admittedly, I did, too.

It's not for any of us to judge the thoughts or fantasies or decisions of others. Running away from the brink isn't necessarily black and white; it can be a complicated decision that can be construed as courageous or cowardly, or perhaps a blend of both. It also doesn't have to involve physically leaving the home. There are many ways women can run away. Some of those choices may be healthy, some not.

*Women on the Brink* was born from my questions about why women, of all ages, choose to stay or decide to make a significant change in their lives. I'd love to hear your thoughts, and your stories, about running away or other ways you've dealt with extreme challenges. You can contact me via my website at http://www.gekretchmer.com/contact/.

Also, as you may know, one of my all-time favorite things to do is to visit with book clubs, in person or via Skype, to talk not only about my work but about books in general. If you have a book club you think might be interested in a visit, please let me know about that, too.

Finally, I've learned how important book reviews are, and I'm tremendously grateful for those readers who've already posted a review of *Women on the Brink* on Goodreads and online retail sites. As it turns out, books are sold mostly by word of mouth, and those reviews go a long way in helping spread the word. (They also factor into all sorts of algorithms that benefit a book's visibility.) So I'm asking you to please keep this in mind as you read, not just my books but those of all authors. If you like a book, please take a couple of minutes to rate it on Goodreads and the online retail site of your choosing with the simple 5-star system and just a couple of sentences describing your thoughts about the book.

With warm gratitude,
G. Elizabeth Kretchmer